Randall Ingermanson
TRANSGRESSION

HARVEST HOUSE PUBLISHERS
Eugene, Oregon 97402

Cover by Left Coast Design, Portland, Oregon

TRANSGRESSION

Copyright © 2000 by Randall Ingermanson
Published by Harvest House Publishers
Eugene, Oregon 97402

Library of Congress Cataloging-in-Publication Data

Ingermanson, Randall Scott.
    Transgression / by Randall Ingermanson
        p. cm.
        Summary: While playing a virtual reality game, Rivka Meyers, an American Messianic Jew visiting Israel for an archaeological dig, becomes trapped in ancient Jerusalem, involved in a plot to destroy the spread of Christianity.
        ISBN 0-7369-0195-7
        [1. Virtual reality—Fiction. 2. Time travel—Fiction. 3. Christian life—Fiction. 4. Jewish Christians—Fiction.5. Israel—Fiction.] I. Title.
    PZ7.I465 Tr 2000
    [Fic]—dc21   99-044488

Printed in the United States of America

00 01 02 03 04 05 06 / BC / 10 9 8 7 6 5 4 3 2 1

To Eunice and our girls: Carolyn, Gracie, and Amy

Acknowledgments

I thank:

- Yoni Adonyi, Rabbi Barney Kasdan, and Hadara Hyman, for teaching me Hebrew

- Don Williams; Jay Hoehn; David, Becca, Sarah, and Daniel Poage; Mark and Gail Lundgren; Jeff and Kristine Magee; Mike and Kathi Peltz; Tony and Kym Halstead; Bob and Lauren Hassan—my friends at the Coast Vineyard, for interest in my fiction above and beyond the call of friendship

- Barney and Liz Kasdan; Gary and Sandy Becker; Ron and Kahanah Farnsworth; John Sabin; Bill and Rene Woods; John Thomley—my friends at Kehilat Ariel, where I learned much more about Messianic Judaism than I can put in one book

- Sherwood Wirt, Lee Roddy, Elaine Colvin Wright, Christine Tangvald, David and Heather Kopp, and a cast of thousands more who have served as faculty at various writing conferences I've attended

- Donna Axelrod, Steve Moore, Patricia Anders, Melinda Reinicke, Peggy Leslie, Mike Carroll, and Denyse O'Leary—my critique team past and present

- Sol Stein, Jack Cavanaugh, Lauraine Snelling, and Kathy Tyers—four pros who've critiqued my fiction and made me a better writer

- John DeSimone, my writing buddy since the Dark Ages

- Jan Collins, director of encouragement in a thousand e-mails

- Claire West, first reader and first critiquer, my nuclear weapon against writing errors large and small

- John Olson, creative genius, writer extraordinaire, and friend

- Chip MacGregor, Carolyn McCready, Betty Fletcher, and Barb Sherrill—the editors who saw this project through from rough draft to clean copy

- Mom and Dad, for making me what I am

- Eunice and our girls, Carolyn, Gracie, and Amy, who have cheered me on through many twists and turns in my writing career

PART I · VIRTUAL UNREALITY

There is much we still don't know, such as what happens to objects and information that fall into a black hole. Do they reemerge elsewhere in the Universe or in another universe? And can we warp space and time so much that one can travel back in time? These questions are part of our ongoing quest to understand the Universe. Maybe someone will come back from the future and tell us the answers.

—STEPHEN HAWKING
In the foreword to *Black Holes and Time Warps* by Kip Thorne

PROLOGUE

Rivka

Rivka Meyers knew something was wrong when she bumped into a wall that wasn't there.

"Ow!" She tugged at the virtual reality headset she had worn for the past half hour. "Dr. West?" she said. "How do I get this thing off?"

No response.

She fumbled with the straps at her chin. "Dr. West? Are you there? Hello?"

The buckle popped loose in her hand. She pulled the headset off and blinked. The lab was much darker than she remembered, and it smelled musty. Why hadn't she noticed that before?

The game had defocused her vision. While she waited for her eyes to adjust, she put her hand against the wall. It felt rough, stony. *Like limestone,* said something deep inside her archaeologist's brain.

But that was impossible. She was in the back part of a physics laboratory. Rivka suddenly felt dizzy, nauseated.

"Dr. West, what's going on?" she asked in a loud voice. "I'm done playing your computer game." Her voice echoed oddly in the stillness.

"Dr. West!" She was shouting now, angry. What kind of a prank was he playing? She didn't like it, and she wanted out. Now.

Rivka turned her head in a slow semicircle, studying her surroundings. In one direction, she could see light from a rough-cut entrance. In the other direction—total darkness. She sniffed. It smelled like…a cave. But it couldn't be. Not on the third floor of a physics building in downtown Jerusalem.

"God, help me!" It wasn't a prayer—just a figure of speech. Maybe it wouldn't hurt to try the real thing.

Lord…help me get back to the lab. I need to find Ari…

A bead of sweat ran down her back. Did she really want to see Ari again, after what he had said last night?

A footstep scuffled at the lighted end of the room. A deep male voice said something muzzy and indistinct.

Thanks, Father. Rivka turned to look.

Right away, she saw that it wasn't Ari. Nor Dr. West. At the moment, she didn't care. Any human being would be welcome. "Excuse me!" she shouted in English and began walking toward the man. "Could you tell me how to get to Ari Kazan's lab?" She repeated this in Hebrew.

The light grew better as she got closer to him. He wore a black beard and rough garb much like a Bedouin's…but different. Rivka couldn't quite place his costume, although she had been in Israel for over a month now and had thought she had seen everything: Arabs in checkered *kaffiyehs*, Hasidic rabbis in black fur hats, Druze villagers in baggy shirts and pants, sabra girls in string bikinis. This man might well be the janitor or just as easily the department chairman.

The man squinted in her direction. The nearer Rivka came to him, the more she slowed. Finally, she stopped. "Hello?" she said. "*Shalom? Salaam?*"

He said something in a language she didn't recognize. The vowel usage reminded her vaguely of Syriac—a notion so ridiculous that Rivka almost laughed out loud. Syriac had been a dead language for centuries.

A little smile formed on the man's face as he stared at her. His gaze ran up and down her body, seeming to peel away her T-shirt and cutoffs. His eyes lit up with an evil glow that needed no translation.

Rivka's heart double-thumped, then began a tap dance of panic in her chest. She stepped backward, clutching the virtual reality headset in her hands as though it were a shield. "Dr. West!" she shouted. "Help!"

The man chuckled softly. He took a step toward her, his hands held out to either side to cut off her escape.

"Who are you?" Rivka asked in a loud voice that grated in her own ears. She stepped back again. "*Mi attah?*" She couldn't remember how to say it in Arabic.

The man took another step toward her.

Rivka backed rapidly away from him. "Don't you dare touch me!" she said. "I'm an American! *Ani Amerikait!*" The words sounded foolish, but she had read somewhere that you had a better chance if you kept talking and put up a fight.

The man gave a yellow smile and kept advancing, catlike.

Rivka stepped back again, and the headset in her hand clunked against something hard. A wall. Her mind spun wildly now, out of control. The man was only a few paces away. Desperate, she lunged forward and screamed, "Get away from me!"

She threw the headset at his face and dodged to her left.

He batted the flimsy missile away with a hairy paw and scooted to his right, keeping between her and the exit. His eyes glowed with animal pleasure. He took another step.

Rivka pulled a key out of her pocket and clenched it tightly. Improvise! Fight! She kept moving sideways, maneuvering for room. *Please, Father, save me!*

The man feinted forward. She skittered sideways, tripped over a huge bump on the ground, staggered. Then her foot stepped on a marble-sized pebble, and her leg shot out from under her. She landed hard on her back in the dirt. Her key dropped into the loose dirt somewhere nearby.

The man grunted in triumph and rushed at her.

She dug her hands into the soft dust for balance and timed her kick perfectly.

Almost perfectly. At the last instant, he twisted his hips. Not much, but enough.

Her sandal thudded into a very solid thigh. The shock ran up her leg and into her spine. "No!" she screamed, and began kicking her feet in the air like windmills.

His hands snaked at her ankles, caught them, locked them in an iron grip. He laughed softly and forced her feet to the ground. He pinned them down with one enormous hand and leaned forward. Rivka smelled his vinegary breath.

She slashed wildly with her left hand, scratching at his eyes. He jerked his head away.

Point-blank, Rivka flung a handful of fine dust into his eyes. He screamed, clawed at his face. Suddenly, Rivka's legs came free.

She rolled away from him. He lunged blindly for her, coughing, spitting.

She scrambled up, grabbed another handful of dust, and pitched it into his gaping mouth.

He choked and fell on his face.

Rivka turned and ran. "Ari!" she screamed. "Help!"

She raced outside into the sunlight, sprinted madly through a dark grove of trees with gnarled branches. Her heart pounded in her chest. Her ragged breath rasped in her ears. Was he following? Faster! Tears fogged her eyes. Her leather sandals tore at her feet. Trying to look back over her shoulder, she tripped and fell. Dust flew up all around her.

Coughing, she clambered to her feet and dared to look back. The man was nowhere in sight.

Rivka panted until she caught her breath. Her left wrist throbbed from the fall. She massaged it while she squinted into the trees, afraid that the man might be lurking in the shadows. Nothing happened.

Finally, she turned around to get her bearings.

She blinked twice and then stared. Across a small valley rose up massive stone walls. Herodian masonry. Jerusalem limestone. Towering white walls. It looked like...

But that was impossible. She closed her eyes, breathed deeply three times, and opened them again. *Absurd.* Had she gone loony or something?

Rivka had visited the Temple Mount twice and studied hundreds of pictures during three years of graduate school. But she had never seen it looking like this. So pure. So spotless.

So new.

On the surface, Thorne's mathematical reasoning is impeccable. Einstein's equations indeed show that wormhole solutions allow for time to pass at different rates on either side of the wormhole, so that time travel, in principle, is possible. The trick, of course, is to create the wormhole in the first place.

—MICHIO KAKU
Hyperspace, chapter 11

CHAPTER ONE

Rivka

Rivka raised her pick high overhead and swung it again into the hard-packed earth.

Crack! She had heard that sound dozens of times in the two weeks she had been on this dig.

"My friend, you are trying to break every pot on this site?" A broad grin covered the face of Dov Lifshutz, her coworker for the week. Dov was a graduate student from Hebrew University with a couple of years' experience digging already. Though only about three years older than Rivka, he had spent those three years in the Israel Defense Forces. Service in the IDF aged soldiers like dog years.

Rivka gave an innocent shrug and held up her tool. "This thing isn't a toothpick, you know." She had learned her first day on the job that you couldn't help breaking things. Like it said in all the books, archaeology was destruction.

She stood to her full height and dug a fist into the aching muscles in her lower back. They had been working half the morning in the middle of a square hole, five meters on each side and now almost a meter deep. Apparently, they were about to hit another layer from the late-Roman period.

Dov knelt in the bare dirt and inspected the mark Rivka's pick had made in the reddish earth. She dropped down beside him. In a minute, they would know if she had found another pot, or something more interesting. Together, they loosened dirt with their fingers and pulled it out of the small hole.

"Can you see anything?" Dov asked.

Rivka pushed her small hand in and plucked out a handful of dirt. Something flashed in the sunlight. Something blue. Rivka gasped. You didn't find blue pottery in the Roman period.

Dov lowered his face until his nose almost touched the dirt. "*Tov me'od!*" he said. *Very good!* He raised his head and hooted with glee.

Rivka felt a sudden rush of adrenaline. "Is it what I think it is?"

"It is never what you think it is," Dov said. "That is the charm of archaeology." He grabbed a triangular steel trowel from her bucket of tools and handed it to her with mock formality. "I leave the honors to you, my brilliant and lovely friend."

Rivka smiled and took the trowel. Carefully, she poked it into the earth around the hole, loosening the dirt. Archaeology was a funny business. You attacked the earth with heavy equipment—bulldozers, picks, shovels—until you hit something. The minute you made contact, you had to treat it like a family heirloom.

When she had broken up the dirt a bit, Rivka began scooping it into a *goofah*, a makeshift bucket recycled from an old tire. Archaeology was a thrifty science, dependent on old tools and volunteer labor and the occasional wealthy donor. She wasn't getting paid for this summer's work; she was paying for the privilege. More precisely, her father was paying.

Rivka took a broad paintbrush and whisked the loose dirt away from a smooth, flat surface, exposing an area the size of her hand. Tesserae—tiny tiles! The colors were still dull and indistinct, except for the brilliant blue crack she had made with her pick. She felt her insides trembling. This looked wonderful.

"We must wash it." Dov jumped up and got a Dixie cup full of water from the jug of ice water resting in the narrow strip of shade at the edge of the square. He handed it to Rivka.

She poured a little onto the patchwork of tiny inlaid tiles and polished them with her wet finger. When she had poured out the whole cup, the edges were muddy but the center gleamed blue and white.

"Beautiful," Dov said. He raised an imaginary microphone to his mouth and made a theatrical gesture with his left hand. "Ladies and gentlemen, I present to you the famous Rivka Meyers Memorial Mosaic!"

Rivka laughed. "Memorial! That sounds a bit morbid."

"Morbid?" Dov said. "What means *morbid?*"

"Mahalati," Rivka said.

"Miss Meyers, you amaze me," Dov said, still using his mock formal tone. "When you started here, you still had your most charming American accent. Now you speak like a *sabra,* mostly."

"Thank you...mostly." Rivka picked up the trowel again. "Now, if you don't mind, I'm going to uncover some more of the famous Lifshutz-Meyers mosaic."

Dov grabbed another trowel. "With your permission, I wish to join you."

Before he could begin, his cellular phone buzzed. He pulled it out of his pocket and flipped it open. *"Hallo, medaber Dov."* He listened for a moment. *"Ken, Imma."*

Rivka smiled. Cellular phones were very big in Israel—much more so than in the United States. It was both common and comical to see a tough-looking Israeli soldier standing on a street corner, an Uzi dangling from his shoulder, a phone pressed to his ear, nodding and saying exactly what Dov had just said. *Yes, Mama.*

Rivka did her best not to listen. Dov's reluctant tone and slouched posture told her that Dov's mother was asking him to do something he didn't like. Finally, he hung up.

Rivka continued working in silence. Dov went to the water jug and poured two cups of water. "Rivka, you should take a break, please. It would be most unfortunate for you to become dehydrated."

She continued work for a full minute, then reluctantly decided he was right. This mosaic wouldn't run away.

"I guess you're right." Rivka dropped her trowel and took the cup he offered. They sat down in the sliver of shade on the north side of the square and drank.

Dov crushed his Dixie cup in his hands and studied it minutely. "Did I ever tell you about my cousin Ari?"

Rivka suppressed a smile. In Hebrew, *Ari* meant "lion" and *Dov* meant "bear." "Did your grandparents own a zoo?"

"No, they lived in one," Dov said cryptically.

Rivka waited for him to explain this remark.

"So, as I was saying, my cousin Ari is a genius," Dov said. "He teaches physics at Hebrew University. Very, very smart, but he studies too hard."

What was Dov driving at? "We all study too hard," Rivka said. "The perils of academia."

"Okay, so let me finish, already," Dov said. "Ari's a nice guy, but he doesn't get out much. So his mother gets worried, and she talks to my mother, and—"

"And so your mother tells you, 'Dov, find Ari a nice Jewish girl so he won't be lonely.'" Rivka wanted to laugh. "Am I right?"

"Not exactly," Dov said.

"Close?"

"Something like that—"

"Sorry." Rivka stood up and dusted the seat of her cutoffs. "Not interested."

Dov laughed out loud. "Hey, little sister, you think I'm *meshuga?* Crazy? I know you have a most excellent gentleman friend back home, yes?"

Rivka mumbled something that even she couldn't hear clearly. Stefan was neither excellent nor a gentleman nor a friend, but if Dov wanted to think so, where was the harm?

"And anyway, you're too short for Ari, my friend. I'm not asking you to go out with him, okay?"

Rivka almost asked what height had to do with it but decided to skip it. "What are you asking me?"

"I'm asking for a little help," Dov said. "That's all, yes?"

"What kind of help?"

"You're a nice girl, and you know everyone on the dig." Dov stood up and stretched. "You find another nice girl—somebody adventurous—"

"And I suggest to this nice girl that she hitchhike to Jerusalem and meet a mad scientist for a little fling?" Rivka stared at him. "You think I'm crazy?"

"Fling? What means *fling?*" Dov said. "Anyway, Ari isn't a mad scientist. He's a nice guy, only shy. And besides, who said anything about hitchhiking? We can take her in my car."

"*We?*" Rivka said. "Where do you get this *we?*"

Dov's face split into an enormous smile. "Ah, I'm forgetting the best part. You can come, too! To help melt the ice, yes? We drive up to Jerusalem for the weekend and stay in the youth hostel. On *Shabbat,* we can go to the Temple Mount, see the mosques. After *Shabbat,* we go out somewhere with Ari. Somewhere safe, okay? We eat at a nice café. Maybe we go dancing, or we go shopping in the *shuq,* or we look at some art, I don't know. Then the next day, we see some archaeological sites in the Jewish Quarter. You've been to the Temple Mount?"

Rivka nodded. "Once."

"But you would like to see it again? And the Burnt House? And the Wohl Archaeological Museum?"

"Of course I would like to see all that," Rivka said. "I haven't had time to visit the Burnt House."

"You'll have lots of time," Dov said. His face broadened into an engaging grin. "So! You'll go?"

Rivka hesitated. She hadn't gone out with any of the guys on the dig, although several had asked. She hadn't come here to meet guys, despite what her mother thought. *A young woman only goes to Israel to meet men or to meet God, am I right? And you already know God, so you're looking for a man. What's to be ashamed of that?*

Nothing, of course, except that it was wrong—a hundred and eighty degrees wrong, to be exact—on both counts. One reason Rivka had wanted to leave Berkeley for the summer was to get away from Stefan. After she tried telling him nicely that they weren't a good match, he had spent most of the spring semester stalking her.

The other reason she had wanted out of Berkeley was to take a break from God. Or rather, a break from fighting His battles.

Ever since she had been a teenager growing up in a Messianic synagogue in San Diego, Rivka had been taking her lumps for God. Somehow, she had never been able to walk away from an argument. Four years of debates in high school, another four as an undergraduate at the University of California, San Diego, and three more in graduate school at Berkeley.

In the last six months, she had lost her fire. She had heard all the easy answers to all the easy questions once too often. She was tired of giving easy answers, tired of too many battles with too many pseudointellectuals, of always being on the defensive. Tired of her own questions.

If God was in control of the universe, then why was her life so out of control? And why had He up and abandoned her for the last six months?

When her father had offered to pay for her summer in Israel, Rivka jumped at the chance, even though she knew there would be strings attached. Her plan was to work hard, play hard, and take a time-out. A time-out from God.

Or maybe she was giving Him the time-out. A time-out for bad behavior. Whatever.

Just for this one summer, she wouldn't tell anyone that she was a Messianic Jew. Why bring it up, when it would just lead to an argument? Why not let somebody else be Supreme Defender of the Faith and First Tiger for a while? Let someone else take the heat. God could get along without her help for a few months, couldn't He?

So far, it was working—sort of. She had actually gone a whole month without alienating anybody. Nobody had called her a liar, a fool, or a phony since she had set foot in Israel.

Which made her feel like a liar, a fool, and a phony.

It also made her feel hungry for God. Not hungry for talk *about* God, but hungry for...

"Hey, little sister, which planet are you on?" Dov asked. "*Hallo*, Rivka?" He rapped twice on her skull.

"Sorry," Rivka said. "I was just...thinking."

"Okay, fine," Dov said. "So think. You have plenty of time to think, yes? You don't have to decide right away."

Rivka smiled. Of all the guys on this dig, Dov had to be the safest imaginable. Like an older brother. And it would be wonderful to see Jerusalem again, to really take some time, to try to imagine the city two thousand years ago, when Yeshua walked those streets, climbed the steps to the Temple Mount, lit a fire in men's hearts—a fire that had gone cold among her own people but had found a home among Gentiles. She wanted fire in her heart again. Real fire. Wanted it bad.

"Okay, I'll go," she said.

Dov's eyes widened in surprise.

"So tell me. What kind of woman would your cousin Ari be interested in?"

Dov shrugged elaborately. "She has to be Jewish, or my mother will kill me, yes? And she should be pretty, of course. Maybe blond? And tall. Ari is a hundred and ninety centimeters."

About six foot three, Rivka calculated. She thought for a moment. "Do you know Jessica Weinberg?"

"Who Weinberg?" Dov asked.

"Jessica. She works in Luke Morgan's area. I think she's what you're looking for. Blond. Jewish American Princess. Adventurous. She's studying at Brown University. And she's a lot taller than I am—maybe five foot eight."

"How much is that in centimeters?" Dov asked.

"A hundred and seventy-three," Rivka said.

"You're very quick with the numbers, my friend."

"My father's an applied mathematician," Rivka said. Then she clapped her hand to her forehead. "Oops! I just remembered something. Jessica doesn't speak any Hebrew—well, hardly any."

"No problem!" Dov spread his hands wide. "Ari speaks very excellent English. He studied at Princeton and MIT."

"Good." Rivka knelt down in the dirt and picked up her trowel. "I'll talk to Jessica at lunchtime. Meanwhile, we have a masterpiece to uncover."

"Very good!" Dov plopped onto his knees beside her. "But *le'at, le'at!*" he said. *Slowly, slowly.*

CHAPTER TWO

Ari

Ari's cellular phone buzzed while he was crossing King George Avenue. He pulled it out of his pocket as he reached the sidewalk. "*Shalom*, Ari speaking."

"*Shalom*, Ari!" said Dov. "The ladies are waiting."

"I'm just turning onto Ben Yehuda Street now," Ari said. "Where are you?"

"Go toward the Hotel Kikar Tzion," Dov said. "We're in a little café out on the sidewalk. You can't miss us."

Ari snorted. "Which means I will, certainly. Remember the first time you told me we couldn't miss?"

"And how could I forget, when you keep reminding me?" Dov asked. "Ah, the waiter is here already. Hurry, Ari."

"*Shalom*." Ari snapped his phone shut and jammed it into his pocket. It was half an hour after sundown. *Shabbat* was over, and the streets had magically filled with people—tourists, students, families, couples. The night air was cool, with just a hint of a breeze. A good night to be alive.

Except that his meddling *Imma* had pestered Dov's meddling *Imma* into setting him up with this blind-date foolishness. Ari sighed. Part of him felt offended by it all.

And part of him felt grateful. After all, you didn't meet many women in the halls of a physics department, and Dov had assured him that both of the "ladies" he was meeting tonight were friendly and attractive. Ari only hoped he would make it through the evening without doing anything ridiculous. He hadn't had much of a social life for years—not since his undergraduate days at Hebrew University.

It was his own fault, he knew. He feared too much that he would do something wrong, so he usually wound up doing nothing at all. A man almost thirty-two ought to have a wife, or at least a girlfriend. But how did you do that? What was the magic trick? His *Imma* said he was too passive, and she was probably right, and it made him furious, but what could he do? Was it his fault he got all the introversion genes?

After a couple of blocks, a bookstore across the street caught Ari's eye. As he came closer, he wondered if he might have time to glance in the window. This section of Ben Yehuda Street was a pedestrian mall. Ari crossed the street.

"Ho, Ari!" shouted Dov from somewhere very close.

Ari spun around.

Dov sat grinning at him from a table fifteen meters away. "Ari, I bet the ladies dessert that you would walk past without seeing us!"

Ari shrugged his shoulders and smiled. "You're a scoundrel, parking yourself just across from a bookstore. The ladies should refuse to pay."

Dov and his friends sat at a round glass table on the sidewalk. Ari studied them as he strode up to his chair. The tall one— that would be Jessica—was very pretty. Blue eyes and blond hair and the deep tan that Americans seemed to think so desirable. The other one was petite, with braided dark hair and glittering black eyes and honey-colored skin. She looked like a *sabra*, a native Israeli.

"Sit, my friend!" Dov said. "Jessica, Rivka, this is my cousin, Ari Kazan. He is a very great physicist, although he is too modest to admit it."

Ari sat down, his ears burning hot.

"Kazan," Jessica said. "I've been wondering all week if you're related to the director."

Ari was used to this question. "Regrettably, no." He shrugged his right shoulder. "Mr. Kazan was born Kazanjoglu, in Istanbul. Whereas my great-grandfather was a Kazan from Kiev."

Jessica looked a trifle disappointed. Then her face brightened. "Dov was just telling us about your adventure in the Arab Quarter."

Ari took a sip of water. "Which adventure was that?"

"The time you saved my life, you *meshuggener!*" Dov said.

"Ah, well this story gets better every time I hear it," Ari said. He shrugged at the two women. "Really, nothing much happened."

Rivka leaned forward. "Did you really wade all the way through Hezekiah's Tunnel?"

Ari nodded. "All the way to the Pool of Siloam."

"Ooooh!" Jessica squealed. "That sounds like fun!"

Fun? Ari hadn't thought of it as fun. He had simply wanted to see the tunnel. To be Israeli was to be an amateur archaeologist. Hezekiah's Tunnel was one of the most ancient unquestionably authentic sites in Jerusalem, a connection to ancestors dead for the last twenty-seven centuries.

"The fun came at the end, mostly," Dov said. "When we reached the Pool of Siloam, a crowd of Palestinians was there. One of them spoke to us in Arabic, and I, being a great *meshuggener* in those days, answered in Hebrew. Five or six of them tried to drown me."

"Then what happened?" Jessica asked in a breathy voice.

Dov grinned broadly. "Ari broke some noses most magnificently."

Ari felt his stomach tighten. He remembered the cold fear in his heart, the sight of Dov's twisted face underwater, the pain in his jaw where one of the Arabs slugged him. Bloody faces, eyes filled with rage, angry shouts. He had been a fool to go on that expedition with Dov, and a bigger fool to get into a fight. Sometimes you had to fight, but it was never a good thing. Even if you won.

"We escaped only because Ari could throw stones better than the Arabs." Dov threw an imaginary missile at a phantom Arab. "He never misses."

Ari cleared his throat, embarrassed. That was an exaggeration. And anyway, throwing stones was not a talent a physicist needed.

"Shall we order?" Rivka said.

Ari picked up his menu, grateful for the diversion. "So tell me about your recent discoveries, my archaeologists."

"Rivka found a mosaic this week!" said Jessica. "It's absolutely incredible…at least what she's uncovered so far."

"The find of the season, possibly," Dov said. "As beautiful as the one that was stolen from Beth Shean!"

Ari looked at Rivka. "You'd better watch this cousin of mine, or he'll be claiming credit for it himself."

"He was there when I hit it with my pick," Rivka said. "He deserves half the credit."

Ari felt a little twinge of surprise. Sharing credit—that was a refreshing attitude to see in an academic.

The waiter arrived and took their orders. The three archaeologists began an animated discussion of mosaics, and how important it was to preserve them, and the dangers of theft, and how each one brought new surprises to the art historians. Ari contributed to this conversation mostly by asking questions. He could learn more by listening than by talking. And besides, he felt just a bit tongue-tied. Jessica looked very pretty, much more so than any girl he had ever gone out with before.

Finally, halfway through their frozen yogurts, a grin spread across Dov's face. He leaned forward. "Ari, you must tell the ladies about your latest theory, yes?"

Ari shook his head. "I wouldn't want to bore them."

"Try us," Rivka said.

"What kind of physicist are you, exactly?" Jessica asked.

"He's building a time machine!" Dov said.

"A what?" Jessica asked, with a giggle that made it clear she thought Dov was teasing her.

Ari winced. "Not exactly," he said. "I'm a theorist. They don't let me handle experimental apparatus for fear I'll break something."

The women laughed.

"So your colleague is building the time machine," Dov said. "But he's using your theory, correct?"

"Not even a theory," Ari said. "Just a non-simply connected solution to Einstein's equations. And you should call it a closed timelike loop, not a time machine, please." He cautiously looked at the women. Jessica was staring at him, her mouth half open, a look of awe in her eyes. Ari hated it when people looked at him like that, as if he were a space alien.

Rivka's eyes glittered with interest. "My father made me read a book last spring vacation when I went to visit him. *Hyperspace* by Michio Kaku. Do you know of him?"

Ari relaxed. "Oh, Michio's book! Very well written, but no mathematics. Did you like it?"

"Yes, it was awesome," Rivka said. "But you're wrong. There was a bit of math. He kept putting in matrix diagrams without explaining what they meant. For example, on page 102, where he started talking about Kaluza-Klein theory."

Ari stared at her. "You remember the page number?"

Rivka blushed. "Yes…I have a fairly good memory."

An understatement. "And did you understand the model?"

"Not really," Rivka said. "I followed the main point, that the universe is supposed to have ten dimensions, or twenty-six, or whatever, but I didn't see what those matrices were all about."

"I can explain." Ari pulled a pen out of his shirt pocket and began scribbling on his napkin.

"Tell us about the time machine," Jessica said.

"It probably won't work," Ari said. "It's based on a little model I cooked up, which nobody took seriously. We have a saying in physics: A theorist writes a paper, and nobody believes it—except he himself. An experimentalist writes a paper, and everybody believes it—except he himself."

"That American friend of yours believes in your theory," Dov said. "He has a very strange name."

"Damien West," Ari said. "He's an experimentalist from Northwestern University. I don't quite understand why he has so much faith in my model. Dr. West is a bit odd, as are all physicists, but he is a very fine pulsed-power experimentalist."

"And he's building a time machine?" Jessica asked.

"A closed timelike loop," Ari said. "He thinks he is building one. As I said, it probably won't work, and he'll go home at the end of the summer."

"But what if it does work?" Dov said. "Then you will very certainly get the Nobel prize, yes?"

"We might have a problem in *proving* it works," Ari said.

"Won't it be obvious?" Rivka asked. "Just take the Nobel committee on a guided tour of the twenty-fifth century. Wouldn't that do it?"

"Oh, no, no, no," Ari said. "Now you've been misled by Michio's book. To go forward in time is a hugely expensive project. You need near-light-speed rockets and other tech... we don't have."

"So what are you going to try?" Rivka asked. "To go backward in time? I thought the book said that was impossible."

"It probably is," Ari said. "But I worked out a model last year, really very simple. It's based on the Casimir effect in a strong oscillating electric field. You create a resonant shell of so-called 'negative-energy matter,' and it forms a condensate of quantum-mechanically created wormholes as a macroscopic object. The very strange thing is that it allows you to go *backward* in time, but not forward. There might be some dangers in going through the device. Also, it would have some stability problems."

"What kind of problems?" Rivka asked.

"If you passed through the device and it then collapsed, you couldn't return."

"No problem," Dov said. "Make two! Then you'll have a down escalator and an up escalator, yes?"

Ari shook his head. "That won't work. The zero-point fluctuations in a volume the size of the earth are only enough to make one wormhole. If my calculations are correct, you can't make two."

"So you might send the Nobel committee back a hundred years, but they might regrettably not return to give you your prize," Dov said.

"And what if they accidentally killed Mr. Nobel before he set up his prize?" Jessica giggled. "Wouldn't that be funny?"

"That can't happen," Ari said. "You can't change the past."

"How do you know?" Jessica asked. "In every time-travel novel I've ever read, you *can* change the past. Otherwise, there wouldn't be much to the plot, right?"

Ari drummed his fingers on the table. He found most science fiction boring or silly. "God is not a novelist," he said shortly.

"You can prove mathematically that the past cannot be changed—not even with a closed timelike loop."

Jessica looked annoyed. Ari wished he hadn't said anything. Wasn't he here to have a good time? Why did he always have to talk about physics? It only ended with people getting angry at him for spoiling their delusions.

"Look!" Rivka pointed down Ben Yehuda Street. "They're going to do some folk dancing. Let's pay our bill and go watch."

Five minutes later, they joined in the applause as the first dance came to an end. The lead musician, a short, bearded bear of a man with a guitar that looked much too big for him, stepped forward. "Who wants to join in?" he shouted in Hebrew.

Rivka stepped forward immediately and joined the women in the center circle. Dov poked Ari. "Let's go! You are coming, Jessica?"

"Can you teach me, Ari?" Jessica asked.

The last thing Ari wanted was to make a fool of himself trying to dance. He shook his head. "I don't know how."

Dov took Jessica's hand. "I'll show you," he said. "It's not so hard."

Ari folded his arms across his chest and leaned against a lamppost. Why couldn't he be more like Dov?

The musicians started playing a slow, traditional folk song, *Oseh Shalom Bimromav.* Ari doubted that Dov had ever danced this song before, but after a few missteps, he picked up the simple rhythm, moving fluidly to the music, if not gracefully. Jessica looked to be hopeless. When the others turned right, she turned left. She watched Dov, trying to imitate his movements, but she kept getting her feet tangled. Ari was glad he hadn't bothered to try.

Rivka obviously knew this dance and also the Hebrew words. She glided lightly around the circle, her hands and feet moving in perfect unity, her face lit up with a smile. Where had she learned to dance like that? Ari found that he could not stop watching her. There was something strange about Rivka. No, not strange. Different. She was intelligent without being arrogant, nice-looking without being a prima donna. But there was something else, too. Ari couldn't quite put his finger on it.

The music ended. Ari joined in the applause. Dov and Jessica stepped out of the circle. As Rivka followed them, one of the musicians stopped her and said something. Rivka nodded and went back into the circle.

"Hey, Dov!" Ari said. "They're stealing your lady."

Dov grinned. "She's good, did you see it? Maybe she was a gypsy in a previous life, yes?"

Jessica laughed.

"Ari, you should have tried," Dov said. "It was easy, mostly."

"Easy!" Jessica fanned herself. "I'm hot. I could use a beer."

"Me, too," Dov said. "Hey, Ari, why don't you stay here and keep an eye on Rivka while we go buy some drinks? Don't let one of those musicians touch her, okay? She's a nice girl."

Ari nodded. "I'll stay."

A moment later, Dov and Jessica had disappeared into the human beehive of Ben Yehuda Street. The next dance was very fast and very complicated. Ari didn't know the words or the melody. But Rivka did. She spun. She clapped. She whirled. She stomped. She sang. And all the while, her face seemed lit up with an otherworldly serenity.

The song ended with a shout. The onlookers burst into applause. Ari clapped loudly.

Rivka came out of the circle, shaking her head to the musicians' pleas that she stay for another dance. She scanned the crowd. Ari waved at her, and she glided toward him, smiling.

"Where's Dov and Jessica?" she asked.

"They went to get some drinks," Ari said. "Are you hot?"

Rivka shook her head. "That was fun!"

"Where did you learn to dance like that?" Ari said. "You're very good."

"In San Diego," Rivka said. "My...synagogue had some classes. You ought to try it sometime."

"Maybe I will," Ari said. Which was crazy, of course. He stood there awkwardly for a moment, wondering what to say next. Finally, he asked, "Which synagogue do you go to in San Diego?"

She hesitated for a moment. "Beth Simcha."

"Is that Reform?" he asked. "Or Conservative?" She was obviously not Orthodox.

Again, a strange little hesitation. "Actually, I don't go there anymore since I went off to graduate school in Berkeley."

Ari suddenly realized that they were both speaking Hebrew. He hadn't noticed because she was so fluent. "How long have you been here in Israel?" he asked. "You speak like a *sabra*."

"That's sweet of you to say so," Rivka said. "I've only been here three weeks, but I try to get Dov to speak Hebrew to me as much as possible. Of course, he wants to practice his English."

"But you've been speaking Hebrew a lot longer than three weeks," Ari said.

Rivka nodded. "I had to learn biblical Hebrew for my bat mitzvah. That's when I discovered I had a little knack for languages. I got some tapes on modern Hebrew, and that helped with my accent."

"How many languages do you know?" Ari asked.

"I forget," Rivka said. "English, of course. And Hebrew. German in high school. Then I took Latin and *koine* Greek at community colleges, also while I was in high school. French in college, and a little bit of Russian. Then the weird ones—Aramaic, Ugaritic, Syriac, Ethiopic. One of these days, I'll get around to Coptic. I've also picked up a little Arabic on the dig from one of the Jordanian students."

"That's amazing," Ari said. "Besides Hebrew, I know only English and Arabic and a little German. That's enough."

"Maybe enough in physics," Rivka said. "But if you study archaeology or the Ancient Near East or the classics, you've got to know a lot of languages. It's not that bad, really. Ancient languages only have a few thousand words. You learn those, and a little grammar, and you've got it."

"No, thanks," Ari said. "Mathematics—now that's a language I can understand."

"That's what my father says," said Rivka. "He's an applied mathematician at AT&T. He wanted me to go into computers."

"So why didn't you?" Ari asked.

"Sometimes I wish I had," Rivka said. "It pays a lot better than archaeology, and you don't have to swing a pick in the hot sun."

"What's wrong with a little exercise?" Ari asked. "I happen to like digging."

"Really?" Rivka studied him, her eyebrows high.

"Yes, really," Ari said. "There's a place southwest of Jerusalem where you can go and plant trees. It's a tourist trap, but I have an arrangement with one of the managers. I like to go there when I get stuck with my equations, and he lets me plant trees until I find a solution."

"Oh, I wish I could do that," Rivka said. "When I go back home, I would love to leave behind some trees that I had planted."

"It's hard work, planting trees," Ari said.

"So is digging up old ruins," Rivka said. "I'm tough. Will you take me tree-planting sometime?"

Ari swallowed. Had he heard right? Had she just asked him for a...whatever? "Sure," he heard himself saying. "When would you want to do that?"

"I'm free tomorrow morning," Rivka said. "Dov and Jessica and I are going to some museums in the afternoon."

Ari felt his head buzzing with a strange mixture of fear and warmth and excitement. He clenched his fists tightly to maintain control. *Stay calm, Ari, you fool. Stay calm.* "Very good, then."

"There they are!" Jessica's voice, shrill, piercing.

Ari turned and saw Dov and Jessica pressing through the crowd toward them. "You would like a Maccabees, yes?" Dov held up a can of beer.

Ari suddenly felt thirsty. He took a can and popped the tab.

Dov pressed one into Rivka's hands. "And now where shall we go?" He punched Ari's arm. "I see you eyeing that bookstore! Not tonight."

"Oh, couldn't we just step in for a minute?" Rivka said. "I hate going past a bookstore without peeking inside."

Jessica took a long pull from her beer. "I'm game."

Dov shrugged. "If the ladies insist. But just a few minutes, yes? There is an art gallery up the street—very, very excellent— not to be missed."

The four headed toward the bookstore. Ari felt as if his head had detached from his shoulders and was now gliding several meters above the street. A warm glow of well-being had settled over him—a glow not due to the Maccabees.

On its heels came fear.

Don't ruin things, Ari. Don't do anything stupid. Don't make a fool of yourself.

He would, sooner or later. He always did.

It was as certain as any law of physics.

CHAPTER THREE

Rivka

"Rivka, do not move." Ari's voice sounded calm and quiet. "There is a hornet resting on your back."

Rivka froze where she stood, bent over a hole. Ari had gone to get another tree. Now she could hear him padding up behind her, moving slowly. It was a breezy summer day, rich with the scent of moist earth and Jerusalem pine. Something tickled her nose. The pollen here must be similar to San Diego. Her allergies had been acting up all morning.

"You'd better hurry, Ari, I'm going to—"

A sneeze shuddered through Rivka's body. An angry buzzing filled her ears. She dropped to the ground, dreading the sudden, sharp sting.

Instead, she heard a string of angry Hebrew words, followed by the sound of swishing air. She spun around.

Ari frantically batted at a hornet buzzing around his head. The insect zigged left, then right, then left again, darting around behind him. He swatted awkwardly at the back of his shoulder, then yelped.

"Oh!" Rivka said. "Did he get you?"

Ari's face had gone very pale. He brushed something off the back of his shirt. "I told you not to move," he said, his voice tight.

"I'm sorry," Rivka said. "It was my allergies."

Ari gave her a hard look. "I have an allergy, too—specifically to hornets."

Rivka gasped. "Do we need to get you to a hospital?"

He shook his head and zipped open his neon-blue backpack lying on the ground. "There isn't time. I could only survive about fifteen minutes without epinephrine." He yanked out a small packet and ripped it open. Inside lay a syringe with a small quantity of liquid inside. He took the syringe, placed the needle on the vein at his left elbow, and pressed it in.

Rivka's knees felt weak. "I...I'm so sorry," she said.

Ari pulled out his wallet and selected a credit card. "Take this and try to scrape out the stinger." He pulled up his shirt, exposing his lean brown back, and pointed at an angry red welt.

Rivka peered at it and placed the card on his skin.

"Apply a steady and even pressure," he said.

She scraped the card over the welt several times.

"There," he said. "You've got it." He seemed to relax as he turned and took the card. "American Express." He held it up next to his face and smiled. "Don't leave home without it, correct?"

"I'm so sorry," Rivka said again. She felt terrible. Why had she gone and sneezed at just the wrong time?

"Please, it is nothing," Ari said. "It wasn't your fault. I am stung frequently. They seem to like my smell."

Rivka attempted a smile. "Are you...going to be okay? Do you want to leave now?"

Ari shrugged his shirt back on. "We still have this tree to plant, correct? I'll be fine, but I will permit you to do the hard work on this one."

Rivka picked up the tree and promptly sneezed twice. "There's something in the air here." She lugged the tree to the hole they had dug, lowered it in, and pushed dirt around its base with her shoes. "Perfect," she said.

"Someday, there will be a forest around Jerusalem, as in days of old," Ari said. "You must come back then and admire it."

"I'd love that," Rivka said. She leaned on her shovel for a moment, happy and tired. They had been working for a couple of hours, and she had lost track of how many trees they had planted.

"Hello, sir, ma'am, excuse me!" It was a young voice.

Rivka turned around. A small Palestinian boy stood there holding a Polaroid camera. He pressed the button, and the tired motor ground out a white print.

"Sir, how are you and your wife today?" the boy asked. "It is wonderful day for planting, yes? Very, very good day." He held up the print and grinned broadly, revealing teeth much too big for his small face.

Rivka guessed he couldn't be more than six years old.

"It is a beautiful tree you have planted," the boy said. He looked again at the print, and his smile widened as the image formed. "And a most lovely lady to help you plant it, sir." He held the print toward Ari. "A bargain for you, sir. Almost free! Ten dollar!" He took Ari's hand and put the picture in his open palm.

"Little boy," Rivka said, "you shouldn't have wasted your film on us. We don't want your picture."

Ari was looking at the picture with an odd expression on his face. He pulled out his wallet.

"Ari!" Rivka said. "This is silly. It's a scam. That's not worth ten dollars. Didn't you see the movie *Terminator?* You remember the ending—"

Ari pulled out two *shekel* coins and handed them to the boy. "We will go now, Rivka."

The boy stared at the coins. "You did not hear me, sir? Ten dollar! It is a very good price, my friends. Almost free!"

Ari gathered the two shovels and took them back to the man supervising the planting.

"Okay, sir, you win!" shouted the boy. "Five dollar! It is like nothing, yes?"

Ari headed toward his Volkswagen. Rivka followed him.

"Two dollar, sir!" the boy screeched behind them. "Like stealing, for only two dollar!"

Ari unlocked the door and Rivka jumped inside. He shut the door and went around to his own side.

"One dollar," the boy shouted behind them. "You win, my friend! One dollar!"

Ari started the car and backed up out of the lot. Rivka turned to stare at him, a hard, cold knot forming in her stomach. "How can you cheat a little boy like that?" she asked.

"Look behind us," Ari said.

Rivka looked back. The boy was running toward a Palestinian man, waving the coins aloft. The man wore a smile.

"He cheated me," Ari said, grinning. "But only a little."

They drove with the windows open because the car had no air-conditioning. The noise made it almost impossible to talk. Rivka sat back and enjoyed the scenery. Ari was a very nice guy, much like Dov, only less exuberant. He didn't seem to be full of his own brilliance, like plenty of academics she knew. And while he pretended to be a tough, gruff *sabra,* under that exterior lay a gentle spirit. Which came as no surprise. *Sabra* was the English version of the Hebrew word *tsavar*, the native desert cactus—tough on the outside, tender on the inside.

Jessica seemed to like him a lot. She had talked of little else last night at the hostel. Rivka hoped that Ari liked Jessica.

Maybe Dov's little matchmaking scheme might actually lead to something. Wouldn't that be hilarious?

Twenty minutes later, they arrived on the campus of the Hebrew University. Ari stopped in the parking lot of the physics department, next to Dov's VW.

"It appears that our friends are already here," he said. "Shall we go up to my office?"

Rivka nodded. "You can show me your time machine."

Ari snorted and spent the next five minutes explaining why she should call it a "timelike self-intersecting loop."

Ari's office was empty. "They must have gone to Damien's laboratory," he said.

When they entered the lab on the third floor, Rivka spotted Dov and Jessica at the far end of the large room. Beside them stood a late-fortyish man with a thick head of blond hair, a linebacker's shoulders, and an enormous smile. The three stood around a personal computer. Dov wore a virtual reality headset and clutched a joystick.

"Hello, Damien," Ari said. "*Shalom,* Dov, Jessica. I have brought your hardworking colleague back from the future forest of Jerusalem." He turned to Rivka. "Rivka, this is Professor Damien West, from Northwestern University in your America. Damien, this is Rivka Meyers, studying archaeology at Berkeley."

Rivka smiled and shook his hand. "You must be the brains behind the infamous timelike self-intersecting loop."

Dr. West burst into laughter. "Ari, have you been propagandizing again? Just call the beast a time machine, will you? How else are we going to get the *National Enquirer* interested?"

Dov yanked the virtual reality headset off his head. "Most awesome, this software. Where can I get it?"

Dr. West jerked his thumb toward the door. "The guys in the next lab are collaborating on this with the archaeology department. It's still in beta, but they ought to be willing to let you play with a copy. They're going to call it *Avatar* when they go commercial."

"*Avatar?*" Rivka said. "As in the incarnation of a Hindu god?"

"That's one definition," Dr. West said. "But *avatar* is a buzz-word among computer geeks for any type of role-playing character, especially in virtual-reality games like this one. Do you want to try it?"

Rivka looked at her watch. "Oh my gosh! I didn't realize we were so late. Dov, have you and Jessica been waiting long?"

"Only an hour," Dov said. "But Professor West gave us a most entertaining lecture on his time machine. Furthermore, we had also the *Avatar* game to amuse us. Rivka, you really must try it. You can walk through the Second Temple, speak with the people, observe the sacrifices, hear the music, everything except smell the incense! Really very good."

"Some other time," Rivka said. "If we're going to see the Burnt House and the Wohl Archaeological Museum and the Gihon Spring, we'll need to hurry."

"Access to the spring is closed today," Dov said. "There was a small incident in the Arab Quarter this morning." He shrugged. "Maybe next weekend, yes?"

"Yes," Rivka said. "You promised a guided tour yesterday, and I'm going to get it!"

"And you can see the lab, too," Ari said. "If Damien ever gets our machine to work, maybe Dov can show you the original Temple Mount."

"Sounds like a deal to me," Rivka said. A number of blue metallic boxes against the wall caught her eye. She wandered over and bent down to inspect one.

A powerful hand clamped on her shoulder. "Miss Meyers, that capacitor can store enough charge to reshuffle your deck permanently."

Rivka stood up slowly.

Dr. West took his hand off her shoulder. "Of course, it has a grounding plate, but did you check for it?"

She shook her head. "I'm not quite sure what that would look like."

"Safety first, Miss Meyers! It only takes one accident to mess up your whole life."

"I'm sorry," she said. "I wasn't thinking."

"In my lab, I want you to think. And when you do, think safety."

Jessica had picked up a brick-shaped object from the table with both hands. "Goodness! What's in this thing? It must weigh fifty pounds!"

"It's a lead brick. For shielding." Dr. West shook his head as he crossed over to her. "I'll take that, Miss Weinberg. If you dropped it on your foot, you'd scream like a burning cat." He took the brick in one hand and idly did a few curls, as if it were a dumbbell.

"Damien's an exercise freak," Ari said. "He's got a black belt in judo."

"Not judo," Dr. West said. "Tae kwan do. And karate. But that's not exercise. It's just for discipline."

Rivka smiled to herself. Dr. West was definitely a bit odd.

"So, Damien," Ari said, "when are we going to get the device working?"

Dr. West shrugged his thick shoulders. "Maybe tomorrow. Maybe next year. That last shot really fubared the components."

"My fault," Ari said. "There was a singular solution that I missed."

"*Fubared?*" Dov asked. "I don't know this word."

Rivka smiled. "It's an acronym—fouled up beyond all recognition. Fubar."

"Which is precisely what happened," Dr. West said flatly. "And I don't have many spare capacitors."

Dov rubbed his hands together. "My friends, shall we leave the physicists to their laboratory? The Burnt House awaits!"

Rivka and Jessica both nodded agreement.

Jessica gave a little wave to Ari and Dr. West. "If you men don't blast yourselves into the last millennium, we'll see you next week. Same Bat-time; same Bat-station."

It wasn't very original, but for some reason, everybody laughed.

(((

That evening, as Dov's car puttered along a narrow two-lane highway back to the dig, Rivka sat hunched in the back seat. In the front passenger seat, Jessica suddenly tittered.

"Did I miss a joke?" Dov asked.

Jessica began chanting in a singsong voice. "Ari and Rivka, planting a tree, K-I-S-S-I-N-G!"

"*Mah zot omeret?*" Dov asked, then switched to English. "Something is wrong with your voice, Jessica?"

Jessica peered over her left shoulder at the back seat. "Come clean, Rivka! What were you really doing with Ari this morning? What took so long?"

"We were planting trees," Rivka said. "And I've got the body odor to prove it."

"Surrrrrrre," Jessica said. "I know another way to work up a sweat."

Dov wagged a finger at Jessica. "Rivka is a very nice girl," he said. "And besides, she has a boyfriend back in the States, yes, Rivka?"

Rivka grunted something, hoping the engine noise would transmute the sound into whatever Dov wanted to hear.

"Well, if you've got a boyfriend back home, maybe you'd better tell Ari about it," Jessica said. "I think he likes you, Rivka. You're just his type."

"That's ridiculous," Rivka said. "You could have gone tree-planting too, if you hadn't been sleeping in."

"If you say so," Jessica said in an airy voice. She turned on the radio. Scratchy music filled the small car.

Rivka leaned back in her seat and closed her eyes. *Pay no attention.* Jessica was probably just jealous that she had missed out on a good time.

Ari was a nice guy, but Rivka considered him off-limits for one simple reason. It was a good bet he didn't believe in God. And it was a given that he didn't believe in Yeshua. Whatever she did, she wasn't going to get involved with someone who didn't share her faith.

Jessica was probably imagining things. But if she turned out to be right, there was an easy way to solve the problem. *Hey, Ari, guess what? I'm a Messianic Jew.* That would nip it in the bud, wouldn't it?

Rivka felt her neck growing hot. Did she really want to tell Ari that? If she told him, he would probably freak out. And then he would tell Dov and Jessica, and they would think she had been deceiving them. Which, by her silence, she had been.

Great. She closed her eyelids, pressed both temples with her hands, and sighed. *Just great.* If it became necessary to tell Ari, she would do it.

Just not right yet.

Ari

Ari studied the text of the e-mail message he had just written. Should he or shouldn't he include the part about Rivka? Would Yoni read between the lines and see how crazy he was about Rivka? After five minutes of intense thought, he decided to leave it in. What harm could it do?

He clicked on the Send button with the mouse, then read the message again.

```
From:akazan@einstein.huji.ac.il
(Ari Kazan)
To:jon34@math.ucsd.edu
(Jonathan Stern)

   Shalom, Yoni:

   We are making progress on Damien's
wormhole device. He tells me that he
has nearly finished rebuilding the
power supplies and we should not
expect a repeat of last week's mishap.
I think you and I were partly to blame
```

for attempting that nearly singular configuration. I am sending an attached file with my guess at the B-field we should aim for next. What do you think? Your guess is probably better than mine. Let me know ASAP, since we expect to be firing the machine early next week. If it works, then maybe we'll see you last year. :)

By the way, my archaeologist cousin brought a couple of his colleagues up to Yerushalayim last weekend. You may know one of them, Rivka Meyers, since she is from San Diego and studied at UCSD. She says that her temple is Beth Simcha. Do you know her, by any chance?

Regards,

Ari

❰ ❰ ❰

When Ari turned on his computer the next day, a flashing icon notified him that he had e-mail in his in-box. He clicked on it and found that he had twelve messages. Eighth on the list was the reply from Yoni. Ari clicked on it first.

From: jon34@math.ucsd.edu
(Jonathan Stern)
To: akazan@einstein.huji.ac.il
(Ari Kazan)

hi ari:

>I am sending an attached file with
>my guess at the B-field we should aim
>for next. What do you think? Your
>guess is probably better than mine.

your equation 17 is wrong there is
a sign error and the solution is even
more singular than that last one. i
suggest you try it anyway. what can go
wrong, you're not going to blow up the
univers you know. keep me posted i
have a student looking at this problem
and he has some ideas for sovling
numercally. we have some;cray timne
saved up at the suprecompjting centre.
dont expect results beofre you fire
tho.

>If it works, then maybe we'll see
>you last year. :)

heehee, right. in stokcholm

>She says that her temple is Beth
>Simcha. Do you know her, by any
chance?

please tell me this is a joke. beth
simcha is a messianic jewish sysna-
gogue here in sd. they are very con-
versionary types and get in the news
once on a while wth their antics. tel-
lyour cousin to crcuify her, ok?

bye4now

yoni

Ari stared at the final paragraph. Yoni's typing was always atrocious, but he never got his facts wrong. If he said Beth Simcha was messianic, then it was. That crack about crucifying her was typical exaggeration. Yoni always talked like that, but he was actually a pacifist and a gentle soul.

A hard knot formed in Ari's gut. He clenched his fist and slammed it down on the table beside him.

Ari Kazan, you stupid meshuggener! *The first girl you fall for since high school, and she's a Christian!*

Damien

Saturday night. Damien smiled. His wife had left him, among other reasons, because he thought Saturday night was for doing physics. Tonight would be the Saturday night to end all Saturday nights. Literally.

Damien drummed his fingers impatiently while he waited for the power supplies to charge. The Sabbath had ended an hour ago, and power had come back on in the lab shortly thereafter. That was how the Israeli government kept the ultra-orthodox happy, by restricting the rights of everyone else.

All that would end soon. If this worked, there soon wouldn't be any electricity to shut off on the Sabbath. No generators. No wires. No engineers. And especially, no more bleeping physicists. Damien grinned. *I'm putting myself out of a job.*

He flipped up the screen on his personal laptop and double-clicked on an icon on his desktop. It was password-protected. A dialog box popped up, requesting the password. He typed it in. A document opened on the screen—the Unabomber Manifesto.

Damien had read this document a hundred times. Each time, he found pleasure in the tightly reasoned logic, the two hundred and thirty-two paragraphs, numbered as if they were theorems. Damien had highlighted the most important ones. He scrolled through the file, picking out his favorites with a practiced eye.

1. The Industrial Revolution and its consequences have been a disaster for the human race.

50. The conservatives are fools: They whine about the decay of traditional values, yet they enthusiastically support technological progress and economic growth.

121. You can't get rid of the "bad" parts of technology and retain only the "good" parts.

140. We hope we have convinced the reader that the system cannot be reformed in a such a way as to reconcile freedom with technology. The only way out is to dispense with the industrial-technological system altogether.

166. The factories should be destroyed, technical books burned, etc.

185. As for the negative consequences of eliminating industrial society—well, you can't eat your cake and have it too. To gain one thing you have to sacrifice another.

202. It would be hopeless for revolutionaries to try to attack the system without using *some* modern technology. If nothing else they must use the communications media to spread their message. But they should use modern technology for only one purpose: to attack the technological system.

Damien leaned back in his chair. The Unabomber's logic was flawless. It was his execution that was wrong. If he had studied his relativity theory and left the bomb-making to the chemists, he might have gotten somewhere. Ironically, he had even nibbled at the solution, and yet missed it. Damien scrolled down a bit more. There! *You had it, you fool, and you missed it!*

> 211. In the late Middle Ages there were four main civilizations that were about equally "advanced": Europe, the Islamic world, India, and the Far East (China, Japan, Korea). Three of those civilizations remained more or less stable, and only Europe became dynamic. No one knows why Europe became dynamic at that time; historians have their theories, but these are only speculation.

Damien scratched at the back of his neck. The answer should be obvious. Europe was Christian; the other three civilizations were not. Christianity in the late Middle Ages was in the process of inventing science.

The Greeks had made a stab at it, but they were too theoretical. Real science was based on experiment, not theory. Not to mention, they had this weird notion about time being cyclic. Of course, that ruled out the idea of progress, of evolution in thought.

The Jews had the right idea about time, that the universe had a beginning, that things were changing, developing, improving. Not to mention they were big on order and reason. But they didn't know a thing about math.

Somehow the Christians had picked up the worst of both Greeks and Jews. The Christians had fubared the world, first with their nut-ball morality plays, and second by inventing scientific method.

It wasn't that science was bad. Damien liked science. The problem was that science caused technology to move forward. In turn, technology pushed forward science. Positive feedback. Bad stuff. And technology was dorking up the world.

Nobody wanted to admit it, but the Unabomber was right. Half right, anyway. Right about technology. Missed the boat on religion.

Too late for that now. What good would it do to cut off a few branches? The thing to do was to get at the root. Historically speaking, you couldn't have science without Christianity. And you couldn't have Christianity without Paul.

Damien had read a book on it. Most people thought Jesus set up the show. Well, they were wrong. Jesus was just a nice little Jewish rabbi kind of guy who got himself killed. Then Paul went and made up all that stuff about the resurrection and communion and all that morality garbage about doing unto others.

Get rid of Paul, and you would shut it down. All the way down.

A beeping sound interrupted Damien's thoughts. He closed the file and went to check the power supplies. If Ari was right, they wouldn't need a huge current, but they would need a high voltage for the initial transient phase—a few hundred kilovolts. Damien didn't fully understand the theory. As an experimentalist, all he had to do was make the thing work. In his field, pulsed-power physics, nobody was better at doing exactly that.

The instruments passed his visual check. He went to the PC monitoring the experiment. Before making a shot, he always ran three diagnostics. The first two checked out. The third registered a hair high. Damien nudged one of the dials down, then rechecked everything. Good. Now throw the switch, and see what breaks this time.

Damien pressed the mouse button.

A loud bang rattled the lab. That was normal. You fired a gigawatt or so of power, even for a few microseconds, you were bound to get some noise. From now on, it would be very quiet. Given the high Q of this system, the steady-state power requirements were only a few hundred watts. Ari was a genius—give him credit for that.

The monitor showed the realtime waveform of the differential voltage between the two Rogowski coils. According to Ari's theory, this was proportional to the length of the closed timelike loop in spacetime. If the waveform showed zero, within the experimental noise, then the experiment had failed. The problem would be determinining whether it was exactly zero.

If it were nonzero, then it would be tiny—on the order of the Planck time, a billionth of a trillionth of a trillionth of a trillionth of a second.

Give or take.

But it wouldn't stay tiny. A positive feedback mechanism kept it growing exponentially in time. In a few hours, if the thing worked, the wormhole would have tunneled back in time by a full nanosecond, at which point Damien's instruments could measure it. Thereafter, the time tunnel would expand steadily, doubling every few minutes until Damien turned off the feedback mechanism. At that point it would freeze, locking in to whatever point in the past Damien wanted.

He had chosen Friday, May 27, A.D. 57.

The reason was very simple. On that date, Paul of Tarsus came riding into Jerusalem. Damien had looked it up in a book. That marked the beginning of the single week in Paul's life when you could pinpoint his location to within a few meters at several different points on the time line. Damien had worked it all out on a chart. A no-brainer.

Pretty soon, Paul would be a no-brainer too, if this experiment worked out.

At the moment, of course, nothing showed on the monitor. Damien checked the time. Barely after nine. Ari wouldn't come in until tomorrow morning. If the beast worked, Damien would be gone by then. And if it didn't, he would have learned something.

He kept a cot at the other end of the lab, which he used occasionally when he had to baby-sit experiments. He set his alarm for 4 A.M. Until then, the signal would be undetectable, so why worry about it?

Damien stretched out on the cot and closed his eyes.

Who knew? Tomorrow might be the last day of the rest of his life. Or rather, everybody else's life.

Rivka

Rivka leaned back in her chair, wondering what had gotten into Ari. He had been distant through the whole meal, leaving Dov and Jessica and her to do most of the talking. Last weekend, Ari had been quiet, but he had at least been there. Now he might as well be on Mars. His face seemed closed, and he picked at his food, ignoring the excited talk about Rivka's mosaic.

Jessica considered the mosaic the find of the summer for the entire dig. Dov thought it might be the find of the season for all of Israel. So far, they had uncovered nearly a third of it, revealing the hands and arms and lower bodies of two persons. The dating was uncertain, but some on the dig speculated early second century.

Rivka felt exhausted after a week of intense work. She simply lacked the energy now to talk much.

Dov fished in his wallet and laid out some bills on the table. "I am still wanting to see that art gallery we missed last weekend, my friends."

"Me, too," Jessica said as she put her money on top of Dov's.

Rivka dug into her pocket and pulled out some *shekel* notes. "Oh," she groaned. "I don't feel up to walking much."

Ari picked up the bill for the meal and handed it, along with a credit card, to the waiter. "Dov, I also am not in the mood to visit the art gallery. Perhaps I could sit here quietly and talk with Rivka?" He scooped up the cash and stuffed it into his shirt pocket.

Dov shrugged. "Ladies?"

Jessica nodded and flung a wink at Rivka.

Rivka ignored her. "I'd rather talk than walk tonight."

"Very good, then," Dov said. He stood and pulled back Jessica's chair. "We will meet you back here, Rivka? Or perhaps Ari would wish to walk you back to the hostel. It is not far."

"Hey! Good idea," Jessica said.

Rivka wondered if there was some conspiracy going on behind her back. "Don't worry about me," she said. "I'll be fine."

By the time the waiter returned with the credit-card slip, Dov and Jessica had disappeared into the thick crowds on Ben Yehuda Street. Ari signed the slip rapidly.

"Are you feeling well, Ari?" Rivka asked.

He clasped his hands on the table in front of him and studied them intently. "Not particularly well."

Rivka had learned long ago that one way to draw out a guy was to ask him about his work. "How is your progress on the wormhole?"

"Fine."

"How's Dr. West? He seems like he might be rather hard to get along with."

"I have no problems with Damien."

Was it her imagination? Had he stressed the word *Damien* just a hair? Was there someone else he was not getting along with? "Are you angry at someone, Ari?"

"No."

Rivka's heart skipped a beat at this staccato sentence. Why was he lying to her? "Are you angry at me?"

Ari unfolded his hands, then folded them again. "Rivka...I make an effort to be at peace with everyone."

So she was right. "And...?"

"And I also insist on the truth. That is something I value very highly."

Rivka gave a little half-laugh. "Um...good. I kind of like the truth too. Is there something I'm missing here?"

"Tell me again about this temple you attend in San Diego," Ari said. "It is called Beth Simcha?"

Rivka didn't really want to talk about Beth Simcha. "I don't live in San Diego anymore. I've been in Berkeley for three years now."

Ari's eyes narrowed, and now he raised them to look at her. "But your family lives in San Diego."

"Yes, that's right." She noticed again how intense his eyes were. Not intense and angry. Intense and sad.

He dropped his gaze again and pushed his chair back from the table. "It is not important. Please forget that I mentioned it."

"Ari! You can't just drop it like that. What's the matter?"

His Adam's apple bobbed twice. For a long moment his eyes drifted down Ben Yehuda Street. Then his features hardened. "So. You grew up in San Diego. And you had a bat mitzvah."

"That's right." Rivka suddenly felt a bit chilly. *Where was he going with this?*

"And this temple of yours is Reform?"

Rivka hesitated. Now she could guess Ari's direction. She just didn't know why. "No, not Reform."

"Conservative, perhaps?" Ari's long fingers splayed out on the glass table. "Not Orthodox, surely?"

"No, neither," Rivka said. "And not Reconstructionist." She swallowed hard. This was as good a time as any to just come out with it. The truth. "There's something I've been meaning to tell you, Ari."

"Yes?" His voice sounded thick. Again, his eyes drifted up, almost, but not quite locking on hers.

Rivka took a deep breath. "My father left my mother and me when I was five years old. Just walked out one day and didn't come back."

Ari's eyes clouded with sympathy. "I'm sorry."

"Neither of my parents was very religious. My mother had grown up Orthodox and hated it. My father was raised in a non-observant home. The amount of religion I got from them was exactly zero."

Ari said nothing.

"My mother wanted to get away from the East Coast, so she packed us up and we headed for San Diego. She got a job with General Dynamics, and a few years later married a supervisor in the Aerospace Division." Rivka paused. "A nice Jewish guy, but no religious affiliation."

Ari nodded.

Rivka hesitated, wondering how much of this she should tell. Would he laugh at her, if she told him all of it? She decided on the short version.

"Right after my eleventh birthday, my parents…decided to start going to temple. They had some personal stuff going on, and…well, they ended up going somewhere unexpected."

"Beth Simcha," Ari said. "Jews for Jesus."

So. He knew it all. Or thought he did. "Not quite," Rivka said. "Beth Simcha is a Messianic Jewish congregation. Jews for Jesus is a para-church organization—"

Something snapped in Ari's face, as if a wire stretched very tight inside his head had suddenly broken. "Yes, church," he said. "Very well put, Rivka. A Christian organization, not Jewish."

"Wrong." She said it firmly, but in a nice tone. "We are very much Jews."

"Do you worship That Man? Do you believe he is a god?"

"Yes, but—"

"Then you are Christians. Therefore you are not Jews."

Rivka pressed her hands to her temples. She was tired and beginning to feel a bit irritable. This wasn't the time to get into a long discussion about Judaism and Christianity. *Why did he think all this was so important, anyway?* "Listen, Ari, can we talk about this some other time? I'm really not in the mood for it right now."

"I only want the truth," Ari said. "Is that too much to ask?"

"No, but why now? Can't it wait?"

"If you are ashamed of the truth…"

That struck a nerve. Because she *was* ashamed. A little bit anyway. She was tired of this kind of thing, had come to Israel precisely to get away from it, and here it came flying back in her face again. Fine. If he wanted the truth, she was going to give it to him—as much as he could stand. She leaned forward. "Ari, did it ever occur to you that maybe you don't know everything? That maybe your preconceptions might possibly be wrong? That the things other people have told you about Yeshua might—"

"Yeshua!" Ari's face darkened. "That is a fraud. Why not call him by his true name, which is Jesus? You put a Jewish veneer on a Gentile concept. Perhaps you can sell it to American Jews who know nothing of their heritage, but not to Israeli Jews."

Rivka knew this gambit. *Big mistake, Ari Kazan! I've got you now.* "You need to study up on your history, Mr. Brilliant Physicist. Yeshua was as Jewish as they come. The earliest so-called Christians were all Jews. All of them! At first, they couldn't believe that Gentiles had any share in the *Mashiach*. Go back and read your history books."

Ari looked stung. "I am not ignorant of history. So let me tell you some history, if you are willing to listen without insulting me."

This was going to be interesting. "Go ahead."

"After the Babylonian exile, our people lived in many lands—among them Persia."

Rivka nodded.

"In Persia, certain Jews became infected with an avatar myth. You are familiar with such things?"

So he wanted to play a weird card here. Rivka leaned back in her chair and folded her arms. "Yes, I took a comparative religion course at UCSD."

"Therefore you know that the myth of a god coming down to be incarnated as a man is not new."

"Nothing's new, Ari. The Greeks thought of atoms twenty-five hundred years ago. They knew the earth was round two millennia before Columbus. There's nothing new under the sun."

"You are correct but irrelevant. Atoms exist, whether imagined by Greeks or not. Likewise, the earth is round, without regard to its geographers. But Jesus is a fraud. He never existed as a man. He is an instance of the avatar mythos perpetrated by quasi-Jewish syncretists. Failing to find an audience among true Jews, they turned to Gentiles with much greater success. Ergo, Christianity."

Rivka laughed out loud. Many educated Jews actually believed Jesus had never existed. She was used to that one. But this avatar stuff was new. And absurd. "Ari, I expected better of you. Do you have any evidence, or are you just making it up?"

"You believe that Jesus is the incarnation of a god?"

"Not just any god. Our God. The living God. The God of Abraham, Isaac, and Jacob."

"So you concede the point." Ari ticked off one of his fingers. "And you believe—"

"No!" Rivka slapped her hand on the table. "I don't concede anything."

"You just did. And you believe in the so-called Trinity, three gods who are alleged to be one. Very nice arithmetic. Perhaps you could educate me on this new type of mathematics?"

Great. That one was complicated. How did you explain the Trinity to someone who would just twist anything you said? Especially if you didn't understand it yourself? Time to veer back, put Ari on the defensive. "We were talking about avatars a minute ago. Why the change of subject?"

"Because I won that point," Ari said. "Your Jesus is nothing more than an avatar myth. He is no more real than those people in the computer game which Dov likes so much."

"Ari, you've got it backward. In that game, the most real character *is* the avatar—the representation of the actual human player holding the joystick. The other characters are completely unreal. They're figments generated by the software, no more real than shadows on the wall."

"So now you give me echoes of Plato, analogical thinking. Unfortunately, not logical thinking. Since you concede that Jesus is an avatar, you must resort to an analogy to make your point. Why do you avoid the truth?"

That got under Rivka's skin. "What is it with you, anyway? What are you, the truth fairy?"

Ari jerked backward as if she had slapped him.

Rivka tried to think of some way to defuse things. How had she gotten into this mess?

"It seems a small request that you should tell the truth," Ari said. His fingers lay clenched on the table, the knuckles white. "It is a lie to call a church a synagogue. It is a lie to call a Christian a Jew. Messianic Jews are an oxymoron."

"You have some problem with Jews who believe that the Messiah has come?" Rivka asked. "Were the Lubavitchers suddenly not Jews when some of them claimed that Rebbe Schneerson was the Messiah?"

Ari's face flashed with anger. "The Lubavitchers are fools," he said. "But they do not slaughter Jews, so they are not a problem. I have a problem with Christians persecuting my people for two thousand years."

"But—"

Ari cut her off with a wave of the hand. "You have heard of what they did to Rabbi Akiva and Bar Kochva? You have heard of Constantine and his forced conversions? You have heard of the slaughter of Jews during the Crusades? You have heard of the torture of Jews during the Spanish Inquisition? You have heard of the strange love for Jews displayed by Martin Luther? You know about Chmielnicki and his pogroms? You think the Holocaust was an aberration?"

"Ari, I know all that," Rivka said. "There are answers—"

"The answers of Christians begin with stones, continue with swords, and end with fire," Ari said. "I am not interested in their answers."

Rivka felt heat rushing through her temples. She had studied the history of Christian dealings with Jews, and it was ugly. Unforgivably ugly. And yes, there was reason to think that the Holocaust was the natural fruit of that history. But it had been sixteen centuries of persecution, not twenty, and long stretches in the middle had been marked by peace between Jew and Christian. Anyway, it was all over now, wasn't it? Mostly over. The pope had even declared back in the sixties that Jews weren't responsible for the crucifixion. Evangelicals had gotten interested in the Jewish roots of their faith. The mainline Protestant churches were increasingly tolerant. Only fringe right-wing groups still called Jews Christ-killers. Things had changed.

Mostly.

"Just tell me this," Ari said, jabbing a finger at her. "Are you a Jew or a Christian?"

Rivka leaned forward, tired and angry. "Wrong question, Mr. Grand Inquisitor. I'm a Jew who believes that the Messiah has come, and His name is—"

"Wrong!" Ari shouted. "If you believe in That Man, then you are not a Jew. Case closed." He slammed his open palm down on the table. Both glasses of water jumped.

Rivka suddenly noticed that people at other tables were staring at them. Fine. If they wanted a show, they'd get one. She was just angry enough to do something crazy. She slowly stood, picked up a glass of water, and tossed its contents into Ari's face.

"Cool off." She slammed the empty glass down hard on the table. "And you can go jump in your wormhole!"

She stalked away without looking back.

Pedestrians parted for her, staring with open mouths. Let the idiots gawk. What did she care? She didn't need any more abuse from Ari. And she didn't need him to walk her back to the hostel. She could find her own way.

One thing was for sure. Jessica wouldn't be doing that stupid chant on the way back to the dig this time.

Ari

Ari stood hastily and tried to brush the water off himself. He quickly gave up and began walking away in the opposite direction from Rivka. After a block, the heat of his anger began to dull.

He had told her the truth, and what had it accomplished? He had alienated her, just like he knew he would. *Poof!* Gone. Whatever it was that she had, that inner fire, that grace he had admired, that wit—all gone.

Because he was a donkey, that was why. A king-size, monumental, dumb-headed donkey. A fool.

Why? Why? Why?

Some questions had no answers. Ari had learned that a long time ago, at the age of three.

Who killed Papa? He used to ask his mother that, over and over, until it drove her wild and she beat him on the head with her wooden spoon.

Why do people hate us? That one had five hundred answers, and none.

Why can I have either the truth or peace, but not both?

Why, why, why?

Once a year or so, Ari went looking for an answer to one of these questions—in a bottle. American whiskey sometimes had the answer. Or Russian vodka. Or English gin. He was not particular about the country of origin, as long as it drowned the unanswerable questions.

After a block, Ari found a small food store, the Israeli counterpart to the American supermarket. He stepped inside and headed for the section that he usually avoided.

The aisle with the liquid answers.

Damien

Eleven-year-old Damien West stared into the murky green lake water, afraid to jump, afraid not to.

"Go ahead," said his brother Stu. "You dive in first. I dare you."

Damien shivered. Why was it always like this? Fear gnawed a hole in his gut. The diving raft swayed gently beneath his bare feet, rocked by small waves. The wind sucked the warmth out of his thin body. He peered into the water again, then backed away from the edge.

"Chicken!" Stu said. "You never want to go first!" He was fourteen, afraid of nothing.

"You show me how," Damien said. "You're better at it than I am." He looked back toward the cabin, where their parents were still changing. Maybe he shouldn't have swum out here with Stu before the adults were ready.

"Okay, watch this." Stu stepped to the edge of the raft, leaped out into space, and executed a perfect jackknife with a half-twist. His muscular body swished cleanly into the water.

"Good one!" Damien shouted. But of course Stu couldn't hear him underwater. Damien waited. Any second now, Stu's head would pop

*up. Had he swum underneath the raft? Damien turned to look, but
Stu wasn't behind him.*

*Five seconds ratcheted into ten, then into twenty. Stu could stay
underwater for almost a minute—much longer than Damien. But
still, he didn't appear.*

*Damien's heart beat faster. Where was Stu? How long had he
been under?*

"Stu!" Damien shouted. "Quit playing. Come on up!"

Nothing.

*Cold dread numbed Damien's mind, and with it came courage.
He stepped off the raft, plunging feet first into the lake. The water had
barely closed over his head before his feet jarred into the muddy
bottom. The shock rattled through his soul.*

"Stuuuuuuuu!"

Professor Damien West woke up shouting. His skin felt
clammy and hot, and his heart galloped madly in his chest.
"Stu," he whispered into the darkness. "Why'd you have to go
first?"

☾ ☾ ☾

Damien couldn't go back to sleep, so he lay on his cot thinking
about his brother until his alarm went off at 4 A.M. He flicked
on the lights, blinked until his eyesight adjusted, and went to
check the monitor.

What the …? Staring at the results, Damien nearly blew a
brain gasket. The wormhole looked like it was growing!

After the first shock, he double-checked everything. It might
be a calibration error or baseline drift. After all, the instruments
showed only a one-nanosecond difference between the front and
back ends of the wormhole.

A few minutes later, it showed two nanoseconds. Then four. Then nine. The time gap doubled in a bit less than three minutes. Exponential growth.

A wormhole condensate.

Damien drank coffee and watched the monitor as his baby grew and grew and grew. It took over an hour to grow the wormhole out to a one-second timespan. In minutes, it stretched out to two, then five, then ten seconds. Beautiful.

In another hour-and-something, the beast had tunneled back a hundred years into the past. Damien realized he had to act fast. At this rate, in ten or fifteen minutes the wormhole would dig its way three thousand years back. He didn't want to go that far.

Damien dialed the feedback down a bit and let things stabilize. He decided to just run it manually from here on in. He would tweak the voltage a bit and see how far the wormhole tunneled into the past. From that, he could work out with a calculator how much to tweak it the next time.

Unfortunately, the wormhole had a natural time delay between the action and the response, and that limited how fast he could work. Also, he had no margin for error. If he overshot his target date, he couldn't shrink the wormhole back. This was a one-way street.

Damien cursed his stupidity. If he had thought about this before, he could have written a control program to do this automatically while he sat back and watched. But he hadn't thought about it. In any experiment, you ran into things you didn't consider in advance, and that led to screwups. People always acted surprised to hear that brilliant physicists made mistakes. Damien liked to respond that physicists weren't all that brilliant, but if you gave them enough chances, they would eventually get it right.

Normally, it didn't matter. If one shot went fubar, you fixed it and made another shot. That wouldn't work here. According to Ari, this was a one-shot deal. If it worked, fine. If it didn't, there would be no second chances. The way Ari had explained it, the machine was tapping into a nonrenewable resource. Damien didn't understand Ari's calculations, but he did understand that he couldn't afford any mistakes.

He also understood that his bladder felt ready to pop. All that coffee had come back to haunt him. He made a rapid calculation in his head, adjusted the dial to a safe setting, and ran for the bathroom.

It took longer than he expected. His kidneys must have been in overdrive, he figured. When he got back, he immediately saw that he had made a slight mistake. The growth of the wormhole had slowed down to almost nil. He dialed up the feedback as high as it would go, but the wormhole made little response. He punched in a quick calculation on his calculator, and then swore. It would take another fifteen minutes at least to get the growth rate up again, and more than that to home in on the date he had chosen. It was already past seven. He would be doing very well to lock in the wormhole on target before eight. And he still had to pack his things.

Ari would come in long before then, if he followed his normal routine. Then again, he might not follow his normal routine today. Last week, he had ditched work to go tree-planting with that girl, the smart one. She was supposed to come back this weekend. Damien resisted the urge to cross his fingers. He didn't believe in superstitions, but he could only hope Ari had gotten lucky last night. If so, he might sleep in for once.

Damien watched the monitor for a while. At last he saw what he wanted. The wormhole had begun advancing again into the past. And still no sign of Ari. Damien went to his desk and rummaged around for his victory cigar. He had seen that in a movie awhile back and decided that if his plan ever succeeded, he would smoke one, too, no matter how bad it tasted.

The cigar wasn't half smoked before he locked the wormhole down on target: May 27, A.D. 57. He shut down the feedback mechanism, ensuring that the wormhole couldn't tunnel even one more millisecond into the past. Now the only way to change the wormhole was to destroy it—let it shrink back down to the Planck size where nobody could ever use it again.

Damien stepped carefully to a reinforced doorway set in the wall. The wormhole lived inside this closet. He hesitated. It might be a good idea to take this slowly. Safety first. He had set the oscillating electric field at a level to just maintain the wormhole. It ought to be safe, but why take chances? And who knew how that exotic matter would behave?

Cautiously, he grabbed the doorknob. Last night, it had led into an empty closet. Now, it should be a dream right out of H.G. Wells. He pulled the door open.

Damien cursed aloud and took a step back, aghast. In front of him waited a great ball of...nothing. Blackness. Emptiness. He shut the door, his hand trembling.

Wormholes diffused electromagnetic radiation. He knew that. You couldn't see through them, though you should be able to walk through. In theory. Kip Thorne's book showed a sketch of a wormhole, and Damien had thought himself prepared.

But he wasn't. Suddenly the victory cigar in his mouth tasted foul.

Rivka

Rivka slowed as she reached the third floor of the physics department. What would Ari say when he saw her? Would he apologize? Ignore her? Start another argument?

She guessed that he would at least be civil, especially if Dr. West were there. It would be nice if they could both agree that they had overreacted last night. For her part, she wanted to tell him she had some doubts herself. If she admitted she didn't know everything about God, maybe Ari would back down a little and admit he didn't know everything about Yeshua. Not that she held out much hope of him coming to know Yeshua anytime soon, but at least they could be friends. You had to admire a man as committed to the truth as Ari.

Rivka's nose twitched as she wandered down the hallway. Why did people smoke those horrible-smelling cigars? And barely after eight in the morning!

She pushed open the lab door and then coughed. It smelled thick in there, and her eyes watered. "Ari!" she said. "Put that thing out. The war's over. Truce!"

Dr. West's laugh echoed from the far end of the room. "Oh, hello. I wasn't expecting a lady this morning, so I thought I would try something stronger than coffee to help me wake up." He strode toward her, his face redder than Rivka remembered it, his blue eyes oddly bright. He stubbed out his cigar in a large brass ashtray. "I'm sorry. You'll have to remind me of your name again."

"Rivka Meyers." She held out her hand, and he shook it.

"If you've come to see Ari, he's not in yet. I have no idea why not."

Rivka tugged nervously at her right earlobe. "I hope he's not too upset with me. We had...a bit of an argument last night."

"An argument?" Dr. West nodded. "He does that once in a while—flies off the handle. He usually forgets the next day. I expect he'll show up any minute. Would you like some coffee?"

"No, I'm wide awake." An awkward silence hung between them. "Maybe you could show me the famous wormhole that you've been working on," Rivka offered.

Dr. West's face took on an odd expression.

"Is something wrong?" she asked.

He shook his head, and then a broad smile creased his face. "No, it's just…I'm a little nervous. I've got the power supplies all ready to charge up for a shot, as soon as Ari gets in. I don't want to touch anything until we fire."

"I won't get too close," Rivka said. "I never did like electricity much."

Dr. West led her toward the far end of the room and pointed toward a doorway. "That's the portal—"

"A *doorway?*" Rivka said. "That's it? Just a doorway?"

"Not *just* a doorway," Dr. West said. "It's wired up to carry some heavy juice through it, and there's a special conduit for exotic matter. Don't ask what that is—I haven't the foggiest. But Ari goes on about it for hours if you let him. Anyway, the doorway's reinforced pretty well to resist the transient forces."

"Where does it lead?"

"Right now, it goes into a closet," Dr. West said. "If Ari's theory works as we think, when we throw the switch, a wormhole will develop inside there that leads to whenever you want."

"When would you like to go to?"

He grinned again. "Last October, so I can bet on the World Series. I lost a lot of money last year. This time I'll earn it all back and maybe break Las Vegas just for grins."

Rivka laughed. "Ari says you can't change the past."

Dr. West shrugged. "Who knows? Nobody's ever tried. Do you believe you can change the future?"

"You mean, do I have free will?" Rivka said. "Sure, I believe that. Most people do."

"Well, if you can change the future, why not the past?" Dr. West said. "Same thing, from a physicist's point of view."

"I'm not a physicist," Rivka said. "I'll let you and Ari argue that one out."

Dr. West smiled. "Ari always wins our arguments," he said. "But once in a while, even a dumb experimentalist like me can prove a smart theorist wrong. In physics, the experiment gets the final word."

Rivka turned around. "Speaking of Ari, where is that guy?"

"He should be here any minute," Dr. West said. "Would you like to play that game *Avatar* we were demoing last week for your friends?"

That sounded interesting. "Sure," Rivka said. "That's the kind of journey into the past I can understand."

Damien

Damien could hardly believe his luck. Five minutes ago, he had thought he had lost everything. The wormhole looked like the high dive to nowhere, and Ari might show up at any minute.

But now, here came Rivka with excellent news. She'd had an argument with Ari. Knowing Ari, Damien guessed he would go plant some of his stupid trees for a few hours.

Furthermore, if he played his cards right, maybe he could maneuver Rivka into serving as a guinea pig. Would she bite?

Rivka looked up from the computer. "Okay, it's finished booting up. Where's this *Avatar* game?"

Damien put on his happy face and came around the table to stand behind her. A few mouse clicks later, he stepped back. While the program loaded, a graphic splashed up on the screen—a fly-through of the Temple in the year A.D. 66. "Pretty, isn't it?"

Rivka nodded. "How does this game work?"

Damien picked up the virtual reality headset. "You put this on over your eyes, and it shows you a 3-D view of wherever you're at in the computer-generated world. The headset has motion sensors, so as you walk around or turn your head, the computer rotates your world or moves you through it, just like you're really there. It's pretty standard as far as graphics go, but the archaeology boys did some really neat stuff with artificial intelligence. You've got a mike in the headset, so you can talk to characters, and they'll respond. Sorry, but right now, it only works if you speak Hebrew."

"That's no problem," Rivka said. "Is there a wire I'm going to trip over?"

"It's got a digital wireless link," Damien said. "The range is something huge, like a quarter mile, but you can't go more than fifty feet in this room, so you won't go out of bounds. By the way, the motion sensor amplifies your forward motion. Even small steps will move you pretty fast, so you don't have to go very far in real space to move a long way in the virtual world."

"My father would love this," Rivka said. "How do you put this gear on?"

"Step over here, away from the computer table, so you won't bump into anything," Damien said. He put the headset on her head and carefully strapped it under her chin. No need to spook her. She was about to perform a great service to the world.

"Awesome!" Her voice came through the computer's speakers. "I can't believe this." She turned her head left, right, and then straight up.

The image on the computer monitor showed a 2-D rendition of everything Rivka saw inside the headset. She stood in the outer courts of the Temple. Thousands of people milled around her, dressed in the garb of ancient Judea. Looking at the display, Damien could hardly believe how much punch computers packed these days—more than a Cray only twenty years ago. "Okay, now just take a small step," he said.

She did. The image on the screen seemed to zoom forward.

"Take it easy," he said. "The software amplifies forward motion."

"What a terrific teaching tool!" she said. "I've got to get this for my machine at home."

"Here's something really inventive," Damien said. "Try talking to one of the people passing by you."

Rivka spoke to one of the female passersby in Hebrew. The woman stopped, turned, and said something in response. Damien caught a few words, but his Hebrew was pretty rusty. He knew enough for his purposes, so why learn more?

Rivka began walking, taking small steps. The inner Temple zoomed toward her on the monitor.

Damien tiptoed toward the doorframe leading into the wormhole. Quietly, he opened the door and pulled it all the way around until it latched, wide open. He couldn't see through the wormhole, but he knew perfectly well what lay on the other side—a cave he had located precisely a month earlier using a global positioning device. The wormhole tunneled through both space and time. It had to. Even Damien understood that the-orem. The cave actually lay a couple of miles away, on the slopes of the Mount of Olives, a convenient place for Damien to emerge into his Brave Old World. But only if it were safe.

Damien returned to the computer monitor. Rivka had made it into the inner Temple and was engaged in a conversation with a fierce-looking priest with a bushy beard and piercing eyes. The man looked a bit like Ari, Damien noted with amusement.

When Rivka finished the conversation, Damien picked up the joystick. He had neglected to tell Rivka one important detail. The program could also be controlled by the joystick. When both the headset and the joystick were in use, the computer simply added both movements together to determine the view. Which allowed Damien to steer Rivka—albeit awkwardly. He had discovered this feature last week when Ari's cousin played the game.

Guiding Rivka was both hard and easy. Hard, because Rivka didn't want to walk in a straight line for very long. Easy, because she took baby steps, allowing him to correct any errors before she got far.

It took several minutes to get her near the door. Then she sneezed.

Damien held his breath, thinking she might have smelled the cave. Would she take off her headset before she went through the door?

She didn't. Instead, she began moving toward one end of the courtyard in the Temple, where steps led up to a huge altar and, beyond that, to the inner sanctum. Damien wasn't very familiar with the Temple geography, but he guessed that all the gory stuff happened in there. Rivka made a beeline for that altar.

Damien rotated Rivka's world just a bit with the joystick. She corrected for this by changing her own direction a hair. Bit by bit, he got her pointed toward the wormhole. Then he used the mouse to lower the sensitivity of the forward motion sensors. This forced her to move her feet more to get the same motion in her imaginary world. Again, he did this gradually, so she wouldn't notice.

In a few minutes, Rivka stood in the doorway.

Damien held his breath. Anything could happen here. Would she be zapped by stray electric fields? Would magnetic fields stir up eddy currents to fry the metal in her cutoffs? Would some weird gravitational gradient rip her apart by tidal forces? He simply hadn't worried about all this until a few minutes ago. Nobody had ever done this before, and nobody would ever do it again. Unless Ari was wrong about only being able to build *one* of these beasts.

Even then, Damien would make him right by the simple expedient of rewriting the last twenty centuries of history with a magic bullet into Paul's brain. With that minor revision, nobody would ever make a wormhole again. There wouldn't be enough science left to blow your nose with.

While Damien wiped the sweat off his palms, Rivka walked through the doorway and into the wormhole. And vanished. Damien kept his eyes glued on the computer monitor. Good! The radio link hadn't broken. Rivka stopped to talk to some fool musician, halfway up the steps into the inner sanctum of the Hebrew god.

Damien slowly exhaled. It worked! The wormhole was safe! Which presented another problem. How would he get Rivka to turn around and come back? She wandered on, oblivious to the fact that she had just walked into a different century. And still, she kept moving.

Somebody knocked at the door of the lab. Damien's heart began racing. Now what? He made a snap decision. Silently, he glided to the wormhole and eased the door shut. He would leave Rivka alone in her little world for a few minutes, and then he would come back and figure out some way to get her back into the present. He didn't need her anymore. She had jumped off the high dive first. The water was safe. Damien felt ready to dive in himself.

The knocking continued, hesitant and unsure. Damien hurried to answer it.

When he opened the door, he saw the mousy new postdoc who had just arrived from China. The young man stared shyly at the floor and then poured out his question in very bad English. "So very sorry to disturb. Laser printer out paper. Where is more?"

Damien put on his most genial smile. "I'm afraid I don't know," he said. "I would suggest you try the department secretary down on the first floor. She knows more than God."

It took three repetitions, with much smiling and gesturing on Damien's part, to get this message into the postdoc's brain. Then the young man mistook Damien's smile for friendliness and asked if he came from the United States, and if so, where?

Damien tried a short answer, but there seemed no way to explain in a few words where Northwestern University was located. No, not in the Northwest. In the Midwest, just north of Chicago. No, he did not know Bill Gates. No, he had never been to the University of Washington, where the postdoc had a friend. And all of this had to be repeated several times.

Damien began getting worried. How long had Rivka been alone? Five minutes? Six? Seven? He didn't know for sure, but he wanted to check up on her. Finally, he simply sneezed three times, right in the postdoc's face.

The young man stepped backward.

"Sorry," Damien said with a smile. "Sick." He pointed at his nose. "Bad cold."

The postdoc nodded and kept backing away. Damien smiled, waved a friendly good-bye, and shut the door. He turned and ran back toward the wormhole. When he reached it, he took a few seconds to catch his breath. Then he eased the door open, stepped into the wormhole, and walked through to the other side.

In the dim light in the middle of the cave, a man lay retching on the ground. Rivka was nowhere in sight.

Damien backed through quickly and pushed the door shut. His face suddenly felt very hot. What had happened? Something bad. Something very bad.

But no time to worry about that. He had to move quickly—finish packing, set the wormhole for a delayed shutdown, and then go. If he found Rivka soon, he could send her back.

Otherwise…that would just be too bad for her. He couldn't afford to let anything screw up his plan. As the Unabomber had pointed out, in order to gain one thing, sometimes you had to sacrifice something else.

Or someone else.

PART III

If I have a time machine (wormhole-based or otherwise), I should be able to use it to go back in time and kill my mother before I was conceived, thereby preventing myself from being born and killing my mother. Central to the matricide paradox is the issue of *free will*: Do I, or do I not, as a human being, have the power to determine my own fate?

—Kip Thorne
Black Holes and Time Warps,
chapter 14

Rivka

Jerusalem. Old Jerusalem!

Rivka kept wondering if she were crazy. Or hallucinating.

The world around her looked painfully real, and yet painfully different. The sky had that brilliant blue hue that she had only seen in parts of the world untouched by the internal combustion engine. The smell of wood smoke hung in the air, just like her San Diego neighborhood at Christmastime. Another smell assaulted her nose too. She stepped around a large pile of mule dung. And straight across this valley, the walls of the Temple Mount rose up high, looking fresh and new, like the model at the Holyland Hotel, but life-size.

What kind of reality had she fallen into? It was more real than that silly virtual reality thing she had been playing. And yet it was unreal. The Temple as she saw it now had not existed for more than nineteen hundred years. Was it some grand illusion?

Rivka could think of only one explanation. Ari's theory of time machines, or timelike self-intersecting loops, or whatever the heck they were called, had worked. Raw joy welled up in her heart at that. He had earned his Nobel prize.

The explanation seemed reasonable, but it raised a disturbing question. If there were a wormhole in the lab, why hadn't Dr. West warned her about it? She was going to ask him some hard questions as soon as she went back.

Not right away, of course. The way back to the wormhole led past an attacker. She would have to wait awhile before she felt safe going back. Anyway, she wanted to do a little sight-seeing first. It wasn't every day you walked into a different millennium. It wasn't every day you came within an eyelash of getting...

Rivka shivered. Her knee throbbed painfully from the fall she had taken. She looked at it again. A long trickle of blood ran down her shin from her knee. She needed some water to wash it off.

She turned and began walking south. Within a hundred yards, she spotted a campground off to her left on the slopes of the Mount of Olives. The last time she had visited here, she had seen a church. Now, black goatskin tents sprawled everywhere, seemingly placed at random. Dozens of children raced among them, screaming while they played a game of tag. As she came nearer, they all seemed to spot her at once. For a moment they simply stared.

Then they disappeared.

Rivka kept walking, hoping to get past without incident.

Suddenly, a score of women emerged from the tent city. They wore modest neck-to-toe garments, somewhat like Bedouin women—but different. One of them shouted at Rivka. Then all of them shook their fists and screamed.

Rivka turned and ran. It had to be Aramaic they were speaking. It definitely wasn't Hebrew, either modern or biblical. She had never heard Aramaic spoken, but she had read plenty. The consonants she had heard seemed to be fairly close to modern Hebrew, though the vowels were inflected in Aramaic patterns. She hadn't quite caught what the women said, but one word stuck in her ears. It kept rattling around now inside her head. *Zonah.*

Whore.

Assuming she really had gone back in time, one point had just become exceedingly clear. She hadn't dressed appropriately for this party.

Damien

Damien carefully packed the pistol into his duffel bag and zipped it shut. Almost ready. He was sweating now, partly in nervous anticipation, partly because he had been rushing around the lab for the last fifteen minutes. Only two things left to do. He opened a file on his laptop, printed it to the laser printer down the hall, then trotted out the door and down to the printer. No good to have curious eyes reading his chronology of Paul's last visit to Jerusalem.

Seconds later, he rushed back into the lab, fuming. The blasted laser printer was out of paper, as he ought to have known. He checked the queues of all the printers in the building. One on the second floor was ready. He printed the document and then dashed out to get the copy. When he returned with the paper, he stuffed it into the pocket of his bag and closed the lid on the laptop.

Now only one task remained. Damien strode to his desk and pulled out an Arab costume. He figured that if he were going into the first century, he had better be dressed to fit in. This was the closest thing he had been able to come up with. He pulled the caftan over his head and down his body, plopped the *kaffiyeh* on his head, stepped out of his Reeboks, and slipped on the sandals. Not perfect, probably, but it would do him until he could buy more clothes. He had packed plenty of gold and silver—

enough to last a lifetime. Which was important, because he wasn't coming back. If his plan worked, there would be nothing to come back to.

He slipped his Reeboks into the duffel bag, shouldered it, stepped to the computer, set the delay for sixty minutes, and clicked the mouse on the Shutdown Wormhole button.

Then he stepped back and smiled. Almost irrevocable now. The wormhole would collapse in an hour. The delay would give him time to come back if he hit any immediate problems. He didn't expect any, but it never hurt to have a fail-safe. He took a last sip of his coffee, marched to the wormhole doorway, and opened it. The empty void didn't spook him now. Rivka had proved it safe. He looked back at the lab for just a moment. The words of a song from the sixties popped into his head. *Stop the world—I want to get off!*

Damien stepped through the doorway and pulled the door shut. In an hour, the wormhole would collapse down to the Planck diameter, too tiny to imagine. If Rivka didn't get back before then, she wouldn't get back at all. Tough luck.

He strode forward through the wormhole and into the cave, smiling. He had a wonderful past ahead of him.

Rivka

Rivka walked rapidly down the road toward the southeast corner of the city. Straight ahead, beyond the Hinnom Valley, a forest of Jerusalem pines shimmered in the sunlight. To her left, the Mount of Olives rose, minus the thousands of tombs she had seen last time she was here. And to her right, the city of her dreams, the city of a thousand songs. *Yerushalayim shel zahav.* Jerusalem the Golden. Her pulse hammered with excitement.

Soon the road intersected with a much busier one coming from the south. Rivka marched into the foot traffic, hungry to reach the city.

Children dashed in and out among the adults, screeching in Aramaic. Women walked more sedately, baskets balanced perfectly atop their heads. All of them were as modestly dressed as the Iranian women Rivka had seen on TV. Even their hair was covered. She felt their disapproving stares burning holes in her T-shirt. She ignored the men who turned to goggle at her.

Ari's wormhole idea had worked. Unbelievable! The evidence surrounded her, pummeling her senses, and yet she almost refused to accept it. Was it tied in to the *Avatar* game somehow? No, that had to be a red herring. Computers were powerful, but they couldn't warp time. Only a wormhole could have brought her to this place, or rather this time—whenever it was.

But first things first. Rivka needed to wash the bleeding gash on her knee. After that, she would try to find some clothes that would help her fit in better. She absolutely had to look around at the sights. This place was just...stupendous. As soon as she got herself presentable, she would be homing in on the Temple Mount.

She would go back to Ari's wormhole later and get Dov and Jessica and bring them here. They would just *freak* when they saw this place. But she wanted to get a good look around first before she went back. And she didn't dare go near that cave for a while yet.

As soon as she passed through the city gates, she saw what she needed—the Pool of Siloam. It lay right where the maps showed it, fifty yards inside the city. Rivka headed straight for it.

The pool was surrounded by a stone wall, with a gate at the west end. Rivka ducked inside the gate and scanned the area. A number of modestly dressed young women stood around the walls, holding clay jars and chatting idly. Every one of them had perfect posture—heads, shoulders, hips, and heels in a straight line. Self-conscious, Rivka stood a little straighter. She guessed that these were servants of the rich, or daughters of the poor, or hired laborers.

The women quickly noticed her, and the chatter around the pool hushed. Rivka gave an uncertain smile and stepped toward the pool. Edged with stone, it looked much like a swimming pool. The north end opened into a cave, the famous tunnel built by King Hezekiah. The tunnel carried water from a hidden spring outside the city, enabling the city to withstand a siege by the Assyrian king Sennacherib in 701 B.C.

Rivka dipped her hands into the pool and scooped up some water onto her bleeding knee. The cool liquid stung her raw flesh. Rivka gritted her teeth and poured more water on it.

"What happened, little sister?" The question, in Aramaic, came from directly behind her.

Rivka turned around. A slim young woman stood there, concern in her eyes. She stood a couple of inches taller than Rivka and looked to be about twenty-five. She wore a loose, boxy tunic of unbleached wool and her hair was completely hidden by a cloth covering.

"I fell," Rivka said, choosing her words carefully and speaking slowly. She had never actually spoken Aramaic before. She had only read it. "A man chased me."

The young woman nodded. "You are lucky twenty men did not chase you, dressed like that. You are new at this, are you not?"

That was putting it mildly. "Yes, I'm new. My name is Rivka."

"My name is called Hana," said the woman.

Rivka noted the idiom. Next time, she would say, *My name is called Rivka.*

Hana turned around and shook a fist at the other young women staring at them. "So what is there to look at?" she shouted. "I will take care of little sister here. Mind your own business, all of you. And I am next—understand?"

Hana must be some sort of a leader here. The other young women instantly averted their eyes from Rivka and formed into little clusters of animated gossip.

Hana led Rivka toward the wall nearest the entrance. Together, they stood in the shade, out of the mid-morning sun. "The first thing you need is some decent clothes," Hana said. "That was very foolish, wearing those. Where did you get them?" She fingered the blue denim of Rivka's cutoffs. "What do you call these?"

Rivka grinned and told the truth. "Levis 501 jeans."

Hana stared at her. "Levites what?"

A man walked in through the gate. He had a thick gray beard, a well-cut linen tunic, and the posture of a man used to giving orders. At once, all the girls around the pool stopped chattering and turned to look at him. One of them started forward. Hana snapped her fingers at the girl, shook her head hard, picked up a clay water vessel, and strode toward the man.

"*Adoni,* do you wish me to carry water for you?"

Adoni, Rivka noted. When you addressed a man in this culture, you called him *Adoni.* Sir.

The man's eyes swept over Hana in a way that sent shivers down Rivka's back. Then his gaze fell on Rivka, and he pointed at her. "You. I want you to carry water."

Rivka felt a rush of panic in her belly. She had no vessel, nor any practice in carrying a jar on her head.

Hana intervened. "*Adoni,* my little sister is unclean this week. Please allow me."

"How much?" the man asked.

Rivka hadn't expected that. But of course! In any primitive culture you negotiated everything.

"Two *dinars,*" Hana said.

Rivka's eyes nearly popped out. Two days' wages, just to carry water? Hana had made a ridiculous offer.

The man shook his head in apparent disbelief. "Two *dinars?* For that, you should carry me and not my water only."

"Very well, *Adoni,*" Hana said.

"One *dinar,*" said the man.

Rivka blinked. What was going on here?

"Two," Hana said, her voice taking on a stubborn note. "And I will carry two vessels of water."

A slow smile spread over the man's face. "Two. Very well," he said. "Follow me." He turned and walked out into the street.

Hana stepped to the pool and lowered her clay vessel into the pool. With a quick, smooth motion, she lifted it atop her head and strode out into the street. "Come with me, little sister."

Rivka hurried to catch up with her, wondering why Hana had promised two vessels of water when she could carry only one at a time. Why not ask one of the other girls to carry one? Was she going to come back? And why the outrageous price?

The man had stopped at a small shop thirty paces up the street, looking at something. Hana walked past him without stopping or speaking. Rivka stared at him as they passed.

"Do not look, little sister," Hana hissed. "Have you no manners? A woman does not speak to a man in the street." Her voice had the tone adults used when talking to children.

"Would you mind explaining what this is all about?" Rivka asked. "And how do you know the way unless he leads?"

Hana said nothing. With quick steps, she sliced through the crowded street, walking at a pace that soon had Rivka trotting to keep up. Rivka looked back once, but a sharp intake of breath from Hana stopped her. They headed uphill toward the Temple Mount. After a couple of hundred yards, Hana suddenly turned right onto a tiny side street that wound its way through a thicket of one-story stone buildings. They took a couple of turns, then stopped. Hana withdrew a large iron key from the cloth belt at her waist. She inserted it into the lock of the front door, turned it a quarter turn and pulled back. The latch clicked open. She reversed the procedure to withdraw the key. A stone bench with no back huddled against the outside of the building.

Hana pointed at it. "You will sit there and wait, little sister. If anyone troubles you, shout loudly."

Rivka sat, thoroughly puzzled.

Hana pushed open the door and stepped inside, leaving the door ajar. A few minutes later, the man arrived. He leered at Rivka for just a moment and then went inside. The door clicked shut behind him.

A horrible thought suddenly formed in Rivka's mind. Shortly, she heard voices through the narrow window slits above her head, and she knew.

Rivka leaned forward and put her head in her hands. So. Hana was a *zonah*. Now everything made sense—the odd negotiation, the high price, Hana leading instead of following. It was all a ritual. In San Diego, men stopped hookers on the street and asked if they were "dating," a precaution against the vice squad. In Jerusalem, men hired women to "carry water."

Rivka felt a mix of pity and anger. She tried to ignore the sounds she heard from within the house. Very soon, it was over. She felt a rush of relief. Now she just wanted the man to go away.

"You promised twice." The man's voice floated through the window slits.

"Just wait a little, *Adoni*," said Hana.

Rivka stood up and walked a little way up the street. She couldn't bear to hear any more. She wanted to scream. What had driven Hana to this? A man came down the street toward Rivka, leering at her. She scowled at him fiercely and retreated to stand in Hana's doorway until he passed.

She paced back and forth in the street, clenching and unclenching her fists. She didn't know Hana very well, but she liked her already. Didn't Hana deserve something better than the life of a *zonah?*

❰ ❰ ❰

After the man finished his business and left, Hana fetched Rivka inside and then went off somewhere on a mysterious errand, warning her sternly not to go outside until she returned.

Rivka passed the time by studying the construction of Hana's house—a classic barrel-vaulted stone house with one room that served as kitchen, bedroom, and living room, all in an area smaller than the master bedroom of Rivka's home in San Diego. Incredible! What an opportunity for an archaeologist!

A key scraped in the lock. Rivka jumped.

Hana opened the door. "I have bought some cloth to make clothes for you." She dumped the material on the dirt floor. It was the same sort of unbleached wool that she wore herself. "Do you know how to sew?"

Rivka didn't know what to say. She could sew well enough—with a sewing machine. But with bone needles? "I'm not sure."

"Why are you so helpless, little sister?" Hana studied her with pity. "Where do you come from?"

Rivka shrugged. "From a far country, where the customs are strange."

"Are you a widow?" Hana asked. "Or were you a slave? How did you become a *zonah?*" She asked this in a matter-of-fact tone, as if she were asking what Rivka had eaten for breakfast.

"I...well, I'm not really a *zonah,*" Rivka said.

"Oh." Hana simply stared at her.

"Is something wrong?" Rivka asked.

"You walk in the streets half-naked, you leave your hair visible to all, you shamelessly look men in the eyes, and yet you seem surprised that a man chased you. Now you claim you are not a *zonah*. Why do your actions not match your words?"

Rivka closed her eyes. Her head was beginning to ache. "I'm just…confused. I think I want to go home."

"You must not go outside dressed like that," Hana said. "And you said you come from a far country. Do you have money to travel? If so, then you should pay me for this cloth. It cost me more than a *dinar*."

Rivka shook her head. She had left her wallet in her backpack—back in Ari's lab. And anyway, what good would her modern *shekels* and her Visa card do here? "I don't have any money."

"Then you cannot travel," Hana said. "How do you plan to live? You do not know how to sew. Can you carry water? Your back is not straight, and you do not stand as a water carrier should. Did your mother not teach you anything? Do you plan to beg for your bread? You cannot; you are not ugly. You would earn many *dinars* as a *zonah*. I will teach you how you must behave so you will not be stoned. You will stay with me tonight, yes?"

"Yes," Rivka immediately answered. Then she realized that long before tonight, she ought to go back to the wormhole.

Hana cocked her head as though listening. "You are lying," she said. "And yet you meant to tell the truth." She shrugged and set to work. "You are a very strange person, Rivka. But you are in danger so long as you walk in the streets without proper clothing. Now be quiet, so I can think how to make you a tunic. Then you can explain why you do not wish to stay with me tonight."

Rivka sat quietly and watched.

Hana cut the cloth with iron shears into the boxy pattern she wore herself. It looked a lot like the illustration Rivka had seen in the margin of the Steinsaltz edition of the Talmud.

Hana threaded a bone needle and began sewing rapidly, her mouth pursed in concentration. Rivka decided that she liked Hana, despite her bluntness. She was a straight shooter, and she just might have saved Rivka from a stoning—or something worse.

Rivka's mind spun wildly. She owed a great debt to her new friend. How in the world was she ever going to repay Hana?

How?

She would find a way, she decided. But she would not become a *zonah* to do it.

Damien

Damien walked swiftly through the cave toward the light at the far end. He felt good, now that he had committed. It was the waiting that twisted your guts. Once you jumped, everything was fine.

Usually.

Outside, the sunlight momentarily blinded Damien. He blinked and waited for his eyes to adjust. He had visited this very cave weeks earlier—or was it thousands of years in the future? On his personal world-line, it was in the past. The difference leaped at all of his senses.

The brilliant blue sky dazzled his eyes. The natural sounds of a preindustrial age soothed his ears. The warmth of the sun warmed his skin. The unpolluted air smelled clean. The Industrial Revolution had not yet spoiled the taste of planet Earth. This was what the Unabomber had been looking for, if only he had had the brains to figure it out.

Damien smiled at the irony. Use technology to destroy technology. The perfect self-referentialism.

He shrugged his duffel bag higher up on his shoulder and began walking toward the city. Somewhere, less than twenty miles away and moving closer every minute, was Paul of Tarsus. Sometime in the next week, his world-line would intersect with Damien's, and then—

A shouted challenge brought him up short. He turned.

A man approached him. Dirt smeared his face. In his hand, he clutched a virtual reality headset. *Uh, oh.* It looked like Rivka hadn't got much of a welcome when she arrived.

Damien smiled at the man and said one of the phrases he had learned from his Hebrew language tapes. *"Shalom. Ani rotzeh l'hagia l'Yerushalayim."* He mentally back-translated to be sure he'd got it right. *Hello. I wish to arrive to Jerusalem.*

The man stared at him and then cut loose with a torrent of unintelligible words.

Damien stepped back a pace. *"Tislakh li, Adoni. Attah medaber Ivrit?"* The tapes had prepared him decently, he thought. *Excuse me, sir. Do you speak Hebrew?*

The man replied with a question. At least, it sounded like a question from the rising intonation. Not a word of it made any sense to Damien.

So this was ancient Hebrew? Damien suddenly wanted to laugh out loud. Those stupid Israelis thought they were so clever in building modern Hebrew on a base of ancient Hebrew. Wouldn't they be disappointed to find out that their language didn't sound a thing like the old days?

He made a gesture to the man, intended to signify, *Sorry, I can't understand you.*

The man's eyes grew wide, and an offended look spread across his face. He spat out a challenge, dropped the headset, and charged at Damien.

At the last possible second, Damien dodged left, planted hard and lashed out a foot, catching the man just below the kneecap. The man squealed like a slit pig and staggered to his knees.

"Sorry about that," Damien said. "Next time, pick on someone—"

The man lunged at him, flailing with his fists.

Damien threw up his arms to ward off the blows. One slipped through and smacked him in the eye. Damien swore at him. Up to now, he had been mostly playing. But eyes were precious. For that, this creep would pay. Damien had a policy of always taking revenge. It was good insurance for the future. Besides, it was fun.

Damien stopped his opponent with a stiff arm to the chest, then jabbed a stiffened thumb into the man's jugular vein. The attacker screeched and stumbled backward.

Damien charged in and body-slammed him into the dirt. The man huddled on the ground, clutching his throat. Damien walked around behind him and kicked him in the kidneys. Hard.

"Have a nice day," he said in English.

He turned and strode away toward the south end of the city. He had found a book in the university library that claimed to map out "Jerusalem, City of Jesus." According to the maps, the best way to get into the city was at the southeast corner. He would test that claim now.

After a short walk, he found the road. Soon it joined up with another one. This one was crowded with people, as he had expected. A Jewish feast was coming up two days from now, on Sunday. There would be lots of visitors from out of town. Including one named Paul.

Nobody paid Damien any attention at all. He took that as a sign that he had chosen his costume well. As he looked around him, though, he could see nobody in an outfit like his—which just proved that all the Sunday school pictures were wrong, as he had always suspected. But his clothes didn't look too out-of-place.

Jerusalem was a big city, and lots of foreigners visited. He ought to be able to blend in.

The language would be a problem, though. He had counted on being able to make himself understood with his pidgin Hebrew. It looked very much like that wouldn't work. He wasn't bad at languages. He had studied German in high school and passed a language exam in both German and Russian in grad school. And he had learned enough modern Hebrew to get by. But a language took time, and he didn't have much right now. No way he could pick up the local lingo in the next week. That gave him two options.

Either he could try to get along by sign language—at the risk of offending the locals. Or he could find an interpreter.

Rivka Meyers.

They taught ancient languages in archaeology school, didn't they? How else could anyone read the inscriptions? Presumably, Rivka had studied whatever they spoke here. And hadn't Ari mentioned what a terrific linguist she was? Hardly any accent at all in her voice, he claimed.

Plus, with a name like Rivka, odds were she was Jewish. Damien had never met a Jew who cared much for Paul of Tarsus. Most of them blamed Paul for the garbage Christians had dumped on them for the last two thousand years. It was a sure bet Rivka Meyers would be all too happy to help track down Paul and do him justice.

Damien smiled. Another problem solved.

But that only led to two more. Where could he find Rivka? And what kind of cock-and-bull story could he give to explain her presence here?

The answer to the first question was as plain as the great wall of limestone rising up into the sky on his right. In that *Avatar* game, Rivka had gone straight for the Temple Mount. Another sure bet. If you wanted to find an archaeologist in ancient Jerusalem, skip the yellow pages. Just head straight for the Temple.

On the way, he would figure out some lie to explain how she got here. *The stork brought you, sweetie.* Or something like that.

Ari

Ari stumbled up the stairs of the physics building. His pulse pounded out an unholy rhythm in his skull, thanks to his binge last night. He ought to have stayed home today, but he wanted to ask Damien's advice about Rivka. Damien knew a bit about women. He had been married at one time, and he had broken off with his latest girlfriend shortly before coming to Jerusalem for the summer.

Ari pushed open the door of the lab. "Damien?"

No answer. He looked at his watch. After nine. Damien must have gone to the bathroom or down the hall to the laser printer. He would probably laugh in Ari's face when he heard about how he had made a fool of himself last night.

A beeping sound came from the back of the lab. The computer. Ari walked over to see what was going on. A dialog box filled the screen. It had a horizontal bar showing the progress of whatever operation Damien had set it to. Ari glanced at it idly.

He froze. *Wormhole will collapse to Planck size in approximately 45 minutes.*

"Oh my…!" Ari said. Then he realized that it had to be a prank. Damien was a bit of a joker. "Very funny!"

The dialog box changed. *Wormhole will collapse to Planck size in approximately 44 minutes.*

Damien must have gone to a bit of work. He had probably gotten bored this morning and hacked something out in Visual Basic. Ari moved around the table and went to see if Damien had finished putting the guts of the pulsed-power driver back together yet.

Everything looked okay. All the cables were in place and appeared to be connected. Ari was not an experimentalist, and he always felt a bit queasy when dealing with electrical apparatus. Especially things Damien had wired. The man was a genius, but sloppy.

Ari stopped in mid-stride. The red power light glowed.

Another joke? Or had Damien gotten impatient and tried the machine early this morning? If so, Ari would wring his neck. They had agreed that they would both be present for all shots— just in case the thing actually worked.

The best he could tell, the device was really conducting current. Damien was going to pay for this. He had no right! Ari heard a knock at the door.

He walked carefully back to answer it. His head felt like he had an axe buried in his skull, his eyes as gritty as a three-day beard. When he reached the door, he found Dr. Hsiu, the new postdoc from China, standing outside.

Dr. Hsiu handed him two sheets of paper and smiled timidly. "Laser printer working now," he said. "I find and bring to Dr. West. Nice man."

Ari looked at the top page. A standard cover sheet for a print job, with Damien West's name plastered all over it. Ari looked at the second sheet—a spreadsheet with eight rows and five columns in a weird mix of numbers, letters, and abbreviations. None of it made any sense.

He looked back at the postdoc. "Dr. Hsiu, have you seen Dr. West today?"

"Yes, yes," said Dr. Hsiu. "Hour ago. Maybe less. He not here?"

"I haven't seen him," Ari said. He held up the two pages. "Thanks. I'll give him these." He took them over to Damien's desk and left them there where he would be sure to find them.

Ari went back to look at the workstation. The dialog box now claimed the wormhole would shrink down to the Planck size in 39 minutes. An insane thought struck him.

He strode to the doorway into the closet where they had planned the wormhole to form. He yanked the door open, hoping to see the inside of a closet.

He saw deep emptiness. The blackness of a highly diffusive object, just like the theory predicted. A wormhole.

Ari's knees went wobbly. "I don't *believe* it." He threw the door shut and raced back to the workstation. He scanned the dialog box until he spotted a *Cancel* button at the bottom. He clicked on it with the mouse. The dialog box disappeared, revealing another one beneath it. Ari scanned it. Sweat slicked his hands and his eyes kept playing tricks on him, causing the screen to look jiggly. Where had that control panel come from?

He would kill West for this. Ari didn't know how he could have put the device back together so quickly, but that question could wait. Right now, he had to stop the wormhole from collapsing. If it went down, it would be gone for good.

It took him ten minutes to figure out how the controls worked. Each time he adjusted the power setting on the screen, he heard the loud pop of electrical sparks inside the guts of the power supplies. *Damien's seat-of-the-pants wiring.* Finally Ari straightened up and massaged his aching temples. Now he could do nothing but wait. If he had guessed correctly, the wormhole would stay open, but it would take some time to find out.

Ari noticed a cup of coffee on Damien's desk. He walked over and stuck his finger in the coffee. Tepid. Damien had not been gone long. Had he actually gone through the wormhole, or was he still in the building somewhere? Ari walked around to sit in Damien's chair. There, hidden under the desk, lay Rivka's backpack.

Ari sucked in his breath. What was she doing here? Had she been here with Damien? Had she seen the wormhole?

Even worse, had she gone through it?

He forced himself to breathe deeply. Rivka was intelligent. She would know better than to go off through a time portal into the past, wouldn't she?

Ari jumped up, unable to sit still any longer. Then he saw the personal computer in the corner. He recognized the *Avatar* software. He strode over and stared at the screen. It showed the interior of the Temple. He grabbed the mouse and clicked on the Status menu. A window popped up. One line leaped out at him. *Current user: Rivka.*

Rivka had been here, and now she was not. She had been playing this game, and now she was not. Ari felt sick with fear.

He scanned the status window. *Current playing time: 1:25.* Rivka had started this game an hour and a half ago. Dr. Hsiu had seen Damien West here an hour ago.

Ari pounded his fist on the table. Then he jerked his cellular phone out of his pocket and speed-dialed a number.

Six rings later, he heard a sleepy voice. "Yes?"

"Dov, this is Ari." He clenched his fists and tried to will his heart to stop racing. "I'm afraid something may have happened to Rivka."

"To Rivka?" Dov suddenly sounded wide-awake. "Has there been a bombing?"

"Maybe worse," Ari said. "I'm in the lab, and Dr. West appears to have created the wormhole without my consent. Both he and Rivka are missing."

"I am on my way instantly."

Ari hung up. *Think calmly.* He went back to check the work-station. The readings looked wrong. He adjusted the power setting again. A crackling noise issued from the power supply.

Now he would have to wait for things to settle down. He left the computer, went back to Damien's desk, and pulled out Rivka's backpack. Something small and hard bulged under his sandal. He reached down and picked it up. A silver coin. Ancient, by the look of it. Since when had Damien West been interested in coin collecting?

Damien's laptop computer lay closed on the desk. Ari flipped it open and hit the spacebar. Good. Damien had left it in sleep mode. Ari stared at the screen, seeking inspiration. If Damien had printed that document, he had either done it from this laptop or one of the other computers in the lab. The document looked personal, though, like something Damien wouldn't keep on a semipublic machine. Most likely, it had come from the laptop. What else was on this machine?

Ari fired up the word processor and checked the File menu. It showed a list of the last five documents Damien had opened. The first on the list was labeled "Manifesto." Ari clicked on it.

A dialog box popped up, asking for a password. Ari stared at it for a minute. If this document was important enough for Damien to protect, then it was vital for Ari to read. But how?

What was Damien's game? What was the weird spreadsheet all about? And how did Rivka fit in? Had Damien taken her through the wormhole with him?

Ari hunched forward in the chair and closed his eyes. The thought made him nauseated. Last night, he had never wanted to see Rivka again. He had almost hated her. Rather, he hated what she stood for—two thousand years of violation of his people. And yet, there was something about her. He cared about her. Was *crazy after her,* as the saying went.

He could make her understand that, if only he could talk to her one more time. This time, with logic. But would she give him a second chance? Or would she cut him off before he could start up?

Start up. Something clicked in Ari's brain. A fragment of a conversation he had had with Damien a month ago. *Start up.*

Ari grabbed the mouse of the laptop, hardly daring to hope.

CHAPTER NINE

Rivka

"Now you must try it on," Hana said. She held up the tunic she had made for Rivka. "Take off those terrible things you're wearing."

Rivka wished she had brought her backpack so she would have a place to stow her clothes until she went back to the wormhole. She pulled her T-shirt and shorts off, slipped the tunic over her head and let it drop down around her body. The rough wool scratched her skin. "Can we go to the Temple this afternoon?" she asked as she tugged the tunic into place. "I would like to watch the sacrifices."

Hana shrugged. "I do not enjoy watching animals bleed and burn, but as you wish. Or we could go tomorrow—on *Shabbat* there will be more sacrifices, if that is what you want to see."

"*Shabbat?*" Rivka felt disoriented. "What day is today?"

Hana gave her a very strange look. "The sixth day, of course. What day did you think it was?"

Rivka felt her face reddening. Where she had come from, yesterday was *Shabbat*. Today ought to be the first day of the week. Obviously, she had left on a Sunday, arrived on a Friday. Weird.

Hana repeated her question.

"I've been traveling lately," Rivka said. "You can lose track of time when you're on the road."

"I have never gone further than Bethany," Hana said.

Two miles away. Incredible.

"We should be leaving for the Temple soon," Hana said.

Rivka's stomach growled. She had eaten only a bagel for breakfast and nothing since. "What about…lunch?" she asked. She didn't want to impose, but she was hungry.

"What is lunch?" Hana asked.

Rivka had used the modern Hebrew word. She tried to think how to explain. "Don't you eat something at midday?"

Hana looked puzzled. "No. Do you? Why do you not eat in the evening?"

"I do," Rivka said. "In my country, we eat in the morning, at noon, and in the evening."

"How very strange," Hana said. "Are all people in your country wealthy?"

Rivka remembered reading that most people in primitive agricultural cultures lived on two meals a day…when they had food. "Yes, many of our people are wealthy," she said.

"Then why do you have no money?" Hana asked.

"I lost it," Rivka said, thinking of her backpack, still in Ari's lab. She went to the door and opened it. "Shall we go? I would really like to see the Temple."

"Wait." Hana took the squarish piece of cloth left over from making Rivka's tunic and folded it into a triangle. "Cover your hair with this. Have you no decency?"

"I'm sorry." Rivka fumbled with it helplessly. Finally, Hana rolled up Rivka's French braid, folded it into the cloth, and knotted it.

Rivka stepped out into the street.

Hana followed her. "You are a very strange person, Rivka. I do not think I understand you at all." She locked the door behind them and secreted the key in the cloth belt around her waist.

"I don't understand you, either," Rivka said. "But I like you."

"You are an honest person," Hana said, as she began walking briskly along the small street. "This evening you must explain to me why an honest person tells so many lies."

☾ ☾ ☾

Rivka stood as near to the front of the Court of Women as she could get. She faced west toward the sanctuary. Immediately in front of her, fifteen semicircular steps led up to an enormous bronze gate. On the steps stood dozens of Levite musicians, garbed in white. Some had wooden harp-like instruments. One held a bronze pair of cymbals. A priest clutched a silver trumpet. The rest were singers. All of them waited in perfect silence, facing the worshipers in the court below, watching the director of music.

Rivka could see beyond them, through the great gate, into the Court of Priests. Several priests led in a ram for the afternoon sacrifices. The animal, smelling blood, struggled. His ferocity shocked Rivka. Rams were stronger than she had thought. The priests fought to drag it up to the slaughtering point—a wooden post with a metal ring. They tugged the ram's horns up through the ring, forcing his head into relative immobility. Two of them gripped the animal's horns and pulled backward hard. The ram bleated in anger.

Or fear.

Another priest came forward with a sharp knife and a large silver pitcher. Rivka guessed it held at least a gallon.

The priest laid the knife across the ram's throat and sliced horizontally. Blood spurted out into the pitcher.

Rivka turned away. Her hands flew up to her mouth.

Hana reached up and put a hand on her shoulder. She turned Rivka's attention back toward the priest.

The ram kicked backward with his hind legs, but the priests stood beside him, not behind. As his blood filled the pitcher, he weakened. Then his knees buckled.

The priests released his horns and lowered him most of the way to the stone pavement. In a few minutes, he stopped kicking. The priests each grabbed a leg and hoisted him onto a slaughtering table, just out of Rivka's line of sight, which suited her just fine. She didn't want to see any more.

"Are you going to faint?" Hana asked.

"No, I'm fine," Rivka said. "It's just...I never saw anything like that before."

"But if the people of your country are wealthy, then they must eat meat often," Hana said.

"Yes..." Rivka wiped her forehead. "But my people don't slaughter their own animals."

Hana merely shook her head in disbelief.

Within a few minutes, the priests stepped back from the table. Had they finished cutting up the ram already? One of them reached forward, grabbed something off the table, and walked across Rivka's field of vision toward the altar on the left-hand side of the gate. In his right hand, he carried a leg of the ram.

Rivka sensed a collective intake of breath around her. Something was about to happen—something anticipated, something important.

She saw the priest step up to the base of the altar. It was huge, something like twenty feet high and wider than that at the base. The priest swung his arm far back, then slung it upward rapidly, underhand. The ram's leg rotated twice as it sailed up onto the altar, landing with a thud.

The crowd began breathing again. The priest turned and headed back toward the slaughtering table. He made several trips. The legs he flung up. The side pieces, shoulders, and head he had to carry up the steps to the top of the altar. Finally, it ended. Another priest appeared with a pitcher containing wine, a drink offering to the living God. Again, Rivka sensed an anticipation in the crowd around her. The priest paused briefly at the base of the altar. Then he poured out the drink offering on the steps leading up to the top of the altar.

Claaaaaaang! The Levite with the cymbals clashed them together.

Rivka jumped.

An instant later, the musicians burst into song.

> *The Lord reigns, He is robed in majesty,*
> *The Lord is robed in majesty,*
> *And is armed with strength.*
> *The world is firmly established;*
> *It cannot be moved.*
> *Your throne was established long ago;*
> *You are from all eternity.*

For the first time in a long time, Rivka felt awe well up in her heart. People all around her fell on their faces on the stone pavement. Rivka did, too. She let the music wash over her in a great wave. She recognized the words as the ninety-third psalm, the song always sung on the sixth day of the week in the Temple. The words of the psalm struck her with new force now. *You are from all eternity.*

Taken literally, that implied God presided above time. He didn't need a wormhole to get from the past to the present to the future and back again. He just *was*. Time limited man. But not the great *I AM*.

Rivka had always believed this—more or less. She just hadn't grasped it. Probably she still didn't, but today's visit to the past had made it all seem a bit more real. She had once read a book about how the kingdom of God was "already, but not yet." At the time, she had dismissed it as a poetic bit of theology-speak. Now it seemed possible, even logical.

Rivka lay there for some time, immersed in tranquility. Was it her imagination, or did a Presence permeate this place? She wanted to stay here forever, enjoying—

"Come, Rivka. It is time to go," Hana said.

Rivka opened her eyes and saw that the Court of Women had begun to empty. She looked at her watch. After four o'clock. Did that mean anything? Her watch also informed her that today was Sunday, and that was certainly wrong. But the position of the sun in the sky told her that her watch was not far off.

She stood up and stretched. "I should be going home now."

"You will not travel far before *Shabbat* arrives," Hana said. "If you truly live in a far country, then you cannot walk there before the sun goes down. Will you not stay with me this evening?"

Rivka didn't know what to say to that. She wanted to go back soon. Dov and Jessica would worry about her. And she had to tell them about this place! They would insist on coming back with her tomorrow to visit—this time with cameras. *Shabbat* in the Temple! What more could anybody want?

Hana studied her face. "You are far away in your thoughts, my friend."

Rivka patted her arm. "Let's go." They began walking toward the exit. She felt anxious to get back to the wormhole soon.

They went through the south gate of the inner Temple and down the steps toward the outer courts of the Temple Mount. At the foot of the stairs stood a waist-high barrier enclosing the inner Temple. Jews considered everything inside this barrier too pure for Gentiles to enter. On the way in, Rivka had seen signs in Aramaic, Latin, and Greek warning *goyim* to go no further, on pain of death.

"Rivka Meyers!" An American accent, a familiar voice.

Rivka's head spun toward the source. There, just outside the barrier, stood a large man in an outlandish modern Arab costume, waving his arms exuberantly. Dr. Damien West. He looked delighted to see her.

But why? Rivka felt pretty sure Dr. West had something to do with her coming here. So why had he come looking for her? It didn't make sense. Perhaps he had come to take her back. Probably right now. She felt a twinge of regret, like a kid when recess ended who wanted to stay out another five minutes.

"Who is that?" Hana asked.

Rivka strode out through the gap in the barrier and up to Dr. West.

"Thank goodness I found you," he said.

"Um, Dr. West...if you don't mind, I have a few questions for you. For starters, how did I get here?"

Dr. West smiled broadly. "First, I have to apologize for allowing Ari to do this to you. Are you all right? You've had no trouble, have you? I've been terribly worried about you, Miss Meyers."

"I'm fine," Rivka said. "What do you mean about Ari? What did he do?"

"I'm not sure, exactly," Dr. West said. "I've had him arrested, and a jury will determine what he did. I'm so very sorry, Miss Meyers. While you were playing the *Avatar* game, I stepped out to go to the restroom. Apparently, Ari came in while I was out. He locked me out of the lab and turned on the wormhole, creating a time portal. I don't know how he got you through it, but obviously he did, because you're here."

"You're telling me Ari...sent me here?" Rivka asked. That didn't make any sense at all. Nothing made sense.

"The best I can determine, yes, he did," Dr. West said. "When I finally got inside the lab, he was trying to—" Dr. West paused, and a troubled look crossed his face. "I don't know how to say this, Miss Meyers, but he was trying to shut down the wormhole."

Rivka's knees suddenly felt like Jell-O. "But...he told me last week that you can only make a wormhole once. How would I have gotten back?"

Dr. West cleared his throat. "I'm sorry, Miss Meyers, truly I am. If Ari had succeeded...you would have been stranded here. For good."

"I don't believe it," she said evenly. "That doesn't sound like the Ari I know. Why would he do that?"

"You told me this morning you had an argument with him last night, is that correct?"

"Yes." Rivka felt her fists tightening at the memory. "He accused me of...some things. I got angry and threw a glass of water in his face. And I'm afraid I made a rather rude suggestion to him. Then I walked off. I came in this morning to apologize."

Dr. West was shaking his head. "You don't know Ari Kazan very well," he said. "He has a temper, really quite remarkable. He never forgets, and he never, ever forgives. Last year, I heard that he completely destroyed the reputation of a postdoc who dared to suggest that his wormhole theory might be wrong. It got quite vicious."

Rivka shivered. This didn't sound right. It didn't square with what Dr. West had told her just this morning. And she knew Ari to be a peace-loving guy. She'd had to drag the truth out of him last night, or he would have just sat there being miserable. He was the classic conflict-avoider.

And yet, Dr. West had come looking for her. Ari hadn't.

"Ari's got a counselor that he talks to about his anger issues," Dr. West said. "It's been kind of a secret. Ari's mother and stepfather are ultraorthodox, you know, and quite wealthy. They would probably disinherit him if they found out."

Anger issues? Now that made some sense. Ari obviously repressed a bit of hostility. He had vented some of it last night at Christians, but maybe it went deeper than that. And yet...

Rivka had to sort this thing out. Either Ari or Dr. West let her go through that wormhole and then left her to fend for herself in a land that didn't treat women with bare arms and legs kindly.

One of them had abandoned her.

Her heart quivered with anger. *But which one?*

Rivka knew she would figure it out if she could get more information. Obviously, she wouldn't get anywhere by making weird accusations. She would keep asking questions. If Dr. West were lying, he would trip himself up eventually. Meantime, she would give him the benefit of the doubt. And Ari, too.

"So," she said brightly, "how did you know where to find me?"

Dr. West smiled. "I guessed right away that you had gone through the wormhole. I used a bit of karate to disable Ari. Nothing permanent, mind you. He whacked me a good one in the eye."

"I see," Rivka said. "You're going to have a nasty shiner there."

"Nothing major," Dr. West said. "Anyway, then I had to stabilize the wormhole—and that was quite a trick, let me tell you. Another two minutes, and you would have been...history." He whiffed the air with his hands.

She shivered.

"So after I called the police and had Ari arrested, I went through the wormhole to see if I could find you. I found a cave of some sort, but you weren't there. I went outside and found myself on the outskirts of ancient Jerusalem. I saw the virtual reality headset on the ground, so I knew you had been there. Then I took one look at the Temple Mount and figured you had probably taken a little sight-seeing expedition."

Rivka shook her head. "I'm so glad you came. This morning was a bit of an adventure. I'll tell you about it on the way back. This is my friend Hana." She switched to Aramaic. "Hana, this is a friend from my country. His name is called Damien."

"Daimon?" Hana flinched. "That is a bad name for a good man."

"No, not *Daimon.* Not an evil spirit. His name is Damien. It is a common name in my country. We speak a different language there. He will help me return to my country."

Hana examined Dr. West with an appraising eye and said nothing.

Rivka wondered if she was sizing him up as a potential customer. "Well!" she said, with forced verve in her voice. "Dr. West, shall we get back to the lab? I've got my camera there, and I'm dying to bring Dov and Jessica back here with me tomorrow. This place is awesome—literally! You can almost feel the presence of God in the Temple."

Dr. West nodded. "We can go back as soon as you want to. I should warn you, though, that the wormhole is likely to collapse if anyone else goes through it. I did some calculations before I left and concluded that I could come through safely and we can both return home, but that will be the end of it. The gravitational field of our bodies is almost certain to send the wormhole into decay mode. We won't be able to come back—and good riddance to this place, if you ask me. The natives here are a bit odd, don't you think?"

Rivka found that she was holding her breath. She wanted to see more of this city—to explore the place a bit and see the sights. If she couldn't capture it on film, at least she could burn it into her memory. "How long would it be safe for us to stay here?" she asked.

Dr. West shrugged. "In principle, decades, I suppose. As long as nobody walks through that wormhole, it should hold together indefinitely. I left some of the physicists there in charge with strict orders to let nobody else through."

"Did you tell them when you would be back?"

"Well, I couldn't be sure how long it would take to find you, so I told them to expect me in a few days. I got lucky and found you right away, but I'd guess they won't get worried unless we're gone more than a week." He shrugged. "Don't tell me you *like* it here? This place gives me the creeps."

"I do like it," Rivka said. "In fact, I love it! It's every archae-ologist's dream to come to a place like this. Would you mind terribly if we stayed for a day or two? This whole city is amazing. I've already seen things that are going to rewrite every book I've read on the cultural anthropology of the Herodian period. And I want to do a really thorough survey of the Temple Mount. Professor Ritmeyer will never forgive me if I come back and can't tell him if his reconstruction is correct. And I want to see..." She threw up her hands, embarrassed. "You probably think I'm nuts."

Dr. West patted her arm gently. "I sort of understand. How long do you want to stay? No, don't answer that. You probably want to stay forever. Sorry, you can't. I want to get back to claim my half of the Nobel prize. And somebody's got to testify against Ari—painful as that will be. Despite his temper, Ari has been a good friend of mine—until today."

Hana tugged on Rivka's sleeve. "Why is your friend dressed like that?"

That was a good question. Rivka jabbed a finger at Dr. West's clothes. "Where did you come by the threads? Did you rob a Bedouin?"

Dr. West gave a good-natured grin. "I went to the *shuq* yesterday to pick up some souvenirs to take back to the States. I'm afraid the guy ripped me off. I've never got the hang of bargaining with these people. Anyway, when I realized I had to come back through time to find you, I decided that a silly costume was better than none. It's turned out better than I expected."

Rivka squinted at the clothes. "Marginally," she said. "You really ought to get a native costume if we're going to hang out here for a few days." Then she remembered that she had no money and was dependent on Hana's charity. "Um, we may have a problem."

"What kind of problem?" Dr. West asked. "I'm good at problem-solving."

"Money," Rivka said bluntly. "I'm flat broke, and it takes money to eat."

Dr. West put his hand in his pocket and pulled out a fistful of silver coins. "I collect ancient coins," he said. "Part of my collection was in my desk in the lab. I raided it, just in case. Guess I'm an overgrown Boy Scout—always prepared."

Who would keep a coin collection in a physics lab? Dr. West's story was beginning to sound just a bit too smooth. But play along.

Rivka gave an admiring laugh. "You've thought of everything, haven't you? That's amazing." She turned to Hana. "How would you like to earn some money? My friend needs a place to stay for a few days. Can you put him up with us?"

Hana shook her head violently. "Keep a man in my house? That would not be fitting."

Rivka wondered how it could be less fitting than Hana's present line of work.

Hana's face flushed a deep red. "My friend, have you no shame? Why do you speak to this man in public? And why does he allow it? Is it the custom in your country to do such things?"

"Yes," Rivka said. "That is the custom, and many other things which you would find strange. I know it is hard for you to understand. My friend needs a place to stay, and he has money. Can you help him find lodgings that would be fitting?"

Hana thought for a moment. "There is a house empty not far from where I live. The husband died, and the wife went back to her family. The landlord has not been able to rent it because people say it is cursed. Is your friend troubled by a curse?"

"No, of course not," Rivka said.

Hana's eyes widened. "He must be a very righteous man that he does not fear a curse," she said. "Come with me, and we shall see if the house can be had. We must hurry. Soon it will be time to make *Shabbat.*" She turned and headed for the south end of the Temple Mount without looking back.

"Let's go," Rivka said. "It won't be the King David Hotel, but you'll have a bed."

"I don't mind roughing it." Dr. West began walking after Hana. He handed Rivka a few silver coins. "I don't know what these are worth in this economy, but take them. You may need some money."

Somehow, that melted a few of Rivka's suspicions. These old coins had to be valuable.

Maybe she could trust Dr. West after all.

CHAPTER TEN

Ari

Ari scrolled down the Unabomber Manifesto. "Dov, look at this garbage!" He pointed to a sentence Damien had highlighted in red. *In order to get our message before the public with some chance of making a lasting impression, we've had to kill people.* What kind of fool would believe this nonsense?

"Your friend is mentally unstable, evidently," Dov said. "How did you guess his password again? I do not understand."

"I didn't guess it," Ari said. "Damien is paranoid about losing data, so he installed a keystroke grabber in his start-up folder. It keeps a record of everything he types, in case his machine were to crash while he was typing something important. It recorded everything he typed, even passwords. I scanned the dump file and found it."

Dov shook his head. "You are very clever."

"No, Damien is stupid," Ari said. "He's overly safety-conscious, and it caught up with him. When I get my hands on him, I'm going to twist his head off." Which went against his pacifist convictions, but everybody had a limit to what they could take.

"What if he changes something in the past?" Dov asked. "He seems to admire this Unabomber very much. Perhaps he will go back a few years and prevent this man from being arrested."

"That's crazy," Ari said. "You can't change history. The trajectory of the universe through phase space is single-valued."

Dov nodded. "I do not understand, but I am sure you are right. And yet, what prevents him from doing something terrible? If he were to assassinate David ben Gurion before our War of Independence, then there would most likely be no State of Israel today, yes?"

"Nothing *prevents* him," Ari said. "But you don't understand. He won't."

"How do you know?" Dov asked.

Ari was beginning to get impatient. "Because I have read the history books. The past has already happened. Wherever Damien has gone, he has done nothing. More precisely, he has done exactly what he must do in order to ensure that the past we have read about in the history books would happen just as those books describe. If only those books had been more detailed, they would have described his actions. Since they do not describe his actions, we know that he did nothing important."

"And you do not know how far back he has gone in time?"

"No, I don't know the calibration constant that relates Damien's measurements to actual time. That is determined by the number of turns in his Rogowski coils, and I have never bothered with such details. Have you been able to decipher that spreadsheet?"

Dov frowned at the document for a moment. "Not yet, I am sorry." He shook his head, folded the sheet, and jammed it in his pocket. "And what about Rivka?" he asked. "I will have to notify the dig director if she is missing. Are you certain that she went through the wormhole?"

"Almost certain," Ari said. His heart hiccuped. "I feel responsible for her."

"Rivka is tough and smart," Dov said. "She will come back. How long can you keep the wormhole alive?"

Ari turned to look at Dr. Hsiu, whom he had pressed into service to keep watch on the monitors. "How is the wormhole, Dr. Hsiu?"

The postdoc wiped his damp forehead. "Very difficult," he said. "Wormhole not stable. Changes this way, that way, very bad. Power supply has bad component."

"And we can't shut it down to change it," Ari said. "We'll just have to keep it alive as long as possible."

The power supply sparked.

"Sorry," Dr. Hsiu said. "I adjust, and then sparks. Very, very bad."

Ari closed his eyes and tried to think. Damien had to be crazy. What was his game? Why had he gone? To change something? If so, he was doomed to failure. Physics said so, and physics was never wrong.

Except when it was.

Who, before the 1960s, would have guessed the universe could allow CP violation? But experiment said it did.

Ari suddenly felt sick.

What to do? Every instinct in his body told him to wait. Damien would come back, fearful that the wormhole would collapse and strand him. Rivka would return, too.

Unless something prevented her. Or someone.

What if Damien had taken her with him by force? What if he didn't mean to come back? What if he wouldn't allow Rivka to return?

Ari might wait for hours, days, weeks, dying a little inside every second.

No!

No, he wouldn't let Damien make the rules. He had already done that, allowing Damien access to the lab when he wasn't around. And now here was the result: an unauthorized wormhole and two people missing. Why had he ever trusted Damien?

But to go through the wormhole after them terrified him. In all likelihood, he would only make things worse by chasing Damien and Rivka. He would make Damien even crazier, Rivka more angry at him. And who knew where the wormhole led, or when? It could take Ari into the middle of the Russian revolution, or a desert island, or the lair of a Tyrannosaurus rex. Also, the device had gone unstable. If it collapsed, he wouldn't be coming back.

Yet if it posed a potential danger for him, then it meant certain danger for Rivka. That he could not allow. He had blundered badly last night, had alienated her, had allowed her to leave. He hadn't intended to do any of that, but she had dragged the truth out of him and then been repelled by that truth. He would never abandon the truth, but if there was any hope of any future with her, he wanted it.

Wanted it more than anything else.

Ari opened his eyes and looked at his cousin. "Dov, I think you should notify your dig director. In my opinion, there is a strong chance that Rivka may never come back. Her parents should be informed." *A small lie in the service of the truth.*

Dov's face turned pale. He slowly pulled out his cell phone and began punching in numbers.

"Not here." Ari pointed at the capacitors. "There will be electrical interference with your phone signal. Make your call in the hallway, away from the power supplies."

Dov nodded and began walking toward the front of the lab.

Ari watched him go. *Shalom, my friend.* His head felt strangely light. He tapped Dr. Hsiu on the arm. "I'm going to have a look at those capacitors," he said. "Don't touch the controls for a few minutes, or you'll fry me."

Dr. Hsiu's eyes widened. "Not safe, not safe!"

Ari shouldered his backpack and walked rapidly toward the power supply. Behind him, he heard Dr. Hsiu saying something, but the blood roared in his ears and he could hear nothing, could feel nothing but the clammy sweat on his back. He reached the power supply and kept walking past it to the doorway. Behind him came a shout. Ari yanked open the door, stepped through, and slammed it shut behind him.

Darkness enveloped him.

I'm crazy, crazy, crazy. What if she doesn't want me?

But it didn't matter what Rivka thought she wanted. He was going to pursue her until he caught her. Whatever it took.

❰ ❰ ❰

Twenty minutes later, Ari walked into a Jerusalem both wonderful and awful—a city he had barely imagined. With each step, he felt more like a foreigner. Men and women in four-cornered tunics turned to stare at him as he walked by. For one thing, he stood almost a head taller than anyone else. Also, he wore blue jeans and a black T-shirt with the Maxwell equations on the front. And who in this world had ever seen a neon-blue backpack? Only his leather sandals seemed in place, but nobody paid much attention to those.

Ari felt intensely embarrassed by the stares. Obviously, he had come far back in time. He had just seen the Temple, destroyed more than nineteen centuries ago. To his eye, it looked like Herod's Temple, the final remodeling begun by King Herod less than a century before its final destruction. Why had Damien come back twenty centuries? Accident or intentional? And how did Rivka fit into this?

It shocked him to see just how big ancient Jerusalem had been. How could he hope to find Rivka? Crowds of people packed the roads. Could they all be residents? If not, why had they come?

Then he saw something familiar. The Pool of Siloam lay just ahead. It hadn't changed in twenty-seven hundred years. That was a fixed point in this crazy world. He had almost got killed in there, once upon a time. Happy memories. Despite that, its relative seclusion would be better than people gawking at him out here on the street.

He ducked inside the walls of the pool area and heaved a sigh of relief. At once, the place grew dead quiet. He saw a number of young women standing around with clay water pots resting on the ground beside them. Several of the women approached Ari, nudging each other, whispering, and pointing at his blue jeans.

"*Shalom*, my friends," Ari said in biblical Hebrew. Years ago, as a teenager, he had read quite a bit of the Bible in its quaint old Hebrew, at the insistence of his ultraorthodox stepfather. The religious instruction had only bored him. Even then, he had read Darwin and knew that Genesis was nothing more than the mythology of desert nomads. He remembered enough of the biblical idioms to make himself understood. "I am looking for a friend of mine. She is dressed somewhat like I am. Perhaps you have seen her today?"

Blank stares greeted him. Then one of the women spoke to him, a torrent of syllables which sounded a bit like Hebrew, only different. Very different. Aramaic, he guessed. He had studied only a little Talmud before quitting altogether. Had he studied more, he would have learned some Aramaic. But he hadn't known that as a fourteen-year-old. Too late now.

"Do any of you speak Hebrew?" he asked. "*Ivrit?*"

The women suddenly backed away from him. One of them shouted something at him in an angry tone. *What was the problem?* Were they allergic to Hebrew? Something must lie behind their strange behavior, but he couldn't fathom it at the moment.

He decided to leave. Obviously, he wouldn't get any information here, much less a warm welcome. It couldn't be any worse out on the streets.

Rivka wasn't here, but she was somewhere nearby. She had to be. And someone had seen her. Many people must have seen her. He had to find one of them who spoke Hebrew. If he could find an interpreter, he would be in business.

And who would speak Hebrew in this city of Jews? Scholars, aristocrats, that sort of person.

Where would they live? Ari could easily guess. In every city he had ever seen, the rich people lived on the hilltops, while the poor lived in the low-lying areas. The Pool of Siloam huddled in the lowest part of the city.

Obviously, he should head uphill. Ari took a last look around the pool, then strode out of the gate and up the long avenue heading west, uphill. The sun hung high in the sky. That should give him plenty of time to find an interpreter.

Dov

Dov downshifted as he approached the tight curve. The engine of his VW whined as the car slowed. Anxiety had knotted up his stomach all day, since the terrible moment when he saw Ari closing the door that led into the wormhole.

"You shouldn't have called the police," Jessica said.

"I did not call them," Dov said, accelerating out of the turn. "I called the department chairman. What was I supposed to do?

Leave the Chinese physicist to deal with it alone? How was I to know that the chairman would call the police?"

Jessica sighed loudly. She had gotten hysterical earlier today, when Dov went back to the youth hostel and told her that Rivka was missing—apparently transported back to some unknown time. And that was nothing, compared to the reaction of Ari's mother.

"Are they really going to shut it off next weekend?" Jessica asked.

"Maybe not," Dov said. "But if you saw the device, you would understand. Every minute, the physicists have to readjust the machine. When they do that, the power supply sparks. According to the rabbis, they are making fire, and that is not allowed on *Shabbat*."

"You're telling me that nobody turns on their lights on *Shabbat?*" Jessica asked. "Nobody drives a car?"

"Most people do." Dov pulled out into the left lane to pass a tourist bus. "The ultraorthodox, which we call in Hebrew the *Haredim,* do not. And therefore, the State of Israel does not. You have not met the *Haredim* on our dig, so let me tell you about them. This is not the United States. Our leaders made compromises with the *Haredim* in 1948, and we continue to live with the results of that now. Had we not done that, there would be no State of Israel. But because we did so, we have an Israel sometimes controlled by religious zealots."

"But...we're talking about a physics lab," Jessica said. "It's ridiculous!"

"Correction," Dov said, pulling back into the right lane. "We are talking about a physics lab owned and financed by the State of Israel, and it must obey the law of the land. Yes, it is ridiculous, but it is the law. You have many foolish laws in your United States also, yes?"

"Can't those physicists write a program to do the adjustments automatically?" Jessica asked. "Then no human would be violating the *Shabbat*. Isn't that the way it works?"

"I asked them that," Dov said. "Unfortunately, nobody really understands the machine very well. They can write software to control it, but the software must be tested. On what? They must test it on the machine itself. If there is a mistake, then…" Dov made a fist and then let his fingers explode outward. "Poof! Are you willing to take that chance, my friend?"

"It would be better than just cutting off the power next Friday afternoon, don't you think?" Jessica sounded angry.

"Yes, it would," Dov said. "They will try it, but they are not confident. The physicists have asked us to seek a legal solution—just in case."

"Legal? As in lawyers?" Jessica said. "That's a different matter. Why didn't you tell me that?"

"You are a lawyer?" Dov asked. He slowed to a stop, then made a right-hand turn onto the dirt road leading to the dig.

"No, but half my family are lawyers," Jessica said. "My mother has some second cousins who live in Tel Aviv and Haifa. One of them is a lawyer. My mother wanted me to look them up before I go home."

"I suggest that you do so tonight," Dov said. "But the dig has no money to hire an expensive lawyer. Is he good? Will he work for free?"

"I hear that *she* is very good," Jessica said. "Which probably means she's expensive. I can ask if she'll help."

"Please do," Dov said. "I have not yet spoken to Rivka's parents. Perhaps they can pay. I already know that Ari's mother will not contribute. She and his stepfather are *Haredim*, members of the Lubavitcher sect. They will not spend a *shekel* to defend a violation of *Shabbat*."

"But...lives are at stake!" Jessica said. "Doesn't that count for anything?"

Dov came to a stop in the dusty, unpaved parking lot of the dig. "Yes it would count, if it were true. The principle of *pikuach nephesh* would apply—the saving of a life. But what evidence can you present that Ari and Rivka are in danger?" He turned to look at Jessica. "I have already considered this line of reasoning. Ari and Rivka are healthy adults who have been inoculated against all major diseases. In a primitive culture without medicine, they might very well live forty or fifty years."

"But Rivka could die in childbirth!" Jessica said.

"Do you have reason to think she is pregnant?"

"Rivka?" Jessica laughed out loud. "I would bet she's still a virgin, to be honest."

Dov sighed. "That is most unfortunate." He pounded his hand on the steering wheel. "I do not feel good about this, my friend. It is likely that Ari and Rivka will come back before *Shabbat*. But we must be prepared for the possibility that they will not. Cases like this often go to the Supreme Court."

"On five days' notice?" Jessica stared at him.

Dov closed his eyes. He suddenly felt very tired. "In the State of Israel, yes, a case may go to the Supreme Court in a few days. But we have only four, not five. If we argue the case Thursday, then they can decide by Friday."

"It sounds hopeless," Jessica said. "Can't somebody just go through the wormhole and have a look around—try to find them?"

"You saw what has happened in the lab," Dov said. "The police will not unseal the wormhole, except to allow Ari or Rivka or Dr. West to return. Nobody will be allowed to go through from our side. It is a hazard, for one thing. Also, they fear that someone might interfere with the past and thereby destroy the present."

"I was hoping there might be some way to change their minds," Jessica said. She sat in silence for a long moment. "What are we going to do?"

"Call your mother's cousin, the lawyer," Dov said. "And if you are religious, I suggest that you begin praying."

ELEVEN

Rivka

Halfway through the Friday evening meal, Rivka fought down a growing sense of uneasiness. The bread was excellent, the wine quite passable, and the company congenial. And yet she wished she had not insisted that Dr. West eat with them.

It had nothing to do with the fact that she had to interpret everything Hana or Dr. West said. What worried her was the remarkable rapport her two friends had developed.

"Miss Meyers, would you be so kind—"

Hana handed Rivka the wineskin. "Please ask *Adoni* if he would like some more wine."

"—as to pass me the wine."

Rivka handed it to Dr. West. *Weird.*

He winked at Rivka and then threw a twenty-four-carat smile at Hana. She blushed.

The whole thing seemed unnatural to Rivka. Tomorrow, after a little sight-seeing, she would tell Dr. West she wanted to go back home. But right now, all she could do was try to point the conversation in a neutral direction.

"Dr. West, do you happen to know what year this is?" Rivka asked. "Did your computer tell you anything like that?"

He took a swallow of wine and shook his head. "I'm afraid not. Actually, I don't understand Ari's theory all that well. In principle, you could make an estimate of the time span of the wormhole, but in practice there's too much experimental noise. When did the Romans burn down that magnificent Temple? That ought to give you a clue."

"Late summer of the year 70 C.E.," Rivka said.

"C.E.?" he asked. "Is that B.C. or A.D.?"

"It stands for Common Era," Rivka said. "Sorry, I keep forgetting you're a layman. It's exactly equivalent to A.D., which stands for Anno Domini—the Year of Our Lord. Jews don't quite appreciate that terminology, so it's common among scholars just to use C.E. No reason to irritate people unnecessarily, right?"

"I guess not," Dr. West said. He gestured toward Hana. "She doesn't seem too irritated. Why not ask her what year it is?"

Rivka had already thought of that. "They don't have a running year count like we do. They normally just date years from the accession of the last king or governor or whatever. But I'll ask her anyway. It can't hurt."

Dr. West poured some wine into his stone cup.

"Hana, I've got a very stupid question for you," Rivka said. "What year is this?"

Hana raised her eyebrows. "All years are alike, yes? Is it not so in your country?"

"In my country, every year is different." Rivka decided to try another tack. "Who is Caesar?"

Hana gave her a very strange look. "Caesar is Caesar, of course. Are you really so ignorant? I am wondering again what country you come from, that you can ask such questions. You are not stupid, but you are very ignorant."

"I'll try to explain sometime," Rivka said. "But I just want to know, what is the personal name of Caesar? Augustus? Tiberius?

Gaius, also called Caligula?" She pronounced each name in *koine* Greek.

At each name, Hana shook her head in puzzlement. "I never heard of these men."

Rivka nodded patiently. The Greek names would naturally sound foreign to Hana. "What about Claudius?"

"Ah!" Hana said. "This name I have heard, but you torture the pronunciation." She said it in Aramaic.

Rivka repeated it several times, until Hana agreed that she had it right.

"So this man Claudius is Caesar?" Rivka asked.

"No," Hana said. "He died. His son is Caesar."

"*Neron Qesar?*" Rivka had a reason to know Nero's name in Hebrew. If you wrote it out in Hebrew letters and added up the numerical equivalents, you got six hundred and sixty-six. Of course, you could get that number from the pope, or Ronald Reagan, or Bill Gates, but there was something to be said for the Nero interpretation.

"Yes," Hana said. "I have heard that name. *Neron Qesar* is very popular."

Which meant they were in the first half of Nero's reign. Obviously, if the people still liked him, he hadn't murdered his mother yet. So the year must be earlier than 59.

"How long has he been Caesar?" Rivka asked.

Hana shook her head. "I do not know. Several years."

Rivka turned to Dr. West. "I've narrowed it down to the late fifties of the first century. With a little luck, I might work her down to the exact year."

He shrugged. "Does it matter? Not much was happening back then, right?"

"Are you kidding?" Rivka said. "The fifties were a critical decade in the history of Judea. They created an intense ferment of discontent that led directly to the Jewish revolt in the late sixties. And even you must know that the destruction of the Temple forever changed the direction of both Judaism and Christianity. Up to that time—"

"Okay, okay, I surrender!" Dr. West grinned at her. "Guess you learn something new every day." He stuffed another hunk of bread in his mouth.

Rivka turned back to Hana. "So tell me, is there a king named Agrippa?"

Hana gave her another one of those smiles that one gives to children's questions. "Of course. Who else would be king?"

"And how long has he been king?" Rivka asked.

"I do not know," Hana said. "Several years."

No new information there. "And who is the high priest?"

Hana rolled her eyes. "Ishmael ben Phiabi. Why do you want to know all these things?"

Rivka ignored the question. She had just remembered something from Jeremias's classic book on Jerusalem. "Do you remember if King Agrippa read the book of the law aloud at the feast of *Sukkot* recently?"

"Yes, he did," Hana said. A look of surprise spread across her face. "But if you did not know he was king, how did you know he read from the law? It happened the year before last. We rejoiced that a king in Israel should read the law again, as in days of old."

"Bingo!" Rivka said. She turned to Dr. West. "I would bet you money this is the year 57 C.E."

He raised his cup and took a sip. "So is anything interesting going to happen this year?"

"Probably," Rivka said. "Nobody knows for sure, but most scholars date the last visit of the apostle Paul to Jerusalem to one of the years 56, 57, or 58."

His eyes went suddenly large and he choked.

"Is something wrong?" Rivka asked.

"Inhaled a grape skin. I'll be fine." He covered a huge yawn. "So, are you telling me you don't know when Mr. Paul shipped into town?"

"Dates are a little fuzzy," Rivka said. "We've got Josephus, and we've got the New Testament, and they're generally talking about different events, and neither one gives very many firm dates. Then we've got Tacitus and Suetonius, and they do give good dates, but they're not talking about Judea much. But the best guess is probably the year 57. I would say it's about fifty-fifty."

"Can't you ask our friend?" He nodded toward Hana. "Who cares what those dusty old boys say, when you've got a lusty young girl right in front of you?"

"This isn't a game, Dr. West," Rivka said. "If you think I'm going to stand idly by while you..."

He grinned at her. "I assure you, my intentions toward the young lady are honorable."

Rivka didn't feel very reassured.

"So ask her whether Paul's been to town lately," he said.

Rivka turned back to Hana. "Did anything unusual happen last year at *Shavuot?* Like a riot in the Temple?"

Hana shook her head. "No, why?"

"Just wondering," Rivka said. She decided to ask another idiot question. "And what month is this?"

Hana stared at her. "It is *Sivan.*"

Rivka felt something hot in her chest. "Is *Shavuot* past yet?"

"No," Hana said. "*Shavuot* is tomorrow. But surely, you came to Jerusalem for the feast, yes?"

Rivka jumped to her feet, unable to contain the rush of adrenaline in her veins.

"What is it?" Dr. West said. "What's wrong?"

"I'm fine, I'm fine," she said. A huge grin had split her face, making it almost impossible for her to talk. "I just can't believe it."

"Believe what?" he asked.

"Tomorrow is *Shavuot*—that's the Feast of Pentecost—in the year 57. If the usual chronology of Paul's life is correct, then he rode into town *today!* Can you believe our luck?" She danced around the room in glee. "I'm gonna find him, if it's the last thing I do!"

Dr. West had a strange expression on his face. "Frankly, Rivka, I'm a little surprised at your reaction. I didn't think you Jews were all that fond of the old boy. Planning to stick a knife in his ribs, are you?"

That irritated Rivka. "No, of course not," she said in a stiff voice. "I'm afraid you're mistaken. I'm Jewish, but I'm also a believer in Yeshua."

Dr. West's mouth fell open. "You mean like Jews for Jesus or something?"

"Or something."

His eyes narrowed. "Does Ari know about this?"

Rivka suddenly felt her mood dampen. She closed her eyes. "Yes, he knows. That's what we had the big argument about last night. He wasn't too thrilled when he found out."

"I can imagine," Dr. West said. "You know, they killed his father."

"What? Who did?"

"The Christians. Bethlehem, early seventies. Ari's father was doing his Army reserve duty. Did you know that a lot of Palestinians in Bethlehem are Christian?"

"Well, of course. Everybody knows that."

"It was news to me, until Ari told me," Dr. West said. "Anyway, a crowd of Palestinians mobbed a squad of the Israeli reservists one night. Ari's father got under the heap. Trampled to death. Terrible way to die. Scarred Ari's whole life, I gather."

"So that's why he's so…" Rivka felt tears in her eyes. "I didn't know."

"I'm not excusing what kind of person he is," Dr. West said. "I still think he's a rat and a half, and you have every reason to hate him—"

"I didn't say I hate him," Rivka said. "I feel sorry for him." Something began nagging at her. Something about the wormhole. She couldn't quite put her finger on it.

"Well, I don't know about you, but I feel a bit jet-lagged," Dr. West said. He shook the crumbs off his clothing. "Listen, I think I'll just go back to my house early tonight, all right? Catch fifty winks, and I'll be as good as new in the morning. You should pack in early yourself. Tomorrow's a big day for you, right? You're doing the big sight-seeing tour?"

"I guess so," Rivka said, trying to remember the thought he had interrupted.

"Tell you what," he said. "Take me along, will you? I'm no archaeologist, but I would kind of like to see the sights, if we can avoid the tourist traps. And who knows? Maybe we'll run into a famous author and we can grab his autograph. Wouldn't that be worth something when we go home?"

"Famous author?" Rivka said. "Oh, you mean Paul." She felt her spirits rise at that. "Yeah, maybe we will. I have a pretty good idea where we could find him, if you don't mind waiting a few days."

Dr. West gave her a most charming smile. "I've always been an autograph hound. For an all-time bestselling author like Paul, I would wait a whole week."

"Well, it's either this week or next year," Rivka said. "I can pretty much guarantee that."

Dr. West stood up slowly, gave a little half-bow toward Hana, and turned toward the door. "Good night then, ladies. I'll see you tomorrow. You know where to find me."

"Good night," Rivka said as he disappeared into the street.

Hana's face wore a dreamy smile.

Rivka sat down again, wondering what she could say to discourage Hana from even thinking about Dr. West.

"He is a nice man," Hana said.

Rivka said nothing.

"You do not agree that he is a nice man?"

Rivka closed her eyes. "I'm just confused, that's all." Somebody had sent her through the wormhole this morning—sent her through and abandoned her. That was unforgivable. But who had done it?

As of now, all she had to go on was gut instinct. She couldn't imagine Ari shipping her off to the first century, no matter how angry he felt. And yet...What if he really did have a mental illness, as Dr. West had suggested? On the other hand, what evidence did she have, other than Dr. West's say-so? And why should she trust him?

"I have known many men," Hana said. "Once, they confused me, but now they do not. This one is a good man, and he speaks the truth."

"How can you be so sure?"

Hana pointed at Rivka's unfinished meal. "Eat. Drink. Enjoy your meal! It is *Shabbat*. When you have finished, I will tell you a story. It is not a happy story. Then you will understand how I can always be sure."

Damien

Damien strode back toward his house, grateful that he had dodged a bullet. He had almost given things away there, talking about Rivka sticking a knife in Paul's ribs. That had been stupid. He had made an assumption—a wrong assumption. Fortunately, Rivka had taken it as a joke.

He could still use her to help him. All he needed was for her to show him around, help him get used to the terrain. He knew roughly where he needed to make the kill, but she could pin it down exactly, if he handled her right.

But was this the year? That had given him a real shock, Rivka's comment about the date of Paul's visit. He had thought he had that one nailed down: A.D. 57. He had found a book in the library with a title something like *A Chronology of Paul*. The book made it seem pretty obvious. Of any date in the whole history of the early church, that was the one certain date. Now Rivka said maybe it was this year, maybe next.

At least he hadn't come a year late—not if that easy-on-the-eyes Hana knew what she was talking about. That would have been a disaster.

If he was a year early, it would be a bit of an inconvenience, but he could deal with it. He would go take target practice out in the desert every couple of months, just to keep his skills up. The gold coins in his duffel bag would keep him fed and housed. He could wait a year, if he had to.

In any event, he couldn't go back to the future and try again. By now, the wormhole had pinholed itself out of existence, and Ari would be ripping out his beard in fury.

Damien's hands began itching. He hadn't fired a gun since coming to Israel. Early tomorrow morning, he would go out into the desert somewhere and shoot up some cactus or whatever they had here. Just to sharpen up for the big day. Not that his skills could evaporate. He had qualified a long time ago as an expert marksman.

And the rest of the day, Rivka would give him a guided tour of the killing grounds. Damien reached his house and unlocked the door.

Whatever he did, he couldn't afford to let Hana come tagging along with them. Damien wanted his mind free to concentrate on the task, and he couldn't do that with a looker like Hana around to distract him. He would have his hands full trying to pump Rivka for information without letting on why he wanted to know.

Rivka might be tricky to manage. She had brains and persistence.

In a woman, that could be a dangerous combination.

TWELVE

Ari

Ari shivered in the cool night breeze. Why hadn't he brought a jacket? Because he was stupid, of course. He had expected to find Rivka quickly.

He hadn't expected that it would be so hard to get along in his own city. He had tried to speak to a number of people in simple Hebrew. Most of them had not understood him and had scurried away with fearful looks. There had been a few well-dressed men who appeared to understand him, but they were surrounded by thuggish bodyguards carrying daggers and clubs, who kept Ari from getting too close. The city didn't seem all that safe these days.

Ari's stomach growled in protest. He had found a granola bar in his backpack, and that was all he had eaten all day. Ari had a few coins in his pocket, but no merchant had been willing to look twice at them. Real coins were made of rough silver or bronze, not the overly shiny *shekels* Ari carried.

He had become a street person—hungry, homeless, dressed wrong by the prevailing standards. And now it was dark. The moon provided a quarter-slice of light in the sky, but in a few hours it would go down. He really ought to just hunker down in some doorway for the night.

The alternative was to go back without Rivka. He could probably find his way back to the cave by moonlight and get to the wormhole. But what chance would he have of coming back?

None. Zero. By now, the authorities would know about the wormhole. Bureaucrats were alike all over the world: risk averse. If Ari ventured back to the lab for even ten seconds, they would keep him there. They wouldn't allow him to come back looking for Rivka.

And without one more chance at Rivka, he couldn't live with himself. A cold gust blew through Ari. He shivered again.

Then he heard footsteps behind him. Quiet footsteps. He spun around.

A scruffy, short man slunk along only a dozen paces behind. A scar ran diagonally across his forehead. Greasy black hair hung down to his shoulders. In his hand, he held a dagger.

Ari bellowed his best imitation of a samurai yell. For an instant, the man froze. Then Ari turned and ran.

He had always been reasonably fast, but his backpack made running awkward. The darkness and the uneven dirt street made the footing dangerous. Ari heard the footsteps of his pursuer slapping on the hard ground behind him. Was he gaining or losing ground?

Ari rounded a corner, skidded slightly, righted himself, and accelerated.

Then his foot landed wrong on a lemon-sized stone in the street, and his ankle twisted beneath him. He cursed just before he hit the ground.

He lost only a second, rolling once, landing on his knees, scrambling halfway to his feet, scooping up the backpack that had fallen off his left shoulder. Too late.

The man slammed into him.

Ari pitched over backward into the dirt. He rolled to his left, grabbed the backpack, and held it up as a shield.

Then he heard another shout from up the street. His attacker stepped back, fear lighting up his eyes. Ari's hands closed on a stone in the dust beside him. It was too small, but it would have to do. Still lying on his back, Ari slung the stone awkwardly at his attacker. Pinpoint!

The man screamed like a woman, turned, and staggered away.

Ari leaped to his feet and spun around to face whatever danger had frightened his attacker. He saw a young man with a black beard running toward him. The man slowed down and then stopped. He said something Ari couldn't understand in a voice that sounded friendly. He looked absolutely unafraid.

Ari held up both hands to show that he was unarmed. *"Shalom,"* he said. "Do you know anyone who speaks Hebrew?"

Surprise flashed across the young man's face. "I do. Don't you understand Aramaic?"

"No," Ari said. "I speak only Hebrew."

"Are you a Pharisee?" the stranger asked. "Who taught you Hebrew?"

Ari grinned at that idea. Pharisees, he remembered, were the precursors to the *Haredim,* who had made his teenage years so miserable. "No, I am not a Pharisee. I learned Hebrew from my parents."

The young man studied Ari for a long moment. The quiet strength in his eyes made Ari feel comfortable, at home. "I doubt that you are a bandit, anyway." He stepped nearer and smiled. "My name is called Baruch."

"I am called Ari."

"A strange name," Baruch said. His smile broadened.

"It is common in my country, and so also is your name."

"Have you come for the feast?" Baruch asked.

What feast? It was too late in the year for *Pesach,* too early for *Sukkot.* Therefore, it must be *Shavuot.* If a feast was on the agenda, he would certainly attend. "Yes, I have come for the feast."

"Why are you alone at night?" Baruch asked. "It is dangerous in the streets when the bandits come to Jerusalem for the feasts."

"I have nowhere to stay," Ari said.

"Did you come to Jerusalem with no money?" Baruch's eyes glowed with sympathy.

Ari nodded. "I arrived late today and could find no food and no shelter."

"Then you will stay with me," Baruch said. "I see that you are honest, although not wise. Come with me and learn wisdom."

Ari smiled. "I would like that, yes."

They began walking back up the street together.

"And why were *you* out so late at night?" Ari asked.

"I was praying with friends in my synagogue," Baruch said. "I do not fear the bandits, nor any man. I fear only HaShem."

Ari smiled. *HaShem.* The Name. It was a term used by the Orthodox to refer to God without despoiling His name. Amazing that so little had changed in twenty centuries. Ari decided that he liked his new friend very much. Baruch had a direct way of speaking that would have sounded arrogant from most men. From him, it was simply the plain and unvarnished truth.

"And what sort of synagogue do you belong to?" Ari asked, just to make conversation. Immediately he realized it was an absurd question. There wasn't any such distinction as Orthodox, Conservative, or Reform in ancient Jerusalem.

"My synagogue is called *Shomrei HaDerech,*" Baruch said.

Ari nodded. *Guardians of the Road.* From anyone else, it would have sounded ridiculous, like one of those strange Islamic zealot groups. But Baruch was clearly not strange, nor Islamic, nor a zealot. He reminded Ari of the old Hasidic rabbi who had tried to teach him Torah, years ago. Simple, kind, fervent, wise.

"I am glad you speak Hebrew," Ari said. "I had some difficulties earlier today."

"We love the Torah in my synagogue," Baruch said. "I am sorry if my speech is awkward. I do not normally speak Hebrew. I only read it and pray the prayers."

"You speak very well," Ari said. His stomach rumbled again.

"Are you hungry?" Baruch asked. He stopped in front of a small stone building and unlocked the door.

"I have not eaten today," Ari said. "I...lost a friend while we were traveling, and I had no money to buy food."

"The day after tomorrow, we can look for him," Baruch said.

Ari resisted the urge to correct Baruch's misunderstanding. There would be time for that later.

Baruch shut the door behind them and locked it. An olive oil lamp burned in a niche inset into the stone wall. Baruch had obviously left it burning before *Shabbat*, so as not to violate the commandments by making fire. Ari's stepfather had always insisted on doing this with the electric lights—a fact which had nearly driven Ari mad as a teenager. For some reason, it didn't bother him nearly as much that Baruch did so. Baruch had an excuse for his superstitions, for his ignorance of modern science. There was no modern science yet.

Ari looked around the room. A pool of water filled the left side of the house—a *mikveh*, for purification. On the right, under the light, he saw a stone table with wooden stools. Bread and cheese and a wineskin lay on the table.

"Sit," Baruch said.

Ari sat on one of the stools and almost reached for the bread. Just in time, he thought better of it.

Baruch sat across from him. *"Baruch attah Adonai, Eloheinu, Melech ha-olam, ha motzi lechem min ha-aretz!"*

Ari had heard the traditional blessing ten thousand times growing up. It had annoyed him mightily at the age of fourteen. It didn't annoy him now. After all, Baruch had never read Darwin, nor Freud, nor Dirac. How could he know that man lived alone in an unfeeling universe? He could not. Therefore, he attributed all things to a nonexistent higher power. Ari could hardly condemn him for his ignorance. And besides, Ari felt truly grateful for this food, so it seemed fitting to express thanks, even if to a nonentity.

"*Amen!*" Ari said. He reached for the bread and tore off a chunk.

"You must explain the writing on your tunic." Baruch pointed at the Maxwell equations on Ari's shirt. "I feel certain that it is important, and yet it makes no sense to me."

Ari wondered how he could possibly explain. The Maxwell equations completely defined the behavior of light, magnetism, electricity. None of this would make sense to Baruch. Except light. "It tells how HaShem created the world."

Baruch's face began shining. "I must understand this wonderful thing, how HaShem created the world. Is it permitted that men should know such a thing? Can you explain it to me?"

Ari thought he could, but he suspected he would get himself stoned as a heretic. "Another time, perhaps. It is very deep wisdom. Tell me the news of Jerusalem."

Baruch's face tightened. "The news is not good," he said. "Renegade Saul has returned."

Ari raised his eyebrows. "I am not familiar with that name."

"It is a long story," Baruch said. Anger flickered in his eyes.

"We have time," Ari said. "Tell me, my friend." He was hungry and thought he would probably be at the table for quite a while. It would be interesting to hear what sort of renegade could upset a man as well-centered as Baruch.

Rivka

"Tell me your story," Rivka said, when she had finished her meal. "Why do you trust my friend Damien?"

"Because he tells no lies."

"Then why do you trust me?" Rivka said. "You told me today that I am an honest person who tells many lies. Why do you say that?"

"Why did you lie?" Hana asked. "You are honest. Your spirit is light, but your words are dark. I do not understand you. When you lie to me, the voices tell me."

"Voices?" Rivka said. A cold feeling settled into her chest. Great. So Hana was a paranoid schizophrenic or something.

"Yes, the truth-tellers," Hana said. "When someone lies to me, the truth-tellers warn me."

"How long have you been hearing these truth-tellers?"

"Since my husband died," Hana said. "That is the story I wanted to tell you. He left me a little money, but it was soon gone to pay my rent and buy food. Then I became hungry. I went to the Temple to ask for a share of the poor-basket, but the priests told me I was too young to register as a widow."

"How old were you?" Rivka asked.

"I was fifteen," Hana said. "So I came home, and I fell asleep crying. I dreamed that I beat the priests with sticks. It gave me happiness to beat them until they cried out. When I awoke in the morning, I heard the truth-tellers. They said that I should go to the Pool of Siloam and wait, and that I would never go hungry again."

Rivka found herself struggling to breathe. "So you..."

"I went to the pool, and there I met a woman named Martha who helped me. She taught me how to stand and how to walk to make men hungry."

Rivka closed her eyes. "And what about the truth-tellers?"

"They protect me," Hana said. "One day, a man came looking for a water carrier. Martha went away with him."

"And…?" A nameless dread clawed at Rivka's insides.

"And her body was found outside the gates of the city," Hana said. "It has happened several times. The truth-tellers show me who can be trusted and who cannot. I protect all the women there. I did not see Martha go, or I would have warned her."

Rivka said nothing for a long time. It was a strange tale. How much was real, and how much fantasy? How could Hana make decisions based on voices in her head?

Probably those were the wrong questions, she decided. To Hana, it was all very real. She would have no concept of fantasy. And everyone made decisions based on voices inside their heads. Most people's stream of consciousness was vocalized in an interior voice. If you could accept one voice, why not several?

Clearly, Hana had had a horrible life, and this was how she protected herself. Rivka felt tears rolling down her cheeks, and she brushed them away. Finally, she asked, "What about my friend Damien?"

"He is your friend, but he is not your friend," Hana said. "He is from your country, but he is not from your country. He is a man who walks backward. I do not know what this means, but the truth-tellers say that he walks backward. Do you understand me, Rivka?"

"Yes," Rivka said.

"You are telling the truth," Hana said. "And you are also lying. How can this be, Rivka? I do not understand it at all."

"It is very difficult." Rivka opened her eyes. "I will try to explain it when I understand better myself."

Hana was staring at her intently. She continued studying Rivka for some time. "You have a question you wish to ask me."

Rivka shook her head.

"You do have a question. Ask it."

Rivka didn't believe in the truth-tellers, but obviously Hana had a very well-honed sense of intuition. It wouldn't do any good to lie to Hana. "I was just wondering something about Jerusalem." She paused, wondering how to phrase this. "Are there any Jews here who are called *Notzrim?*" That was the modern Hebrew word for Christians. What would it be in the first century?

Hana's face twisted in puzzlement. "No, who are these people?"

"It is a sect," Rivka said. "Like...Pharisees, or Sadducees, or Essenes."

"There are many sects," Hana said. "Every year, a new prophet arises, claiming to be Elijah or Messiah." Bitterness edged her voice. "Every year, the Romans kill a prophet. Last year, there was a man from God who came out of Egypt."

Rivka nodded. The so-called "Egyptian" mentioned in Acts and Josephus. The man presumably came from the huge Jewish community in Alexandria, the biggest city in Egypt.

"He was lucky," Hana said. "The Romans chased him away into the wilderness. Many of our people died."

Rivka felt like weeping. She had read about all this in her history books and had felt bad about it. But it was different when you heard about it firsthand.

"Now you must tell me, who are these *Notzrim?*" Hana said.

"There was a prophet, about thirty years ago, who came from Nazareth," Rivka said. "His name was called Yeshua, and many of our people thought He was *HaMashiach.*"

"Was He killed by the chief priests for sorcery?" Hana said.

"The Romans killed Him," Rivka said. "But yes, the chief priests gave Him over to them."

Hana nodded. "I know of this man and His followers. They are not called *Notzrim.* They are called *HaDerech.*"

HaDerech. The Way. Rivka saw it at once. How obvious! The Book of Acts mentioned "The Way" or "this way" several times, early on. Then the term disappeared, as the story moved from Jerusalem to Samaria to Antioch, and on to the empire at large. But it made sense that the original name had stuck, at least in the city of origin.

"Tell me about *HaDerech,*" Rivka said.

Hana shrugged. "There is not much to tell. They are known to be righteous men. Many of them are Pharisees."

That went with what Rivka knew. The Book of Acts made it clear that a large number of Pharisees had entered the Jesus Movement in the forties and fifties. The reasons for this were unclear, given the running battles between Jesus and the Pharisees during His lifetime. However, if you took Acts seriously, then you had to accept that things changed at some point.

Not everyone took it seriously, of course. It was an uncomfortable claim. Modern Jews preferred to believe that the early Christian movement was essentially pagan in origin—ergo, Ari's notion of Jesus as an avatar myth. Conservative Christians found it hard to believe that the "early church" could have found room for "legalistic Pharisees." Liberal Christians didn't take any of Acts seriously—too many miracle stories.

It seemed that only two groups took any notice of these Pharisees in the Jesus Movement: Messianic Jews and historians. And nobody paid much attention to either of them.

"So tell me more," Rivka said.

Hana shrugged. "Most of the followers of *HaDerech* live near David's tomb. That is all I know. Are you a member of *HaDerech?* Why do you ask me for information?"

"Because I am new to Jerusalem," Rivka said. "I would like to meet some of them."

"I can show you where they live," Hana said. "But I will not go there with you." She wrinkled her nose. "I do not care for Pharisees, and they do not care for me."

Rivka reached out and touched Hana's arm. "I care."

Hana looked at her sadly. "Yes, you are different. You are not a Pharisee, yet still you are a righteous woman. They will not hate you. Shall I show you where they live tomorrow?"

"Yes," Rivka said.

"It is late," Hana said. "We must sleep now."

Rivka stood up and yawned mightily. Who knew what tomorrow would hold? Would she meet James, the brother of Yeshua? Shimon, cousin of James? The apostle Paul?

And what would Dr. West do if he met any of these men? Maybe one of them would convert him.

Ari

"Tell me about Renegade Saul," Ari said.

Baruch's eyes narrowed. "I only know what I hear, but the stories are very bad."

"So tell me."

"I am a Pharisee, and the son of a Pharisee," Baruch said. "I love Torah. Torah tells us how to live for God and how to live with our brothers."

"With all men?"

"Not all men, of course not. The *goyim* are evil. We are not commanded to live at peace with them. But we are commanded to live at peace with our brother Jews. The way of Torah is the way of peace and life."

Ari nodded, though he didn't believe it. Not much had changed in the last couple of thousand years. Baruch would feel perfectly at home in the ultraorthodox synagogue of Ari's stepfather. It all sounded nice in theory, but this talk of "the way of peace and life" ended the minute you disagreed with them. At least, that was how it had been for Ari, growing up in Haifa in a community that rejected the rational and embraced authoritarianism.

"Renegade Saul claims also to be a Pharisee, and yet his actions are not those of one who follows Torah. He travels among the *goyim*, and we hear that he eats with them. We hear that he urges our brothers who live among the *goyim* to abandon the commandments. We hear that he teaches Jew and *goy* to pray together."

Sudden realization flashed through Ari's brain. *Renegade Saul!*

In Princeton, Ari had known an Israeli named Meir who went by the name of Mark. At MIT, he had met a Leah who called herself Lynn when not home in Brooklyn. Many Jews had Gentile names that sounded like their Jewish ones. Ari had never read the Christian New Testament, but he did know about a man named Paul. Which sounded suspiciously like Saul. Coincidence?

Ari cleared his throat. "My friend, does this Renegade Saul have another name among the *goyim?*"

Baruch frowned. "I have heard that he is sometimes called by a Greek name—*Paulos*—which means *little*. It is a fitting name because he is very short."

Paulos. Paul. It had to be him! Ari smiled a little. Well then. That explained Baruch's antagonism to Renegade Saul. So here he was, the great avatar mythmaker himself, Paul of Tarsus, alienating real Jews. No wonder Baruch was upset. "Why has Renegade Saul come to Jerusalem?"

Baruch shrugged. "For *Shavuot*, of course. The same reason you have come."

Ari nodded impatiently. He didn't want to get into that right now. "So tell me more about Renegade Saul. Is there some man he admires very much?" That would be called a leading question in a court of law, but Ari didn't care. He wanted to find out if the whole mythmaking scheme had begun yet, or whether it was still future. Whatever, this would be interesting to take back to Rivka. If he could prove to her that Jesus was just a myth, she might rethink her position.

Baruch looked puzzled. "There is only one man Renegade Saul talks about. Did I not tell you? He teaches the Way of Rabban Yeshua."

Rabban? Ari shivered. That had to be Aramaic, but it was close enough to the Hebrew word *Rabbenu* that Ari understood it. Our Great One. Our Teacher. Our Rabbi. It was a term used by a community which universally recognized the authority of one man. All over the world, Ari knew, the Lubavitcher Hasidim recognized the alleged greatness of the Lubavitcher Rebbe, the late Menachem Mendel Schneerson.

That didn't prove the Lubavitcher Rebbe was really the *Mashiach,* as some of his followers had believed. But the title did provide powerful evidence that he had existed.

That he was not a myth.

Ari felt light-headed and realized that he had stopped breathing. He forced himself to take in a lungful of air. "Tell me about Rabban Yeshua."

Damien

Damien groped around on the lake bottom, his lungs desperate for air. His foot kicked something fleshy. He whirled in the water and pulled himself toward the thing.

A leg. Stu's leg. Damien tugged himself along it to the torso. He snaked his hands under Stu's armpits and pulled. Nearly weightless in the water, Stu's body lifted easily.

Damien gathered his legs and pushed off the bottom. His head broke the water, and merciful air rushed into his chest. The raft bobbed on the surface, two arms'-lengths away.

He frog-whipped his legs frantically, all the while trying to raise Stu's head above water. His own ducked under the surface, and water rushed into his mouth. He found that he was more buoyant underwater, and he used the opportunity to kick himself toward the raft. His heart hammered in his chest.

But Stu's heavier body would not stay above him. They rolled in the water, and Damien found himself breathing air again. Now he had the raft within reach. He grasped it with his left hand while he clutched Stu around the upper body with his right.

It was impossible to haul himself onto the raft while holding Stu. Nor could he let go. His grip hardened, as he fought to keep Stu's head

*above water. If he was still alive, he would be able to breathe. And if
not...*

*Damien shook his head in fury. Stu would live. He had to.
Damien would not let him die.*

*Then he was shouting. "Mom! Dad! Help! Help us! Help us
now!"*

When Damien woke up in the morning, he found that his
arms ached, his cheeks were wet, and his heart was steeled for
what he had to do.

Ari

"You will need decent clothes, if you are going to pray with us,"
Baruch said. They sat on the floor in the sleeping room upstairs.
Baruch owned remarkably little furniture. A thin bedroll on the
floor. A wooden bench, on which he kept his clothes. A table
and stool, with some papyrus sheets, an inkwell, and one pen.
Some window slits high up on one of the walls let in a little
light.

Baruch handed Ari a worn four-cornered tunic made of
wool. Each vertical seam ended in a ritual fringe, a cluster of
blue threads, knotted together exactly like the fringes on the
prayer shawl in Ari's closet back home in Jerusalem. He hadn't
worn it in years.

"Put this on," Baruch said. "It is forbidden to pray in clothes
that do not fulfill the commandments."

"Do you obey all the commandments?" Ari asked.

"As many as HaShem gives me the strength to observe,"
Baruch said. "Why do you ask?"

Because you're a Christian! Ari wanted to shout. *You can't keep
the commandments!*

Which was true, and it wasn't.

True, Baruch belonged to a sect which followed the teachings of the man he called Rabban Yeshua—Jesus of Nazareth. Therefore, Baruch was a Christian.

And yet he was fully a Jew. He prayed the *Amidah* every morning and every evening. A *mikveh*—a ritual bath—filled up half of his downstairs. He observed *Shabbat* and the feasts as religiously as Ari's stepfather. He kept every commandment that he could. And he believed that HaShem had raised Rabban Yeshua into a new life as *Mashiach* of Israel, and that he would soon appear to rule the earth.

Baruch was as Orthodox as any of the *Haredim* who had made Ari's early life so miserable. He was as Christian as any televangelist who had ever thumped a Bible on TV.

Despite all this, Ari respected Baruch. He had a quick mind, a quicker wit, and eyes that reflected suffering without bitterness.

Baruch repeated his question. "Why do you ask? Of course I try to observe all the commandments. I am a Jew."

Ari pulled the tunic over his head. "I think that you are more a Jew than I am."

"That makes no sense," Baruch said. "You are a Jew, or you are not a Jew. There are no halves in the kingdom of HaShem."

"In my country, some men do not observe the commandments," Ari said.

"You mean some *goyim?*" Baruch asked. "But of course *goyim* do not observe the commandments. HaShem gave the Torah to Israel, not to the nations."

"No," Ari said. "I mean that there are Jews who do not follow the Torah." *For example, me.*

Ari expected Baruch to look shocked. Instead, he looked confused. "You are saying they are renegades? *Apikorsim?* They do not observe the commandments, and yet they are called Jews? Why do men in your country misuse language?"

"A Jew is one born of a Jewish mother," Ari said. "One who loves Israel—"

"That is nonsense," Baruch said. "A Jew is one who lives within the covenants which HaShem made with Avraham our father and with Moshe our teacher." He wrapped a broad woolen belt around Ari's waist several times and knotted it once, like a scarf.

Ari was beginning to get impatient. "In my country, many Jews do not live within the covenants. They are—"

"They are *apikorsim*," Baruch said. "Renegades. Apostates. Men like Renegade Saul—may the living God deal justly with him!" He glanced up at the window slit. "It will be dawn soon. Let us go and pray, my brother. I thank HaShem that you are not a renegade, like those wicked men in your country."

By now, Ari's head was spinning. He followed Baruch quietly down the stairs and picked up his backpack from the floor where he had left it the night before.

"Leave it here," Baruch said. "It is *Shabbat*, and you may not bear that."

Ari decided not to waste time arguing. He unzipped the pocket of the backpack, pulled out his emergency adrenaline kit, and slipped it inside his belt.

"What is that?" Baruch asked.

"It is medicine that would save my life, if I need it," Ari said.

"Then you must carry it with you," Baruch said. "Torah requires it."

They went out into the dark street. Baruch locked the door behind them and they set off. The houses were built very closely together. Ari lagged behind Baruch by a step and stretched out his arms. His fingertips brushed the houses on either side of the street. A sense of awe welled up inside his chest. This city was his city, these stones his stones, these people his people. Strange, primitive, ignorant—yes. But still his. For no reason at all, he loved this place, these people. Even though he was an *apikoros*.

"Will we meet Renegade Saul at your house of prayer?" Ari asked.

"Of course not," Baruch said. "I am told that he does not pray as we are commanded to do."

"Suppose he does it secretly," Ari said. In some strange way, he was beginning to identify with Renegade Saul. Rivka would no doubt find that amusing. She would be less delighted to learn that her coreligionists were roughly the equivalent of the *Haredim*.

They arrived at the house of prayer and went inside. A number of men already waited there. They greeted Baruch, who introduced them to Ari. Within a few minutes, they began the morning prayers.

☾ ☾ ☾

The day passed slowly for Ari. After the morning prayers, he and Baruch returned to Baruch's house and ate the morning meal. Then they returned to the house of prayer for more prayers and readings from the Torah and the Prophets. As a guest, Ari was invited to read. He declined, saying that he did not know how to chant the Hebrew. Nobody seemed surprised by this. Not all of them could even read Hebrew, much less chant it.

The *Shabbat* worship service continued long past what Ari considered lunchtime. In the early afternoon, he learned that there would be no lunch. Apparently, the concept was unknown here. Baruch promised that they would be invited to a *Shavuot* feast at the home of one of his married friends. That came as a shock. The traditional celebration of *Shavuot* always fell on a Sunday. Apparently, that tradition hadn't been born yet.

They spent the afternoon talking. Ari carefully skirted the issue of Torah observance. Finally, Baruch went upstairs to use the chamber pot.

Then there came a knock at the door.

Ari opened it. Outside stood a man and a woman.

The man said something in Aramaic.

"I'm sorry," Ari said. "Do either of you speak Hebrew?" He smiled at the man, then at the woman.

She blushed violently and turned away to face the street.

The man's face stiffened. Ari wondered what he had done wrong.

"Who is at the door?" Baruch asked as he came down the stairs.

Ari stepped aside. Baruch went out and greeted the man. He did not speak to the woman.

All of them came into the house. Ari retreated into the corner.

Baruch turned to him and beckoned. "Come, Ari, my brother. The woman has a headache, and we must pray for her. Please do not look the woman in the eye again. It is not done in Jerusalem, although you tell me the customs are different in your country."

Ari stepped closer, wondering what would happen next. What would he do if Baruch asked him to pray?

Baruch spoke to the man. The woman pointed to her temples and her forehead and spoke in a quiet voice, looking only at her husband.

"She has had pain for many hours," Baruch said. He took the husband's hands and laid them on the woman's head covering. Then he laid his own hands on top of these. "Ari, you may put your hands on mine. Of course, you must not touch the woman."

Ari did as he was told.

Baruch began praying in Aramaic.

Ari listened intently. He was beginning to catch a few words of the language. It wasn't so different from Hebrew—the two languages were closer than German and English, he decided.

After a few minutes, Baruch stopped praying and asked the man a question. The woman answered to her husband.

Baruch nodded. "It is good, Ari," he said. "Do you feel the Presence? The *Shekinah* is here. She will be healed."

Ari felt nothing at all, but he decided not to say anything. The woman seemed to be in a relaxed state and that would certainly help her. What harm would it do to play along?

There followed a long period in which Baruch prayed in a quiet voice. Then he asked the man another question. The man repeated this to his wife. Ari didn't see why. She had obviously heard Baruch ask it the first time.

The woman responded in a drowsy, detached voice.

Hypnosis, Ari thought. Or some sort of altered state. Really very interesting. It was amazing how the mind could heal the body, if you let it.

"She says that the pain has diminished very much," Baruch said. His own voice also carried a dreamlike quality. "The Spirit is here, Ari. Do you feel it?"

Ari didn't. "Yes." Some sort of spirit of good feeling had fallen on the group. Except himself, of course. He felt nothing at all, but he had not expected anything. From what he had read about this sort of thing, the expectation led to the reality. It wasn't any big mystery. The mind was the body. The body was the mind.

Baruch continued praying, very softly. Ari noticed that his eyes had closed and his eyelids fluttered. An altered state.

And then, suddenly, it ended.

Baruch opened his eyes and smiled. He and Ari each pulled their hands away at the same time. The husband took his hands away also, and then threw his arms around Baruch and kissed him on the lips.

For a moment, Ari feared that he might get a kiss, too. However, the husband still did not seem to have forgiven him for his previous breach of etiquette. The man took his wife and escorted her to the door.

Baruch followed them out into the street. When he returned, his step was light and springy. "So, my friend. Are you ready for evening prayers?"

Was there any choice? Ari shrugged and nodded. "Let's go."

Baruch locked the door, and they set off. The streets were crowded. Ari stayed close to Baruch. He was tired of the enforced tedium of the day. Tomorrow, they would see some action. Tomorrow, Baruch would help him find Rivka. Ari already had a plan. Somebody in Jerusalem must have seen Rivka wearing her denim cutoffs. Ari had seen enough of the city to know that nobody would forget a woman dressed like that, with naked legs and arms. Somebody knew where Rivka was. He needed to find that somebody.

Once he had found Rivka—well, he had a lot to tell her. She wasn't going to be happy to hear it, either. Her apostle Paul—rejected by his own people as a renegade. And her fellow "Christians" were ultraorthodox Jews who followed their Rabban Yeshua as tightly as any Hasidic sect followed its *tsaddik*.

Where did Damien fit into all this? Why had he brought them to this place, this year?

They reached the house of prayer and went in.

Ari sat quietly on a bench and closed his eyes. *You are a filthy, stinking, stupid man, Damien West. If you harm a single cell of Rivka's body, I will forget that I am a pacifist.*

FOURTEEN

Rivka

Rivka studied the northern portico of the Temple Mount. Incredible! What she wouldn't give for her camera and a hundred rolls of film.

She pointed at a stone stairway leading up from the outer court of the Temple onto the roof of the porticoes, forty feet above them. "Dr. West, you see the head of the stairway? That's where Paul will stand when he gets arrested."

"You really think it'll be this next week?" Dr. West asked. "I wish I had my video camera. When we go home, nobody's going to believe we saw the old coot himself."

His tone was jovial, but still it annoyed Rivka. "Don't call him an old coot. He died before he got to be what we would call old, and no coot ever had as many friends as he did."

"Well, he was quite the uptight preacher, from all I've heard," Dr. West said. "And you're the last person I'd expect to be defending him. Wasn't he an anti-Semite and an antifeminist and basically anti-fun? That's the way I learned it in college."

"Antifeminist?" Rivka said. "The guy who said, 'There is neither male nor female in Christ Jesus?' Sorry, I don't think so. It's true that he expected men and women to fill different roles in society, but have a look around you, Dr. West. How many female rabbis and priests do you see? Within his culture, Paul strikes me as pretty liberated."

"Whatever," Dr. West said. "But you're not denying that he was anti-Jewish."

"I am too denying it," Rivka said. "But I can only answer one of your absurdities at a time." She was trying to be nice and having a hard time of it.

Dr. West's laugh had an edge to it. "So answer."

"Okay, for starters you need to go read the books of Romans and Galatians. That's where he explains most clearly his views on the law and freedom in Christ and all that."

"So you're telling me that's where he declared his independence from Judaism?"

"No, *you're* the one saying that," Rivka said. "Let me finish. Do you have any clue why he came to Jerusalem this weekend?"

Dr. West shook his head. "I'm not even sure what I'm doing here, much less a guy who's been dead for two thousand years."

"Paul came for the feast of *Shavuot*," Rivka said. "That's Pentecost in English. He came to do what every Jew wants: to celebrate one of the great feasts in Jerusalem. Next week, he's going to stand before the Sanhedrin. Guess what he's going to tell them?"

"I'm dying to find out," Dr. West said flatly.

Rivka ignored his tone. "When we get home, you can read about it in the Book of Acts, chapter 23. Paul's going to tell them, 'I am a Pharisee, the son of a Pharisee.' Does that sound like the words of an anti-Semite?"

"Um, I'm not quite sure what a Pharisee is," Dr. West said. "Sorry, Miss Meyers, the last time I went to Sunday school was a long time ago, when I was a kid." He tilted his head apologetically. "Go on, this is all very interesting."

"The Pharisees were one of the sects of Judaism, kind of analogous to the modern Orthodox. There were other sects—the Sadducees, the Essenes, the apocalyptists, and so on. Most of them died out after the Jewish revolt, when the Temple burned. For people in this century, that's all coming up in less than a decade. The Pharisees will survive and transmute into Rabbinic Judaism."

"I understand," said Dr. West. "But what does this have to do with our man Paul?"

"Right now, in this city, many of the believers in Jesus are Pharisees or sympathetic to the Pharisees. That's Paul's biggest problem, and he's probably only just finding out about it."

"I don't get it," Dr. West said. "If he's a Pharisee, why is he catching flak from the other Pharisees?"

"Because he preaches to Gentiles," Rivka said. "He's not anti-Jewish; he's pro-Gentile. He wants the nations to receive what the Jews have had for ages: a knowledge of the God of Israel. Right now, that doesn't set too well with Jews. Gentiles are unclean."

Dr. West looked skeptical. "I thought you Jews were all a bunch of bleeding-heart liberals. Democrats and all that."

"Nineteen centuries of persecution will do that to you," Rivka said. "But that hasn't happened yet for these people. In this century, Jews are like every other primitive ethnic group in this world. They consider themselves to be the only pure race, and all other peoples are impure. It's basic anthropology—us against everybody else. Really, it was the Greeks who thought up all that liberal stuff about how all men are created equal."

"So Paul got it from them," Dr. West said.

"Maybe," Rivka said. "But it's a funny thing that he didn't get it from them while he was growing up in a Greek city in Turkey. He didn't get it until God knocked him off his horse on the way to Damascus. It took Jesus to change Paul."

"Or an epileptic fit," Dr. West said. "That'll knock you off your horse, all right."

Rivka laughed out loud. It was incredible to hear such naiveté from a university professor. "Dr. West, that is absolutely absurd," she said. "Paul's life changed profoundly on the Damascus road. He's spent his whole career getting chased, beaten, starved, and imprisoned! You're telling me he's doing it on account of a fit? And he's going to get his head chopped off in a few years. For what? Look me in the eye and tell me with a straight face that it's all just a bad case of the shakes."

Dr. West held up his hands. "Peace, Miss Meyers! I surrender, okay? Maybe we can ask when we meet him—how's that sound?"

"That might be tricky," Rivka said. "I doubt either of us would have a chance to talk with him. I'm a woman, and you don't speak the language."

"So you're a woman," Dr. West said. "What's the big deal? You just told me Paul is the great women's libber, or whatever."

Rivka resisted the urge to whack him. Why this deliberate sarcasm? She took a deep breath. "To paraphrase Bill Clinton, it's the culture, stupid."

"Meaning what?"

"Meaning, have a look around, will you? This is a different world here. Everyone's staring at us. Staring at *you,* actually, because you're talking to a woman in public. In this culture, you don't do that."

"So what?" Dr. West said. "Maybe you're my wife. Why wouldn't they think so?"

"Because men don't speak to women in public," Rivka said. "Not even to their wives. Jewish men don't, anyway."

"So how do they set up their little flings?" Dr. West asked, almost laughing at Rivka's shocked look. "And speaking of that, am I correct in believing our friend Hana is a lady of the night?"

Rivka felt her neck getting hot. "She's a nice girl trapped in something she doesn't like."

"That's what they all say," Dr. West said.

"So why do you ask?" Rivka said sarcastically.

"I just thought it was interesting, your choice of roommate. You're a nice Christian girl. She doesn't seem your type."

For some reason, that tipped Rivka's anger over the edge. She hated being pigeonholed. "I don't have a type, and neither does Hana." She turned and stomped away, heading toward the south end of the Temple Mount.

She heard footsteps behind her, hurrying to catch up.

"Miss Meyers?" Dr. West said.

She was too angry to answer.

"Miss Meyers, listen, I'm a bit of a joker," he said. "It's a weakness of mine. Sometimes I push people too far."

"So push off."

"What I'm trying to say is, I'm sorry," Dr. West said. "I hadn't realized it, but you're a lot like Ari, you know. One little thing, and you blow up."

It wasn't just one little thing, Rivka thought, but a whole succession of little things. She was tired, and far from home, and yet dazzled by her surroundings. And it annoyed her to hear this sarcastic stream of uninformed skepticism.

Real skepticism she could understand. There were plenty of things she found hard to believe in. The Bible wasn't a simple book, and God wasn't a simple god. For that matter, the universe wasn't a simple place, or wormholes would be impossible and she wouldn't be here.

But she hated the shallowness reflected in Dr. West's questions. She had heard it all before, in late-night dorm discussions and undergraduate seminars. It was all so sophomoric. People would question anything having to do with God, but they wouldn't question their own questions. They would challenge the authority of a theologian, but they wouldn't challenge the authority of their buddy who claimed he had read a book that disproved the Bible.

And the final straw was that remark about Hana. Rivka hated seeing people put down, especially those who couldn't defend themselves. In a sense, she felt that was her mission in life, to be the defender of the defenseless.

"Miss Meyers, are you going to talk to me?" Dr. West said. "I messed up, okay? I'm asking you to…forgive me. You can't just walk away from me when I'm asking you to forgive me, can you?"

Oh great, he was doing the noble stuff, taking blame, asking forgiveness. He had beaten her to the punch, and that annoyed her. After all, it was partly her fault. She had been awfully touchy today. And while it was true that Dr. West had been needling her, followers of Yeshua weren't supposed to respond in kind, were they?

She stopped and turned to face him. He looked penitent enough. Rivka sighed. Seventy times seven, and all that. Sometimes, she wished Yeshua had cut the forgiver a little more slack, and the forgivee a little less. But He hadn't.

"Okaaay," she said, dragging out the word to put off the next part. This stuff never got any easier, no matter how much practice she got. "I forgive you. But cut the snide remarks about Hana. And next time you want to argue about my religion, bring some live ammunition. Nothing ticks me off more than hearing nonsense from an intelligent person. I'm sure you get annoyed when some dork spouts off about how Einstein was wrong."

"Einstein was wrong," Dr. West said amiably. "On a lot of issues. He never did swallow quantum mechanics. But I get your point."

They walked together in silence for some minutes. The outer courts of the Temple Mount were huge—a rectangle some three hundred yards by five hundred. Rivka knew this perfectly well in her head, but it was something else to experience it, to be here. You could put a hundred thousand Jews in this vast esplanade, and there would be plenty of room left over.

"I have another question," Dr. West said. "You were telling me about that Sanhedrin thing a while ago. That's what exactly? The government?"

"Close. It's a Jewish advisory council that answers to the Romans on local matters. The Romans are actually quite good about respecting provincials' rights to self-government. In theory, anyway. In practice, they shoot themselves in the foot quite a bit."

"Say, are you up for continuing our guided tour? Maybe we could have a look at where the Sanhedrin meets."

"Honestly, I don't really know where it met," Rivka said. "There was a place called the Chamber of Hewn Stone mentioned in the Mishnah. Unfortunately, nobody left any maps showing its location. The Sanhedrin met there for many years. Supposedly, they later met somewhere on the Temple Mount. We don't really know, but my money's on the Chamber of Hewn Stone, wherever that is."

"We could stop at a gas station for directions," Dr. West said.

"Go ahead," Rivka said. "How's your Aramaic and Greek?"

Dr. West laughed. "Men aren't allowed to ask directions, even when we speak the language. Can't *you* ask somebody?"

Before Rivka could answer, he thumped the side of his head. "Oh, that's right. You woke up on the wrong side of the Y chromosome."

"I suppose I could ask a woman," Rivka said. "But if they're all as well-informed as Hana, I might not learn anything."

"Oh well, we've got time," Dr. West said. "The trial doesn't start for a few days, isn't that what you said?"

"Right," Rivka said. She turned and gave him a curious look. "But you don't seriously want to go, do you? It won't be till next week sometime, and neither of us has any chance at all of getting in."

"That's okay," Dr. West said. A little smile played around his lips. "I know you're dying to see Paul. Maybe we could just hang around outside. I…well, you've given me some things to think about. Maybe Paul is different than what I've been taught. I'm open-minded. I would kind of like to get a look at him, too."

Rivka found herself grinning. Maybe this debating with skeptics was worth it after all. Maybe Dr. West would come to believe. A long shot—but worth trying.

Now that she thought about it, she did want to see Paul. She had come back two thousand years, and by blind chance had landed practically in his lap. She *had* to see him.

More than that, she would love to spend a day with him, picking his brain. She had a number of doubts in her own mind—real doubts, not the manufactured kind that you got in dorm room bull sessions.

She wanted to ask Paul what was his source of information on the life of Yeshua. She wanted to ask his opinions on the afterlife, given that the Hebrew Bible said so little on the subject. She wanted to ask about the sovereignty of God, and how He could be in control of the universe, when her life was so out-of-control.

She had a thousand questions, but no hope of ever asking Paul any of them.

No hope at all. Because she was a woman.

Ari

Ari had never been kissed by a man before. Surprisingly, he found that he didn't mind it.

He and Baruch had gone to a large house for the feast of *Shavuot*. He still hadn't figured out why they were celebrating the feast on the evening of *Shabbat*, rather than on Sunday. Baruch had explained that the Pharisees interpreted the Torah differently on this point than the Sadducees did. Ari didn't follow the reasoning, but he didn't really care. The important thing was that he would eat a good meal tonight. A land where nobody ate lunch was not his idea of a hospitable country.

The women busied themselves in the kitchen preparing the food. The men stood in small circles in the outer courtyard, enjoying the coolness of the evening air. Ari had already begun to get a feel for Aramaic, although he still couldn't express himself very well.

"Brother Ari, you must meet Brother Yohanan and Brother Yoseph," Baruch said. "My friends, Brother Ari has come to Jerusalem from a far country to celebrate the feast with us. He is a learned man who knows the secrets of how God created the world."

Ari smiled at the two men. Brother Yohanan threw his arms around Ari and kissed him. On the lips. Before Ari could recover from this shock, Brother Yoseph did the same.

Somehow, this strange and simple gesture changed things for Ari. Until now, he had thought of himself as an outsider in this little community, an observer. Now he felt welcome, part of the family. A brother. Whether he liked it or not, he had become an honorary member of the community of Rabban Yeshua.

"Tell us about how God created the world," Brother Yoseph said. A small cluster of men gathered around, looking expectantly at Ari.

Ari wondered how in the world he could get out of this. If he told them about the Big Bang, they would stone him for heresy, if they understood him. He cleared his throat, waiting for inspiration to strike. What could he say that would make sense in their reference frame? Would they have a clue what he meant if he said that in the first nanosecond after the Big Bang, photons had outnumbered matter by a billion to one?

Photons. Electromagnetic radiation.

Light.

"In the beginning was Light," Ari said.

"The Light of wisdom," said Brother Yohanan.

Brother Yoseph smiled. "The Light of the Word."

"The Light of Yeshua," said Brother Baruch.

Heads nodded all around the circle. "Rabban Yeshua was the Word and the Light," someone else said.

That started a discussion too rapid for Ari to follow. Never mind. He had told the truth and had not been stoned for it. He stood quietly, enjoying the sound of excited, happy voices. Voices arguing about Torah. It reminded him of his boyhood, when his stepfather's friends would argue Torah on *Shabbat* afternoon. Except that those friends rarely talked about That Man. These new friends ate, slept, prayed, and dreamed Rabban Yeshua.

Ari shook his head in disbelief. He had been so sure That Man had never existed. A legend. A syncretistic avatar myth. But that idea didn't work. He might just as well go back to his modern world and argue that Elvis Presley had never existed. That would be absurd. Too many people remembered the King. And in this world, too many people remembered Rabban Yeshua.

Of course, their memories were faulty. They talked of miracles, healings, prophecies, resurrection. Ari didn't believe any of that. When he had lived in America, the supermarket tabloids had carried at least one story every month on Elvis sightings. People believed what they wanted to believe. Not everybody took care to pursue the simple, unvarnished, uncomfortable truth.

Ari did. And the truth was that the carpenter from Nazareth was just as dead as the crooner from Nashville. Nothing could change that simple truth. Nothing.

❨ ❨ ❨

Ari lay on the hard floor, trying to sleep. After the feast, he and Baruch had come back to the house for the night. Then Baruch had gone somewhere for an emergency meeting, leaving Ari alone. Apparently, it was an internal affair to figure out what to do about Renegade Saul. Ari had not been invited, nor would he have gone if given the chance. He didn't want anything to do with Paul of Tarsus.

It had to be midnight by now, and yet Ari couldn't sleep. He had grown up believing that there was one traditional Judaism, Orthodoxy. Not that he liked the *Haredim*, but he had always assumed they represented the teachings of the fathers from antiquity.

Well, here he was in antiquity, and obviously somebody had forgotten to clue these people in on their traditions. One group said one thing; another group said another. And they attacked each other in the harshest terms imaginable.

Ari found it all disconcerting. He had imagined that Jewish religious rivalries were a modern phenomenon. Dead wrong! Judaism in this century had no center—just a bewildering variety of sects, subsects, and countersects.

And in the middle of it all sat these Jewish Christians, blithely unaware that they were a contradiction in terms. Ari wanted to sit down with Baruch and ask some pointed questions. Do you believe that your Rabban Yeshua is literally and genetically the Son of HaShem? Do you believe that his death cancels your sins? Do you believe HaShem is one—or three?

Ari once had a neighbor in Boston, a blond born-again airhead, who tried to convince him on all these points. Such questions were important to modern Christians. He had a feeling Baruch would not even have thought of these issues. These people were not theologians or philosophers. They lived in simple obedience to the Torah and to their Rabban Yeshua, and they seemed to have no inkling of any contradiction.

Ari heard the door open. He opened his eyes and squinted into the deep darkness.

"Brother Baruch, is that you?"

"Did I wake you, Brother Ari?" Baruch asked. "Please forgive me. I tried to be silent when I came in downstairs."

"You did a good job being silent," Ari said. "I didn't hear a thing until you came through this upstairs door. I've been awake thinking since you left."

Baruch grunted something. Ari could hear the swish of his cloak coming off his shoulders.

"So what happened at your meeting?" Ari asked. "Did you decide to send Renegade Saul away?"

"If it had been my choice, we would have," Baruch said as he knelt down. Ari heard him fumbling for his bedroll on the floor.

"So you've got some liberals among you. Is that the problem?"

"I do not know what you mean by *liberal.*" Baruch's voice tightened with anger. "We had a plan. Brother Yaakov was to give Renegade Saul an ultimatum—something impossible to perform."

"And it went wrong?" Ari asked.

"Two things went wrong," Baruch said. "First, Renegade Saul was permitted to speak. So he spoke, and he spoke, and he spoke."

"Was he boring?"

"No, unfortunately not," Baruch said. "Renegade Saul is a very entertaining speaker, and very persuasive. He told of his work with the *goyim,* how they have come to a belief in our *Mashiach* and a knowledge of HaShem, how they worship in our synagogues on *Shabbat,* how they have their demons cast out and their diseases healed."

"And you don't approve?"

"No, of course I approve!" Baruch snapped. "How can any Jew disapprove of such things? I shed tears when he told of the jailer who beat him and then repented within hours and became a believer."

"Then why are you angry?" Ari asked.

"Because Renegade Saul is content with too little," Baruch said. "The *goyim* leave their idols and confess belief in HaShem and learn the prophecies of Rabban Yeshua, our *Mashiach.* And that is all! He does not bring them into the community of Israel, nor teach them to obey the commandments which bring joy. He does not make them walk in the way of Torah."

"Why should he? They are *goyim*," Ari said. An instant later, he mentally scolded himself for defending Paul. Paul was the enemy.

"If they wish to become our brothers, let them join the community," Baruch said. "Let them be circumcised as we and our fathers are, and let them learn Torah."

"Did Renegade Saul persuade anyone?"

"No, but he weakened our resolve."

"You said that letting Renegade Saul speak was the first mistake. What was the second?"

"Brother Yaakov asked Renegade Saul to purify himself in the Temple with four of our brothers," Baruch said. "We believed that he had renounced the Temple and Torah—that he was an *apikoros.*"

"And?"

"And he agreed!" Baruch said. "He had no right to do that, if he does not keep the commandments."

"Rope-a-dope," Ari muttered, lapsing into English.

"I do not understand," Baruch said.

Ari hesitated. How did you explain Muhammad Ali to a first-century Jew? Or boxing? "It is a saying in my country. It means to give way before your opponent, causing him to waste his strength."

"That is what Renegade Saul has done," Baruch said. "This week, he will go with our brothers to the Temple, and then all our people will see him, and they will say that Saul is no renegade, but a righteous man, a Pharisee, an observer of the commandments."

"Does it matter what people say?"

"Yes. The truth matters. And it matters what Renegade Saul does in foreign countries," Baruch said. "We hear that he teaches Jews to forsake the ways of the fathers, to eat meat sacrificed to idols, to abandon Torah."

Ari saw nothing wrong with any of those things. He could forgive Saul for abandoning Torah. But he could never forgive Saul for establishing a Gentile Christianity which would someday rise up and persecute his people. Why wasn't Baruch concerned about that?

Obviously because he couldn't see the future. But Ari had seen the future, and it was ugly beyond belief. Because of Saul, an endless stream of Jews had met violent deaths. Because of Saul, the blood of Jews stained the pages of history. Because of Saul, his countrymen had met the sword and the stake and the rack and the oven.

And because of Saul, Christian feet had trampled Ari's father to death in a village only a few kilometers from here. For all that, Saul was guilty. Indirectly, yes, but still guilty.

"You are quiet, Brother Ari," Baruch said. "Are you sleeping?"

"I am thinking." Ari yawned mightily. He decided to change the subject. "I fear for my friend, whom I lost outside Jerusalem. I do not know where to begin looking. The city is very crowded."

"That is an advantage," Baruch said. "There will be many witnesses. Was he dressed in strange clothing like yours?"

"She was dressed somewhat like me."

"A woman!" Baruch said. "You did not tell me you were married!"

"She is not my wife."

"Brother Ari, is it the custom in your country to travel with a woman who is not your wife?" Baruch sounded shocked.

"We were not traveling together." Ari wondered how best to explain this. "She came first, and then I meant to follow and meet her."

"Then why did you have no money?" Baruch asked. "I do not understand. Your country is so strange, I cannot even imagine this place."

"It is late," Ari said. "I will explain tomorrow."

"Sleep well, Brother Ari."

"And you also, Brother Baruch."

Ari smiled into the darkness. Already, he was beginning to talk like these people.

Tomorrow, he needed to find Rivka and go home before he started thinking like them, too.

SIXTEEN

Ari

"Brother Ari, you must wear the clothes you wore when you arrived," Baruch said.

Ari pulled off the tunic Baruch had loaned him and stepped into his blue jeans. The T-shirt with the physics equations was dirty and wrinkled, but it was all he had. He put it on. "Aren't you going to take off your phylactery?" He pointed to the small, black leather box strapped to Baruch's forehead.

Baruch looked surprised. "I wear this always, except on *Shabbat*. Do they not do so in your country?"

"Only during prayers," Ari said. And of course he himself never wore phylacteries, but he saw no point in saying so.

Baruch accepted this without question. He seemed to be getting used to the bizarre customs of Ari's country. "In which language is the writing on your tunic?" he asked.

"The language of the wise men of my country."

"Please read to me how HaShem created light." Baruch pointed at the four lines of equations.

Ari quoted them from memory. "The curl of the electric field equals the negative of the time-derivative of the magnetic field. The curl of the magnetic field equals the time-derivative of the electric field plus the current density. The divergence of the electric field equals the charge density. The divergence of the magnetic field equals zero."

Baruch's face shone with delight. "I would like you to teach me this language sometime," he said. "It seems that you have many words for each letter."

"The language is very powerful," Ari said. And that was a mystery he would never understood. Why was mathematics so "unreasonably effective," as Wigner had put it? But he had no time to think philosophy right now.

"It is time for us to find my friend." Ari looped his backpack over his left shoulder. "Her name is Rivka, and I fear for her safety."

"Which gate did you enter the city from?" Baruch asked, as they went out into the street.

Ari pointed in the general direction of the southeast corner of the city. "Near the Pool of Siloam."

Baruch nodded. "We will start there."

They spent twenty minutes walking to the pool. It wasn't very far—less than a kilometer—and the crowded streets buzzed with a festive atmosphere.

Children dashed in and out, playing games. Men stood in the streets, gossiping in little clusters. Women talked in their own small groups. Ari saw virtually no mixing of the sexes. Merchants hawked their wares on the street. Everywhere, the smell of roasting meat and pickled vegetables filled the air. Ari loved it.

Baruch said little as they walked downhill toward the city gate. When they came near the gate, Ari caught Baruch's arm and pointed toward the Pool of Siloam. "I went in there first, right after I entered the city. There were many young women, and they tried to speak to me, but I could not understand them."

Baruch hesitated a moment.

"Is something wrong?" Ari asked.

"It is said that many of the water carriers here are *zonaot*," Baruch said.

Obviously, Baruch had lived a sheltered life in a Pharisee home. If he actually talked to a *zonah*, Ari decided, maybe he would learn that they were real people too. "We must go in there. When the women saw me, they pointed at my blue clothes. I think they may have seen Rivka. We should ask them."

Baruch's face tightened. "Surely there are others who may have seen your friend."

"Yes, but it makes sense to try first where Rivka was likely to go. And I now remember that Rivka once asked me to show her this pool. It is almost certain that she came here."

"Very well." Baruch didn't look happy. He threaded his way through the crowd to the gate leading into the pool area.

Ari followed him. Once inside the gate, he looked around the area again. He recognized several of the faces.

Evidently, they recognized him also, because they shrank away. He still hadn't figured that out. "Brother Baruch, I don't think they like me."

"Then stand here near the entrance and I will speak to them alone," Baruch said. He walked toward the nearest group of women.

Ari stayed, trying to look harmless.

Baruch spent some minutes talking quietly with the women. Remarkably, they did not appear to fear him, and several of them even seemed quite friendly. Ari found this amusing.

Baruch turned and pointed at Ari, and then asked the women another question.

Several of them answered at once, nodding their heads in excitement. One of them pointed out of the gate and up the hill toward the Temple. Another interrupted, and then a third did, too, each correcting the one before.

Finally, Baruch nodded and turned away from the group. One of them called after him in an unmistakably ribald way. Baruch's face reddened, and he hurried toward Ari.

"They saw the woman Rivka here about noon on the day before *Shabbat,*" he said. "She left with a *zonah* named Hana. The women have given me exact directions to her house."

Ari grinned. "It seems that they were willing to give you much more than directions, Brother Baruch."

Baruch turned toward Ari and his face darkened. "Please do not speak of it again, Brother Ari. I am a man, subject to the lusts of the flesh. I do not wish to sin against HaShem and against my own self."

Ari swallowed. "Forgive me, Brother Baruch."

"Of course," Baruch said. "Now let us find your Rivka. It chills me to think that this woman Hana may be teaching her the arts of the *zonah.*"

It chilled Ari, too. Together, they walked up the hill as quickly as they could push through the crowds.

After some distance, Baruch turned to the right onto a side street. Ari followed him.

Two more turns, and then Baruch stopped. He pointed at a small house. "That is the place. I do not wish to enter the house of a *zonah,* my friend. If any brothers of the Way saw me, I would have difficulty explaining myself."

Ari thought that the explanation would be rather easy. And they were far from Baruch's house. What would one of the brothers of the Way be doing here? But he had already given Baruch enough grief for one day, so he asked, "Will you wait here?"

"I…would rather return home to pray," Baruch said. "When you have found Rivka, you must bring her to visit me. Can you find your way back to my house?"

"Easily," Ari said. He slapped Baruch on the shoulder. "I respect you, my brother. You are a righteous man. I want very much for Rivka to meet you." And wouldn't she be shocked when she found out what Jewish Christians were really like?

"Shalom," Baruch said. He turned and hurried back the way they had come.

Ari waited until he disappeared. Then he turned and went up to the door and knocked. Rivka was going to be so incredibly relieved when she saw that he had come to rescue her.

Damien

Damien had spent half an hour waiting impatiently while Rivka and Hana discussed possible locations for the Chamber of Hewn Stone where the Sanhedrin met. He had no rational reason to be impatient, he reminded himself. He had worked out the chronology of this coming week a long time ago. Paul wouldn't show up in the Temple for two more days. Damien would make his first attempt there. Only if that failed would he need to know about the Chamber of Hewn Stone. This whole little excursion today would be a fail-safe, just in case. A precaution. You could never be too careful.

He didn't understand what was taking them so long, but at least it gave him a chance to admire Hana.

A knock sounded on the thin wooden door.

Damien stood closest. "I'll get it." He stepped to the door, slipped the latch, and pulled it inward.

Ari Kazan stood in front of him.

For a second, both of them stared at each other in stunned disbelief. Then Ari dropped his backpack and charged at Damien, hands groping for his neck.

Damien backpedaled into the room, wondering how on this green earth Ari Kazan had come through the wormhole before it vanished. Not possible! Damien's back slammed against the wall of the house. He raised his arms to protect his face. An instant later, Ari hit him hard. Damien absorbed most of the force with his arms, but his head smacked painfully against the stone wall behind him.

He heard the women screaming. Ignore it. Focus on this fight. Ari had just wasted all of his force—foolishly. Now he would pay for that mistake.

Damien jerked both elbows up, catching Ari's chin, popping his head back. Ari gurgled and swung, but without any real power.

Damien lifted his left knee, taking the easy groin shot. Ari staggered backward, his breath hissing.

Damien followed, bunching his right hand into a tight fist. He jabbed hard to the solar plexus. Ari toppled over into the dirt.

Now what? If he were alone with Ari, Damien would have simply killed him. Lying there on the ground wheezing, Ari had no more defenses than a snail on the sidewalk.

But Damien had the women to think about. Women didn't like violence. He still needed Rivka Meyers. No sense alienating her.

Time to do the sweet-reasonableness thing. A dog and pony show. "Ari, Ari, Ari." Damien shook his head slowly. "You can't let go, can you? Why have you come here to attack us? And how did you escape the police?" He turned to face Rivka. "Miss Meyers, I'm terribly sorry that I had to use force on him. I told you he had gone crazy, didn't I? Such a waste of a brilliant mind."

Rivka's face showed stark disbelief. Her legs wobbled, and then she sank to her knees.

She looked ready to faint. "Miss Meyers, are you all right?" He hadn't anticipated this response.

But no, that presented an opportunity. He could escort Ari away from here by force, take him to his rented quarters, and kill him there. Five minutes and he would silence Ari for good.

"Ari, are you hurt?" Rivka asked.

Damien began worrying. Women always sided with the loser. The underdog thing. He had to do something.

"More to the point, Ari Kazan, why did you do it?" Damien said. "Why did you create the wormhole without my permission? We had an agreement that we would both be there. Why, Ari?"

"What are...you talking...about?" Ari's voice came out in little gasps. "You powered up the wormhole yourself, without asking—"

"It won't do to lie," Damien said. If he could bait Ari into attacking again, that would help his case. Women didn't like aggressors. "Miss Meyers already knows the truth. You were going to strand her here, weren't you? Why, Ari? Over one little argument? That's truly pathetic."

Ari lunged up off the ground, swinging wildly.

Damien stepped sideways, caught Ari's right arm, twisted it around, and kicked Ari's legs out so that he fell in the dirt face-down. Damien sank down on his back, twisting the arm high and hard behind Ari.

"You jerk!" Ari gasped. "What's your...game, West? Why did you make...the wormhole? And why drag Rivka into this?"

Damien ratcheted Ari's arms up another notch. "Ari, that's a strange gambit. A man of your intelligence can do better than that. What I'm wondering is how you escaped from the police. What did you have against Miss Meyers? She's really a very nice woman. I don't like it when you mistreat people, Ari, and I'm not going to stand by and let you get away with it."

Ari began to say something, then coughed violently.

Damien's brain raced. Time to pack Ari out of here. He looked up at Rivka. "I'm terribly sorry that he's attacked us like this, Miss Meyers. If we tie him up, I could take him back to the house I'm renting. Then I could hold him there peacefully while you take a few minutes to decide what to do."

"Yes, I would like that," Rivka said. "I'll ask Hana to find us some rope." She spoke rapidly to her friend. Hana nodded and went out.

Ari finished coughing and lay still, his chest heaving. "Rivka."

Danger, Will Robinson! Damien couldn't afford to let Ari talk. He yanked on Ari's arm. "Sorry, I can't allow you to verbally abuse Miss Meyers."

Rivka came over to look at the prisoner. "Dr. West, I want to hear what Ari was saying. Could you ease up on him just a little?"

Damien winced internally. That was exactly what he didn't want to do. But he couldn't see a graceful way to refuse. "Right, Miss Meyers."

"Rivka." Ari coughed again. "I came to ask you...to forgive me."

Instinctively, Damien yanked again on Ari's arm. He couldn't let Ari talk like that. Women ate up that kind of thing.

Ari cried out in pain.

"Dr. West, will you *please* back off just a little?" Rivka sounded agitated.

Hana returned just then with a length of rope.

Very good. Damien felt his pulse slowing a little. He would get things under control in a minute. Damien tied Ari's hands behind his back.

"Rivka." Ari's voice sounded desperate.

"Don't listen to him, Miss Meyers."

"Dr. West, I'm a big girl, and I'll decide who to listen to. Got it?"

Damien cleared his throat. He had gone overboard, and he knew it. "I'm sorry, Miss Meyers. You're quite right. Whatever you say."

"Good," Rivka said. "Now I want you to leave for a while. I need to—"

"I don't think that's a very good idea," Damien said. An ice cube of panic shivered down his spine. He could not let her—

"I'll decide what's a good idea and what's not."

She was getting uppity again. Dumb chick. If he didn't need her, he would... Never mind. That line of thought would get him in trouble. Be cool. Be rational. Think calming thoughts.

"Dr. West, I want you to leave. Right now."

Damien stood up.

Hana began jabbering at Rivka. Rivka argued back. Damien waited, hoping Hana would talk some sense into her. He suddenly felt angry at himself. He ought to have killed Ari at once, then tried to sweet-talk Rivka afterward. Too late for that now. Hana just had to win this argument.

The women talked for several minutes. Damien put on his most humble, aw-shucks face. Finally, they finished the argument.

Damien shrugged apologetically. "How about if I take Ari away for a few minutes and just talk to him quietly?"

"No," Rivka said. "I want you to leave now."

Damage-control time. "As you like," Damien said. "Please be careful, Miss Meyers. Don't believe anything Ari tells you. He's dangerous."

"Don't worry," Rivka said. "Hana and I will get the truth out of him."

Which was exactly what Damien was afraid of.

SEVENTEEN

Rivka

Rivka picked up Ari's backpack and closed the door behind Dr. West. Ari lay on his face in the dirt, his arms tightly bound from wrists to elbows. Why had he come? If he were really a madman, as Dr. West said, then what was all this about forgiveness? That didn't sound like a guy gone bonkers.

"Who is this man?" Hana said. "I do not trust him."

"His name is called Ari," Rivka said.

"He is truly from your country," Hana said. "He wears the same strange clothes." She reached down and touched the blue denim of Ari's pants.

"Rivka," Ari said.

"What is it?" she asked.

"I treated you badly the other night, and I am sorry. Please forgive me."

"What's got into you?" Rivka asked. "You're talking in biblical Hebrew!"

"It is a long story," Ari said. He began coughing again. When the fit subsided, he said, "Could I beg you for some water?"

Rivka went to the water jar and dipped a stone cup into it. Then she took the cup and knelt down in front of Ari. He still

181

lay on his stomach. She gripped his shoulder, rolled him onto his side, and held the cup to his mouth. He drank greedily.

"Thank you," he said. "It is better than the last cup of water you gave me."

"You're acting more the gentleman this time." Rivka felt a little tremor run through her.

"I am sorry," Ari said. "For the last two days, I've been looking for you, thinking what a fool I've been, wishing I could change what I said."

"You've been looking for me for two days?" Rivka said. "How did you escape from the police?"

"There were no police," Ari said. "Although I will certainly call them when we return. Damien violated our agreement. Why did you come here?"

"I don't know exactly how I got here," Rivka said. "I was playing the *Avatar* game, and then somehow I wound up in a cave, and..." She closed her eyes, wincing. "Long story. Dr. West says you turned on the wormhole and sent me through it and then tried to shut it down."

"That's ridiculous," Ari said. "It would have taken hours for the wormhole condensate to form. Overnight, at least. Damien must have created it Saturday night—when I was being rude to you at the café. I'm sorry, Rivka."

Rivka had no idea what had come over Ari, but he seemed very different from the man she had talked to last Saturday night. "Have you really been looking for me for two days? Were you out on the streets the whole time?"

"I met a friend—Brother Baruch," Ari said. "He rescued me from a bandit and took me into his home. I stayed with him over *Shabbat.*"

It all sounded terribly plausible, even the part about being rescued from a bandit. Ari didn't seem ashamed that he had needed rescuing. That had the ring of truth.

But was it the whole truth?

If Ari was telling the truth, then Dr. West had to be lying. And vice versa.

Hana brought a drink from the same cup Ari had drunk from. Rivka gulped it down.

"I do not trust him," Hana said. "He has the face of a man who takes his pleasure and does not pay."

Now Rivka felt very confused. She had never been all that good at spotting liars, whereas Hana owed her life to the fact that she could spot one. But Hana was telling her exactly the opposite of what her own instincts said. Somehow, she preferred to trust Ari over Dr. West, but she couldn't explain why.

She needed more facts. "All right, Ari," she said. "I don't understand what's going on between you and Dr. West, but I've heard his side. Now you tell me yours. Start with our friendly parting on Saturday night."

Ari did. It took a quarter of an hour, with Rivka asking numerous questions. Each he answered patiently.

"...so then I ended up here in Jerusalem two days ago, trying to find someone I could talk to," Ari said. "I was attacked by a bandit, and a man named Baruch scared him off."

"So where is this Baruch?" Rivka asked. "Why didn't you bring him?"

"He brought me here and then went back home," Ari said. "I would like you to meet him because he's an interesting person."

"What did he say just now?" Hana asked. "He is lying."

Rivka pondered this briefly. "Something tells me you're not telling the truth, the whole truth, and nothing but the truth, Ari."

"And why are you cross-examining me?" he asked. "I want you to meet Brother Baruch. Neither he nor I will harm you— ever."

"Hana, he wants me to go with him to meet a man," Rivka said. "Should I trust him?"

"No," Hana said. "He has some hidden reason for wanting you to go."

Rivka hesitated. What did Hana know? She had to be making this stuff up. Rivka took a knife from the table and walked around behind Ari.

"What are you doing?" Hana asked.

Rivka said nothing. She carefully slit the rope, one strand at a time, until Ari's arms came free. She put the knife on the table and began massaging his forearms.

"Thank you," Ari said.

"Rivka, you are making a big mistake," Hana said.

"Stop it!" Rivka shouted.

Hana shrank away from her.

"Hana, I'm sorry."

"You will be more sorry if you go anywhere with this man," Hana said darkly.

Rivka simply kept working on Ari's arms. Finally, he put his right hand on the floor and pushed himself to a sitting position. He turned his head slowly from side to side, rubbing his neck. Dirt matted the left side of his beard. "I keep thinking this is an evil dream," he said. A trickle of blood ran down his left arm from elbow to wrist.

Rivka fetched another cup of water and poured it over the blood. "Does it hurt?"

"I'll live," he said. "Let's go." He slowly stood up, bowed awkwardly to Hana, and then went to the door.

Rivka followed him. "I'll be back this evening," she said to Hana.

"No, you will come back crying before it is noon," Hana said. "The truth-tellers tell me so."

"If I do, then I'll concede that your truth-tellers are wiser than I," Rivka said lightly, as she and Ari stepped out into the street.

Damien

Damien could have gone back to his rented house for his gun, but he dared not risk letting Ari out of his sight. He waited in the shadows of an ugly stone building fifty yards up the street from Hana's house. Rivka was going to let him go—Damien would bet money on it. But would she believe Ari's story?

If she did, then she would be no more use to Damien, and he might as well kill her. But he wanted to be certain of that before taking such drastic action, because she had useful information. With any luck, she would vacillate for a day or two, trying to figure out who was lying.

And all he needed was a few more days. Today was Sunday. He would have a possible shot on Tuesday, but the better chance would come Wednesday. At the Chamber of Hewn Stone, wherever that was. Rivka could tell him, if she would.

How much did Ari know? Could he win over Rivka during the next few days?

The door of Hana's house opened. Damien stiffened, freezing in the shadows.

Neither Ari or Rivka looked in Damien's direction. Ari's arms were unbound. Bad news. That meant Rivka trusted him.

Ari pointed across the city in a generally westerly direction. Then he and Rivka began walking. Hana didn't come out. Damien waited a few seconds then hurried after them. If they were heading west, they weren't going back to the wormhole.

Which meant they had some other destination. Why?

Which meant they had some other destination. Why?

Far ahead, he saw Rivka sneeze twice. That reminded him of something.

It took another ten minutes to remember. The other day in the lab, he had sneezed in the face of that Chinese postdoc, the one who had come to ask about—the printer! The laser printer had been out of paper. The same printer Damien had tried to print to a few minutes later.

Damien ran through a possible scenario. When a laser printer ran out of paper, it queued up the documents until somebody put paper in. Then it printed out everything. Which meant that somebody in the department had come across his chronology of the last days of Paul in Jerusalem. They would know it was Damien's, because of the header page, which would have his name all over it.

He cursed under his breath. What if Ari Kazan had found that paper and brought it with him? He wouldn't be able to understand it. The document was intentionally cryptic. It wouldn't make sense to anyone who didn't know the story of Paul's last journey to Jerusalem exceedingly well.

But Rivka was an expert in all that. If anyone could make sense of that chronology, Rivka could.

Damien tried to calm himself by breathing deeply, slowly. A lot of ifs had to come off for that to happen. If Ari found the page in the printer. If he brought it with him. If he showed it to Rivka. Then Rivka might figure things out.

It was a long shot. Then again, Ari coming through the wormhole was a long shot.

If lightning could strike once, it could strike twice. But stay calm. First get as much information as possible. It made no sense to go leaping to conclusions until you had data.

Especially in light of the gold mine of information between the ears of Rivka Meyers.

EIGHTEEN

Rivka

Rivka hadn't visited the Upper City yet—at least not in this century. In her own century, she had seen many of the sights, some of them clearly bogus. One of them came quickly to mind: David's tomb and the Upper Room, both housed in the same building.

This, however, was not bogus. It took her breath away. When she got home, she would have a few dozen papers to write, breaking new ground in first-century architecture, linguistics, cultural anthropology, and Judaic studies. This experience would make her career as an—

Rivka sneezed. Twice.

"Are you well?" Ari asked.

"It's just my allergies," Rivka said. "Whatever's in the air is pretty much the same as it will be two thousand years from now."

Ari sniffed. "With one addition. Do you smell the Jerusalem pines? We have a real forest outside of this city."

Rivka breathed in deeply. Delicious. She sneezed again. "And what about you? Have you seen any of those hornets you're allergic to?"

Ari shrugged. "Of course, but not to worry." He patted his backpack. "I have two doses in here."

"How far is it to your friend's house?" Rivka asked.

"Not far. Less than a kilometer."

"Tell me everything you know about Dr. West," Rivka said.

Ari spent the rest of the walk telling her. Rivka listened intently, not so much to learn about Dr. West, but to learn about Ari. You could tell a lot about someone by listening to him talk about his enemies. By the time they arrived at the small two-story house in the Upper City, Rivka felt certain of one thing: Ari respected Dr. West. That is, he had respected him until two days ago, when one of them had powered up the wormhole without the other's permission.

But which one? According to Hana, who claimed to be a human lie detector, Damien was truthful and Ari wasn't.

So why did Rivka trust Ari so much more than Dr. West?

Ari knocked on the wooden door of the house. "Brother Baruch!" he shouted. "I have found her!"

The door swung inward. A lean young man with a thick black beard stepped to the doorway. His eyes skimmed over Rivka without making contact and settled on Ari. His mouth fell open. "Brother Ari, what happened to you?"

"I had a fight with a dirt floor," Ari said.

"And lost very badly," Rivka said, using the same biblical Hebrew that the two men spoke. "Brother Baruch, it's very pleasant to meet you."

Baruch's eyes widened, but still he did not look at Rivka. "Your friend speaks our language very well, Brother Ari."

"Which implies I do not," Ari said, sounding very pleased to have caught his friend in a minor gaffe. "She is a scholar, Brother Baruch. She can even speak to you in Aramaic."

"A scholar?" Baruch looked puzzled. "Do you mean she is a scribe? She can read?"

Rivka stopped herself from laughing out loud "Yes, and I can write and do arithmetic, too. My calculus is a bit rusty, but that is acceptable, since it has not yet been invented."

"Your friend speaks in riddles, Brother Ari."

Baruch's habit of speaking only to Ari bothered Rivka more than she had expected. She knew it was just a cultural thing. Still, she felt just mischievous enough to try to shake up Baruch's worldview a little bit.

Rivka grabbed Baruch's hand and shook it. "My name is called Rivka."

Baruch stared at her. When she let go of his hand, he stepped back a pace. "Brother Ari, is it the custom in your country for women to be so familiar with men?"

Rivka answered in Aramaic before Ari could speak. "In our country, men treat women with respect. They do not speak over women's heads as if they were children."

Baruch shook his head in disbelief and answered in Aramaic. "You have very strange customs in your country. It is not done in Jerusalem. Please forgive me for appearing to be rude." Then he actually looked Rivka in the eye. His ears glowed bright red.

Rivka lowered her eyes, sorry she had embarrassed him. "Ari," she said in Hebrew, "please tell Brother Baruch that I, too, ask forgiveness for seeming rude. I will try to learn the ways of Jerusalem."

Ari shrugged. "My friends, you have much to learn about each other. Brother Baruch, would you mind if I wash myself in your *mikveh?*"

Baruch looked surprised. "Brother Ari, the *mikveh* is for purifying from ritual impurity, not for bathing."

A sly grin spread across Ari's face. "Very well. I had a dream last night, and I awoke ritually unclean."

Baruch shot a nervous eye toward Rivka, obviously shocked that Ari would say such a thing in the presence of a woman.

"Very well, then. You must use the *mikveh,* but please remember next time to purify yourself when you arise from bed. Rivka and I will wait outside."

"Couldn't we go upstairs?" Rivka asked. She wanted to see the rest of the house. It was more elaborate than Hana's one-story structure, and she wanted to see as much of the architecture as she could.

"It would not be proper for a man and a woman to be alone," Baruch protested. "Surely, even in your country such things are not allowed."

Rivka mentally whacked the side of her head. She ought to have guessed that it wouldn't be proper. The modern ultra-orthodox had similar restrictions. "I understand. I guess we can stand out here in the street where everyone can see us. I do have some questions I would like to ask you."

"And, please, you will not speak to me in public," Baruch said. He spread his hands in apology. "It is the custom here in Jerusalem."

"I am sorry." Rivka stepped into the street. Baruch came out and shut the door behind them.

Rivka sat on a stone bench in front of the house. Baruch went a little way down the street and simply stood there.

The warmth of the late-morning sun made Rivka feel sleepy. Old Jerusalem. So familiar, so strange. In many ways, it was exactly what she had expected. The architecture, the street layout, the Temple, the material culture—all of these were simple extrapolations of what she had seen in her books. But the people, the customs, even the pronunciation of Hebrew and Aramaic—all were different from what she might have guessed.

It wasn't any one thing exactly, but the sum total that shocked her. A large number of little surprises that all added up to something radically different from her expectations. The stale-tasting water. The lack of soap. Human waste running in the gutters.

The male supremacy. Thank goodness Baruch was genuinely trying to accommodate her forwardness. It must be hard on him, too. She had assumed that merely knowing about the culture would enable her to get along here. It wasn't working out that way. Head knowledge was one thing; experience another. But she could put up with anything for a few days, especially in view of the payoff.

She was going to write one dazzling report on all this when she got home. What would the tabloids say? She could imagine the headlines: *Archaeologist Walks with Jesus. Alien Abduction Through Wormhole. Time Travelers Return with New Dead Sea Scrolls.*

"Brother Baruch!"

Rivka turned her head at the sound of an unfamiliar voice. A man limped up the street toward Baruch. He wore an untrimmed gray beard, and his right leg looked to be a couple inches shorter than his left, but his eyes shone with determination.

Baruch greeted him warmly and kissed him on the lips. "*Shalom*, Brother Mattityahu. It has been too long! How is life in Samaria?"

That struck Rivka as odd. Why would an old man move to Samaria? It was only thirty or forty miles, but you couldn't exactly take a bus to get there.

"HaShem is good," said the man named Mattityahu. "But I am not well." He parted his beard. "See what the Evil One has done to me."

Curious, Rivka stood up and edged closer. From this distance, it looked like some kind of an ulceration on the man's face. Or possibly...skin cancer. A cold shadow touched her heart.

"Let us pray," Baruch said. He laid hands on Mattityahu's face.

Rivka moved closer.

Baruch began praying. *"Baruch Attah, Adonai, Eloheinu, Melech Ha-Olam, Adonai, Rafayenu."* Blessed are You, Lord our God, King of the universe, Lord our Healer.

Rivka felt a rush of excitement. Baruch might be some kind of holy man—a thaumaturgic healer like Honi the Circle-Maker or Hanina ben Dosa. Or possibly some other category of charismatic figure not known from the literature.

Baruch switched to Aramaic. "Oh Lord, our God, let the power of Your servant fall upon Brother Mattityahu. Heal, oh Lord! Undo the work of the Evil One. Restore this face to reflect Your glory."

Rivka heard a sound behind her. She turned. Ari came out of the house, his hair dripping wet, his clothes clinging to him. Apparently, Hotel Baruch didn't come with towels.

"What's going on?" Ari asked.

Rivka shushed him with a finger to her lips. "Baruch's performing some sort of healing ritual on the gentleman there," she whispered. "He just got started, and I'm trying to watch without intruding."

"I think Baruch is the local doctor," Ari said. "Some woman came by yesterday and he prayed over her."

"Did she get better?" Rivka asked.

Ari shrugged. "Headache. Probably psychogenic. She said she felt better, and that's what matters, isn't it?"

Rivka wanted to say that the patient's actual physical condition mattered more than a changeable mental state, but she wanted to see as much of the ritual as she could. She turned back to watch.

"...in the name of Yeshua *HaMashiach*," Baruch said.

Rivka blinked twice, astounded. Had she heard right? Yeshua? Baruch had to be a member of *HaDerech*—The Way! Wouldn't it be incredible if he healed this Mattityahu right here in front of Ari? *Oh, God, let this man get well! Let Ari see Your power, Lord.*

Baruch took his hands off the man's face and examined the skin. From this distance, Rivka could see no change at all.

"Looks bad," Ari said. "That one doesn't look psychogenic. I hate to tell Baruch, but I don't think he's going to get anywhere."

"And how do you know?" Rivka asked. She was offended by his tone, although privately she had her own doubts. This case didn't look easy.

"You don't believe in that stuff, do you?" Ari said.

"In what stuff?" Rivka asked, stalling. Her mind raced ahead. Should she tell Ari? Would he believe her? And if she did tell him, should she tell the whole truth?

"Sorry, maybe we had better not discuss it," Ari said. There was a note of discomfort in his voice. "I don't want to get into another big argument over nothing."

"No, I want to discuss it," Rivka said. "I promise not to get mad."

"Okay, fine." Ari switched to English. "But let's keep this in a language the neighbors won't understand, shall we? And I'm already wet, so you may forego the water this time." A crooked grin played across his face.

Whatever his flaws, Ari certainly had a forgiving spirit. Rivka smiled to show that she was going to be a good sport. She took a deep breath. "To answer your question, yes, I do believe in that stuff. Not that I care for the Holy Rollers on TV who promise a miracle every ten seconds, but I think God does occasionally intervene."

"Intervene—as in He violates the laws of physics?" Ari asked.

It was a trick question, and Rivka had been down this line. "I don't really care if God obeys the laws or breaks them," she said. "But I do believe that people sometimes get unexpectedly healed after prayer."

"That's not a very strong statement from a statistical point of view," Ari said. "There is a small rate of spontaneous remission in cancer, for example."

Bingo. He had jumped into this one with both feet. She might as well hit him with her big guns. "Okay, let's take an example," Rivka said. "Joe Schmoe is diagnosed with skin cancer, malignant melanoma, advanced. Too late for chemo or radiation. Too extensive for surgery. No hope. The doctors send Joe home to die. Joe's neighbor comes over and lays hands on him and prays. The next morning when Joe wakes up, he is healed. Totally. No traces in his system. He goes back to the doctors, and they say they've never seen anything like it. It's not spontaneous remission. It's a miracle. Direct quote from the doctor. Now how does that fit into your theory?"

Ari shrugged. "Offhand, I would say it sounds pretty strong, though it's only one instance. This is a hypothetical case, I assume?"

Rivka shook her head. "Joe Schmoe was David Goldberg. My stepfather."

Ari scratched at his nose. "When did this happen? Did you see it yourself, or is this a family legend somebody told you about?"

"It happened when I was eleven years old," Rivka said. "I told you a few days ago that we started going to a Messianic synagogue in San Diego when I was in sixth grade. That was after David got healed. Our neighbor was a member of Beth Simcha, and he came over and prayed, and boom! It was pretty weird, really. I still can't believe, sometimes, that it really happened. But I also remember exactly how I felt when I woke up the next day and that huge ulcerated patch on his arm was just gone."

Ari shrugged. "Interesting."

"So, you believe me?" Rivka said.

"Sure, why would you lie?" Ari said. "But I would like to meet your stepfather, anyway. You know—seeing is believing."

Which was exactly the problem. Rivka wondered how to explain the rest of it. She still didn't understand it herself.

"Brother Ari!" Baruch said. "You must come and help me pray for Brother Mattityahu. I am concerned."

Rivka sighed. Off the hook for now. But that would only make it worse later.

Ari went over to have a look. Rivka followed him. The closer she came, the less she liked what she saw. It didn't look good. Baruch put his hands over Mattityahu's face again.

Ari said nothing. Quietly, he laid his hands on top of Baruch's. He gave Rivka a little shrug, as if to say, *It can't hurt, can it?*

Which was true and it wasn't, as Rivka had learned.

Baruch continued praying in a soft, yet intense voice. Sweat popped out on his forehead. Ari closed his eyes. Rivka could not guess what he was thinking.

They stood like that for quite a long time. At last, Baruch stopped praying. He and Ari lifted their hands away at the same time. Rivka stepped forward, afraid to look, unwilling not to.

Nothing had changed.

"It is the same," Baruch said. "You agree, Brother Ari?"

Ari nodded. "Yes."

"We will pray again tomorrow," Baruch said. "You will come back, Brother Mattityahu?"

The old man tugged at his beard. "I will come back. We will be here in Jerusalem for yet a week." He gripped Baruch's arm and then leaned forward and kissed him. He did the same to Ari.

Rivka wondered what she would do if Mattityahu tried that on her, but of course there was no such danger. He hardly seemed to notice her at all.

"Have you heard the news about Renegade Saul?" Brother Mattityahu asked.

Rivka felt a little rush of adrenaline in her veins. Renegade Saul! She had never heard of that particular name applied to Paul, and yet her instincts filled in the gaps in her book knowledge.

"He will be going to the Temple with the four young men on the day after tomorrow," Baruch said. "I did not believe he would go, but he promised that he would. He is an *apikoros*, but he is no liar. What he says, he will do."

"Perhaps he is not an *apikoros* after all, if he will go to the Temple," Mattityahu said.

"No, you are wrong," Baruch said. "I heard him last night with my own ears. He eats with *goyim*. He teaches them to follow Rabban Yeshua, but he does not teach them to observe the commandments."

"But does he obey the Torah?" Mattityahu asked. "Does he teach our brothers in the Diaspora to forsake the customs? That is what I want to know."

"He denies it," Baruch said. "He calls himself a Pharisee, a son of Pharisees."

"So?" Mattityahu said. "Is he a liar, or is he not? If he is a Pharisee, then he is a true follower of the Rabban."

"I asked him this question," Baruch said. "I asked if he eats meat sacrificed to idols."

Rivka held her breath. Paul had tread a fine line on that one.

"And what did he say?" Mattityahu asked.

"He says he does not know," Baruch said.

"How can he not know?" Mattityahu's face showed bewilderment.

"He does not ask," Baruch said. "He simply eats the food set before him by his host."

"And he is never told?" Mattityahu asked. "I do not believe that."

"Sometimes his host will say, 'This was sacrificed to an idol,'" Baruch said. "In that case, he will not eat it."

"Don't ask; don't tell," Rivka said on impulse.

Both men turned to stare at her—actually at some fixed point above her head.

She blushed. "I am sorry. I did not wish to intrude." She knew her friends back in Berkeley would be freaked by her kow-towing to this patriarchal system. But she had a simple answer to that, one which Paul himself would endorse. When in Jeru-salem, do as the Pharisees do. And why not? Much of human behavior was culturally conditioned, not some grand moral absolute. No way in the world could she force gender equality in a cultural matrix like this one.

Brother Mattityahu looked up at the sky. "My friend, I must be returning to my daughter's house. But I will visit you tomorrow, if HaShem wills it." He nodded to Baruch and Ari, but not to Rivka, then turned and strolled away up the street.

"Something is not right," Baruch said in Hebrew. "I must go to my room and pray. I do not understand why nothing hap-pened." He walked back toward his house, tugging at his beard.

Ari had been standing to one side quietly. "Did you follow what they were saying?" he asked Rivka. "I caught most of the words, but I can't follow full-speed Aramaic yet."

"It was about a certain man named Saul," Rivka said care-fully.

"Ah, yes," Ari said. "Renegade Saul. Baruch told me all about him last night." He hesitated. "Did you catch what they call him here? *Apikoros*. Renegade." He seemed almost apologetic about scoring a debating point.

Rivka laughed. "Did you think that was news to me? I read all about it when I was a kid. It's in the Book of Acts. Saul comes back to Jerusalem, and the first people to make a fuss are his own fellow Christians. Not the Jewish leaders. Not the ultra-orthodox. But his own Christian brothers. Yes, I knew that. I didn't know they called him Renegade Saul, though."

"I would hardly call these people Christians," Ari said.

Rivka stared at him in surprise. She had used the word *Christians* only because Ari had insisted a few days ago that Messianic Jews were not real Jews. He had obviously done some rethinking in the last few days. Good for him. She saw no reason to hammer the point home. Ari wasn't stupid. "You're right, Ari. They're Jews who believe in Yeshua *HaMashiach*, and yet they're still part of the community of Israel."

"But what about the Christian creeds?" Ari asked. "How do those fit in?"

"What about them?" Rivka said. "They don't exist. The Nicene Creed is almost three centuries down the road. The Apostles' Creed is fifty to a hundred years in the future. Even the New Testament isn't written yet, except for a few letters by Renegade Saul. There aren't any stained-glass churches yet, Ari. No pope, no pulpits, no pipe organs. No Christian anti-Semitism, because nobody has figured out yet that Christians aren't Jews."

"Except Renegade Saul," Ari said. "He's figured it out. Don't tell me he hasn't blasted 'the Jews' in his writings."

"Paul? I don't think so. He comes down on the law, but not on Jews."

"It's in your New Testament. My next-door neighbor at MIT used to quote it to me. All about how the Jews killed Jesus."

"Sounds like John," Rivka said. "His name is Yohanan in Hebrew. He's referring to Jews who disagree with him. It's an old tradition, arguing among ourselves. Two Jews, three opinions, remember? You want an example of some real vituperation, read the Dead Sea Scrolls. They make John look like a purring pussycat. Paul, too."

"I...guess I would like to meet Saul," Ari said.

That makes three of us. Rivka closed her eyes. *You, me, and Dr. West.*

"Don't fall asleep," Ari said. "I still have some questions for you."

"Fire away."

"Please," Ari said, "we are not at war, correct?"

"Sorry. Bad choice of words."

"As I told you, I am interested in your stepfather's story," Ari said. "Could I have his e-mail address, please? I would like to get his account in his own words."

Rivka sighed and took a deep breath. Now she had to tell him.

"There's a problem," she said.

"Problem?"

She nodded, and then the whole sorry last six months of her life came rushing in on her. Something snapped in her heart. Not now—she couldn't face it, couldn't talk about it, couldn't even think about it.

"What kind of problem?" Ari asked.

Rivka shook her head, annoyed—no, angry. At God. Tears blurred her vision, and her voice choked off so she couldn't talk. She turned and began walking away in the general direction of Hana's house.

She heard Ari's footsteps behind her. "What kind of problem, Rivka? I...didn't mean to intrude, but—"

"He's dead!" Hot grief squirted up through her insides as she said it. "Pancreatic cancer. Last winter. Last *Christmas!* How's that for ironic, huh? He died on Christmas, and God wasn't there to make it all right." She smeared at her eyes with the sleeve of her tunic.

"I'm sorry, Rivka—"

"Well, I'm angry!" she shouted. "Now leave me alone."

"Rivka, please—" He touched her elbow.

She shook him off. "Just give me a little space, will you? I need some time by myself."

"If you want to talk—"

"I don't!" She knew she was acting like a spoiled brat, but right now she didn't really care. "Look, Ari, if you want to bother me, come do it tomorrow morning. Right now, I just want to go back to Hana's. Alone."

"If you insist." He stopped. "I'll see you tomorrow, my friend."

Rivka kept walking, half-blinded by her tears. She hadn't asked Ari to come looking for her. And now he had stirred up this, which she had been trying to bury for the last six months.

God had dealt her a raw hand. If He hadn't healed her step-father way back when, she wouldn't have expected anything this time. But He had—He had done a miracle. Once. So why did He have to stop with just one? If God was sovereign, why didn't He do a better job of running His kingdom? Why did He get her hopes up and then walk away?

That was one question she would ask Paul, if she somehow managed to cross his path. Assuming he would bother to talk to a woman.

When Rivka arrived back at Hana's house, she was still crying. Hana opened the door, reached out her arms, and simply hugged her.

"Cry, my friend," Hana said. "I have been waiting for you. Now you must cry until you are finished."

So Rivka did.

Damien

The moon gave a little light, enough to see by in the deserted streets. Damien strode up the hill, guided by his memory. Rivka and Ari had hung around outside that house for a while this morning. Damien hadn't seen them looking at any papers, but that didn't prove anything. If Ari had Damien's spreadsheet, they would get around to it sooner or later. And Rivka would see through Damien's cryptic notations quicker than pig Latin.

Damien had to prevent that. At any cost. He clutched the lock pick he had fashioned out of stiff wire. He had brought a lot of things that might come in handy in his duffel bag. It paid to plan ahead. He had spent the evening practicing on the door of his rented house. Dead easy, compared to modern locks. The hard part would be dealing with Ari and his friend. Two against one might be tricky.

He turned right, then left, then right again. There. The moon threw weird shadows in the street. Damien wasn't spooked. He feared only one thing in life: the sight of his brother, lying in that wretched bed. That he couldn't stand. But he could now do something about it.

At the door, Damien listened intently. Nothing…not even a snore. He eased the pick into the lock. In. Twist slightly. Tug gently.

Click!

Damien's heart pounded in his chest. He listened again. If anyone had heard him, they would come to investigate.

But he heard no sound. After sixty beats of his heart, Damien eased the door open. It must have been greased with fat lately, like his own door, because it swung in silently on its iron hinges. He opened it all the way and peered inside.

He saw…nothing. No bodies, anyway. He flicked on a pen-sized flashlight and swung the beam around the room. No people. A stairway led up into darkness. So maybe they slept on the second floor. The neon blue of Ari's backpack caught Damien's eye.

Yes!

If Ari had any information, it would be in there. That was practically his office. He never went anywhere without it.

Damien hesitated. Should he go upstairs and put a bullet through Ari's head and be done with it? No. Rivka would figure that one out in a millisecond. And she had information that could help the mission. If he had any chance of getting that information out of her, he had to wait.

Damien silently lifted the backpack and slung it over his shoulder. He stepped backward out into the street, pulling the door shut behind him. He even took a minute to lock it. No need to leave a mess. Why give Ari any clues at all?

Fifteen minutes later, Damien arrived back at his rented house. It was an easy walk when the streets were empty.

Inside, he lit the olive oil lamp with his cigarette lighter and opened the backpack. On top lay a bee-sting kit. Damien dropped it on the floor. On impulse, he crushed it under his heel. Then he dumped the rest of the contents of the backpack onto the floor. What a load of junk! A calculator. A battered address book. Red and black Uni-ball pens. A checkbook. Paper clips. A multifunction screwdriver. A clipboard with two dozen loose pages of calculations. Good grief, the guy must do tensor calculus in his sleep. A phone bill hung half out of its envelope. And what was this?

Damien held up a Polaroid photograph. Ari and Rivka, standing in a field next to a small tree. That must be the day they went tree-planting. What kind of a loser took a girl planting trees on a date? On a whim, Damien ripped the photo in two, neatly separating Ari and Rivka.

What else was in that pile? Damien pawed through the rest. Junk. Plenty of junk, but not what he was looking for.

So either Ari had that spreadsheet in his pocket, or he hadn't brought it along. Most likely the latter.

Excellent. One less thing to worry about.

Damien scooped the dregs of Ari's pathetic life into the backpack, zipped it shut, and tossed it into the corner near his duffel bag.

So Ari had no real evidence. It would be his word against Damien's. There had to be some way to persuade Rivka that Ari was a liar.

Come to think of it, Ari had got her crying real good this morning. Maybe the job was already done. Damien lay down on his bedroll. He would give Rivka until noon tomorrow to come to him. If she didn't, then he would go looking for her.

He needed Rivka's knowledge. If she wouldn't tell him voluntarily, he would *make* her volunteer.

And if a few eggs got broken along the way—tough.

NINETEEN

Ari

When Ari arrived back at Baruch's house, the sun had risen and he felt famished. He had gone to the morning prayers with Brother Baruch before sunrise and then taken a walk alone around the streets while the city woke up.

The streets of old Jerusalem resonated deep within his soul, rousing some yearning he hadn't known. These ancient, strange people—these were his family. However deeply you probed into the universe, you had to come home sometime to your family. This place was home, these people his family, and Baruch his brother.

"*Shalom,* Brother Baruch!" Ari shouted. "I'm hungry as a bear!"

Baruch smiled at that and pointed to the table, where bread and cheese and pickled vegetables were laid out. "I have already eaten. Your friend Rivka came by looking for you. She wishes for you to come visit her when you are ready."

That was a good sign. Ari sat down and tore off a chunk of bread. Then he caught himself and said the blessing over the bread. If he wasn't careful, all this praying and blessing was going to become a habit.

Ari ate quickly, fending off questions from Baruch about the country from which he and Rivka had come. When he finished, he washed it all down with a stone cup full of good kosher beer and then stood up.

"Baruch, thank you for the delightful meal. I'm going to go see Rivka now."

Baruch nodded. "And I shall be praying in my room upstairs. I am much disturbed about my Brother Mattityahu. Something is very wrong."

"Pray for Rivka also, my friend," Ari said. That surprised him. Just a few days in this environment, and already he was adapting to the local speech patterns. Very strange.

"I shall pray for Rivka," Baruch said. He tilted his head for a moment, as if listening to a voice far away. "And I believe I shall pray also for you, Ari. There is a whisper of fear in my heart."

"I'll be all right," Ari said. As long as he didn't run into Damien West. If that happened, there would be trouble. He walked around the table and reached for his backpack, which he had left on the floor the night before.

It was gone.

"Baruch, have you seen my pack?" he asked.

Baruch shook his head. "You did not take it when we went to pray this morning?"

"It was dark and I forgot it," Ari said. "Which was stupid, because it has my medicine. I need it." He went upstairs. The pack was nowhere in sight.

When he came down, Baruch stood out in the street, looking around.

"Baruch, is it possible that Rivka might have taken it with her when she came by this morning?"

Baruch shrugged. "Possible, yes. I do not remember. She did not stay here long."

Ari felt a surge of annoyance. Why would she do that? In addition to his medicine, that backpack contained a lot of personal things. He didn't want anyone rummaging through it.

Just to be sure, he searched the entire house again. The backpack was gone. Rivka had to have taken it.

"*Shalom,* my brother," Ari said. He turned and began walking briskly down the hill toward Hana's house. It was still cool, and the streets weren't yet busy, so he made good time.

When he reached the bottom of the hill, he saw three boys throwing stones at the eaves of a building. They kept throwing as he came nearer.

He held up his right hand. "Hold, hold!"

They stopped throwing and let him pass.

A stone whizzed past his head the instant he had gone by.

He spun around and shouted in Hebrew, "Too close, boys!" forgetting that they would only understand Aramaic.

But the boys hooted in glee, pointing. Ari turned to look. Hornets' nest! A gaping hole hung open. Out of it gushed dozens of buzzing hornets.

Ari backpedaled as fast as he could. He heard the boys yammering behind him. He tripped over one of them, and they both fell in the dirt. Ari rolled off the boy and scrambled away on his knees as fast as he could.

One of the boys screamed. Ari sprang to his feet. Before he could take a step, another boy barreled into him. Ari staggered wildly, then fell. The boy yelped.

Something settled on Ari's neck. He brushed at it frantically, then pushed himself off the ground. Something tickled his right arm.

He swatted at it wildly with his left.

A needle of poison lanced his arm, just below the elbow.

Ari smashed it an instant later. A dead hornet fell out of his hand to the ground. And then he was running.

He had only one hope in the world. Rivka had better have his backpack.

He looked at his watch. 7:12 A.M. Without his medication, he could survive till 7:30.

Possibly.

Rivka

Hana had been gone for an hour when Rivka heard her name being shouted out in the street. Footsteps followed and then the door flung itself open. Ari stood there, a look of stark terror on his face.

"Ari. What—"

He held up his red, swollen arm. "Hornet sting!" he shouted. "Do you have my backpack?"

She stared at him stupidly. *Backpack?* "Um...no, Ari. Why—"

"I've got to have it!" he shouted. "Now! I need a shot of epinephrine!"

"Oh my gosh!" she said. "I...I haven't seen your backpack, Ari."

"You didn't take it when you dropped by Baruch's house?"

"No, of course not!" Her heart pounded in her chest. "What can I do for you? There's got to be something—"

Ari's face went completely white, and then he slumped down on the floor. "Rivka," he said, "I want to tell you something before I..."

She knelt down beside him. "No, you're not going to die, Ari! Please, no!"

"Rivka, listen to me!" Ari swallowed hard. "I've never told a woman this before, so please don't laugh."

"Yes?"

"I'm...in love with you, Rivka."

Rivka stared at him, stunned. *Love?* That hadn't occurred to her. The past few days, she hadn't even been sure they were friends. Wasn't it only yesterday they had been arguing yet again about something they were never going to agree on, while they watched Baruch—

"Baruch!" Rivka said, jumping up. "Don't move, Ari! Is Baruch at his house?"

"Yes, he's praying," Ari said. "Rivka, will you kiss me? I'm going to die."

Rivka bent down and kissed him hard on the lips. The smell of fear clung to his body like a vapor. She wanted to tell him that he could know he had eternal life. The four spiritual laws and all that. But what if he didn't buy it? *Move, Rivka, now!* She dashed out the door and down the street.

How far to Baruch's house? Maybe half a mile, maybe a little more. She knew that a good runner could run half a mile in two minutes. In running gear, on level ground.

Rivka was not a good runner, and she wore leather sandals. And after a short downhill stretch, it would be uphill all the way.

Soon she was gasping and had to slow down. Women stared at her as she ran past. A group of men shouted filthy remarks at her. Children pointed. Rivka didn't care.

God, please don't let me get lost. Please let Baruch be where I can find him. Please let me be on time. Please, God, save Ari Kazan.

By the time she reached Baruch's house, her breath was coming in ragged gasps and her chest ached. She pounded on the door, found it unlocked, and charged in.

The lower room was empty. Rivka staggered up the stairs and tried the door. Latched! She beat on it and tried to scream, but she could not catch her breath.

The door swung open. Baruch stood there, his eyes wide, his phylactery askew. "Why have you interrupted me during my prayers?" he said. "And where is Brother Ari?"

She pointed back in the general direction of Hana's house. "Not here," she gasped out.

"It is not fitting that you should be here alone with me," Baruch said. "You must—"

"No!" she said. "Listen!" But that was all she could get out before having to pant again. Finally, she caught her breath enough to gasp out a few words. "Ari is dying! You must pray for him!"

"Where?" Baruch dashed past her down the stairs and out into the street. "Brother Ari!"

Rivka followed him down. Her knees felt weak, and she wanted to collapse.

"Where is he?" Baruch shouted.

Rivka pointed toward the east. "In the house of my friend Hana. I'll have to show…" She fought for air. "I'm so tired!"

Baruch turned and ran.

"Wait!" Rivka tried to shout after him, but her voice would not carry. She stared at his retreating back. How could Baruch find Hana's house without her to show him the way?

Ari

Ari checked the time again. 7:28.

His arm fell weakly to his side. He lay flat on his back. His throat tightened up so hard he could barely feel the air moving in and out. Dark spots quilted the stone vaulted ceiling of the house. If God existed, Ari would soon meet Him.

He was a fool, of course. He shouldn't have come through the wormhole looking for a woman who couldn't possibly care for him. He should have looked to see what the boys were throwing stones at. He shouldn't have told Rivka that he loved her. No, on second thought, he felt glad he had told her. Truth mattered, even intensely personal truth. He had done right to tell her, though perhaps she thought him a fool.

The dark spots closed together. The lights flickered out.

In his mind's eye, Ari saw Damien West come into the little house.

Was it a dream? In the dream, or whatever it was, Ari felt himself start crying.

"Why are you crying?" Damien asked.

"Because I love you." As Ari said the words, he knew that they were true in some strange sense which he could not fathom.

From outside the room, far up the street, came a faraway voice like the sound of an angel's trumpet, filling the room. Damien vanished. Ari opened his mouth, but no air would come in. A strange, muzzy lightness pressed down upon him, squeezing out consciousness. Then that voice again—Brother Baruch—shouting, "Yeshua!" The door flew open.

Ari felt something hot explode in his heart. A packet of pure heat surged down through his legs. When it reached his feet, it bounced and raced up toward his head. One heartbeat later, the heat slammed into his lungs, his airways, his throat.

Instantly, the iron bands choking him shattered. Light flooded his eyes. Cool air washed into his lungs.

Ari lay on the floor, afraid to move. It was an illusion. A dream. A near-death experience.

In a minute, he would see the famous white tunnel, find himself vacuumed through into another mode of existence. Or more likely, into the final darkness. Or even—

"Brother Ari, can you speak?" Baruch said. "Rabban Yeshua, save him!"

Ari pushed himself up to a sitting position and turned his head to look at Baruch. "I...don't understand it, but—"

"What has happened?" Baruch said. "Rivka said you were dying."

"I was dying," Ari said. "And now I am not." He shook his head in disbelief. "You've healed me, Brother Baruch."

"I have no power to heal," Baruch said. "Give glory to the God of our fathers, Brother Ari. *Adonai, Rafayenu.* The Lord our Healer. Rabban Yeshua."

Ari reached up. "Help me stand."

Baruch pulled him to his feet.

Ari shook the dust off his clothes. He fingered the welt on his right elbow. Almost gone. The pain had gone. If there was any such thing as a miracle, this must be it.

"Blessed be HaShem," Ari said. "Blessed be HaShem."

Baruch threw his arms around Ari and kissed him. "The Lord our Healer. The Lord our Healer."

The sound of a woman screaming echoed outside, far up the streets. The sound of hysterical wailing. Rivka.

Baruch stepped outside and waved his arms. "Rivka! Here, Rivka! He is alive!"

Ari felt his heart lurch. How in the world was he going to face Rivka Meyers now, after admitting that he was in love with her?

You're a fool, Ari Kazan. But at least you're a live fool. Blessed be HaShem.

TWENTY

Baruch

Baruch felt only pure, holy joy. HaShem had saved Brother Ari's life. Blessed be HaShem. And in healing Brother Ari, HaShem had shown him a vision. It must be true. So why did Brother Ari resist the truth? "It was a vision," Baruch said again. "Brother Ari, you received a vision from the living God."

"It was like a dream," Brother Ari said. "And yet I was awake and I saw my enemy."

"He was your enemy," Baruch said. "But now HaShem has restored him to you. You must make peace with him."

Rivka looked skeptical. "It requires two in order to make peace. Yesterday, they fought like tigers. Today, will they make peace? Only if Damien is willing."

That name offended Baruch. "You must not call any man a *daimon*." No man could be compared to an evil spirit. Man was made in the image of HaShem.

"Not *daimon*," Rivka said. "Damien. It is a common name in our country."

Baruch shook his head. "It is a strange country, and I would not wish to visit it. But, Brother Ari, you must do your part to make peace with this Damien."

"For my part, I have made peace," Brother Ari said. "Something happened, and I do not understand it. I do not hate him anymore."

That proved it a true vision of HaShem. "It is the work of Rabban Yeshua in your heart," Baruch said. "He commanded us to do a hard thing—to love our enemies."

Brother Ari turned a piercing eye on him. "And yet you hate Renegade Saul."

Brother Ari's words rang on Baruch's heart like a hammer on hot iron. He lowered his gaze, unable to meet those bright, burning eyes. Had not Brother Ari seen a vision from the Holy One, blessed be He? And now he had spoken a prophetic word. When a prophet spoke a word into your heart, you ignored it at the risk of your own soul.

"Why do you hate a man who does not hate you?" Brother Ari asked.

Brother Ari spoke truth, and Baruch knew it. Yet he did not want to follow that truth to its logical conclusion. "Brother Ari, you do not understand who this man Renegade Saul is."

Brother Ari gave a harsh laugh. "You are wrong, my brother. I know better than you ever will who Saul is. I know what he has done, and I know what he will do, and I know the effects of his deeds for many years. And yet I do not hate even him any longer."

Brother Ari was telling the truth. Baruch could feel the pain in his words, and it wrung his heart. But what must he do? What must he do?

A woman's voice from behind startled him. "Why are *you* here?" The voice sounded at once angry and aggrieved. A woman's voice. "You must leave."

Baruch slowly turned. Before him stood his worst nightmare.

Rivka

At the harsh tone in Hana's voice, Rivka felt her heart lurch. "Hana!" she said. "Why so angry?"

Hana's eyes locked on Baruch, and her mouth quivered with rage. "You!" She jabbed a finger at him. "Have you come to pay for your last visit? A year is a long time to wait! I should make you pay double."

Rivka thought Hana must be joking, but one look at Baruch's face told her that Hana was completely serious.

"Forgive me," Baruch said in a tiny voice. "I was not myself in those days—"

"Which is a clever way of saying that you do not have to pay," Hana said. She snorted in disgust. "Please leave my house, all of you. I have a man waiting down the street who will give me real silver."

Baruch fumbled for something hidden in the folds of his broad cloth belt. At last he pulled out a leather purse and extracted two coins. His hands shook as he held them out to Hana.

She snatched them away and studied them intently. "Two *dinars*," she said. Her face broke into a smile. "That is more than I deserve, since you were gentle." She dropped the coins into her belt and went out into the street.

Rivka locked her gaze on the ground, unwilling to humiliate Baruch further by looking at him. Nobody said anything. A minute later, Hana returned. "You may all stay," she said. "I have money. I do not need to carry any man's water today." She brought in a full jug from outside and poured herself a drink into a stone cup.

Rivka wondered what Baruch was thinking. Abruptly, he yanked open the door and strode out.

Ari started after him.

"Wait," Rivka said. "He needs some time alone, Ari."

"Why did he come here?" Hana asked. "I have not seen him in over a year, but I carried his water often before that."

Rivka spent the next several minutes explaining what had happened. She stopped twice to ask Ari questions in Hebrew, and she then translated the answers into Aramaic for Hana.

"What will happen if he is stung again?" Hana asked.

"I don't know," Rivka said. "Ari, don't you think we should go back to our own time now? If you're stung by another hornet, it might be presumptuous to expect God to heal you again."

"You're right," Ari said. "I would like to say good-bye to Brother Baruch, and then we should go back as soon as possible."

"Dr. West says the wormhole will collapse the minute any of us goes through," Rivka said. "We'll have to warn him we're going back, so he can come, too. We can't leave him stranded here."

"He said what?" Ari asked. "Rivka, that is nonsense. The wormhole's stability is determined by the presence of exotic matter threading the wormhole, which depends on the power supply in our lab. It has nothing to do with people going through it."

"That's not what he told me, and I would think he knows something," Rivka said. "You're not trying to leave him behind, are you?"

Ari shook his head. "Of course not. I told you I am reconciled to him in my heart. I agree that we should ask Damien to go back with us. But more than that, we need to have a long talk with him. Something funny is going on here, and he needs to give us some straight answers."

"No way. I know what happens when you two get in the same room," she said. "There would be another fight in ten seconds."

"Things have changed," Ari said.

"Not for him," Rivka said. "Maybe you've really changed. If so, prove it. Stay away from him. I'll go talk to him myself."

"I don't trust him," Ari said.

"I thought you were reconciled to him," Rivka said.

"That doesn't mean I should trust him. I don't think you're safe with him alone."

"Dr. West is a bit strange, I admit," Rivka said, "but he's been a perfect gentleman around me. And I'm not going to let your paranoia keep me from having a talk with him."

"Rivka, I'm just saying—"

"I know what you're saying." Rivka turned to Hana, who had been watching this conversation with blank eyes. "Hana, can I borrow your knife? I want to go talk to Damien, and Ari does not trust him."

Hana picked up the knife on her table and handed it to Rivka. "It is the way men are—when they love a woman, they instantly become jealous."

"How do you know about that?" Rivka asked. Nobody had told Hana anything about Ari being in love.

"How could I not know it?" Hana said. "I have seen the eyes of many men. And the truth-tellers confirm it."

Rivka was beginning to feel very curious about these truth-tellers. "Do they tell you whether I'll be safe with Damien?"

"Yes, you will be quite safe," Hana said.

Rivka slid the knife up the long sleeve of her tunic. "Ari, I'm going to see Dr. West. Hana and I think I'll be very safe. You need to stay here."

Ari gave a wry smile. "You're leaving me alone with this woman? Brother Baruch would be shocked, shocked."

Rivka went out into the street, thinking about that. Baruch was in big trouble—mostly with himself, but also with his community. What would happen when all his friends found out who he had been fooling around with?

She felt just a bit sorry for him. After all, he seemed to have repented. And he had healed Ari.

This was something Baruch would have to sort out for himself. By this afternoon, she and Ari and Dr. West would be out of here.

Damien

Damien had slept late after his night's adventures and then gone shopping for his breakfast. After that he had taken a leisurely stroll through the streets, just trying to get a better feel for the territory. You could never know it too well. The day had gotten quite warm and humid, and Damien felt lazy and sluggish. The hurry-hurry-hurry of modern life was already beginning to fade. This would be a permanent vacation, as soon as he finished Job One.

When he turned the corner near his rented house, he saw Rivka just stepping away from the door. Good. She had come to him, as he had expected.

He mentally geared himself to be the courtesy king for a while. And wasn't that the story of his life? Always having to playact a role. When this was all over, would he even remember what it felt like to be real?

"Hello, Miss Meyers!" he said. "How are you this morning?" He watched her closely. Was she suspicious? What had she and Ari guessed about his mission?

"I'm...a little frazzled," she said.

She looked it. Dust and sweat streaked her face. "You look a little under-the-weather. Are you coming down with a bug?"

"No," she said. "But I'm afraid Ari did."

"I'm very sorry to hear that," Damien said. He was very glad to hear it. "Summer cold?"

"A hornet."

"No!" Damien fought hard to contain his joy. "He's terribly allergic to them, isn't he?"

"Yes, it nearly killed him," Rivka said.

Excellent. Ari was probably lying in a bed somewhere in a coma. Damien allowed his voice to quiver with shock. "Is there anything I can do? Where is he?"

"He'll be all right," Rivka said. "But I think it's time this little adventure ended. Ari wants to go back through the wormhole this afternoon."

That didn't compute. Ari had told him weeks ago that a hornet sting could kill him. Maybe a couple millennia of evolution had changed the venom just enough to save his life. Too bad. Damien nodded sympathetically. "It's fine with me if he goes back. You and I are still on for some sight-seeing and autograph-hunting, right?"

"But we can't." Rivka looked puzzled. "If Ari goes, then we need to go, too. Isn't that what you told me Friday? The wormhole will collapse as soon as the next person goes through it."

Damien cursed himself for getting caught in a trap of his own making. Nothing to do but backtrack. "You know, I've been puzzling over that ever since Ari appeared yesterday."

"Puzzling over what?" Rivka asked. She fanned herself and pointed up at the sky. "Is there any chance we could go in out of the sun? It's boiling out here."

"Forgive me," Damien said. "Of course." He produced a key and took his time opening the door while he tried to remember what condition he had left the room in. Was Ari's backpack out of sight? Had he let any scraps of paper fall on the floor?

The lock clicked. Damien hesitated. "Miss Meyers, could you find us a small stone or stick to prop this door open? It gets awfully hot in this house."

"Sure, let me look around," she said.

Damien pushed open the door and scanned the room. Ari's backpack lay in the corner. He ran over and threw his duffel bag over it.

But he had left his bag's zipper half open, and inside he could see a box of ammo. He yanked at the zipper, but it jammed.

Before he could unstick the zipper, Damien heard the door opening. He tugged together the flaps of the bag as best he could and stepped toward the table near the door. He would have to keep Rivka distracted at this end of the room. His face felt hot when he plopped onto a stool at the table.

She came in and eyed him quizzically. "Is something wrong?"

"Have a seat," Damien said, motioning toward the stool nearest the door. "It's coolest there."

Rivka sat. "So where were we? Oh, yeah. You've been puzzling over something."

Damien stroked his three-day growth of beard. "It's very odd that Ari didn't disrupt the wormhole when he came through. Evidently, it's more robust than I would have guessed."

"How do you know?" Rivka asked. "Maybe it collapsed an hour after he came through."

"No, it would have happened in a few seconds," Damien said. "And it would have made quite a bang. Ari would have heard it. Obviously, he didn't, or he wouldn't think he could go back. Therefore, the wormhole has survived. Ergo, it is stable." He gave a hearty laugh. "Sometimes these machines work *better* than we expect!"

"Maybe," Rivka said. "But I want to go back home now. It's not safe here for Ari."

"Fine," Damien said.

"Are you coming with us?"

Damien was beginning to feel trapped. If he said no, Rivka would want to know why. He tapped his fingers on the table. "Actually, I'm just a little suspicious of Professor Kazan. This feels like a chance to pick a fight with me."

"I don't think so," Rivka said. "Ari's changed a lot. He says he's not angry at you anymore." She stood up and began pacing.

Damien felt a needle of panic jabbing at his gut. If Rivka saw what was in that duffel bag, she might make some guesses that would be most unfortunate. *Promise her anything, but get her out of the house. Now.*

"All right, then." He stood up and stepped toward the door. "Let's all go to the cave at noon. I would rather not get anywhere near Ari—no sense in him picking another fight, right? I'll hang around outside, and you take Ari in first and make sure he's gone through the wormhole. Then come out and let me know, and we can go back together."

At the far end of the room, Rivka turned and studied Damien.

He put on his most sincere smile. "Miss Meyers, I'm really glad that this nightmare is coming to an end for us. I won't be happy until we're safely back in our own century."

"Noon, then." Rivka looked at her watch. "It's 9:05 by my watch. That gives us time to say good-bye to our friends." She went to the door and stopped short. "Ouch! It's bright out here."

"And hot, too," Damien said. He followed her to the door. "Thank you for coming, Miss Meyers. I do hope Ari and I can be reconciled. I think when he starts seeing his counselor again, he'll settle down."

"I thought you said he *is* seeing one."

"What I meant," Damien said, trying to make up something while he spoke, "is that he was seeing one until recently, but then he stopped for a few weeks. It's an ego thing, you know. Ari's a proud man."

"Um…right," Rivka said.

One thing Damien still wanted to find out. What had Ari told her about Paul, if anything? He allowed himself a faint snort. "Such a pity, we won't be collecting that autograph, after all."

"Autograph?" Rivka asked.

"You remember." Damien watched Rivka's face very closely. "Saint Paul."

He saw only disappointment, not guilt or fear or any other out-of-place reaction. "You're right. I really wanted to see him. I've heard through the grapevine that he really is in town."

That was news to Damien. Great news. His heart began thudding in his chest. He forced his voice to stay calm. "Oh well, if we came back with his autograph, who would believe it anyway?"

Rivka nodded absently. "I had better hurry if we're going to say good-bye. Ari's got a friend in the upper part of the city." She stepped out into the street. "Don't forget—noon today."

"I couldn't possibly forget," Damien said.

He watched Rivka walk down the street. Of course, he was not going to meet her outside the cave at noon. She would send Ari through then come looking for him. He wouldn't show. She would eventually get tired of waiting and go through herself. And if she stayed, what could she do without Ari?

That meant a slight change in his plans. He obviously wasn't going to find out from Rivka where Paul's trial was going to be. He would have to find out himself. And only two days left to figure out how.

But first he had another task. He went back into the house and pushed his duffel bag aside. Ari's backpack had to go. If Rivka or Ari came back here for any reason, he didn't want to risk them seeing it. He would never be able to lie his way out then.

Damien shoved the backpack into his duffel bag and zipped it shut. A minute later, he was out on the street, going in the opposite direction from Rivka. He had read once that somewhere outside the city were garbage pits. Once he dumped the backpack, he would be home free.

Hana

From far up the street, Hana watched Rivka leave the good man's house. She felt sad that they would all be returning so soon to their own country. She might never see any of them again.

The good man left his door open and ducked inside his house. Hana wondered whether she should return to her own home now. She wanted to speak to the good man, but the truth-tellers said that she must return home at once.

Then the good man came out of his house with a large bag. He locked the door and started down the street in the opposite direction.

Hana did not want him to go away. The truth-tellers raised their voices, insisting that she turn back. She stopped.

The good man kept walking. She must decide now or lose sight of him.

The truth-tellers began shrieking. The terrible sound hurt her ears. She wavered, torn by fear and doubt. The good man disappeared around a corner.

With a rush of nausea in the pit of her stomach, Hana decided to disobey the truth-tellers. She trotted forward after the good man. The truth-tellers would be angry, but she would ignore them. Just this once, for the sake of the good man, she would ignore them.

TWENTY-ONE

Rivka

It did not make sense. Rivka had seen it, but she could not understand it.

Why did Dr. West have a box of ammunition in his duffel bag?

Rivka's stepfather had been a gun enthusiast. He had insisted that she take a basic gun-safety course years ago. She had never owned a gun and didn't want one. But she knew what ammunition looked like. And she knew it was heavy.

Why had Dr. West brought something like that through the wormhole with him?

If he had bullets, then he must have a gun. How had he gotten possession of a gun in Israel? Either he had smuggled it in, or he had bought it illegally. Neither one spoke well for his intentions.

When Rivka reached Hana's house, her mind was buzzing. She opened the door.

"So what's the news?" Ari asked. "Did Damien behave himself?"

"Where's Hana?" Rivka laid Hana's knife back on the table.

"Out somewhere." Ari took a sip of water from the stone cup. "She said she didn't want to stay in the same house alone with me. Maybe she thinks it doesn't look good."

Rivka managed a smile, but her mind had latched onto a question and wouldn't let go. *Why did Dr. West need all that ammo?*

"Is Damien coming back with us to the wormhole?" Ari asked.

"Have you been seeing a counselor?" Rivka didn't believe what Damien had told her, but she wanted to hear Ari's reaction.

"Of course not. Did Damien tell you that?"

She nodded.

He laughed. "I don't understand what game he's playing. I really don't."

"Tell me something." She hesitated. Ari would hit the roof when he heard this.

"I'm listening," he said. He held up the stone cup. "Like a drink? You look like you could use one."

"Suppose someone carries something heavy somewhere, and that something has only one use," Rivka said. "Do you think that someone would use that something?"

"Say again?" Ari said. "I got lost with all the someones and somethings and somewheres."

"He's got a gun," Rivka said. Suddenly, she felt fear gnawing at the inside of her skull. "At least, I think he does. There's a box of ammunition in his duffel bag, and I saw it, and then he lied to me about how you need counseling and how proud you are, and I'm scared, Ari, I'm really scared. What is he going to do with a gun?"

It happened so quickly that she hardly noticed. Ari was up on his feet, holding her in his arms, and she was crying. She felt a strange mixture of terror and trust.

"Tell me everything," Ari said. "Everything he said. Everything you did. Everything you saw and heard and felt."

Rivka told him. They sat down together on the floor, and she went over the entire conversation in minute detail. Ari just listened.

When she finished, they sat in quiet thought for a long moment.

They both heard the soft footfall at the door at the same time. Ari rose silently to his feet. He motioned for her to move to the far corner of the house.

Rivka wanted to scream. She could see in her mind's eye Dr. West crouching outside with a gun, preparing to storm in and shoot them both.

Ari pressed himself against the wall just inside the door. Rivka stuffed her knuckles into her mouth.

The door opened.

Ari lunged.

Hana screamed and dropped something on the ground.

Ari's backpack.

Then Ari was gabbling out an apology, and Hana stood there quivering with fear, and Rivka rushed to her and hugged her and tried to explain what was going on.

Finally, Ari picked up the backpack, pulled Hana in, and shut the door.

"Where did you get that pack?" Rivka asked.

"Your friend," Hana said. "I watched when you went to his lodgings. Soon after you came out, he also went out with a bag. I followed him. The truth-tellers told me not to, but I went anyway."

"To where?" Pieces of this puzzle were falling into place, but Rivka wanted to get it all.

Hana pointed toward the south. "To the refuse pits in the Valley of Hinnom. He took out this strange pack and threw it in."

"Translate, please." Ari unzipped the backpack and opened it. He pulled out a crushed packet of epinephrine. A broken hypodermic needle dangled from its syringe. Sheets of paper had been wadded up and jammed into the pack. Ari lifted them out. Two halves of a Polaroid photo fell to the floor. Ari stooped and picked them up, his face tight with fury.

Rivka summarized what Hana had said.

"I don't believe it," Ari said. "This is malicious, pure and simple. What's he up to?"

"He was looking for something," Rivka said.

"Like what?"

"I don't know, but I think he's afraid. When I went to his house, he acted nervous. Almost like he was afraid of me."

"Why? He's got a gun. Even without one, he could rip you apart. What's to be afraid of?"

"Physically, nothing. So he has to be afraid of what I know."

"What do you know?"

Rivka shook her head. "I have no idea. After living here for a few days, I know a lot less than I thought I did."

"If he was afraid of you, then why did he steal *my* backpack and trash it? There's nothing in it."

"Does he know that? Obviously, he thought something was there. Is anything missing?"

Ari sighed. "It's hard to say. He didn't exactly put it back in alphabetic order."

"But if he found it, why was he nervous just now when I went to visit him?"

"It doesn't make sense," Ari said.

"It has to make sense," Rivka said. "He created the wormhole for a reason. He came back to this particular time for a reason.

He's lying to me for a reason. Why the gun? Why the lies?"

Ari's face turned pale. "Isn't it obvious?"

"Isn't what obvious?" Rivka felt the blood rushing through her temples. She didn't want it to be obvious. *Please, God, no.*

"He came here to kill somebody."

"That's...crazy."

"Of course it's crazy. Damien's crazy. And I just remembered something." Ari tugged at his beard. "Back in the lab, when I discovered you were gone, Dov and I looked through Damien's laptop."

"And...?"

"He had a copy of the Unabomber Manifesto. It was one of the most recent documents in his word processor. I remember one of the phrases was highlighted in red. Something about, 'That is why we had to kill people.'"

"No!"

"And there was something else." Ari closed his eyes in concentration. "One of the postdocs brought in a printout Damien made on the laser printer. Weird stuff, unreadable."

"You saw it?"

"I did, but it made no sense. A spreadsheet. Some columns had just numbers. Others had letters. Neither Dov nor I could figure it out."

"Did you bring it?"

Ari shook his head. "Dov walked off with it just before I came through the wormhole."

"We need that paper."

"We need a gun," Ari said.

Hana stood staring at them, her eyes wide. "I have done something very wrong."

"No, Hana," Rivka said. "You did exactly the right thing."

"But you are going back to your country, and I will not see you again."

Rivka didn't know what to say to that.

"We've got to find Brother Baruch," Ari said. "Before we go back to the wormhole."

"He may not want to come with us," Rivka said. "I mean, with the three of us."

Ari looked at Hana. "Oh," he said. "That's a problem."

Rivka pushed him toward the door. "Go find him. He needs you right now. We have time. Bring him with you and meet me at the cave at noon." She turned to Hana and explained what they were planning.

Ari shouldered his backpack and then hesitated. "I don't want to leave you unprotected."

"I'm not worried," Rivka said. "Dr. West is afraid of me. And if he's got a gun, you wouldn't be much protection anyway."

"Do not worry, Rivka," Hana said, smiling brightly. "The truth-tellers say that you and I will be quite safe."

TWENTY-TWO

Damien

Damien sat sweating in the shade of the Temple Mount and adjusted his compact binoculars. The mouth of the cave came into focus. There! Rivka and Hana appeared from the south. From the opposite direction came Ari and someone else—a tall man with a thick beard and one of those bizarre contraptions that the Orthodox wore on their foreheads when they prayed.

Damien checked his watch. 11:55 A.M. They were just a hair early.

The foursome met outside the cave. Rivka hugged Hana. Ari's friend kissed him. On the lips.

Damien almost gagged. What a fruit.

Ari and Rivka and Hana went inside the cave. The other one, Ari's boyfriend, stood stiffly outside, his head turning this way and that, as if looking for someone. *Me.* Damien smiled. *He's on the lookout for me.*

Damien checked the time again. 12:01. When he looked again at the cave, Rivka had come outside. She spoke briefly to the fruit. Damien couldn't read her lips. He was going to have to learn the language eventually, but that would have to wait until he had accomplished his mission.

Minutes ticked by, and Rivka was obviously getting agitated. She paced back and forth. The fruit stood motionless, except for his head, which slowly swiveled back and forth, his eyes scanning the area. He looked just like one of those CIA spooks who used to come to international physics conferences in the bad old days before the Cold War went kaput.

Rivka kept looking at her watch and talking to the fruit.

Then Hana came running out, her face flushed with excitement. She shouted something at Rivka and pointed inside.

Rivka gave one last look around, then shouted one word. *Damien!* Even through a jiggly pair of binoculars, he could lip-read his own name.

Rivka turned and scurried into the cave. Hana followed her in. A minute later, she came back outside. Alone. Crying.

The fruit turned and asked her something.

She nodded and buried her face in her hands. The fruit moved to comfort her, but she pulled away and stepped back into the cave. He made no move to follow her.

Damien put his binoculars back in their case, pocketed them, and stood up. He had seen enough. Ari and Rivka were gone.

Very good. He was alone again.

Somewhere, less than a mile away, was Paul of Tarsus. With luck, he would have a bullet in his head by sundown tomorrow.

And if that failed, Damien would have a second chance the day after. Rivka wouldn't be there to help him find the Chamber of Hewn Stone, but he had figured out a solution anyway. Like a lot of things, the answer turned out to be obvious when you changed the question.

Rivka

Rivka rushed into the cave. Hana had told her to hurry.

Ari knelt at the far end of the cave, almost in the wormhole, his cell phone jammed against his ear. His knuckles looked white, even in the faint light. When he spotted Rivka, he beckoned her frantically. She ran the length of the cave.

"What is it?" she asked.

"Dov," Ari said into the phone. "Tell her what you told me." He handed her the phone.

Rivka pressed it to her ear. "Hello, Dov."

Dov's voice was a whisper, barely audible. "Rivka, *shalom*. The whole world knows you are gone. It is disaster here. When you come back, you will be quarantined for three weeks. Your American president commands that you and Professor West must return at once, lest you disturb the past and destroy the world."

"Dov, Dr. West won't come back unless we force him," Rivka said. "What we need is a weapon—a gun. Can you get us one?"

"I do not know," Dov whispered. "The door to the wormhole is guarded. No one may go through from this side. If you return now, it will be permanent. So please to take excellent notes, yes?"

"Yes," Rivka said. "It's…awesome here, Dov. I can't wait to tell you about it."

"You must hurry," Dov said. "There is a problem. The *Haredim* are fighting to shut down the time machine before *Shabbat*. You have two days left. You must persuade Professor West to return before then."

"I'll pass that along," Rivka said. "But Dr. West is acting strangely. He has a gun. We think he plans to use it."

"I would suggest that you prevent him, Rivka. There is much fear here, and they watch me like an eagle."

The sound of a toilet flushing filled the earpiece. Rivka yanked the phone away from her ear. "What the—?" She turned to Ari. "Was that what I think it was?"

He grinned. "We were fortunate. Dov was in the gentlemen's room when I placed my call."

She held the phone to her ear again. "Good luck, Rivka," Dov said. "I must also speak to Ari again, please."

Rivka handed Ari the phone and stood up. The door to the lab was how far away? Three or four feet? It might as well be three or four light-years. If she went through it, she would not come back.

"Dov!" Ari shouted. He stood up and stared at the phone. "Dov!"

"What happened?" Rivka asked.

"We were cut off," Ari said. "He may have been interrupted."

Rivka began pacing. "Now what do we do?"

"We must do our duty," Ari said. "As a reserve officer in the Israel Defense Force, I have my orders from the prime minister."

"You're in the reserves?"

He gave her an odd look. "Everybody is in the reserves. Except the *Haredim.*"

"What are your orders?"

Ari speed-dialed a number and waited, holding the phone between them. "Answer the phone, Dov!" he whispered at the device. It rang and rang and rang.

Finally Ari snapped it shut. "Perhaps he was discovered. I do not think we can speak to him again."

"What are your orders, Ari?"

Ari jammed the phone into his pocket and stood up straight. His black eyes glowed. "To return with Damien West and you as soon as possible, doing no damage to the fabric of history."

Rivka felt light-headed. "And what if we can't?"

"Then I am to do what is best for the State of Israel," Ari said. "If that requires me to kill Damien West and you and myself, then I am ordered to do so."

❨   ❨   ❨

They sat just inside the cave waiting for dusk. For all they knew, Dr. West might be watching the entrance. If he came to the cave...Rivka shivered. They would have no defense at all. The best they could do was wait awhile and then sneak back into the city when it got on toward darkness.

Meanwhile, they had sent Baruch and Hana to complete a special task. Rivka worried that Baruch would feel ill-at-ease with Hana. But nobody but Baruch could do his part; nobody but Hana could do hers. They would have to work together.

Rivka and Ari passed the time talking, sitting on the floor of the cave with their backs against the wall, not too close together, not too far apart. Even here in the cave, the heat of the day sapped their energy.

"Dov will have a chance tomorrow at 4 A.M." Ari said. "He'll smuggle us the document and a gun. Two guns."

"Why didn't the prime minister just send in the army to find us all?" Rivka asked.

"He is afraid." Ari gave an ironic smile. "They are all afraid that you or I or Damien will do something to disrupt history. If three of us are a danger, how much more so a squad of soldiers." He shook his head. "They are fools, of course."

"You're pretty confident, aren't you?" Rivka asked.

"Because I am correct," Ari said. "It is a logical impossibility that we can change the past. There are only two possibilities to describe our situation. We have tunneled back in time, either within our own universe or into some other."

Rivka smiled. "I can't argue with that. So?"

"Suppose we have gone back in time within our own universe," Ari said. "We know that the trajectory of the universe through phase space must be single-valued."

"Um...what?" Rivka said.

"In simple terms, the past must be globally consistent. The past cannot be both one thing and another. If we have returned to our own past, it is because in that past, three persons arrived from the future."

"And their names were Ari Kazan, Rivka Meyers, and Damien West," Rivka said. "So what happened to them?"

"We do not know. They interacted with people and did things which possibly appeared to them to influence their own past. However, they were merely performing the very acts in that past—this present in which we now find ourselves—which would ensure that the world will take the course which you and I know it will take."

"So they were necessary."

"Exactly," Ari said. "Without them, the ensuing twenty centuries would have been different, and they most probably would not have existed."

"Okay—" Rivka said, not at all sure that this made sense. "But you said there were two possibilities."

"Suppose we have entered a different universe," Ari said. "Then, by definition, we can do no harm to our own."

"Does that make any sense, to go to another universe?"

"It makes perfect sense," Ari said. "There could be infinitely many universes that we know nothing about. It is a well-known theory of quantum mechanics, the many-universe theory. And Hawking's quantum cosmology begins with a wave function of the universe, involving an infinite number of possible universes."

Rivka hesitated, afraid to press. "Could…HaShem be in one of those universes?"

A thin smile creased Ari's face. "It is possible. Or He could be in all of them, or none of them, or above them all."

"Where do you think HaShem lives?" Rivka felt her heart pounding, but she had to know.

"I think…" Ari scratched his beard and then cleared his throat. "Rivka, I have never denied the logical possibility of God. Einstein's God. Reason. Beauty. Truth. Above the universe, ordering it. But not a personal God. Not one who intervenes, not one who answers prayer. Not HaShem of the Bible."

Rivka felt two thin beads of sweat roll down her sides.

Ari coughed. "But a physicist never trusts to logic alone, Rivka. A physicist requires experimental evidence. It need not be much. Einstein won the Nobel prize on the strength of a single observation of the gravitational lensing of starlight during the solar eclipse of 1919, confirming a prediction of his theory."

Rivka studied her fingernails.

"This morning, my life was saved," Ari continued. "I do not have a natural explanation. One could construct some such explanation that excludes HaShem, but it would be absurd. The facts are plain. I stopped breathing. Brother Baruch prayed to the God of our fathers. Something healed me—on a time-scale too short for any normal self-healing process. It is enough proof for this simple and foolish physicist."

Rivka felt a rush of joy in her veins. Suddenly, tears filled her eyes. *Thank You, Father.*

"I do not understand why HaShem should be a personal God," Ari said. "For that matter, I do not understand why quantum mechanics should be statistical, nor why the universe has survived to macroscopic times. But one does not argue with experiment."

There was no doubting Ari had changed in the last few days. Changed a lot. Rivka liked the new Ari. She couldn't forget what he had told her this morning. He was in love with her. It felt nice, in a way. Kind of like that old movie, *Terminator.* Ari had come back in time for her. Just for her.

That was really sweet. There was one little problem, though. She had a rule about guys, based on the hard and cold experiences of a few friends. She didn't get romantically involved with unbelievers. Period. Not today. Not tomorrow. Not yesterday.

And yes, it was wonderful that Ari had now conceded a belief in God. But that wasn't enough. The *Haredim* believed in God, too. But they foamed at the mouth over Yeshua.

"Can I...ask you a question?" Rivka felt a gust of fear blow through her.

"Please."

"What do you think about...Yeshua?"

Ari's face hardened. *"Ze davar aher,"* he said. *That's something else.* "Do you know how many of our people have been murdered in the name of That Man?"

Rivka felt her face flushing. "Yes, I know, Ari. I'm a historian, remember? But I'm not talking about His followers, I'm talking about Him! Yeshua—a real man who died in this city less than thirty years ago. What do you think of Him?"

Ari's black eyes glowed with anger. "Rivka, listen to me. I have no need to think of That Man. The actions of His followers for the last two thousand years drown out all else. I will never worship That Man as a god. Never! I would rather die than be a Christian."

"Okay, okay," Rivka said. "Sorry I brought up the subject." *What an idiot I am!*

Ari

Ari felt thoroughly sick to his stomach. If he had had any chance of earning Rivka's affections, he had shot himself in the brain with that last outburst. But it was true. Wasn't that the important thing? He would never lie about his beliefs. Never.

Footsteps sounded at the entrance to the cave.

Ari jumped up. If it was Damien—

Brother Baruch strode in, his face tight with self-control. Hana followed, her eyes aloof, her mouth set primly. Ari didn't think they had enjoyed their task.

"Blessed be HaShem," Baruch said. "I have found a woman who can keep Sister Rivka. Her name is called Sister Miryam, and she is a follower of Rabban Yeshua."

"I took your old clothes to the woman's house," Hana said to Rivka.

Ari felt gratified. It was the first sentence he had understood completely in Aramaic. Not that it mattered much. They would only be here another day or two.

Ari saw that Hana was crying.

Rivka hugged her. "My friend, it is not safe for me to stay longer in your house. We must not allow Damien to see me, and he is lodging close to your house."

Hana nodded. She understood, but she clearly didn't like it.

"What now, Brother Ari?" Baruch said.

Ari shrugged. "When darkness falls, we will go back into Jerusalem and try to sleep. Early tomorrow morning, we will receive the document and the weapons we need."

God of our fathers, King of the universe, the first and the last, HaShem! Ari clenched his fists. *If ever you answered a prayer, answer this one. Send a weapon. Without a gun, we are powerless.*

TWENTY-THREE

Dov

Four in the morning was not Dov's best time of the day, but it would provide his best chance, he thought. At this hour, Binyamin, the night-shift guard at the door to the wormhole, would be tired. Dov had gotten to know him fairly well in the last few days and thought he might have a weakness.

Dov stood at the door to the lab, took a deep breath, and pushed open the door. "*Shalom*, my friend!" he shouted.

"Who goes there?" The voice did not belong to Binyamin. Dov's heart sagged. He would have turned back if he could, but that would look suspicious. He would have to bluff his way through. Ari and Rivka depended on him.

"Binyamin, is that you? I have brought you a cup of coffee."

"Binyamin fell sick with food poisoning," said the guard. "I replaced him at midnight."

Dov walked toward the back of the lab. The Chinese physicist stood at the controls to the wormhole, dozing on his feet, his hands ready to correct anything amiss. Dov would ask the prime minister to give the physicist a medal when this all ended. "*Hallo*, Dr. Hsiu!"

The physicist nodded at him. And winked. He was ready to play his role in this terrible game.

Dov strode toward the man on guard. "*Shalom,* I am called Dov. Dov Lifshutz."

"I know who you are, Lifshutz," said the guard. "You and Kazan are responsible for all this trouble." He wore an untrimmed beard. Ritual fringes hung down below his army shirt.

Sweat ran down Dov's back until it reached the hard metal gun wedged in the small of his back inside his belt. "It is no doubt we are to blame," Dov said, forcing himself to smile. "We failed to keep watch on that wicked *goy,* the American Professor West."

"West only did what Kazan gave him the knowledge to do."

"Oy!" Dov said, trying frantically to think of what a *Haredi* would say. "All is in the hands of HaShem, yes?"

The guard looked taken aback.

"And what is your name?" Dov asked.

"Mordecai."

"*Shalom, aleicha,* Mordecai. You are not Binyamin, but would you care for his coffee?"

"Is it kosher?"

"Yes." A lie, but for the good of the world. Dov extended his gift. *Now, Dr. Hsiu, please now.*

Mordecai reached out to take the Styrofoam cup.

A blast of sparks shot out from the power supply.

Dov dropped the cup. Both he and Mordecai dove for cover. *Thank you, Dr. Hsiu.* Dov covered his head while sparks flew. By coincidence, he found himself wedged up against the door leading to the wormhole. His hand reached into his jacket pocket, pulled out the sheet of paper, and eased it under the door.

"Hey! Lifshutz! Away from that door!"

He looked up. Mordecai stood with his M-16 leveled at Dov's head.

Dov put on his most innocent face. "The power supply is a terrifying thing, yes? I do not know how you can stand to remain here for many hours through the night." Slowly, he stood up and gestured apologetically at the mess on the floor. "I am sorry about dropping your coffee, my friend."

"Step away from that door and come around this side. Now!"

"Tov me'od," Dov said in his most calming voice. *Very good.*

"Quickly, quickly!"

Dov stepped forward. Too fast. His foot skidded on the wet floor and he staggered forward, then slipped and fell. The hot coffee scalded his palms. He rolled away and beat his hands frantically on his jacket to cool them.

Had Binyamin been there, he would have gone to get some rags to mop up the mess. And Dov would have opened the door and tossed his pistol into the wormhole.

"Up!" Mordecai said. He gestured with his rifle.

Dov stood as quickly as he could and backed away toward Dr. Hsiu.

"Lifshutz, I believe you have a mess to clean up. Be quick about it, and then leave."

Dov blew on his burned hands. They hurt, but not very badly. There would be no serious damage.

Except to the plan. That lay in ruins.

Ari

Ari lay on his belly next to Rivka in the very heart of the wormhole, his ear pressed up to the door, listening. A thin crack of light leaked under the door, allowing him to see a little. Tears ran down Rivka's face. Ari wanted to cry, too.

Dov had failed.

Ari gestured with his head. "Back!" he whispered.

Rivka nodded. Together, they crawled backward until they were safely in the past. Here it was pitch-black, the radiation-diffusing properties of the wormhole eliminating the light from the door crack.

Ari clutched the folded sheet of paper. For now, this was all they had. He pulled his flashlight out of his backpack and shined it on the paper.

	A	B	C	D	E
1	1/F	5/27	5/S	21:17	P. 2 Jer.
2	2/S	5/28	6/S	21:18	P.2 Ja.
3	3/S	5/29	7/S	21:26	P. 2 T. 1
4	5/T	5/31	9/S	21:27	P. 2 T. 2*
5	6/W	6/1	10/S	22:30	P. @ S.*
6	7/T	6/2	11/S	23:12	P. exit Jer.*
7	8/F	6/3	12/S	23:32	P. 2 Cae.
8	12/T	6/7	16/S	24:01	P. @ F.*

It didn't make much sense to Ari.

"Let's go outside," Rivka said. "I want to get as far away from that wormhole as possible."

They went outside but found it too dark to see without Ari's flashlight. At four in the morning, the sun wouldn't rise for another hour or so. And today being the ninth day of the lunar month, the moon had gone down a few hours ago.

They sat on the ground and shined the light on the paper. "What do you think?" Ari asked.

"Column B is obviously a set of dates," Rivka said. "May 27 to June 7."

"Agreed," Ari said. "You Americans put the month first, contrary to all reason."

"And column D looks like times," Rivka said. "It's very strange. 21:17—that would be 9:17 P.M. They go all the way up to one minute past midnight. What does that mean?"

Ari shrugged. Something nagged at his brain, but he couldn't quite place it.

"Then column A has to be a set of numbered days, starting with Friday, then Saturday, Sunday." Rivka did some silent counting on her fingers. "Yes, they correlate all the way down the line."

"Then perhaps column C is the set of corresponding dates in the Jewish calendar," Ari said. "5 Sivan, 6 Sivan, down to 16 Sivan."

"Is that possible, that Dr. West calculated the Jewish calendar for this year?" Rivka said. "Why would he do that? What's special about these dates?"

"Anything is possible," Ari said and then hastily corrected himself. "Except for those things which are impossible."

"What a genius!" Rivka said, a smile in her voice. "Is that what they gave you the Ph.D. for?"

Ari laughed out loud. "Touché, my friend. I was thinking of the saying in physics that everything not forbidden is required. I believe Gell-Mann said it first."

"Weird idea," said Rivka. "I don't care who said it."

"Very well, we must yet explain column E," Ari said. "It makes no sense to me."

They both stared at the paper for several minutes.

"Oh! I see it!" Rivka said.

"What do you see?"

"Those numbers in column D," Rivka said. "Those aren't times. They're verse numbers."

"Verses?" Ari said. "Like in the Bible?"

"The New Testament," Rivka said. "The Book of Acts. Look at column E and read down. 'P. 2 Jer.' That means Paul to Jerusalem."

"And the next one? 'P. 2 Ja.' What does that mean?"

"Paul to James. Paul met with a man named James the day after arriving in town. I would guess that was Saturday night."

"Brother Yaakov," Ari said. "He gave Renegade Saul an ultimatum after *Shabbat* ended."

"How do you know?"

"Brother Baruch told me."

"Yaakov is James in Hebrew. That confirms it then. And look at the rest of these. I can read them all. 'P. 2 T. 1.' That's the next day, Paul's first visit to the Temple. Then two days later, 'P. 2 T. 2 *.' That's his second visit to the Temple."

"What does the asterisk mean?"

"I don't know. But the next day, P. @ S.*, means Paul at the Sanhedrin."

"And another asterisk," Ari said. "We still don't know what that means."

"Then the next day, Paul exits Jerusalem—with an asterisk. The next day, Paul to Caesarea, no asterisk. Then four days later, Paul at Felix."

"Asterisk."

"Oh my gosh!" Rivka said, grabbing the spreadsheet.

"What, Rivka?"

"Oh my gosh! Oh my gosh! Oh my gosh!"

"What is it?"

"Every one of those asterisks marks an incident in which Paul's location is known precisely."

Ari stared at her. "Are you serious?"

"He's going to kill Paul." The spreadsheet in her hands began to shake. "That's why he brought a gun."

Ari closed his eyes. His pulse hammered in his skull. What if Damien really succeeded in shooting Paul? What would that mean for the subsequent history of Christianity? Without Paul, could there have been Augustine? Luther?

Hitler?

All of which was useless speculation. You couldn't change the past. It was mathematically impossible. As a physicist, Ari felt dead certain that Damien must fail.

But as a Jew, Ari wished him all the luck in the world.

Damien

Damien locked the door of his rented house and strode down the street. *Here I come, Paul, ready or not!*

Today was Tuesday, May 31, in the year-of-somebody-else's-Lord 57. Today, Damien was going to throw a giant monkey wrench into the gears of history. The past would never be the same again.

Damien grinned. He enjoyed making bad puns about time.

He wondered what would happen to the future world to which Ari and Rivka had returned. He guessed it would be like in that movie *Back to the Future*. The future would simply... never happen. More correctly, the future would turn out different from the one he remembered.

The death of Paul several years early would have a ripple effect. If a butterfly sneezing in Beijing could cause a tornado in Kansas, then a bullet in the brain of Paul would derail the whole history of the church. He wouldn't live to write all those books that messed with people's heads. He wouldn't convert anybody in Rome, so you could kiss the papacy good-bye. As the years passed, the new future would diverge more and more from the old one.

Luther, Bacon, Newton—they would be different men, uncontaminated by the evil effects of Christianity. There would be no Western rationalism, no rise of science, no industrial revolution. No physicists. Not even a Dr. Damien West. Wasn't that a pretty little paradox?

Not really, Damien decided. He had already ceased to exist within the old future. Therefore, his existence didn't require that future. He was here, and it made no difference how he got here. You could tie yourself in knots worrying about philosophical nitwittery. What mattered was what you could touch, see, measure.

Such as the kinetic energy of a hollow-point +P loaded nine millimeter bullet. That was reality. Philosophy was garbage.

A few minutes later, he arrived at the southern entrance of the Temple Mount. He went in through the giant gates and climbed the many dozen steps ascending through the belly of the Temple Mount. Finally he emerged in the bright morning sunlight in the outer court of the Temple.

Rivka had been good enough to show him the exact spot where Paul would address the crowd sometime today. The place was at the north end of the huge court. Damien took his time walking there. He had plenty of time. It would be hours before Paul got himself arrested.

Then things would happen quickly. Damien wanted to spend the time scouting the killing ground. Preparation was the key.

If you anticipated everything, you would be ready for anything.

Ari

Ari felt a cold knot tightening in his stomach. "Rivka, this is crazy. We don't even know Damien's going to be there today."

She quickened her stride. "I'll bet you anything that Paul's going to be there," she said. "And if Dr. West doesn't show, he's a fool. It's his first chance."

"Rivka, this is useless. Damien has a gun. What good can we do?"

"We can do more good there than we can sitting in Baruch's house," Rivka said. "Besides, I thought your orders were to prevent Dr. West from messing anything up."

"Yes, correct." *But since it is logically impossible for Damien to change the future, why should I do anything?* Ari cleared his throat. "Very well, then, what exactly do you plan to do?"

"I don't know," Rivka said. "I know Paul will be arrested in the inner Temple, and I know Dr. West won't try anything there."

"How do you know that?"

"Because he's a *goy,* and he looks like one," Rivka said. "If he tried to get into the inner Temple, he would be stoned on the spot. Oddly enough, that's the charge Paul will be facing—that he's trying to take a *goy* in with him."

"Is he really going to try that?" Ari asked.

"No, of course not," Rivka said. "He wouldn't get ten feet beyond the barrier with a *goy.* Even if he did, the Levite guards would kill them both on the spot. The *goy* would provide all the evidence you would need that Paul was guilty. The fact is that Paul will be held for two years, and then he'll be released for lack of evidence."

"That's crazy," Ari said. "They can't do that."

"Political prisoners were held much longer in the twentieth century," Rivka said.

"Will be held," Ari said. "None of that has happened yet."

"Whatever." Rivka stopped suddenly.

"What's up?" Ari asked. They were standing at the southwest corner of the Temple Mount. It looked far more impressive than he remembered it from modern Jerusalem. At this corner, the glistening white limestone towered above them at a height equal to a fifteen-story building. Amazing.

"We have a choice of several entrances," Rivka said. She pointed toward the largest one: the Huldah Gates on the south side. "I definitely don't want to take that one."

"Why not?"

"Because that's the one I took Dr. West through the other day, when we went on our little tour of the Temple Mount. Odds are he'll go that way, since it's familiar to him. I really don't want to run into him just yet."

"You gave him a tour?"

She winced. "I was stupid enough to show him the exact spot where Paul is going to stand when he addresses the people."

"When Paul does what?" Ari asked. "You'll forgive me for my ignorance, but I don't quite understand the sequence of events."

"It's simple," Rivka said. "A riot starts in the inner Temple around Paul. The mob carries him out and down the steps into the outer court, presumably on the north side."

"How do you know?"

"I don't know for sure," Rivka said. "But it's a good guess. The Romans are standing watch over the Temple Mount on the north side, which adjoins their Fortress Antonia. They see the riot and intervene, arresting Paul. They take him north to the Antonia, and then Paul gets permission to speak to the crowd. It's quite a long speech—five or ten minutes at least."

"Standing still the whole time?" Ari asked.

"Yes, at the top of some stairs."

"Totally exposed to anyone with a gun."

"That's right."

"Then what happens?" Ari asked.

"The crowd riots again, and Paul gets hauled into the Antonia. For the next few days, he's in Roman custody. He comes out briefly for one quick trip to the Sanhedrin, but mostly he's locked up out of sight."

"I thought you said he would be in prison for two years," Ari said.

"Yes, but not here in Jerusalem," Rivka said. "Today is Tuesday. Tomorrow, he goes before the Sanhedrin. Thursday night, the Romans sneak him out of town."

"How did you pin down the dates?"

"I didn't," Rivka said. "Dr. West did, or rather he made some good guesses which are turning out to be correct. He got the year right, and he got the date of *Shavuot* nearly right. He missed it by a day, but it doesn't matter. I went over every verse in my head and made a little table of possibilities. With some reasonable assumptions, it turns out that you can narrow down the day of the arrest to one day. Today."

"What kind of assumptions?"

"Well, we have a record of a number of events happening over about two weeks' time. Some of those events can't happen on *Shabbat*, because Jews wouldn't be doing such things on *Shabbat*. There's a funny gap in the middle, but you can bridge it because you know the whole episode runs twelve days, start to finish."

"And you're sure today's the day?"

"I'm not sure," Rivka said. "But Dr. West is, and that makes me nervous. If he's right, he'll have Paul lined up in his sights before the sun goes down tonight."

"He'll fail," Ari said.

"Darn right, he'll fail!" Rivka said. "I'm going to make him fail, if I have to take a bullet to stop him."

Ari felt a cold stab of fear in his soul. If anything happened to her he would go crazy.

He was already going crazy, seeing her so close, knowing she was so far from him. He had chased her through time to get a second chance, but as far as she was concerned, he had never even had a first chance. Not that she disliked him. So far as he could tell, she rather enjoyed his company. It was nothing personal—just religion. Because she was a Christian. Because he wasn't. Because she would never change, and neither would he.

Suddenly Rivka grabbed Ari's arm. "Don't move."

Ari wouldn't have moved if all the hornets in Jerusalem had been after him.

"You won't believe this," Rivka said, releasing him, breathing again. "Dr. West just passed by, maybe sixty yards behind you. He's heading toward the gates of the Temple Mount."

"Did he have a gun?" Ari asked.

"I didn't see one," Rivka said. "But I know he has it."

"How do you know?"

"I just know."

"Did he see us?" Ari asked.

"If he had, we would be in deep trouble right now."

"We're already in deep trouble," Ari said. "How are you going to stop a man with a gun, Rivka? Seriously."

"He's gone in through the southern gates." She grabbed Ari's hand and pulled him toward the corner stairway. "Come on, we're going up a different way, and then we'll follow Dr. West."

Ari followed, but only because she was leading him by the hand.

Crazy, crazy, crazy.

Rivka

They had followed Dr. West for a quarter of an hour. "He's not going anywhere until Paul comes, I'll bet," Rivka said. Dr. West had scouted all around the stairway leading up to the Antonia Fortress. He had taken up a position in the shade of the northern portico.

"Let's get out of here, then," Ari said. "I don't want him to spot us here. Right now, he thinks we're about two thousand years away. We might as well keep him thinking that as long as possible."

Rivka shivered. *How am I going to stop a nut with a gun?* "Okay, let's go back to the inner Temple. I want to keep an eye out for Paul."

"You're not thinking of warning him, are you?"

"No, it wouldn't do any good," Rivka said. "But if we stay near Paul, we can go along with the mob and have a reasonable chance of not being seen by Dr. West, right?"

"I suppose so." Ari's voice sounded doubtful. They walked along in silence until they reached the foot of the stairs leading up to the inner Temple. "Rivka, are you really going to try to stop a bullet?"

Rivka swallowed hard. "If I have to...yes." *Oh, God, I hope I don't have to. Please, Father, help!*

"I can't allow you to do that," Ari said.

Rivka stopped walking and stared at him. "Just what do you mean by that? I don't recall you being appointed my legal guardian."

Ari's face reddened. "I mean that I...have feelings for you. Strong feelings. It will be physically impossible for me to watch you take a bullet."

"Oh, great!" Rivka said. "Just listen up, Mr. Soldier in the Israel Defense Force! I'm going to do what it takes to stop Dr. West. If that means getting hurt, then I'll take my chances. I thought you had orders from your prime minister? Or doesn't that matter when you're infatuated?" Furious, she spun on her heel and marched up the steps. If Ari wasn't going to help, then why had he even bothered to come along?

She heard Ari's footsteps behind her. "Rivka, please!"

Ignore him. Rivka kept going. It was one thing that Ari had a crush on her. But it was another thing to let him mess up all of history.

"Rivka!"

This argument would rip her apart if she let it. Everything within her told her to leave Dr. West alone. She could stop one bullet, but she couldn't stop more. Obviously, God had some plan. The sensible thing would be to sit back with Ari and watch this movie play out. But what if God had chosen her to play the lead? Maybe Ari was the leading man—wouldn't that be nice? Or maybe he was the bad guy. God hadn't given her the script. But He had given her a gut instinct, and that told her to fight. Fight Damien. Fight Ari.

Right now.

She reached the top of the stairs, went in through the massive iron gate, and suddenly broke into a run.

"Rivka, stop!"

The thin mid-morning crowd didn't slow her much. Rivka sprinted through the people dotting the Court of Women. All she could think of was ditching Ari. The court was huge—you could play soccer in there. By the time she reached the other side, Rivka was out of breath. Where was Ari? At the south gate, she stopped to look back. Ari had stopped thirty yards behind her, and was now helping an old man to his feet and apologizing. He turned to look at Rivka.

She spun around and ran blindly.

And slammed into someone.

Together they staggered down several steps. Then a strong pair of hands gripped her arms.

"*Zonah!*" Rivka looked up into the angry black eyes of a young Temple guard.

An absurd thought flashed through her mind.

Go to jail. Go directly to jail. Do not stop Dr. West. Do not collect two hundred dollars.

TWENTY-FOUR

Ari

One minute, Rivka had been in sight. The next minute, she was gone. Ari felt panic stabbing him in the gut. He dashed toward the south gate. Where was Rivka?

When he reached the gate, he stopped short. Several steps below, a young Temple guard held Rivka at arm's length, a look of distaste scrawled across his face.

Rivka said something to the guard and then kicked at his shins.

In response, the young man shook her hard and said something that sounded like *zonah*. Which meant she was in big trouble.

Ari had no time to think. He marched down the steps and jabbed his finger at the guard's face. "You will take your hands off my wife at once," he said in his best biblical Hebrew.

A look of enormous surprise washed across the young guard's face. "You are a scholar, *Adoni?*" he said in excellent Hebrew.

"Yes, of course," Ari said. It was true and it wasn't, depending on how you defined a scholar. Right now, he just wanted to get Rivka out of this thug's claws.

"And how do I know she is your wife?" said the guard.

"Very simple," Ari said. He turned to Rivka and whispered in English, "Kiss me." He leaned toward her.

She spat in his face and hissed something in Aramaic.

How dare she? Ari felt like turning around right then and walking away. Instead he wiped the spit off his face and smeared it on her tunic.

The guard laughed harshly. "Very well, my scholar. She is obviously your wife. Take her home and beat her well." He shoved her into Ari's arms.

Ari stared at him stupidly. *What was going on?*

"Get me out of here," Rivka whispered in English.

Ari seized her arm and yanked her away. Together they marched down the stairs toward the outer court. When they reached the lower level, he said, "What happened back there?"

"Were you trying to get me stoned?" Rivka asked. "In this culture, a wife never kisses her husband in public. The only woman who would do such a thing is a *zonah.*"

"Oh." Ari suddenly felt light-headed.

"You could have got me killed," Rivka said. "You would have got off with only a warning, of course."

"Forgive me," Ari said. "I was only trying to help."

"If you really want to help, you'll let go of my arm so I can do my job," Rivka said.

"And your job is…?"

"The same as yours!" Rivka said. "Stop Dr. West."

Ari released his grip on her arm. "At any cost?"

"Yes, of course." Rivka rubbed her upper arm. "Ouch, that hurts."

"It is nothing compared to a bullet."

"Listen, Ari, there's one thing you should know about me." Rivka put both hands on her hips and tilted her chin up at him. "I never give up. When I decide to do something, I just go do it. And I've decided to stop Dr. West."

"And how do you know you will succeed?"

She smiled at him, and he felt his heart do a double back flip. "Simple. You told me I'll win."

"I told you?" Ari laughed out loud. "Perhaps we should not speak English anymore, my friend. Evidently, I do not express myself well in that language, if you are so misguided—"

"Just follow through on your own logic, Mr. Hotshot Physicist," Rivka said. "You already told me that two thousand years before our own century, three time travelers arrived in Jerusalem. One, Dr. Damien West, came on a mission to kill Paul of Tarsus with a gun. And you claim that Dr. West failed. Some nonsense about a single-valued trajectory of the universe, right?"

"Yes, but—"

"Let me finish," Rivka said. "How could he possibly fail, Ari? He has surprise on his side, and a weapon against which Paul has no defense. How did he fail?"

"Something…happened," Ari said. "How should I know?"

"Exactly," she said. "Rivka Meyers happened, that's what. Rivka stopped him. Don't ask me how, but she did it."

"You are forgetting one thing, my lovely logician," Ari said. He liked her spunk, her tenacity, her willingness to fight for what she thought right. He just didn't like where she was going with this particular fight.

She simply looked at him as if he had said nothing.

"It is possible that we have not traveled back into the past of our own universe," Ari said. "It is mathematically possible that we have transferred to a parallel universe—one in which Paul of Tarsus is assassinated by a man with a gun."

Something seemed to deflate in Rivka. Her shoulders sagged, and the fire went out of her eyes. "In that case…is our own universe safe?"

"Oh yes," Ari said. "Quite safe. It is you who is not safe—in either scenario."

"And how do we know which universe we're in?" Rivka asked.

Ari shrugged. "We don't yet. We can perform a little experiment to find out."

"And that would be…?"

"We watch Damien," Ari said. "If he kills Paul, then we are not in our own universe, but some other."

"And if he fails?"

"Then we do not know," Ari said. "We can only know if we see events diverging from the actual history of our own universe."

Rivka's black eyes closed for a long moment. Then she opened them. "Fine then, Ari. Take a seat and do your little experiment. If you think this is like some computer simulation where nobody really gets hurt, then you're wrong. This is reality, even if it's somebody else's reality."

"And what makes you so sure you're the one to stop Damien?"

"Because I'm here. Because I know his plan. Because I want more than anything to stop him." She smiled serenely up at Ari. "I've figured it out. I'm God's avatar."

"So God controls everything you do, like a puppet?"

"No, I still have free will. God tells me what to do, and I can choose whether to obey or not. Right now, He's telling me to go stop Dr. West, whatever it takes."

Whatever it takes. Ari had to admit that one of the reasons he liked Rivka was her gung ho spirit, her willingness to just go do whatever she had set her heart to do. But the idea of her stopping bullets terrified him. "Aren't you afraid of dying, Rivka?"

She pushed past him and began walking along the perimeter of the dividing wall that marked the area forbidden to *goyim*.

"Of course I am," she said. "I don't enjoy pain, Ari. Nobody does. But I'm not afraid of being dead."

Ari trotted after her. "Neither am I," he said. "I'm afraid of being alive if you're dead."

"How romantic," Rivka said.

"Don't be sarcastic," Ari said. "I don't want anything to happen to you."

"I'm flattered," she said. "Really, Ari, I am. And not only that, I like you. Did I tell you that yet? You're the most interesting guy I've ever met, although we have a serious difference of opinion on religion. That's a problem. But I have a job to do right now. So please, if you're not going to help me, just don't get in my way, okay?"

Ari didn't say anything. They rounded the corner, and the whole northern half of the outer court came into view. Rivka hadn't said she wouldn't have him. She had said they had a difference of opinion. A woman could change her mind about religious differences. All he had to do was—

"Okay, Ari? Promise me you won't get in my way?"

Ari was about to answer when he heard a shout above them, in the inner Temple. A loud shout. His head spun around. "What did they say?"

"Men of Israel, come to our aid!" Rivka said in Hebrew. "Ari, it's starting!"

"What's starting?"

Rivka grabbed his hand and tugged. "Come on, we're in the way. There's going to be a riot, and we need to get ready for it."

"Ready? How do we get ready for a—"

She pulled him toward the west. "In a minute, there's going to be a mob standing right here. I want that mob between us and Dr. West."

Ari followed her. *What was he supposed to do?*

The noise above them grew louder. A minute later, several young men dashed out of the gate and down the broad expanse of steps into the outer court. "Find some stones!" one of them shouted.

"Bring out the lawbreaker!"

A knot of men appeared at the gate, arms thrashing at someone, feet kicking. Ari tensed. He hated to see violence. The memory of Dov struggling underwater in the hands of the Arabs flashed through his brain. He started forward.

Rivka caught his sleeve. "Don't interfere," she said. "The cavalry is on the way."

Damien

Damien had been preparing for this moment for the last two years, and still it caught him by surprise. One minute, the vast outer court of the Temple hummed with peaceful activity—men standing in clusters gossiping, scholars and students arguing under the shade of the giant open-air porticoes.

And now, from nowhere, a riot had come spilling out of the inner Temple and down into the outer court.

He had not expected so many people. Where was Paul in all that mess?

Shouts suddenly issued from the portico roof above Damien. Latin. He relaxed. The Romans were coming, right on schedule. The clatter of iron-soled boots on wood rang out overhead. A dozen soldiers dashed down the stairway from the portico roof and into the outer court.

Damien remembered a Campus Crusader who had once given him a pamphlet with a title something like *You Can Trust the Bible*. Sure enough, this little story was playing out just like it said in the Bible. Too bad for Paul. Damien held his place and waited.

Now the soldiers had covered half the distance to the still-escalating riot. Damien raised his binoculars. This would be interesting. A handful of Roman soldiers against a mob. How were they going to handle this?

They handled it like Los Angeles cops.

Forming into a wedge, they rammed through the crowd with shields forward. The people trampled each other to get out of the way. An old man, clipped by a shield, actually became airborne. In less than a minute, the Romans arrived at the mob scene, a couple of hundred yards from where Damien watched.

He studied the Romans. Each of them had a short, broad sword of iron. At the sight of the naked blades, the mob calmed down in a hurry.

If these Jews were cowed by mere swords, wait till they saw what a gun could do.

The soldiers formed into a circle. Presumably, Paul was in the center, but Damien couldn't see him. According to the historians, Paul was supposed to be short. But no worry. In five minutes, he would be standing still at the top of the stairs, waiting to catch some lead.

Damien lowered his binoculars.

Uh, oh.

He remembered reading in the Bible that the crowd would be large and noisy. He just hadn't expected it to look like hooligans at an English soccer match.

Damien watched while the mob spilled around the circle of Romans on all sides, a swarming human anthill. The noise beat on Damien's ears. The violence had resumed, worse than before. It would be impossible to aim a gun while in the middle of all that.

Damien fought panic. *Stay calm.* According to the Bible, things would settle down and Paul would give a speech. For the first time in many years, Damien hoped something in that book was true.

The red-feathered helmets of the soldiers stood out above the crowd, marking ground zero. For several minutes, Damien watched them come closer. Time to join the party. *Now.* He moved forward and muscled his way into the mob. The only thing that could go wrong would be to drop his gun. He kept it buried in his left armpit, smothered in his strong right hand.

The Romans began ascending the staircase. The noise grew louder—a physical pain in Damien's ears. When the soldiers reached the top of the steps, they stopped. An officer stepped forward and entered the circle. Damien held his breath. Would he really get a chance for a shot? He stood only about fifty yards away from the soldiers, close enough to make a guaranteed kill in a shooting range. But this wasn't a shooting range. This wild, roiling crowd made him feel like a cork in a blender. And even if these fools settled down, he would never find room to extend his arm to take aim.

Suddenly, the circle of soldiers broke open and two men stepped forward: the Roman officer and a small man with one of those Jewish prayer shawls over his head. Paul of Tarsus. Damien couldn't even see his eyes, but that didn't matter. Pumping a couple of hollow-point bullets into his chest would do the trick.

The Roman held up his hand, and then pointed to Paul.

Magically, the crowd began to quiet. Not all at once, but much faster than an English soccer crowd would have. Or an American one. Obviously, primitive cultures lacking microphones had to behave differently, or their public speakers wouldn't be audible.

Paul made a gesture with his right arm, and this seemed to quiet things down even more. Damien was astounded. Within half a minute, the mob turned into a bunch of pussycats. It was still densely packed, and Damien had no way on earth to get his gun up to aim.

But he saw an obvious solution to that problem. Get to the front of the crowd. That would put him within fifteen or twenty yards of the target. At that range, it would take half a second to raise his arm, aim, and double-tap a couple of rounds.

Piece of cake.

On the steps above the crowd, Paul began speaking. Damien looked at his watch. If he remembered right, Paul was going to give quite a little monologue here—at least ten minutes.

Damien chose a spot with his eyes at the base of the steps, less than forty yards away. Could he cover that distance in ten minutes?

No problem.

He twisted his shoulder in between the two men in front of him and pushed.

Rivka

Rivka massaged her left arm above the elbow. Someone had slugged her there before things had settled down. "Ari, do you see anything?"

Several people turned and glared at her. Evidently, when these people listened to a public speaker, they *listened.*

Under most circumstances, Rivka would have loved to hear this sermon. Paul himself! He had a strong voice and spoke in an educated style, but without the rhetorical flourishes that were currently in vogue among professional orators.

But these were not ordinary circumstances. *Where was Dr. West?* Rivka's heart thumped out a double-time dance, without benefit of flutes or lyres. She and Ari stood at the very back of the crowd. That was fine for Ari—he rose a head taller than most anybody out here. But Rivka was only five foot two—the wrong height for the task at hand.

And Ari was completely useless. His lips had compressed into a thin line, and an utterly aloof expression masked his face. Rivka wanted to strangle him.

At least he had given up on trying to keep her out of the action.

But what could she do? Probably ten or twenty thousand people jammed this area. Only one of them had a gun.

God, help me!

Rivka closed her eyes and tried to focus on God. If she was ever going to hear from Him, now would be an excellent time.

But she heard only the voice of Paul. "I persecuted the followers of the sect called The Way."

She concentrated on the words. She could see them in her mind's eye on the printed page. In English.

Acts chapter 22.

Paul was playing out his part, and Rivka had read the script. But Dr. West would try to rewrite the ending.

Could he do that? Ari didn't think so. But Dr. West thought he could.

How could she stop him?

The words stood out sharp in her mind's eye, black letters on white paper. She scanned ahead. How was it *supposed* to end?

Suddenly, Rivka couldn't remember. Panic burned through her veins, and she couldn't focus anymore, couldn't think. What had gone wrong with her mind? She opened her eyes and looked around. Ahead of her loomed a wall of heads. Behind her...

Behind her was nothing. Up ahead, off to the west side, lay a pile of debris—large paving stones, loose dirt, small rocks. Evidently, the feast had interrupted some construction project, and the workmen had just shoved it all into one big pile, rather than doing a decent job of cleaning up.

"...You will be his witness to all men of what you have seen and heard..." Paul said.

How much time left? Rivka couldn't think. On impulse, she scampered to the debris pile and scrambled up onto it. It rose only a few feet, but it raised her above the crowd. She shaded her eyes from the bright sunlight and scanned the assembly.

And saw movement.

Near the bottom of the stairs, Dr. West's pink cheeks stood out in a sea of dark faces. He wedged his left shoulder between two men and shoved forward. Two heads spun around, glared at him, and then...

And then moved aside.

Dr. West was moving.

About five yards separated him from the base of the stairs.

And now Paul was talking about Stephen, martyred for Yeshua. The crowd stood silent as sleepwalkers.

Get mad, you fools!

Only three yards to go, and then Dr. West would have a clear shot.

"I stood there giving my approval and guarding the clothes of those who were killing him," Paul said.

No reaction from the crowd.

Do something, people!

Two more yards.

"Then the Lord said to me, 'Go; I will send you far away to the *goyim*.'"

One yard.

Do something yourself, Rivka.

Rivka bent down, scooped up a handful of dust, and flung it into the air. "No!" she screamed. "Kill him! Kill him! Kill him! He's not fit to live!" She grabbed some dirt clods and threw them into the crowd, in the general direction of Dr. West. People might get hurt, but she had to think of Paul right now.

Dr. West spun to his left and caught her eye. His jaw dropped open, and shock slashed across his face.

"Kill him!" Rivka screamed again. She threw more dust in the air.

Suddenly, the mob came to life—a mad, writhing thing at the foot of the stairs. Dust flew in the air. Shouts of rage shook the court.

A vortex of violence caught Dr. West off balance. He stumbled, fell.

On the stairs above, the soldiers closed around Paul again. In seconds, they whisked him away toward the Fortress Antonia.

An instant later, Ari arrived beside Rivka. He grabbed her shoulders and pulled her away from the madness toward the shadow of the western portico. "That was crazy," he said. "Why did you do that? You started a riot!"

"I saw him," she said. "Dr. West! He was really close to Paul. And I stopped him."

"Oh, you stopped him all right," Ari said. "And if anything could mess up history, it was that little stunt."

Rivka gave him her winningest smile. "I'm surprised at you, Mr. Fatalist Physicist. We're part of history, you and I. Part of that self-consistent history of the wave function of the single-valued trajectory of the universal phase space. Did I get that right?"

Ari laughed out loud. "Not exactly."

"Okay, whatever. All I'm saying is, if you had read the script, you would know this act was *supposed* to end in a riot."

"Rivka, it would not have turned out that way without you."

"Exactly. I'm feeling very self-consistent today, very single-valued. Very in touch with the wave function of the universe." She dusted her palms off on her tunic, giddy with relief. She had done it! Thank God. "Now let's get out of here before Dr. West comes looking for us. I have a feeling he's not going to be very happy with the way I directed this scene."

TWENTY-FIVE

Damien

Damien stared at Rivka Meyers. What the…? A shower of dirt rained down around him. *Move! Now!* Damien shoved forward, jamming an elbow into somebody's back. The man in front of him turned, bellowed something, and slugged Damien in the face. Then the whole world went berserk. Somebody pushed the wrong way, and half a dozen people went down, with Damien in the middle.

He lost his grip on the gun. A knee caught him in the mouth. He pawed for the weapon furiously, found it, checked the safety, clutched it to his belly, and huddled up, protecting his face. He wouldn't be able to move until these fools got off him.

What was Rivka Meyers doing in this century, anyway? Hadn't she gone home with Ari yesterday? Did she come back? Or had she not gone after all?

Whatever, she had ruined his shot. For that she would pay. For that, he was going to kill her. Tonight.

He would get another chance to shoot Paul tomorrow.

Ari

"Rivka will be safe here for another night," Brother Baruch said. "Your Damien has no way to know where she is staying. Sister Miryam will take good care of her."

Ari stepped out of the stone house and into the street. He thumped his hand against the solid wood door. Strong. Still, he felt worried. Two women alone in this house? He would have preferred to keep Rivka at Brother Baruch's house, but that was impossible. It would scandalize Baruch and his friends. Nor could Ari stay with Rivka and Sister Miryam. "I still think we should go back tonight," he said. "Damien's got to be furious at you."

"Relax, Ari, we'll be fine," Rivka said. "Dr. West won't have a clue where to look for either one of us in this city."

"Promise me you won't go out alone tomorrow," Ari said. "I'll come for you early, we'll say our good-byes to our friends, and we'll go back to where we belong."

Just then, Hana clutched at Rivka's arm and said something in Aramaic.

Rivka shook her head. "No, Hana, I am not worried."

Ari had caught most of Hana's sentence. "Please repeat her last phrase."

"She says that the truth-tellers warn her that I am not safe here, that the bad man will find me and kill me."

Ari felt annoyed. It was one thing to base your fears on reason, but this sort of silliness irritated him. "She will be fine," Ari said in his broken Aramaic. "Do not fear." Somehow, saying so made him feel better.

Hana didn't look convinced.

Baruch tugged at Ari's sleeve. "Come, Brother Ari, we must go to evening prayers. We will pray that no harm will come to

Rivka, and it will be so. And then you will continue explaining to me this evening about how HaShem created the universe."

Ari grinned. Baruch had taken an absurd interest in quantum physics. He probably understood none of what Ari had explained over the last few days, but still he kept hammering him with questions. So far, they had covered atomic theory and the nucleus. "Very well, Brother Baruch." Ari winked at Rivka. "I'll come find you tomorrow morning."

"Not too early," she said. "I want to sleep in."

"Fine," Ari said. "It'll give me time to finish my lectures."

"Say about eight o'clock," Rivka said.

Ari shrugged. "As long as it's before early afternoon. Dov says we need to come back before then, at the very latest. And you know how the *Haredim* go around with their loudspeakers at four in the afternoon, announcing *Shabbat*."

"We'll go back in plenty of time," Rivka said. "Now go say your prayers, Brother Ari."

Ari liked the way she said that. Brother Ari. He turned and headed up the street with Brother Baruch.

"So explain to me again, from what did HaShem build the nucleus?" Baruch said.

"Quarks," Ari said. "It's really very simple...."

Damien

Damien twisted the silencer onto his gun and laced up his heavy boots. By this hour, Rivka would be asleep in Hana's house. The night air hung heavy and humid and uncomfortably warm around him, making his skin crawl. Nights like this drove him crazy.

He slipped out of his house, locked the door, and thudded down the street as quietly as he could in his thick boots. He wore his Arab robe, as he had since coming through the wormhole. It had no pockets, but he had grown to like using the cloth belt that the natives wore. His gun nestled in a shoulder harness inside his robe.

When he arrived, he listened at the door for a full minute. No noise inside. Excellent. The women would be asleep. He would break in, shoot them both, and leave. He felt wound up like an overcharged capacitor. Adrenaline shot through his arteries.

The door looked poorly made. Damien pulled out his flashlight and studied it, choosing his spot carefully. He wanted the door to break on the first or second kick. No reason to give Rivka time to prepare her defenses.

Damien took out his gun, flicked the safety off, raised a booted foot, and kicked hard at the door. It cracked sharply, but held. He kicked again, then twice more in quick succession.

The door flew inward.

Damien stepped in, his gun extended, moving quickly but without panic. Find the women first, before they had time to react.

His flashlight beam skittered around the room. Movement at the far end, on the floor. One head lifted. Hana's voice.

Damien lit up her face for an instant, then danced the beam in quick patterns all around her. Where was Rivka?

Hana said something again.

"Rivka," Damien said. *"Eyfo Rivka?"* Pidgin modern Hebrew, but he hoped the meaning would carry over. He shone the light full on her now.

She cowered on her bedroll, gabbling hysterically. Rivka was sleeping somewhere else tonight, that was obvious.

Damien stepped across the room in three strides and kicked Hana. Not hard enough to make her useless, but hard enough to get her attention.

"Eyfo Rivka?" he demanded. If she didn't lead him to Rivka, he would kill her. And if she did lead him to Rivka, he would still kill her.

She huddled into a ball, shielding her head.

Still holding back, Damien kicked her again, once in the side, once on the back of the head. The idea in any interrogation was to inflict pain, not unconsciousness.

Hana sobbed and began talking again. Damien couldn't understand her. But that didn't matter. She would take him to Rivka. But first, a little business discussion...

Dov

Ten minutes before midnight on Thursday night, Dov came out of the Israeli Supreme Court building with Jessica and her lawyer cousin. A tidal wave of flashbulbs nearly blinded him. Further back, the steady glare of TV lights provided backup. Twenty microphones almost magically appeared in front of his face. A hundred questions battered him, most of them variations on the same theme.

"Mr. Lifshutz, what have they decided?"

Dov heaved a sigh and tried to think what to say. He had been an international celebrity for three days, and already he hated it.

"They have heard all the arguments, and they will announce their decision tomorrow."

"Before the beginning of the Sabbath?"

A stupid question, but Dov saw no point in saying so. The Court would never announce a decision on *Shabbat*. "Yes, before *Shabbat* begins."

"Mr. Lifshutz, have you received any more calls from Professor Kazan? Is it true you were romantically involved with

Miss Meyers? Could you comment on reports that you have sold your story to the *National Enquirer*?"

Dov threw up his hands and shook his head. *Idiots.* Beside him, Jessica was getting the same treatment.

"Miss Weinberg, do you think the government will shut down the wormhole before the time travelers return?"

"God knows," she said, and suddenly she began crying. She covered her face with her hands.

Dov wrapped his arm around her shoulder and pulled her toward the waiting car.

Come back before Shabbat, Ari and Rivka. And do no harm!

Hana

Hana walked through the dark streets, too numb even to hate the bad man who walked close behind, twisting her arm. Pain burned through her shoulder. Her rough woolen tunic scraped at the raw flesh on her back.

The bad man had done a wicked thing to her. Even a *zonah* should have the right to say no.

The bad man jabbed the metal thing into the small of her back at every step. What was it? She had never seen such a tool before. It could not be a weapon, because it was not sharp like a knife, nor heavy like a club.

The bad man wanted Rivka. Inside Hana's head, the truth-tellers screamed at her to obey him. She did not like what the voices told her. They had protected her for many months. Now why did they urge her to betray Rivka?

The bad man would kill her if she did not obey him. But if she did obey, he would kill Rivka instead.

Hana did not want to die. But if she took the bad man to Rivka, then what? He would kill Rivka. Would he then spare

Hana? He had done a wicked thing to her already. Most certainly he would kill her.

The truth-tellers cried out louder. *Go to Rivka! Go to Rivka! Go to Rivka!*

Something had gone terribly wrong. The truth-tellers were telling lies. They had told her the bad man was a good man. A terrible lie. Now they told her to go to Rivka. If she took the bad man to Rivka, he would kill them both.

For a moment, Hana felt fear rushing through her chest, chilling her bare arms. Then she felt free. Whether she obeyed or not, she would die. Therefore, she must neither obey nor disobey.

She would have to fight the bad man.

Damien

Halfway up the long hill, Hana abruptly stopped walking and started screaming. It sounded like *"Esh!"* That meant what? Fire, or something?

"Shut up or I'll shoot!" Damien said in English. Which was stupid. *"Sheket!"* He jabbed the barrel of the gun into her kidney.

She only screamed louder.

Damien suddenly realized she probably didn't know what the gun could do. Therefore, it was not a threat. But if he shot her, then she couldn't take him to Rivka. The gun would only be useful as long as he didn't actually use it.

Meanwhile, she kept screaming her head off.

Damien jammed the gun into the shoulder harness inside his robe, twisted her arm hard with his left hand, and clamped his right over her mouth.

She bit down hard and held on.

Cursing, he released her arm and punched her hard in the small of the back.

Instantly, she quit biting and darted forward out of his reach.

Damien clomped after her.

She leapt ahead, just out of his reach.

He sprinted hard, lunged for her, and missed.

By now she had a slight lead on him. He tried to run faster, but found it impossible in the heavy boots. He slowed a little, conserving his energy. He would just have to wear her down. She was probably dumb enough to try to find safety with Rivka.

Suddenly she zigged to the left down a side street.

Caught off balance, Damien slowed to make the turn. Somehow, she had put ten yards between them, running lightly on bare feet. He wished he had worn his running shoes.

She continued pulling away from him. Worry began to nibble at the back of his mind. She was at least twenty years younger than him, and more lightly shod.

Forget that! No way was a female going to outrun him. He had been second best on his high school football team in the forty-yard time trials.

A minute later, she had doubled the distance between them. Damien's breath began coming in ragged gasps. They had now covered a good quarter mile—ten times the forty yards of a football drill.

Hana turned right. She was going to get away if he didn't do something.

Damien yanked out his gun and thumbed off the safety.

He reached the corner and stopped, dropping into a shooter's crouch. There she was, easily within his range. He sighted down his arm. Steady...aim...

A drop of sweat rolled into his right eye.

He swore and wiped his eye with his sleeve. He aimed again, switching to a two-handed grip to steady the gun, despite his heaving chest. Finally, he squeezed the trigger.

Abruptly, she darted left, just before the pop of the silenced gun told him that he had fired.

Missed!

Frustrated, Damien fired again without aiming. Almost certainly, that was a miss, too. She disappeared down a side street.

He safed the gun and trudged down the street after her, wondering how he could have got so out of shape. When he reached the corner, she was gone. No traces of blood marked the dust.

He had missed twice. No great surprise. On TV, a guy running at full tilt could shoot from the hip and hit a moving target at fifty yards. But this wasn't TV. In real life, even when you did everything right, even in natural sunlight, you couldn't always hit a moving target.

So Hana wasn't going to take him to Rivka.

Might Rivka be staying with that fruit, Ari's boyfriend? Possibly.

And what about Ari? Was he also still in Jerusalem? Damien hadn't seen him this afternoon, but that didn't prove anything.

If Ari were still here, with or without Rivka, it would be worthwhile to eliminate him. Even better to get them both.

Damien patted his cloth belt. He still had the pick he had used to break into Ari's lodgings the other night.

He smiled to himself. *Ari Kazan, if you're still here in Jerusalem, you're a dead man.*

Baruch

Baruch woke from a sound sleep all at once. Something felt wrong. Ari's light snoring continued on an even rhythm.

Baruch heard a scratching sound downstairs. He instantly realized that he had heard it just moments before, in his sleep.

He silently rose and opened the door that led downstairs. He padded down on bare feet and studied the heavy wooden door leading to the street outside. A faint metallic scratching sound issued from it. Something clicked, and then he saw the door begin to move.

Baruch sat down quietly on the stairway. *Blessed are You, Lord our God, King of the universe, who created the quarks and gluons. Blessed are You, who watches over Your children...*

Damien

Damien finally felt the latch give. Excellent! He pressed on the door, and it began to move inward. He nodded and pulled his gun out. Releasing the safety, he then checked the street behind him. Silent and empty.

Ari Kazan, ready or not, here I come.

Damien quietly pressed forward on the door.

It moved inward a quarter of an inch, then stopped. He pressed harder.

No response.

He pulled the door back and tried again. The heavy thud of wood against wood told him all he needed to know.

This door now had a thick bar on the inside.

Damien stepped back into the middle of the street to study the situation. The house had stone walls, a strong wooden door, and no decent windows. Nothing short of dynamite would get him in.

He was not going to kill Ari tonight.

Furious, he turned and stalked away. He had failed three times in one day, and that had to be some sort of a record.

But never mind all that. Tomorrow, he would take on Paul of Tarsus. Paul didn't have a weapon. Paul didn't know what was coming. Paul would never know what hit him.

Ari and Rivka had gotten lucky today. They had had the benefit of surprise.

Tomorrow, that wouldn't happen. Now that he knew they were still here in Jerusalem, he could plan for them.

They would be watching for him—a white man wearing a modern Arab costume.

And that's exactly what they wouldn't find. He would need a disguise, but that should be easy. He had money, he knew what he wanted, and he knew where to buy it. By the time Paul's trial started, Damien West would look more a Jew than Ari did.

TWENTY-SIX

Rivka

Rivka slept badly, dreaming of Dr. West firing bursts from an Uzi at every older man he met on the streets of Jerusalem. She awoke just at daybreak.

"Sister Rivka!" It was the voice of her new friend Miryam. "Your friend is here to see you!"

"Ari?" Rivka said. "I told him not to come until later. Tell him I'm sleeping."

"I cannot," Miryam said. "You are not sleeping. And besides, it is not Brother Ari. It is Hana."

"Hana?" Rivka sat bolt upright. Hana was a late riser. She wouldn't have come without a very good reason.

"She is hurt and crying and very tired," Miryam said. "She told me not to wake you. I have put her to bed in the other room and tended her wounds—"

"Wounds?" *Oh, God, please! No!* Rivka jumped up and ran into the other room of the house, the one that led out onto the street.

Hana lay huddled in a corner, shaking.

Rivka ran to kneel beside her. "Hana! What happened?"

Hana told her in bits and pieces. "...and finally, when I thought he was far behind me, something hit a wall near my face, and chips of stone sprang out and cut me." Hana pointed at the gashes in her face.

"From a bullet," Rivka said.

"I do not know what a bullet is," Hana said.

"The thing he poked you with is called a gun," Rivka said. "It throws pieces of metal very fast. He could have killed you."

Hana's face turned a shade paler. "He *will* kill you, Rivka. You must go back to your own country. Promise me you will go back!"

"As soon as I can," Rivka said. *But Dr. West is going to try to kill Paul again. This proves it. I've got to stop him.* She patted Hana on the shoulder. "You must be exhausted after staying up all night. Sleep for a while. I need to go out."

"You are in danger!" Hana said. "The voices said so yesterday. And now, they say…" Tears filled her eyes.

"Don't tell me," Rivka said. "I don't want to know." She stood up and headed toward the door.

"The voices say you are going to die," Hana said.

"Everybody is going to die," Rivka said. "Tell me something new, please."

"They say you will die today," Hana said. "Where are you going? Please…it is not safe out there."

"I'm going to buy a disguise," Rivka said. "I can't go back to my own country safely without a disguise, can I?"

"You are lying," Hana said. "Why are you lying to me, Rivka?"

Rivka shivered. Hana had pegged her every time she had stretched the truth. *Every time.* It was…unnatural. "I am going to find a disguise. I'll come back as soon as I've got one." That was the plain and simple truth.

Hana's face relaxed a little.

"Sleep, my friend," Rivka said. She opened the door and peered out carefully. The sun had risen and the streets would soon be humming with activity. Good. In a crowd was an excellent place to hide. She fingered the coins Dr. West had given her. They should be enough to buy what she needed.

She stepped out into the street and shut the door.

Damien

Damien did not know what time the trial would be. Nor did he know where. But he knew exactly where Paul was staying. Sometime today, a squad of Roman soldiers would escort Paul out of the Fortress Antonia and take him to his trial before the Sanhedrin.

At some point on his way to or from that trial, Paul would cross paths with a large, dark man in workman's clothing. Lead would explode inside flesh and bone. History would be made. Or rather, history would be unmade.

The dye on Damien's arms felt itchy, and he had already begun sweating inside his day-laborer's costume. Never mind that. In a few hours, he could change into something more comfortable.

The streets were already crowded, chaotic. That annoyed Damien. The history books didn't tell you how cramped ancient cities were. This place was worse than Tokyo, worse than Hong Kong. It made planning difficult. By definition, you couldn't control chaos.

Which meant you needed a fallback plan. Damien had one. Several, in fact.

He arrived at the gate to the fortress soon after dawn. The Antonia butted onto the northwest corner of the Temple Mount. A stairway led down to the street level right at a T-intersection. The two arms of the T pointed north and south; the leg pointed west.

This intersection formed the hub of the busiest section of this city. Already customers thronged the shops lying here in the shadow of the Temple Mount. The tiny cubicles were crammed with merchandise. The real business took place out here in the street.

Damien chose a likely position and stopped to wait for Paul. Maybe one hour, maybe six. Sooner or later, Paul would come out. He would have to pass near Damien. And that would be the chance of a lifetime—

A string of gibberish cut in on Damien's thoughts. A beefy, red-faced shopkeeper stood in his face, gesticulating at a tiny shop crammed with cloth. Silk. Satin. Linen.

Damien shook his head. "Sorry, not interested," he said in English.

The shopkeeper scowled at him and made a gesture that could only mean, "Move along then and let the real shoppers in."

Damien nodded politely and moved down the street a little. No use alienating the locals. He needed to get along with them for just this one day.

But it was the same story at the leather dealer in the next shop, and the ivory goods merchant in the next.

Damien hadn't counted on this. The street was a good twenty feet wide, but it had no place to loiter. You couldn't simply smile and say, "Just looking," as if you were in some Chicago boutique.

Damien made up a Plan B on the spot. He had found the best possible general location, but he couldn't stay standing in any one spot. He would just have to keep moving, ceaselessly drifting along with the foot traffic, walking up and down in front of the Antonia, waiting for the Romans and their guest.

It was going to be a long day.

Ari

Brother Baruch's face shone with delight. "Explain to me again, Brother Ari, how HaShem made the universe from three colors of quarks. Have you seen these quarks?"

Ari sighed. How could you explain quantum chromodynamics without resorting to mathematics and without discussing the experimental evidence—at least the parton model? He shook his head. "No, I have not seen the quarks. They cannot be seen, because they cannot be separated."

"But then how can you know they are three, and not one or five or twenty?"

"I cannot see your bones, but I can feel that you have more than one." It was a bad answer, but the best Ari could come up with.

"But you could also remove my bones and count them," Baruch said. "Why can you not remove the quarks?"

The answer was that Ari did not know. The theory required quarks in a triplet representation, but nature apparently allowed only singlet representations to be stable—which required two or more quarks stuck together. And the reason was not clear, although you could make some plausible arguments. "It is a mystery of HaShem," Ari said. "They are three and they are one, both at the same time. I do not know why."

Baruch gave him an uncertain smile. "Brother Ari, I think sometimes you are joking with me. It is not possible to be both three and one, is it?"

Ari shivered. If Rivka heard him talking like this, she would be sure to make some absurd theological point.

He looked at his watch. Almost 9 A.M.! Incredible! Where had the time flown? He should have gone to find Rivka an hour ago. This always happened when he discussed physics.

"Brother Baruch, I am not joking with you, but I think I have told as much as you can hear for one day. Now I must go to find Sister Rivka."

Baruch nodded. "I will come with you, and you must explain this wonderful thing, that three can be one, and one three. Is it like this—that a box can have one weight, though it has height and width and length?"

Ari stood and reached for the door latch. "It is like that, yes, but not quite." He stepped out into the street.

Baruch followed him and locked the door. "You must explain how it is not like a box."

Ari walked along in silence, trying to sort that out. Finally, he said, "Three dimensions, one weight. It is close enough." Mass was a scalar, a singlet representation of the three-dimensional rotation group, whereas vectors lived in a triplet representation. Really, it was not a bad analogy at all—

Ari's ears perked up. From the direction of Miryam's house, he heard a woman's voice.

Screaming.

Rivka

Rivka had fully intended to keep her promise. When she finished buying her disguise, she meant to go back to Miryam's house to check in on Hana.

And yet she was afraid. Hana had told her she was going to die. Hana's voices. Her protectors. Her truth-tellers.

Rivka had put up a brave front, just as she had done yesterday when arguing with Ari. But when you got right down to it, dying was not likely to be pleasant.

Dr. West was going to try to kill her.

If she went back to Miryam's house, Hana would argue with her, and Miryam also. And possibly Ari, if he came early.

She could not argue with all three of them. Better not to think about it. Just pray.

A public bathhouse for women stood near Miryam's house. It served women who had finished their monthly *niddah* uncleanness. Rivka had just enough money to pay for a bath.

She spent five minutes in the cool water, praying for strength and for courage. When she came out of the water, she felt clean and cool and terribly weak. She also knew that she had to stop Dr. West again. And she couldn't tell Ari or Hana or Brother Baruch. They would try to talk her out of it, and they would succeed, because she was terrified already.

She dressed herself in her newly purchased costume. It was a young woman's white linen tunic, complete with a light cloak and a two-piece veil that covered both her face and her hair. She felt like one of the Iranian women she had seen on TV, except that she wore white, not black. This was the normal clothing worn by a young Jewish woman—a virgin who had never been married.

Which Rivka was.

Never mind that most girls in Jerusalem wearing this costume were under the age of fifteen. Nobody would know her age. Nobody would even notice her. And especially not Dr. West. At least not until she had stopped him. After that...she wasn't going to think about what would happen after that. If she stopped Dr. West today, Paul would be home free, safely in the custody of Roman soldiers for the rest of his life.

First she had to find out where the Sanhedrin met. The books were fuzzy on that. For much of its history, the Sanhedrin met at a place called the Chamber of Hewn Stone. At times, it may have met somewhere on the Temple Mount.

Unfortunately, no historian knew the precise location.

Rivka had been thinking about this while shopping, and she now had a plan. She knew the names of several of the men on the Sanhedrin, some of the great rabbis: Rabban Shimon ben Gamaliel, Rabban Yohanan ben Zakkai, Rabbi Tsaduk. If she could find one of these men, she could simply ask him.

But how to find one of them? Future generations would judge them as great. But did their contemporaries? Or were they relative unknowns in their own city?

One of these men, Rabban Yohanan, worked as a merchant. Rivka guessed that he would run a shop near the Temple Mount. She had seen a long row of shops at the western foot of the Temple Mount, near the site where the Wailing Wall would someday be located. She also guessed that merchants wouldn't be too fussy about talking to females. After all, if women did the shopping, how could they communicate with male shop-keepers? So she would bet good odds that Rabban Yohanan would talk to her.

Rivka headed for that shopping district. Somebody there had to know where to find the shop of Rabban Yohanan ben Zakkai.

Fifteen minutes later, she stood before a small olive oil shop. Inside, she saw two slave girls arguing with a tiny man. The man had gray hair and a wispy gray beard and wore a black leather phylactery strapped to his forehead. A Pharisee.

When the slave girls came out, Rivka went in.

"Good morning, my daughter," said the man. "What can I do for you today?" He had a kind smile, and the peace of God seemed to light up his face.

Rivka immediately felt at home with him. "You are Rabban Yohanan ben Zakkai, who sits on the Sanhedrin?"

A look of puzzlement came over his face. "I am Yohanan, the son of Zakkai, but I am not called *Rabban*. I am not worthy for such a title."

He would be judged worthy, Rivka knew. He just didn't realize it yet, and probably never would. "My father, you are a member of the Sanhedrin, am I correct?"

He shrugged. "Only when that scoundrel Hananyah ben Nadavayah thinks to include me."

Rivka smiled. The high priest Hananyah—Ananias in English—had been written up as a first-class scoundrel in the history books. "My father, you have a meeting today. I wish to know where the Sanhedrin will meet."

He smiled indulgently. "My child, you are mistaken. I have not been invited to a meeting today. Why do you believe—"

"*Shalom*, Yohanan!" A man's voice boomed out in the street behind Rivka.

She turned to look at him. He was a big man, built like a bear, with a thick gray beard and piercing eyes. The phylactery on his sweating forehead hung slightly askew.

"*Shalom*, Shimon," said Yohanan ben Zakkai. "What news?"

"We have been summoned by that prince of fools, Hananyah ben Nadavayah," said the man named Shimon. "We are to appear at the Chamber of Hewn Stone at the sixth hour. He claims that it is urgent, but we are not informed as to the reason."

Rivka checked her watch. It was just after nine o'clock. The sixth hour meant noon. That gave her some time yet.

Yohanan frowned. "If it were really urgent, Hananyah would not schedule it at such an awkward hour. I am unable to attend. My young helper Gamaliel is sick at home. I have no one to mind the shop."

Shimon shrugged. "Very well, my friend. I think I, too, will find an excuse to avoid this meeting." He turned and disappeared up the street.

Yohanan studied Rivka with narrowed eyes. "There is more to you than I can see with my eyes, child. Who are you, and why are you here?"

"My name is called Rivka, and the God of our fathers has sent me to defeat the plans of Hananyah."

"And what are his plans?"

Rivka wondered how much she should tell him. She knew exactly what would happen today in the Sanhedrin. A fistfight would break out between the Sadducees and the Pharisees, with Paul in the middle. But how could that happen, if none of the Pharisees showed up?

"There is a man named Saul, born in Tarsus, who studied with Rabban Gamaliel here many years ago."

"Not so many years ago," Yohanan muttered. "Shimon and I studied with him at the feet of Rabban Gamaliel. What of my fiery young friend?"

"He is here in Jerusalem and he has been arrested—"

"What?" Yohanan cried. "Why have I not heard?"

"—and he will be tried today before the Sanhedrin on charges of desecrating the Temple."

"Saul?" Yohanan shrieked. "Never! He was a zealot for Torah. Surely this is a lie?"

"It is a lie," Rivka said. "But Hananyah intends—"

"I know what he intends." Fire lit up Yohanan's eyes. "Hananyah never loses an opportunity to make fools of us Pharisees. Out! Out! We must catch Shimon and inform him."

Rivka backed out of the shop. Yohanan tumbled out behind her. He locked the shop, beckoned her to follow him, and began pushing north up the crowded street.

"With respect, my father, I am needed elsewhere," Rivka said. "If you could kindly direct me to the Chamber of Hewn Stone, I have been given a small task." *Nothing major. I just have to stop an assassin.*

"It is on the way, my child," Yohanan said. "I will point it out as we pass. And may the God of our fathers bless you with every good thing for what you have done today."

Five minutes later, Yohanan pointed toward a large square on their left. "My daughter, the Chamber of Hewn Stone is that large building with the great wooden door. I must hurry. There is just time. We will need Tsaduk and his zealous friends."

And with that, he disappeared into the crowd.

Rivka felt sadness wash over her. She would have liked to spend more time with this man. She had read Jacob Neusner's two books on Rabban Yohanan ben Zakkai. But the man behind the legends was so much more real than what you could learn from a book. And now she had no time to get to know him.

She stepped into the square and looked around. Nearly empty, with clear lines of fire from many different directions. If you planned to assassinate someone, this would be a great place to do it.

She saw no sign of Dr. West. An odd little nook nestled on one side of the square between two buildings. Deep shade nearly filled it, and a bench sat against one wall.

Rivka sat down to watch and wait.

Now what? It seemed a good moment to start praying.

Father, it says in Your Word that Your strength is made perfect in weakness. Prove it, Lord. Right here. Right now. I'm ready, Lord. Ready to…come home to You, if that's what it takes.

God, I'm scared. Really scared. Help me do what I've got to do. And…take care of Ari. Maybe I won't be able to, after this. He's a very special son of Yours. Special to me, anyway, and I know he's special to You, too. Help him to know You, and to get back to our century safely.

TWENTY-SEVEN

Ari

Ari wanted to cover his ears. The screaming that issued from the house of Miryam cut to his marrow.

Baruch pounded on the door again. "Sister Miryam! It is Baruch! Let me in."

Finally the door cracked ajar. Miryam peered out. "Brother Baruch! Thanks be to HaShem." The door opened wider.

Baruch stepped in. Ari hesitated a moment. He heard something unnatural in that scream—primal, animal. Did he really want to go in there?

But Rivka was in there. If she could stand that horrible noise, so could he.

The door began to close. Ari pushed his way in. Miryam shut the door behind him.

Hana lay curled on the floor in a fetal position, her clothes in shreds, cradling her head in her hands and shrieking. Not words, just raw sound.

It took a moment for Ari to realize that Rivka was not in the room. Before he could ask about that, Baruch stepped toward Hana, extending his arm as if in blessing.

Hana's eyes lit up with fear. She rolled away from him into the corner, screaming louder.

Ari had once lived in a cheap apartment in Princeton. One day the Vietnamese man who lived in the unit directly above him went insane and began screaming. For a solid week. The landlord had been unable to evict the man, and Ari couldn't eat or sleep or study. When the man's family finally came to take him away, Ari had watched them bundle him into a car—screaming all the while, flailing his arms, foaming at the mouth.

Hana looked worse than that man had.

"How long has she been like this?" Ari asked Miryam.

She shook her head and stepped nearer, cupping her hand to her ear.

Baruch moved toward Hana. Ari could see his lips moving, but Hana's ungodly wailing drowned out all other sound.

But where was Rivka? The house had only two rooms. Ari stepped to the doorway and peeked into the other room. Empty.

He began to feel worried. Rivka ought not to have gone out. What if she ran into Damien?

The screaming rose in intensity again. What was Baruch doing to Hana? Ari turned back to look.

Baruch stood above her, both hands extended in blessing. She twisted this way and that, writhing like a snake in a net, ripping at her tattered clothes.

Ari felt a rush of embarrassment.

Baruch waved his hands in the air far above her, as if brushing away unseen cobwebs.

Suddenly, the screaming stopped. Hana's body quit writhing.

The silence struck Ari like a hammer. After the sustained noise, it felt almost painful.

Baruch said something to Miryam in Aramaic, too rapidly for Ari to catch.

Miryam rushed into the other room, returning a moment later with a cotton blanket. She laid it over Hana's body, covering her.

Baruch nodded to her. "Sister Miryam, please bring me olive oil."

"I have none," she said.

"Then borrow some from your neighbor." He motioned to Ari. "Brother Ari, please come and help me."

Miryam hurried out the door.

Ari stepped closer, anxiety welling up inside him. He did not want to get too close, especially with her being the only woman left in the house. "What is happening, Brother Baruch?"

Hana's eyes locked on him. "I know you," she said in a low, rasping voice which sounded almost male. "Ari, who is no lion, but only a mouse, a double-minded man who walks in two lands, who looks for truth and believes a lie, I say to you—"

"Silence!" Baruch said. "I forbid you to prophesy, you child of Satan!"

Hana's mouth went slack. She screwed her eyes shut, as though in pain. When she opened them, they glowed—the eyes of a seductress. "Baruch, my lover, my delight. Why have you not returned to my bed? Is it because—"

"Stop!" Baruch said. He placed his hand on her head. "I command you to come out of her, you spirit of adultery!"

Hana's body convulsed, and her face twisted in shock. She coughed violently.

"Leave her!" Baruch said.

She retched three times, and then lay still.

The door opened, and Miryam returned with a small clay jar of olive oil. She held it near Baruch. He dipped his finger in it and brushed it on Hana's forehead.

"I anoint you in the name of Yeshua, *Mashiach* of Israel, who shall reign on David's throne—"

"No!" Hana screamed. She flung the blanket in the air and flailed her arms.

"I forbid you to fight me," Baruch said. "In the name of Yeshua, I forbid you!"

Hana's body relaxed. Miryam knelt beside her and rearranged the blanket.

"I command you to tell me your name," Baruch said.

Ari almost laughed out loud. Baruch knew Hana's name perfectly well. What was this about?

"I am Truth," Hana said, again assuming the low, rasping tone that she had used earlier. "I know all things, and I reveal them to my servant."

"You will leave her now," Baruch said.

"Let me stay and I will tell you about quarks," Hana said. "I will explain how HaShem created the universe. I will warn you of the left-handed man with no sons. I will—"

"No!" Baruch shouted, and panic lacerated his voice. "Come out of her and come out now! I command it."

Hana roared. Her head whipped back and forth in a frenzy. She retched again. Black bile squirted out of her mouth.

"Come out of her, father of lies!" Baruch said. "Now!"

She shook one last time, screaming a high, wailing note. Then she lay still, panting, her face a mask of exhaustion.

Ari backed away from her, his mind spinning. Quarks? Where had she heard that word? Could she have overheard him talking to Baruch yesterday?

Miryam turned and followed him. "Do not be frightened, Brother Ari. Brother Baruch knows how to deal with the evil spirits."

"Where is Sister Rivka?" Ari asked.

"She went to buy something," Miryam said.

"When was this?"

Hana screamed again, a cry of pure, unadulterated terror.

Miryam dashed to her side.

Ari suddenly felt claustrophobic. He could not stand being in this strange house with these primitive rites. A sick feeling clawed at his insides.

He went outside, shutting the door behind him. He leaned against the wall and closed his eyes.

God of our fathers, God of Abraham, God of Isaac, God of Jacob, and God of Brother Baruch, bring Rivka back to me safely.

Ari felt a sense of warmth enveloping him. The objective side of his mind told him that he was entering some sort of altered state. His intuitive side—that part of his brain that he used for doing physics—told him to continue praying and to do nothing to disturb this state. Something important was happening, though he did not know quite what.

God of our fathers...

Time flowed over him.

Ari could not tell whether ten minutes passed or ten days, but at last he sensed himself returning to a normal state. He heard a woman's voice speaking to him. Blessed be HaShem, it must be Rivka.

With an effort, he opened his eyes.

Sister Miryam stood before him. Concern etched her face. "Please come," she said, speaking in slow and simple Aramaic. "There is trouble."

Damien

The sun hung well up in the sky when the cluster of Roman soldiers emerged from the gate of the Antonia.

Damien had guessed the soldiers would take their prisoner south along the row of shops, so he had been walking north and south with the human currents all morning. But the Romans went west—the wrong direction. That put him at least fifty yards out of position.

He tried to hurry after them, but he could go no faster than the crowd jammed around him. He couldn't just shoot his way through. He didn't have that many bullets.

Finally, he reached the avenue leading west and dashed after the soldiers. This street was broader and less densely packed, but not so straight. He could not see the Romans.

Cursing, Damien pushed through as fast as he could. At the first intersection, he followed his instincts and turned left onto a street less crowded. Wouldn't the Romans be looking for the path of least resistance?

The street rapidly thinned out as it led into a district with a number of warehouses and granaries. Damien picked up speed until he was running.

The street curved toward the left, following the contour of the valley. Before long, Damien could see his way straight ahead for a hundred yards.

There were no Romans in sight.

No sense following a blind alley. He skidded to a stop, spun around, and ran back the way he had come.

When he reached the main avenue, he turned west. The Romans must have continued straight down this avenue. They could have at most a two-minute lead on him. A man running alone could move faster than a group of men with a prisoner. Ergo, he only needed a little time to catch them.

Five minutes later, he came to a wall, one of several that cut through the city. The avenue ran through a gate into a less-populated district. Had the Romans continued through? Or had they turned left onto the large north-south street that ran parallel to the wall?

This was a time for logic. Rivka had told him that the Sanhedrin was composed of the elites of Jerusalem. Also that the rich people lived south of here. The Sanhedrin would most likely meet near where its members lived.

Damien turned left and headed south.

He made rapid progress. This street was not so crowded. The buildings here appeared to be combination homes/workshops for small tradesmen—sandal makers and leather workers and weavers. Damien ran past a bakery and a small synagogue and reached the end of the street. Ahead of him, another internal city wall ran east-west. To the left were more workshops. To the right a gate cut through the wall he had seen earlier. Beyond that, another gate led south into the wealthy district.

Damien zigged right through the first gate, then zagged left through the second. He took a moment to size up the situation. Foot traffic headed south on a very large avenue. To the right stood a large palace. To the left, a nearly empty street.

Nowhere could he see any Romans.

Damien spotted a beggar sitting in the dirt by the gate. He decided to try his Hebrew. It couldn't hurt. "*Eyfo Romaim?*" he asked.

The beggar stared at him vacantly.

Damien tried again, accenting the words differently.

The beggar ignored him.

Damien slid a hand into his belt and grabbed a coin. He waved it in front of the beggar's eyes. "*Eyfo Romaim?*"

The beggar's face lit up. He pointed east, along the nearly empty street, and jabbered something.

Damien dropped the coin in the dust and ran. If the beggar had lied, he would come back and kill him.

Five minutes later, he learned that the beggar had told the truth. As he arrived in a small square at the foot of the hill, he saw the Romans disappearing into a large hall with a thick wooden door.

Damien took a minute to estimate his chances of shooting his way in. He decided the probabilities were low. But no matter. According to the Bible, Paul would be in there only a short time before starting a big fight between the two main factions on the Sanhedrin. In the uproar that followed, he would get hauled out by his armed guard.

The square was quiet and nearly empty. Damien could loiter here as long as he needed. He took a cue from the beggar he had seen and sat down in the shade with his back against the stone wall of the Sanhedrin's building. He draped his workman's headgear over his face and peered out at the world.

Go ahead, Rivka Meyers. Try to stop me now. Try to see through my disguise. Try anything. I win.

Rivka

In the shadows of the little nook, Rivka felt her whole body stiffen. Roman soldiers coming down the hill! She stood and walked toward them.

There! In among the soldiers walked a short man, his head and face obscured by his headgear. Damien hadn't killed him yet. Thank God!

The soldiers reached the great wooden door of the Chamber of Hewn Stone. One held open the door. The others entered.

Rivka retreated to the safety of her nook in the shadows. Bare minutes later, a huge, dark man in workman's clothing and Reeboks raced into the square. He looked around, smiled, and sat down with his back against the wall of the building—midway between Rivka and the door.

Rivka began praying.

Ari

Ari squinted as he ducked back inside Miryam's house. What sort of trouble could Hana be in, that Baruch needed his help?

In fact, she looked normal. She sat on a stool at Miryam's table with the cotton blanket wrapped around her, staring at a chunk of bread in her hands without interest. Baruch hovered behind her, as though afraid that something terrible would happen if he let her out of his sight.

"What is going on?" Ari said. "And how long has Sister Rivka been out shopping? I am worried about her."

Hana's face tightened. "The bad man came to kill Rivka last night. He did a wicked thing to me, and then he tried to make me lead him to her."

"Is that why…" Ari hesitated. *Is that why you've gone crazy?* But that wouldn't be polite.

"He hurt Hana," Baruch said. "He would have killed her and Rivka both, but Hana escaped him. This morning, she came here and warned Sister Rivka. Soon after that, Sister Rivka went out, and now it has been some hours."

"And the truth-tellers lied to me," Hana said.

"The evil spirits," Baruch said. "You should not marvel that they lied to you, Hana. You should wonder that they ever told the truth. They tell the truth only when they must, to steal your friendship, but they lie whenever they can, to bring you to ruin."

Or to bring Rivka to ruin. Ari felt his throat tightening. Hana had told him yesterday that Damien would try to kill Rivka. He had laughed at her. *But she had been right.* "So what is the trouble then?"

"Just before Baruch made the truth-tellers leave me, they told me something," Hana said. Tears began rolling down her cheeks. "The bad man will kill Rivka before the sun is high today."

"How?" Ari asked. An icy fist grabbed at his insides, twisting until he could not breathe. "When? Where?"

"I saw her on the ground. The bad man stood over her, holding a thing in his hands. It threw fire and smashed her head to bits." Hana covered her face with her hands.

"We must find her," Baruch said. "Brother Ari, do you know where she might be?"

Ari tried to think. Damien still lurked in the streets with a gun. Apparently, Rivka would not rest until she confronted him again.

He suddenly remembered Damien's spreadsheet. The second asterisk—today! How could he have forgotten?

"Brother Baruch, do you know where the Sanhedrin meets?" Ari asked.

"Yes, in the Chamber of Hewn Stone," Baruch said.

"I think she will be there," Ari said. "Take me."

Suddenly, Hana began wailing. "I saw it! I saw it! Just now, the bad man threw fire at her!"

"Leave her!" Baruch shouted. "Lying spirit, I command you to come out of her!"

Hana collapsed on the dirt floor, retching.

Despair washed through Ari. He slumped against the wall, unable to feel, to think, to act.

"No!" Baruch grabbed Ari's arm and slapped him hard in the face.

A pulse of anger shot through Ari. "Leave me alone! Can't you see—"

Baruch slapped him again. "Brother Ari, the Evil One whispers always to your heart that it is better to do nothing than to do something. And you are foolish enough to believe. In the name of Yeshua, I command you to be bold, Ari. Bold as a lion. Do not listen to the lies of the Evil One." He yanked Ari toward the door. "Sister Miryam, stay with Hana and pray. We also will pray on the way."

Ari held back. "It is hopeless, Brother Baruch."

"So were you!" Baruch said. "You were dead, Ari. Now run with me, or the lies will be found true because you delayed."

Baruch turned and ran out the door. Ari dashed after him, glancing at his watch. Almost 1 P.M.

Outside, the sun blazed high overhead. Baruch loped ahead, shouting something that caused heads to turn and people to move aside. Ari raced after him, his breath scorching his lungs. Two days ago, he had reconciled himself to Damien. But that was then. This was now.

If Damien had harmed so much as a fingernail on Rivka's body, he would die.

Rivka

Rivka sat on her bench, every nerve taut with anticipation. Dr. West sat between her and the door, but she dared not move closer. That risked having him notice her.

How would the scene play out? In the last half hour, Rivka had imagined half a dozen scenarios. In some, Dr. West won. In some, he lost. Each of them ended with a bullet coming at her with nightmarish slowness. She shook her head. Don't think about that. Just think about—

The door began opening.

It's him! God, tell me what to do next!

Damien

The instant the door began opening, relief washed over Damien. He had been here quite a while, and still no sign of Rivka. His biggest fear was that she would be able to mobilize another mob, like yesterday. But she couldn't do that unless she could see him. Obviously, his disguise had worked. Now it was too late. Anything Rivka could do now would be irrelevant. She had run out of time.

He stood up slowly, so as not to arouse the attention of the soldiers. They clustered tightly around their prisoner, herding him across the square in the direction they had come earlier. As they turned their backs on him, Damien began moving forward. They were only twenty yards away, but he needed to get a bit closer. To kill Paul, he would have to shoot a few of the soldiers. He had ten bullets in his Glock nine millimeter semi-automatic, plus a couple of spare clips. He could be sure of killing Paul with only two bullets, so he had plenty for the Romans.

Damien pursued the soldiers and quickly closed the gap. Ten yards behind them, he reached under his cloak and yanked the gun out of his shoulder harness. He assumed the shooter's stance, released the safety, raised his arm, sighted on the back of the rearmost soldier, and—

Something leaped on his back, lashing at his arms, spoiling his aim. "Nooooooo!" someone shrieked in his ear.

Rivka Meyers! Damien staggered forward, caught his balance, then jerked his left elbow back hard, trying for her solar plexus.

She scratched at his face. Damien safed the gun and allowed himself to fall over backward. Rivka tried to support his full weight, but couldn't. Together, they collapsed into the dirt.

He heard the air whoosh out of her. Her death grip on him relaxed.

Damien rolled to his right and leapt to his feet. Rivka still lay there on the ground, gasping for breath. Damien risked a look back at the Romans.

They had all kept marching straight ahead without even bothering to look back. Nobody else in the square seemed to show much interest. It occurred to Damien that this probably looked like a typical domestic spat.

Rivka staggered blindly to her feet.

Damien let her stand all the way up. Then he slammed his heavy hand into her chest.

She fell back into the dirt and lay there for a moment, panting.

Time to put her out of her misery. Two bullets should do it, and then he could be on his way.

Rivka's eyes focused on something behind Damien and she began screaming, "Ari! Ari!"

"That's an old trick," Damien said. "Sorry, Miss Meyers, you lose." He raised his gun and thumbed the safety off. "Say your prayers."

Ari

Fear drove Ari like a madman. By the time he reached the lower city, he had made up some of the distance, but still Baruch led him by ten paces. They burst into a small square. Ari's blood froze in his chest. Just as Hana had said, Rivka lay on the ground. Damien stood over her.

She tried to rise. Damien slammed a fist into her chest. She collapsed in the dirt. Then she caught sight of Ari, and foolishly began screaming his name.

Damien raised his gun and pointed it at her face.

Too far away to stop him, Ari veered sharply to his right and played the only card he had left.

"Damien!" he bellowed.

TWENTY-NINE

Damien

"Damien!" roared a familiar voice.

Damien's head whipped around. *Ari Kazan.*

Instantly, Damien recalculated his situation. Ari was thirty yards away, and not even running directly at him. *Coward.* But his presence changed nothing. A couple of bullets for Rivka, then a couple for Ari. After that, follow the Romans and load a fresh clip on the way.

No problem.

Damien turned back to Rivka.

Something slammed into him from behind and riveted onto his back.

Damien staggered to one side. The gun flew from his hand.

The thing on his back pummeled him in the face. Damien twisted, threw a glance over his shoulder. He caught a glimpse of the fruit—Ari's boyfriend!

Damien jabbed his fist over his shoulder into his attacker's face. The boyfriend hollered, relaxed his grip. Damien stutter-stepped backward, still throwing punches over his shoulders. His attacker let go and jumped off. Though off balance, Damien immediately spun around and kicked straight out. His foot made only a glancing impact on the boyfriend's thigh. *Bad timing*. Damien stepped back, caught his balance, and waited, sizing up his opponent—who also waited.

Time for the kill. Damien feinted twice, then stepped forward—

A bundle of fury cannoned into him from behind.

Damien fell to the dirt with a monster atop him.

Ari Kazan. Wild with rage.

Rivka

Rivka could think of only one thing. The gun! Get the gun!

She rolled away from the fighting men and stumbled to her feet. Where was it?

There! Against the wall.

Rivka ran to the gun, scooped it up. This was Dr. West's only weapon against Paul. Without it, he was defeated.

Filthy gun!

She pointed it at the dust and pulled the trigger.

It made a small popping sound, but it kicked very hard.

She gripped it with both hands and fired again. And again. Every bullet fired was a bullet that could not kill Paul. After she had fired ten times, the next squeeze of the trigger produced only a click.

Empty! She yanked the clip out and pounded on it with the butt of the gun until it bent. Then she field-stripped the weapon, laid it all out on a flat stone, picked up a rock half the size of her head, and dropped it onto the slide.

There! Nobody would ever fire this gun again.

She looked back at the men.

Dr. West lay on his back in the dirt. Ari sat on Dr. West's belly, pounding his face. Baruch leapt in the air and stomped down hard on Dr. West's right hand. Dr. West screamed.

Hadn't they hurt him enough? Without the gun, he was powerless. Rivka strode over and shouted into Ari's right ear. "Ari!"

He stopped hitting Dr. West and looked up at her.

"I've disabled the gun," she said. "He can't do anything now."

Baruch said, "We must tie him—"

Dr. West's left hand snaked out, grabbed Rivka's ankle, and jerked her feet out from under her.

For an instant, Rivka felt herself in a strange, weightless free-fall. Then her shoulders slammed into the ground. An instant later, her head thunked against dirt and the world went dark.

Ari

The sound of Rivka's head hitting the ground thudded through Ari's skull. She lay very still.

Ari jumped off Damien's chest and knelt beside her. "Rivka!" *She's not moving!* Frantic, Ari looked up. Damien was staggering to his feet. Baruch threw a flurry of punches at him with both hands. Damien somehow parried the attack with his left arm only, his right hanging limp at his side.

"Brother Ari!" Baruch said. "Is Sister Rivka hurt?"

"Yes, very badly."

Baruch seemed to lose all interest in fighting.

Damien backed several paces away from them both, then turned and ran.

Baruch stared at Rivka. "She is not moving."

Ari put his hand on her chest. The slow beat of her heart pulsed into his soul. "Blessed be HaShem, she is alive."

The gun lay nearby. Ari picked up the slide and stared at it. Ruined!

"What is that?" Baruch asked.

"It is a weapon from my country," Ari said. "The thing Hana saw in her vision, which throws fire. Rivka broke it."

"That was foolish," Baruch said. "We could have used it against the evil man."

Ari nodded. "At least he cannot use it against us. Without it, he is like other men."

"He is not like any man I ever saw before," Baruch said.

Ari stuffed the parts of the gun into his belt. "We must help Rivka. And the hour grows late. She and I must return to our own country." He checked the time. Well after 1 P.M.

"She must not be moved," Baruch said.

"If we can take her to my country, we have doctors with power to heal her."

"Only HaShem has the power to heal," Baruch said.

"Sister Rivka!" shouted a woman's voice.

Ari looked up. Hana and Miryam ran toward them.

"What happened?" Miryam asked.

"Thank God, thank God, the truth-tellers lied to me," Hana said. "The bad man did not kill her."

"She is hurt," Ari said. "Help me." He knelt down and began gathering her into his arms.

"What are you going to do?" Miryam asked.

Ari straightened his back and grunted. Rivka was a small woman, less than fifty kilos. Still, it was awkward to lift her, especially since any move might cause more damage. He slowly stood to his feet.

"What are you going to do?" Miryam asked again.

Ari shrugged. There was only one thing he could do. Rivka needed medical attention at once. And the wormhole might close forever in a couple of hours. "I am going to carry her back to my own country."

Dov

The phone in Damien's lab rang. Dov picked it up on the first ring. It was Jessica's cousin, the lawyer calling from the Supreme Court building.

"They have made their decision," she said. "The wormhole must close at three in the afternoon to honor *Shabbat.*"

Dov's heart skipped a beat. "No exceptions for health? *Pikuach nephesh?*"

"Only if their lives are in danger. Otherwise, no exceptions."

"Thank you for calling," Dov said. He hung up.

The physics department had allowed only a single television crew into the laboratory, along with several print reporters, Ari's family, a few physicists, and a dozen representatives of the *Haredim.* The camera crew moved in on Dov now.

"What is the news from the Supreme Court?" the reporter asked in English.

Dov responded in Hebrew, so that his countrymen would be first to know. "The wormhole will close at three in the afternoon to honor *Shabbat.*"

Cheers erupted around the room. Foolish *Haredim.* Like most secular Israelis, Dov hated them all.

When the shouting died down, the reporter asked, "Could you repeat your answer in English, Mr. Lifshutz?"

Dov did. He looked at the large clock that the department chairman had hung on the wall. Two-thirty. Half an hour to go.

Hurry, Ari! Hurry, Rivka! Curses on you, Professor West!

Ari

By the time they reached the cave, Ari felt exhausted and sick at heart. Baruch had been praying the whole time, with little effect. Rivka had stirred twice, but still showed no signs of consciousness. The second time, she had vomited.

The stink of it filled Ari's nostrils, but he would not stop to allow Hana to wash Rivka. He had not much time left. He stole a look at his watch. Almost three. That would put them very close to the deadline, if there was one. Had Dov managed an extension?

Inside the cave, Ari let Baruch hold Rivka so he could use his phone. As he pulled it out of his pocket, he heard Baruch and Miryam and Hana praying loudly, fervently. He stepped into the wormhole and speed-dialed Dov's number.

It rang only once. "*Hallo,* this is Dov. Is that you, Ari?"

"This is Ari. What's the latest news?"

Shouts broke out in the background. The sound of cheering.

"Ari, you almost missed the deadline! We have less than a minute. Are you both well?"

"I am, but Rivka is badly hurt."

"Quickly, Ari! Is her life in danger?"

What kind of a question was that? "Yes, I would say that is an accurate—"

"Wait, Ari!"

Ari heard a thump over the line, the sound of a phone being slammed on a table.

"Are you there, Dov?"

No answer.

In the background, Ari could hear Dov shouting for someone to call a doctor. Then he said in what seemed an almost-triumphant voice, "Miss Meyers is in mortal danger! By order of the Israeli Supreme Court, the wormhole must remain powered up until she and Ari have come safely through. Stand back from the device, please!"

There followed noises that could only be described as disgruntled. Ari wondered what that was all about. While he waited, he stepped out of the wormhole to look at his friends.

The sight caused him to drop the phone in the dirt.

Damien

Damien limped into his lodgings, fuming. His swollen right arm throbbed with each beat of his heart. If that fruit hadn't broken it, he had damaged the tendons or something. Damien could not possibly hold a gun with his right hand, much less squeeze a trigger.

He went to his duffel bag and rummaged around until he found some painkiller tablets. He swallowed two, then wrapped up his damaged right hand as best he could.

That finished, he gathered his belongings and walked out the door. If Ari and the fruit came looking for him, they wouldn't find him here, because he wasn't coming back.

An hour later, he had found a new room in the northwestern corner of the city. He paid in gold, and the owner was only too happy to personally bring a clay jar of cold water to his room and set it beside the one-legged stone table.

Damien sat down at the table and plunged his arm into the water. The cold would help bring the swelling down.

After soaking his arm for twenty minutes, he reached into his duffel bag and pulled out his backup gun: a classic Colt .45—simple, beautiful, powerful. He found it awkward to clean the gun with one hand, but he managed the job. He held the piece up in his left hand, sighting down the barrel.

Two years ago, he had qualified as a marksman with his left hand—not as good as his expert marksman rating right-handed, but good enough for this job.

"Scarlett O'Hara had it right, after all," he said aloud, enjoying the sound of his own voice in the quiet room.

"Tomorrow really *is* another day."

THIRTY

Ari

Ari stared at his friends in disbelief. Baruch slowly lowered Rivka into a standing position. Hana leapt in the air, a huge smile on her face. Miryam said, "Praise the God of our fathers!"

"What are you doing?" Ari asked. "She can't walk in her condition."

"I'm fine," Rivka said.

"Does your head hurt?" Baruch asked.

"No, not at all." Rivka rolled her head around in a slow circle, then shook it gently. "It feels fine. Where are we? What happened to Dr. West?"

"He escaped," Ari said. "You broke his weapon." He reached out and shook her hand. "Congratulations, Rivka. You won. You've defeated Damien. Now we must go home. The wormhole is to shut down at once."

"How do you know?" Rivka said. Worry lines etched themselves across her face. "I don't think we should go back yet."

"We have to!" Ari turned and raced back to the phone, which had fallen in the dirt. The connection had broken. Hastily, he punched in Dov's number again and stepped into the wormhole. "Rivka, please come stand with me and speak to Dov."

Dov

Dov answered the phone after half a ring. It was now connected to a speaker system so that all in the room could hear both ends of the conversation. His whole body ached with anxiety.

"Ari! Do not play any more games, please! The *Haredim* are very unhappy. *Shabbat* is approaching, and we have passed the deadline to cut off power to the device. I have given orders to open the door."

"No!" Rivka's voice squawked through the phone.

"Rivka, is that you?" Dov shouted. *What was going on?* "Ari said you were severely injured." Beads of sweat slid down his face. He looked up nervously. The *Haredim* crowded round him, dark suspicion in their eyes. Dov had never hated anyone the way he hated these black-coated men.

"I'm fine!" Rivka shouted.

"Not true," Ari's voice cut in. "She had a serious head injury, Dov, a concussion. Apparently, the effects are wearing off, but—"

Dov wiped his forehead with his sleeve. Ari and Rivka were making a fool of him, and the *Haredim* would not stand for this.

"I'm fine!" Rivka shouted again. "And I'm not coming back yet."

"Yes, you are," Ari said. "Dov, please open the door. We are coming through at once."

"No!" Rivka shouted. "I have to stay! Dov, can you keep the wormhole open for one more day? I just know Dr. West has another trick up his sleeve. I've got to stop—"

"Open the door, Dov!" Ari said. Then the line went quiet.

Apparently Ari had covered the mouthpiece with his hand. A black-suited *Haredi* dialed up the amplification on the sound system until the static roared. Dov heard the muffled sound of Ari's voice. "Rivka, this is serious. The idiot *Haredim* want to shut down the wormhole right now. You are coming with me now. Is that clear?"

Dov's ears burned. The circle of Haredim glared at him, fury smoldering in their eyes. "Ari, Rivka, please listen! I am going to open the door and let you through, and then we will shut down the device." Dov stepped toward the door. Nobody moved to stop him.

As Dov passed by Dr. Hsiu, the stoop-shouldered physicist tweaked the knobs again. The power supply sparked wildly for a moment. "Now, go!" Dr. Hsiu said. "Safe for another minute, maybe. Hurry!"

Dov leaped to the door and flung it open.

Ari

Terror clawed at Ari's heart. "Stop it, Rivka!" Ari said. "We've got to go now." He pulled again on her hand.

He heard the door to the laboratory fly open behind him.

"I won't go," Rivka said. "I've got to stay for one more day."

"We don't have another day," Ari said. "We have one minute. They are serious, Rivka!"

Rivka yanked her hand free from Ari and hit him in the chest. "Go! Go get your precious Nobel prize, Mr. Great Physicist! I'm staying."

Baruch and Hana and Miryam stepped into the wormhole. Blessed be HaShem! One of them could talk sense into Rivka. "Hana! Please speak wisdom to her. Sister Miryam! Brother Baruch! Say something."

"I'm not a child, Ari Kazan," Rivka said. "This is my decision. I am staying. Now go. You have thirty seconds. Save yourself."

"Ari!" his *Imma* shouted from inside the laboratory. "Ari, come home!"

Dov's voice joined in. "Quickly, Ari. Rivka, come!"

"Go!" Rivka said.

Ari turned to look into the laboratory. Dov stood barely two meters away, restrained by two soldiers of the Israel Defense Forces. "Come now, Ari!"

He took a step toward the lab. There was no point in staying. Damien's quest had proved hopeless, just as the mathematics required. Rivka had gone crazy or something. She wasn't going to return, and he couldn't force her. On the other side of that door waited his family, his friends, and very likely a Nobel.

And on this side?

Only the woman he was unfortunate enough to be in love with.

Which was crazy. She didn't love him, and she wouldn't have him even if she did love him. Because of religious differences. Ridiculous religious differences.

Ari made his decision. Quickly, he stepped onto the threshold of the doorway.

"He's coming!" someone shouted. "Step back and let him through!"

Dov and the soldiers backed away from the door.

Ari could see his *Imma,* hysterical, held back by his stepfather and younger brother. Around them, the black-suited *Haredim.* Dr. Hsiu grinned at him from the console of the power supply.

Ari leaned into the lab and grabbed the doorknob.

"I'm sorry," he said. "I won't come back without her. May the God of our fathers bless you all."

He stepped backward and shut the door. The last sound he heard was his *Imma* screaming.

Ari turned and pushed his friends back, away from the wormhole. "Hurry!" he shouted. "Get out of the cave."

They fled before him. Rivka tripped and fell on the ground. Ari scooped her up and set her on her feet. "I love you," he said.

Hand in hand, they staggered toward daylight.

Mordecai

Mordecai was sick to death of this godless *apikoros,* this Lifshutz, who thought himself more important than the Torah. And Kazan, crazy after a foolish woman.

"Just wait another day!" Dov shouted. "Rivka is not well! She has lost her sanity."

But Mordecai had no more time to waste. *Shabbat* would soon appear—Queen *Shabbat,* the delight of all the week. It would be an abomination to allow the atheists to violate *Shabbat.*

Mordecai signaled to his friends. Avner muscled the Chinese physicist away from the power console.

"What are you doing?" Dov shouted. "Get away from that thing!" He rushed forward. Arik and Shmuli stepped in front of him. Tsvi and Shaul grappled him from behind.

Mordecai stepped to the power supply and pulled down on the red power-off switch.

A shower of sparks flew up from the device. Something behind the door made a tremendous bang. Mad with glee, Mordecai spontaneously raised his M-16 and fired into the power supply. The shot echoed through the lab.

Silence followed—the peace of approaching *Shabbat.*

Blessed be HaShem!

Dov

When the switch closed, Dov involuntarily shut his eyes. He heard a bang, followed shortly by a rifle shot. Then silence. He dared to look. The red light on the power supply had gone out.

Cheers erupted around the room. Dr. Hsiu rushed at the man with the gun, jabbering at him furiously in Chinese. It took several minutes for the confusion to die down.

The CNN crew made its way forward. "Mr. Lifshutz, can you tell us what this means?"

Dov's vision blurred with tears. He wiped his sleeve across his eyes, but he could not stop crying. He turned to face the blaze of the TV lights. "It means they're gone," he said. "Gone forever."

He stepped to the door which Ari had shut a minute earlier. Before anyone could stop him, he flung it open. He saw the inside of a closet. Empty.

Dov turned back to face the camera. Bitterness slashed through his soul. *"Shabbat Shalom."*

PART IV:
ENDGAME

The next morning the Jews formed a conspiracy
and bound themselves with an oath not to eat or
drink until they had killed Paul. More than forty
men were involved in this plot...But when
the son of Paul's sister heard of this
plot, he went into the barracks
and told Paul.

—Acts 23:12-16
New International Version

THIRTY-ONE

Damien

The room stank of urine and antiseptic. An IV ran from overhead into Stu's arm. Damien stared at his brother. Ten years of hell.

Almost ten years exactly, since the day Stu had broken his neck. Damien had just come home from his graduation from Michigan State. The funny thing was, college graduate or not, whenever he came to see Stu, he reverted to talking like a junior high school kid. Stu hadn't done a lick of schoolwork since his accident, and somehow, Damien was afraid to act too smart around his brother.

"So you made it," Stu said. "Congratulations, kid. Now what?"

Damien shrugged. "Ain't much you can do with a bachelor's degree in physics. I'm going to graduate school."

"Great," Stu said without enthusiasm. His voice sounded hollow. "Do me a favor, kid, okay?"

"Sure," Damien said. "Just name it, I'll do it."

"Anything?" Stu said. "Close the door and promise me you'll do anything I ask."

317

That shouldn't be hard. There wasn't much Stu could want, anyway. Damien nudged the door shut with his foot. "Okay, yeah," he said. "Anything."

"Get me out of here," Stu said.

Damien looked around the room of the nursing home. "You mean, like in a wheelchair or something? You want to go outside for a while?"

"No, I mean like off me," Stu said.

Damien sucked in his breath. "You're kidding."

"No." Stu's voice turned hard and cold. "Kid, this place is a hole. I ain't nothing but a lump of meat, and I can't stand it no more. Get me out."

"You're talking about murder," Damien said. "I could get in a lot of trouble." It was a lousy excuse, but the best he could think of.

"Kid, you promised. Carry through." Stu's chin jutted at him.

"Why do you need me?" Damien said. "You got control of your own life. Nobody's making you eat."

"Think again, braino," Stu said. "See that IV in my arm? It ain't there to improve my looks. I quit eating six weeks ago. Fat lot of good it did me. They got the technology to make me eat, whether I want to or not."

Damien stood silent, wondering what to do. A promise to kill someone wasn't really a promise, was it?

"It's Dullsville here," Stu said. "I ain't got squat to do."

"You could watch TV."

Stu laughed harshly. "You know what's on TV? Probably not—you're too busy studying. I'll tell you. On daytime TV, you got your idiot talk shows and your soaps. On the weekends, you got sports. Evenings, you got action shows. So you get a chance to watch morons blab, or you get to watch people getting married and divorced, or playing games, or going to war, or shooting up the bad guys. Guess what, kid? I ain't never going to marry nobody. I ain't never going to play baseball or football. I ain't never going to war. Nothing, kid. All I get to do is watch. I hate it."

Damien shivered. What a life.

"Know what the problem is?" Stu said. "America's too civilized, that's what. In the bad old days, someone got hurt and what did the people do? Stuck 'em out on the mountain to freeze to death or get ate by wolves. Nowadays, we're too goody-goody for that. We got the technology. We got to keep those vegetables alive. Run food in their veins, pipe dreams in their rooms. Not that we got enough technology to do anything practical, like fix their spinal cords. Sorrrrrrry, that would be too much trouble. We got just enough technology to maximize the misery." Stu shook his head in fury. "I hate this country."

Damien sighed. And decided.

"Okay, Stu, I'll do what I can. I got an idea. They give you anything to make you sleep?"

"Like sleeping pills? They stick something in my IV to put me out at night."

"I'll find out what they use," Damien said. "I got a couple friends in med school. They can get me a bunch of stuff like that."

Stu's face relaxed. "Thanks, kid."

"The other thing is, we need to figure out how I can get in here at night, when nobody's looking," Damien said. "You're my brother and all, and I promised, but I don't want to go to jail over this."

"We're on the ground floor," Stu said. "I'll have the orderly leave the window open every night."

Damien hesitated. "Um…when you want to do it?"

"How soon can you get the med?"

"Couple of weeks," Damien said.

"Fine, then. Two weeks from tonight."

"Hey, Stu?"

"Yeah?"

"Would you do the same for me?"

Stu snorted. "Kid, I'd have left you underwater. You didn't do me no favors by hauling me out, you know."

"Sorry," Damien said.

"Well, now's your chance to make it right."

Damien swallowed hard. "Right."

Ari

"Brother Baruch, I want you to teach me to be a scribe," Ari said as they returned from prayers the next morning.

Baruch turned to look at him. "So you have given up hope of returning to your own country and your own time?"

Ari sighed deeply. "It is not possible." He had explained as much of the wormhole as he could to Baruch.

"With HaShem, all things are possible."

"Very well. It is not likely. I cannot continue to impose on you for all my needs. I want to learn a skill for which I can earn money."

"It is not easy to read and write," Baruch said.

"I can already read and write," Ari said. "But I cannot form the letters with a reed pen the way you do. Please teach me."

"It may not be possible."

"With HaShem, all things are possible."

They turned the last corner on the way home. A wealthy woman stood in the doorway of Baruch's house. She wore a dashing outfit of some kind of finely woven red cloth. A gorgeous veil completely covered her face and hair. Ari's mouth fell open. "Brother Baruch, do you have a rich girlfriend?"

"Please explain. What is a girlfriend?"

Ari sighed. "Never mind. I don't have one either."

They reached the door and stopped awkwardly. Ari didn't want to talk to a strange woman, and Baruch clearly wouldn't either.

The woman flipped her veil away from her face.

Rivka! Somehow she was the last person he had expected to be wearing such a gaudy outfit. A mix of emotions shot through him. For her, he had decided to live out the rest of his life in this century. For her, he would learn the art of the scribe. For her, he would do almost anything—except convert to her religion. "Rivka, where did you get that outlandish costume?"

Rivka smiled. "Do you like it? We couldn't get my clothes clean, so I had to take a little charity. One of Sister Miryam's friends is rather wealthy. You should see what she gave Hana!"

"I fear to imagine it," Ari said.

"Brother Ari, I have a question for Brother Baruch," Rivka said. They had reverted to Jerusalem customs, with both Baruch and Rivka communicating through Ari.

"I will be happy to answer Sister Rivka's question," said Baruch.

"This man Saul has a nephew who lives in Jerusalem," Rivka began.

Baruch's mouth fell open. "And how do you know that?" Immediately, he caught his error. "Brother Ari, ask Sister Rivka how she knows this thing. I only learned it myself last *Shabbat.*"

Now Rivka looked surprised. "What? Brother Ari, ask him if he knows this nephew."

"I studied with him in the school of Yohanan ben Zakkai," Baruch said. "I knew him for six years and never suspected that he was the nephew of Renegade Saul until I saw them together at the house of Brother Yaakov. How does Sister Rivka know of him?"

"He is famous in our country and our time," Rivka said.

"Gamaliel the dreamer is famous?" Baruch said. "Nonsense! He will never be a great Torah scholar."

"Perhaps not, but I must find him, Brother Ari," Rivka said. "Ask where—"

"I do not know where he lives," Baruch said, "but he works in the shop of Yohanan ben Zakkai."

Ari broke in. "Rivka, why do you need to know all this?"

Rivka switched to English. "This nephew is going to save Paul's life today."

"So?" Ari said.

"So I would bet you money Dr. West is going to try to stop him."

"Damien hasn't got a gun, and he's in no shape to stop anybody," Ari said. "What is this thing you have for Damien, anyway? It's over. You won. Let go of it, will you? We need to start thinking about how we're going to survive in this century."

"I'll think about that tomorrow," Rivka said. "Paul will get safely out of town tonight. He's leaving from the Antonia around 9 P.M.—if this Gamaliel does his job. I'm going to make sure he does."

"Promise me you won't go near Damien," Ari said. "Even with one arm disabled, he could break you in two."

"I've got this new disguise; even you didn't recognize me," Rivka said. "He won't notice me and—"

"Promise you won't go near him."

Rivka put her hand on Ari's arm and smiled straight into his soul. "I wouldn't go within shouting distance of him if my life depended on it. All I want to do is go see this Gamaliel and warn him, okay? That's all."

Ari bit his tongue. Rivka must be having trouble coming down from the excitement of helping to save Paul. Maybe the best thing to do would be to humor her for a day or two. What harm would there be in her running around town trying to be

Cassandra? She would talk to Gamaliel, save the universe or whatever, and then be happy.

"Okay, Ari?" Rivka asked.

"Yes, fine," he said. "Would you like to eat supper with Brother Baruch and me this evening? Then you can tell us all about your adventures."

She smiled. "Of course. I'll see you then." With that, she turned and headed down the street in the direction of the Temple.

"She is a strange woman," Baruch said. "I do not see why you should be attracted to such a one as her, Brother Ari."

Ari smiled. "Even King Solomon could not understand the way of a man with a woman, so how can I explain it?"

A strange expression crossed Baruch's face. It vanished almost immediately. "Very well, Brother Ari. We shall make a bargain then. You will teach me how it is *Shabbat* in your country, when it is only the fifth day of the week here in Jerusalem."

"And in exchange?"

"In exchange, I will teach you how to write the letters of the Torah according to the ways of the scribes."

"You drive a hard bargain," Ari said, wanting to laugh. "Agreed."

☾ ☾ ☾

The morning sped by. While Ari practiced the maddening art of scratching letters with a reed pen on a piece of thrice-scraped parchment, he and Baruch discussed HaShem and physics and Torah and philosophy and the nature of spacetime.

Baruch had no trouble understanding that time could be curved. Apparently, people here didn't think of time as a straight line anyway. They thought of it as a spiral. But Baruch could not understand how time and space could be the same.

For that matter, Ari had never understood it either. At a certain point, you couldn't really understand physics anyway. You accepted the results of experiments that proved space and time were linked. You developed mathematics to describe what you observed. After lots of playing around, you developed intuition for the equations. But did you then understand the physics? Yes and no.

"I do not understand, Brother Ari, and yet I believe it," Baruch said. "I believe you, and that is enough. You are a man of truth."

The reed pen in Ari's hand slipped, turning his carefully constructed *aleph* into gibberish. He felt frustrated and tired after hours of hunching over the table. His mind had begun to wander. What had possessed him to stay? Rivka, of course. But what if she wouldn't yield in the matter of her religion? What if—

A commotion out in the street yanked Ari back to reality. He heard the sound of men shouting. But what terrified Ari was not the men. It was the high-pitched shriek of a woman's voice.

Wailing in wordless grief.

THIRTY-TWO

Rivka

Rivka hurried down the hill toward the shop of Rabban Yohanan ben Zakkai. What a coincidence that Paul's nephew should be working in the shop of Rabban Yohanan!

Or was it such a coincidence? Paul and Yohanan were about the same age. Both had come to this city as young men to study at the feet of the great master Rabban Gamaliel. The nephew would hail from a Torah-loving family; why else would his parents name him Gamaliel? And if Paul and Yohanan had once been good friends, that would explain how young Gamaliel got his job. Scholars looked out for other scholars.

Rivka hadn't really thought about it until now, but Paul and Rabban Yohanan must have known each other very well thirty years ago. That explained Yohanan's actions yesterday. But did Yohanan know of Paul's current theological position? Probably not.

Rivka smiled. Come to think of it, even with two thousand years of scholarship at her disposal, did she really know where Paul stood? On every issue? She based her understanding of Paul on a few tens of thousands of words he had written. In Greek. Not her native language and not his. Was that enough to know somebody?

The only way to get inside Paul's head would be to go talk to him. And her odds of getting an audience with him were about the same as her chances of getting back to her own century with Ari.

Ari. Guilt shot through Rivka's heart. All because of her, Ari was now stranded here in the past. To be with her. But why had *she* stayed?

She didn't really know. When she had regained consciousness yesterday, a certainty had filled her heart that she must stay. She was God's avatar in this surreal city. Without her, Paul would be dead. And he might still be in danger, though she didn't quite see how.

Dr. West no longer had a weapon with which to kill Paul. Furthermore, Brother Baruch had practically maimed him yesterday, stomping on his arm like that. Baruch, normally so mild, could be ferocious when he had to be. There was more behind that man than met the eye.

But Ari!

Why had *he* stayed? Okay, so he was in love with her. That was sweet, but impractical. He was a nice guy. Attractive, in his own way. Wonderful to talk to.

But he had a problem with her religion, and that made a problem for Rivka. She wasn't going to get involved with a guy who couldn't even talk about Yeshua without foaming at the mouth. *Father, could You make Ari just a little more tolerant? Please?*

Come to think of it, Ari had changed—some. After that amazing hornet-sting episode, he was convinced God existed. And Brother Baruch was an excellent influence. If Ari stayed here long, who knew what might happen? Maybe someday he would lose his antagonism to Yeshua. If he did that, well…something might develop.

But if he didn't?

Rivka suddenly stopped. Up to now, she hadn't thought much about her future here. She had been concentrating on saving the world, fixing up the mess Damien had created. She had another day of doing that. And then what?

According to Ari, they were stuck here permanently. They were going to live out their lives in first-century Judea. They were going to die here.

And Rivka didn't want to die a single woman.

But that presented a problem. Who here *wouldn't* have religious differences with her?

Christianity as she knew it didn't exist yet. No Catholics, no Protestants, no Jehovah's Witnesses. Even Messianic Judaism as she knew it didn't really exist.

For that matter, science didn't exist. Historical-critical study of ancient literature didn't exist. A fair bit of what she considered ancient literature hadn't been written yet.

Who in this world could she marry? Who would have a clue what she was thinking? She wasn't much of a feminist by modern standards, but she had about two millennia head start on anyone now living. Except Ari.

Rivka, you are in deep trouble. You have no chance of a happy family life, no chance of finishing your education. And how are you going to make a living?

Rivka shivered. Her prospects certainly looked bleak. If she was going to live in this century, she didn't have many choices. She could get married. She could live on charity. She could work as a domestic servant or sell herself as a slave.

Don't think about any of that. For today, do what you have to do. Worry about tomorrow tomorrow.

She arrived at the bottom of the hill and turned left onto the street of shops running alongside the Temple Mount. The door stood open at the shop of Yohanan ben Zakkai. Rivka went in.

The old man looked at her with his merchant's face. "How may I help you?"

Rivka pushed her veil aside. Yohanan's face lit up with joy. "Bless you, my daughter. Your new clothing fooled me. HaShem must have sent you yesterday. Let me tell you what happened."

Rivka nodded. What good would it do to tell him that she had already read the book and knew how it would end?

For the next fifteen minutes, the old rabbi paced back and forth in his tiny shop, recounting his adventures in finding the other Pharisees, how they had barged into the meeting just before it began, how Paul had made a fool of that scoundrel Hananyah, and finally how Yohanan himself had nearly punched one of the Sadducees. Rivka wished she could have seen it. But, of course, a woman would never have been allowed to watch a session of the Sanhedrin.

But no matter. Everything had gone the way it was supposed to. Rivka had interfered with history, but her interference was precisely that required in order to make the history work out the way it was supposed to. So far, Ari had been right.

Finally, Rabban Yohanan interrupted his tale. "My daughter, you seem not the least surprised."

Rivka smiled. "All is in the hands of HaShem, my father."

Yohanan's face darkened. "I have heard that used as an excuse to do nothing."

"My father, it is not an excuse to do nothing; it is a reason to do what HaShem would have me to do, confident that He will guide my weak hands to do what I cannot do in my own strength."

The sage tugged at his thin gray beard, his eyes astonished. "You are wise, my daughter. Who taught you? Are you a prophetess?"

"My teacher is the God of our fathers," Rivka said. "And He has given me to know a little of what must happen. I know that Hananyah will call Saul to another trial tomorrow."

"That is correct," Yohanan said. "But how did you know he did not call this trial for today?"

"And I also know that Saul is in great danger, but not from Hananyah."

Yohanan's eyes narrowed. "You know more than I do, my child. What must be done?"

"Saul has a nephew who works for you, correct?"

Yohanan did not even look surprised. "Yes, Gamaliel. Like a son to me, since they killed his father. But he has been sick since the day after *Shabbat*. What has he to do with this?"

"You must tell me where he lives," Rivka said. "It is urgent."

"I will take you there," Yohanan said. "But tell me this. How is it that you know everything about Gamaliel except where he lives?"

Rivka stepped out into the street. What could she possibly say to that?

While she tried to think of an answer, the old rabbi produced a key and locked his shop. When he turned to Rivka, his probing eyes studied her.

The only answer she could think of was to tell the truth. "I have been given a part of the truth, and you also, my father. But HaShem alone can bring us together to make the truth into a whole that gives life."

Rabban Yohanan sighed deeply. "Alas, that you are only a woman. I would have welcomed a mind and a heart like yours into my school."

Rivka bit her tongue.

With the Rabban leading and Rivka following, they walked in silence along the avenue that led north along the western wall of the Temple Mount. When they reached the Fortress Antonia,

Rabban Yohanan turned west along a broad street. Shortly, this forked. He took the right fork, heading northwest. Five minutes later, they turned right on a narrow street. The houses here were large and well-built, with spaces between the buildings. It was a far cry from the crowded slum where Hana lived, or the jammed district that Baruch called home.

Rabban Yohanan stopped at a beautiful home and knocked at the door.

They waited. Nobody answered the door.

"It is likely that Gamaliel is sleeping," Yohanan said. "His grandmother may well be out shopping."

"What about the rest of his family?" Rivka asked. "His mother? His brothers and sisters?"

"He has no other family," Yohanan said. "His mother died many years ago, and he is an only child."

"I will wait for his grandmother."

The old sage raised his hand over her head. "The Lord bless you and keep you, the Lord make his face to shine upon you and be gracious to you, and give you success in all the works of your hands."

"I will find you tomorrow and tell you what happens," Rivka said.

Rabban Yohanan nodded. "*Shalom*, my daughter." He turned and began walking back toward his shop.

Rivka watched the old sage until he disappeared around the corner. Thank God an old merchant would talk to a woman. She paced back and forth in front of the house. Sometime today, Gamaliel would walk out of this door and down the street toward the Antonia.

And then what?

Then Dr. West would do something. But what?

Whatever he had planned, she would have to fight back.

Baruch

Baruch opened the door. Outside his home stood half a dozen of his friends—good men, followers of Yeshua, doers of Torah and not hearers only. With them stood two women. Hana wore the elegant yet modest white silk tunic of a wealthy older woman, but her face had gone stony and cold.

Sister Miryam wore a look of anguish. The shouts of the men told Baruch everything he needed to know.

Baruch had been dreading this moment ever since Hana came back into his life. Now they would all learn the truth, and his old sins would be exposed. He had been raised strictly, according to Torah. All his life, he had tried to do right, to walk in the ways of truth and righteousness, to stay far from sin.

And he had failed. Miserably.

He had a weakness for the women who carried water. Many times, he had broken the commandments on account of those women. Then, about a year ago, something terrible had happened.

The woman he hired that day had been this Hana. She seemed no different from the others. But after he left her, he found that he could not forget her. Voices repeated her name inside his head, over and over again. He could not sleep. He could not eat.

Every day he went back for more of her. And every day his obsession grew. It filled all his mind and darkened his soul and gnawed his spirit. He knew what had happened, and it terrified him. An evil spirit had entered him on account of his sin.

One day, after using her, such a terror entered his heart that he left her without paying. He ran through the streets, fear stabbing at his heart, driven mad by the evil spirit.

The voice in his head shouted that he must die. Frantic, he ran toward his home, intending to find a knife and kill himself.

And then he ran into Yaakov the *Tsaddik*. Literally ran into him, knocked him over. Yaakov was a *tsaddik*, a righteous man, a holy man. Yaakov had no fear of evil spirits, and he had the power to make them flee.

After a few hours in the quiet of Yaakov's home, HaShem restored Baruch's mind. And more. Yaakov the *Tsaddik* was the brother of a man named Yeshua, at whose name evil spirits begged for mercy. Yaakov explained how Yeshua had lived as the Servant of HaShem, how He had suffered and died by the will of HaShem, how He rose from the dead, was seen by many, and then returned to the right hand of HaShem to await the final judgment. Soon, He would return to reign as the anointed King, as the *Mashiach*, and He would crush the evil *goyim* under His feet.

For Baruch, the last year had been a year of peace. He had not suffered from the evil spirits. Nor had he gone near the women who carried water. He had confessed his sin to Yaakov, and that was enough. He did not wish to tell his new friends in The Way of his previous shameful life.

And then he had met Ari and Rivka. Now Hana was back, and he knew that soon his friends would learn the truth and despise him.

Today, his fears had come true. Evidently, Hana had told them his sins. Here they stood, ready to condemn him. What could he say?

Brother Yoseph spoke first. "Brother Baruch, we have learned that this woman Hana is a *zonah*. It is not fitting that she should stay with Sister Miryam anymore."

Sister Miryam shook her head. "But Hana is in danger! An evil man tried to kill her."

"She deserves it," said Brother Yonatan. He was a large man, with thick, wet lips, and he blinked frequently when he talked. "She must not contaminate Sister Miryam."

Baruch felt a strange sense of relief surge through his heart. They did not know of his violation of the commandments. But their sneering at Hana angered him. Hana had shown generosity and compassion to Sister Rivka. "I do not think Sister Miryam would be easily contaminated." He fought to keep his voice even. "I have cast many evil spirits out of this woman. It would be good for her to remain with Sister Miryam."

"Brother Baruch, you are too innocent," Brother Yoseph said. "It is the good who are contaminated by evil, not the other way around. She must be put out. The life she has chosen—"

"Chosen!" Hana shouted. "You fool! Who would choose the life I have been forced to live? I was once a respectable wife, but then my husband died. I had no family, no money, no nothing. I had only my body, which men paid for. Some of them were righteous men." She scowled around the circle, glaring at each man until he looked away.

Her eyes fell last on Baruch. He could not bear to look at her. Now she would expose his sin and he would be disgraced. And he deserved it, because he had sinned. His eyes fell, full of tears.

"You men have many choices in life," Hana went on. "I had none, except to die with honor or live in shame. A man can use a *zonah* for his pleasure one day, and the next go his own way. But a woman who is a *zonah* once is a *zonah* always. No man will have her, nor can she find honor ever again, while she lives under the sun. You fools! Tell me who would choose such a life?"

Baruch felt his heart cut to the quick. She was more honorable than he. She could expose him now, and yet she did not. He was as great a sinner as she, and yet he lived in honor while she lived in shame. Until yesterday, she had lived in bondage to the evil spirits, just as he had once. Now she lived free. Could she not be forgiven, purified, made new, as he had been?

No, she could not. Such things were not possible. And yet…

And yet, since yesterday, Baruch had felt his heart burning with compassion for this woman, wondering how she could receive a new life, when her old life lashed at her so cruelly.

But was it compassion only that he felt? Suddenly, he realized it was something more.

"Brother Baruch, you are wise," said Brother Yonatan. "Tell us what you think should be done with this *zonah*."

Something broke deep within Baruch's soul. He felt an anger rising within his heart—a righteous anger, the anger of Yeshua at injustice.

"I will tell you what must be done," Baruch said. "We must find a husband for her."

Dead silence ran around the circle. Brother Yonatan's fat lips fell open in disbelief. Brother Yoseph's eyes bulged out. Hana laughed out loud, mocking Baruch. "That is foolishness. I am a *zonah*, a wicked sinner. Who would be fool enough to take me?"

Words formed inside Baruch's head, molded his tongue, poured out of his mouth. Even as he spoke the words, he could not believe his own spectacular folly. "I will take you, Hana."

Hana stared at him.

A nervous snicker escaped Brother Yonatan. "That is a foolish joke, Brother Baruch! Do not say such things, even in jest."

Baruch swallowed hard. Brother Yonatan had just offered him a way out. But he could not take it. "It is no jest. Hana, I ask you to be my wife."

"You have lost your wits!" Brother Yoseph said.

Brother Yonatan licked his thick lips. "You have an evil spirit."

Behind him, Brother Ari whispered in his ear. "What kind of trick are you playing, Brother Baruch? This is craziness."

Hana jutted her chin at him. "You are playing me for the fool." She hesitated, and a secretive smile crossed her face.

Now she will tell them all about my sin. Baruch shuddered. *And I deserve whatever humiliation she heaps on me.*

Abruptly, she turned her head away from him and folded her arms across her chest. "But I have made up my mind. I will go back to my own house and not trouble you righteous people anymore, lest I contaminate you. If the bad man kills me, it will not matter, since I am only a wicked *zonah.*" She stepped backward.

The men behind her leaped out of her way.

Baruch was sweating now. Fury raced through his veins. Why would they not believe him? "Stop it, all of you!" he shouted. "You are mocking me, and I will not have it!" He stepped out of his house. "Hana!"

She stopped and turned to look at him.

"Hana, I am speaking the truth before HaShem. I am not lying. Now make your decision. Will you be my wife?"

Hana's eyes bored into his for a long moment. Then she looked around the circle at the others, and her face hardened into a sarcastic smile. "No. Only a witless man would marry a *zonah,* and I would never marry a fool."

She turned and stalked away down the street.

Baruch felt his ears burning. How dare she humiliate him?

Uneasiness hung like thick fog over the group. Brother Yonatan studied something in the dirt, all the while taking tiny steps backward. Brother Yoseph cleared his throat several times and then looked away down the street. Sister Miryam seemed ready to say something, but she kept silent.

"Friends," Brother Ari said, "I must speak to Brother Baruch in private." He took hold of Baruch's shoulders and gently pulled him back into the house.

Relief showed on every face. Then Brother Ari shut the door. Baruch collapsed onto the floor. He had not known he loved Hana until he had asked her to marry him. Now he knew it all the way to his marrow. And he also knew that he would never have her.

He clutched his beard and began to wail.

THIRTY-THREE

Rivka

After waiting an hour, Rivka began to get tired. How long would this take? She hadn't counted on standing out in the hot sun all day.

An old woman marched briskly up the street. In one hand, she carried a lump of goat cheese. In the other, a loaf of flat bread. She stopped at the door of Gamaliel's house.

"Shalom!" Rivka called. "Are you the grandmother of Gamaliel?" What had Yohanan said her name was? Oh, yes— Marta.

The old woman turned and looked at her suspiciously. "Who are you?"

Rivka hesitated. "I am a friend of Rabban Yohanan ben Zakkai." Instantly, she realized she had just made two blunders.

"A friend?" Marta said, her face openly skeptical. "And is he calling himself *Rabban* now? Old fool."

"No...I mean, it was my idea to call him that," Rivka said. "And actually, he's a distant relative." *He's Jewish. I'm Jewish. So we're related, right?*

Marta cackled. "Oh, now he's your relative, is he? When he gets to be your nephew, let me know."

337

Rivka felt her cheeks burning. She had really fouled this one up in a hurry. She decided to change the subject. "I need to speak to Gamaliel."

Marta took a key from her belt and unlocked her front door. "Perhaps you are Gamaliel's cousin? His sister? If so, then you have a right to see him. Otherwise, no. He is sick and must sleep. Two days ago, he was near death."

Rivka gasped. "What sickness is he suffering from?"

Marta stepped inside the house. "The summer fever. Now go away." The door thudded shut behind her.

The summer fever. It sounded harmless, but Rivka knew better. Modern scholars weren't quite sure of its identity. Malaria, maybe. Or typhus fever. Something dangerous. People died from it.

If Gamaliel had the summer fever, then he was in big trouble.

And therefore, Paul was in big trouble. Somewhere in this city, a group of forty or so young men had taken an oath to kill Paul. They planned to kill him tomorrow when the high priest summoned him to a second hearing.

The Book of Acts wasn't quite clear, but the Greek text seemed to say that Paul's nephew was one of the conspirators. Most English translations didn't even allude to that possibility, but the better commentaries mentioned it.

Conspirator or not, tonight Gamaliel was supposed to go tell Paul about the plot. By 9 P.M. Paul would be on his way out of town with several hundred Romans guarding him.

But if Gamaliel didn't do his task, those forty young men would kill Paul. Dr. West wouldn't have to lift a finger. Rivka didn't have a clue how she could stop forty young zealots armed with stones and clubs and daggers.

If Gamaliel was as sick as Marta said, then he wouldn't go anywhere tonight.

Rivka began pacing outside the house, sick with worry. *Please, God, heal Gamaliel!*

Hana

Hana's eyes blurred as she rushed down the hill toward her house. He was cruel. She had thought Baruch was a kind man, but he was cruel. Why else would he have played such a game with her, taunting her with an empty promise of marriage?

Until now, she had respected him. He had shown great kindness to Rivka, had probably saved her life. And he had allowed Hana to stay with Miryam, even knowing she was a *zonah*. Until now, she had thought him a righteous man. He was changed from a year ago, when his appetite for her had twisted him into evil.

But now, she could see it was all a farce. He had mocked her before his friends, waiting for her to accept his false offer of marriage. Then he would withdraw it, and they would make sport of her and drive her away.

If the bad man returned, he would kill her, and she no longer cared. Better to die than to live the life of a *zonah*. She could no longer tolerate this life, constantly having men violate her, eating the strange herbs that caused her body to feel so restless. No more.

The easy way to die would be to find the bad man. He would kill her at once, and her suffering would end. Hana passed her own house and continued walking toward the house where the bad man lived.

When she reached it, she pounded on the door.

No answer.

She beat on it again.

Still nothing.

Hana stepped back and waited. Some moments passed before she realized why she waited. Ordinarily, the truth-tellers would tell her what to do.

But the truth-tellers were gone. Baruch had banished them. He had chased them away.

Baruch had power over the evil spirits. He had meant it as a kindness, but now she was alone—powerless and without knowledge in an evil world pitted against her.

At last, Hana gave up. The house of the bad man was empty, and the truth-tellers were silent. Uncertainly, she turned and trudged back toward her own house.

Baruch had power over the evil spirits. Only HaShem could give a man that power. So perhaps Baruch was truly a good man. Then why had he mocked her?

But what if he had not mocked her? What if he had told the truth? Would a good man swear falsely? No. It was not possible.

Then was it possible that he really wanted her? But why? For the pleasure she could give him? If so, why did he not merely pay for an hour and be done with it?

No, it was not simply for the pleasure.

Then why?

He was a compassionate man—that was it. He must be thinking to do her good.

But what man would make such a sacrifice as to marry a *zonah*? What foolishness was this? And besides, he had sworn that he loved her. A good man would not swear falsely. Baruch was a good man. Therefore, he must love her.

He would have been a good husband.

But she would have been a very bad wife. She would have loved him, of course. He was a good man, a kind man, a gentle man. But still, she was a *zonah*. He would live his life in humiliation before his friends, and so she would also. She could not bear such a life.

No, that was not true. She could bear it, because she had been bearing it. All her neighbors knew what sort of woman she was, and they despised her for it and scolded their men for looking at her with hunger in their eyes.

Hana could bear such a life. But Baruch could not.

He was a good man. She could not allow him to live his life married to a *zonah*. It was best that she had humiliated him. He would come to his senses before he ruined his life.

By the time she reached her house, Hana was crying again.

Ari

"Brother Baruch, if I may make a suggestion—"

"No!" Baruch shouted. "I do not want your suggestions. Just...leave me in peace."

"Very well then." Ari went to the door and stepped out. A minute later, he was striding down the hill.

You're meddling, Ari Kazan. This is a job for a woman, not you. Who are you to interfere in the lives of these two people?

Ari hushed the voices of dissent in his mind. All his life, he had been too ready to do nothing. Take the passive road, the path of zero resistance. And that was wrong. Rivka did no such thing. When she thought a thing right, she did it, at the risk of her own life. He admired that. He didn't deserve such a woman as Rivka. And now here was a small task, a woman's job, and he feared to do it.

Ari Kazan, you are a mouse!

No more. He would no longer live his life in fear. Brother Baruch was not afraid to do a generous thing. Nor Rivka. Nor Hana. He was not worthy of such friends.

Today, just one time, he would not think about himself. He would think about doing what was right.

The sun hung high and warm overhead, and he did not hurry. There was no point in hurrying, anyway. No clocks troubled this city. The watch on his wrist was now worthless. Life in this century was not measured in the microseconds of the computer age, but in hours and days, in months and years, the slow turning of HaShem's time in the city of HaShem.

Except that it would not be HaShem's city much longer. In less than ten years, a war would begin here. It would end in the destruction of the Temple, the death of many tens of thousands, the exile of those unlucky enough to survive.

And he would live through it. Rivka perhaps still had some hope that they would yet be rescued by a second wormhole. Ari knew better. They could not get back. They would live and die here.

When he reached the street where Hana lived, he saw her fumbling at the door, tears streaming down her face.

He stopped. Should he interfere?

Because of him, Baruch and Hana had already been reintroduced. He had already interfered. Nothing he could do would make things worse. He had nothing to lose by trying.

"Sister Hana!" he called.

Just then, Hana managed to get her door open. Her head spun around to look at him. She said nothing, only stared blankly.

"Sister Hana, may I speak with you?"

She shrugged. "If you wish."

Ari suddenly realized he did not know what to say. He had been so afraid of actually doing this that he hadn't thought through what he intended to tell her. They went into the house. Hana shut the door and they sat down on the floor.

He said the first thing that came into his head. "Tell me how you feel." Immediately, he knew it was the wrong thing to say.

But Hana began talking anyway.

Ari had a hard time following her. He was still not very fluent in Aramaic. But what did it matter, as long as she talked?

She talked for a quarter of an hour. Baruch was a good man. A kind man. But his friends were not good, not kind. They did not look at the heart; they looked only on the outside of a person. Baruch could see into her heart. Baruch knew she was not wicked. If it were not for his friends, she would be only too happy to marry him.

But his friends would make life a misery for her. And worse, they would make Baruch's life a misery. It would be a torment for him. His friends would see to that.

Ari let her talk and talk and talk, until she finished.

When she stopped, Ari simply sat quietly for some time. "He is a good man," he said at last.

Hana nodded, and again launched into a long monologue on what a good man Baruch was.

When she wound down, Ari again said nothing for a long time. Finally, he asked, "Do you love him?"

This prompted another outburst. Ari had a very hard time understanding any of this, but one thing was clear. Yes, she did love Baruch. Loved him too much to allow him to suffer on her account.

"So you love him, but you do not love his friends?"

Hana sniffled and buried her face in her hands.

Ari repeated the question.

"Yes," she said in a hollow voice.

"He loves you," Ari said. "It seems that he also loves his friends, although I do not see why. But it may be that he loves you more than his friends. Suppose he were willing to move to a different place, far from his friends?"

Hana uncovered her face. Slowly, she raised her head and looked up at him. "Would he do that for me?"

In truth, Ari did not know. A surge of panic nearly choked him. To speak at all would be to lie. "Yes, Brother Baruch would do that." *May HaShem forgive me if I have guessed wrong.*

Hana's eyes filled with uncertainty. By that, Ari knew that she had really lost her "truth-tellers." It seemed inconceivable to him that such things as evil spirits could really exist. What did it even mean to talk about disembodied personifications of evil? If they had no physical existence, how could they interact with material beings such as humans? And yet, something had caused those voices in Hana, had given her knowledge she should not have. Now that knowledge was gone.

He sighed. There was a limit, perhaps, to what physics could tell him.

"I am afraid," Hana said. "I am not sure that he really loves me more than his friends."

"Then come with me, and we shall ask him." Ari's heart skipped a beat. Had he really said that? What if Brother Baruch refused? What if—?

Stop it.

Ari could not say with certainty what Brother Baruch would do. And yet he knew Baruch. His knowledge of his friend's character gave him faith in how Baruch would act.

Ari stood up. "Come with me to the house of Brother Baruch and I will prove it to you."

Hana remained motionless, looking at him with enormous eyes.

Ari found that he could not breathe.

Then she stood up.

They went out of the house. While Hana locked the door, a meek little old woman hobbled down the street toward them. As she passed by, she spat at Ari's feet.

A wave of humiliation slapped Ari in the face. Did that woman honestly believe that he had done business with Hana?

Obviously, yes. Hana was a *zonah*. Ari was a man. He had been alone with her in her own house.

Brother Baruch would get this sort of treatment all his life—or worse. Infinitely worse to know your friends talked behind your back about your filthy wife, the *zonah*.

Ari shuddered. Was he crazy to be taking her back to Brother Baruch?

Hana put the key in her belt.

"Let us hurry," Ari said.

They walked in silence back up the hill.

The closer they drew to Brother Baruch's house, the more dread filled Ari's heart. It was foolishness to think that this could work.

He knew from his own experience how Hana must feel. He had felt the same way about HaShem. Like Brother Baruch, HaShem had friends Ari loathed. The *Haredim*—those joyless men wearing black, so quick to hate others who did not observe Torah in exact accordance with their tradition. The Muslim fanatics who bought a ticket to Paradise with a suicide bomb strapped to their backs. And especially the Christians—ever quick with the cross, and quicker with the sword and the stake and the oven.

All these were friends of HaShem, but they were not friends of Ari. How could HaShem tolerate such friends?

How could Brother Baruch tolerate his friends? Ari knew the answer as soon as he asked himself the question. Brother Baruch was a compassionate man. For that reason, he loved his friends. For that reason, he had taken Ari, a stranger, in off the street.

So, too, HaShem. He had healed Ari, who had kept himself a stranger all his life. Was it possible that HaShem also loved the *Haredim*? And the Muslim bombers? And…the Christians who had killed Jews in His name down the long ages?

They reached the house of Brother Baruch. Ari knocked at once, fearing that he would back out if he took time to think about it.

No answer.

"Brother Baruch!" Ari shouted. "I have met someone who needs you! Someone who needs care!"

A moment later, the latch clicked. The door swung slowly open. Brother Baruch stood there, his beard gray with dust, his eyes red and bleary.

Ari stepped to one side.

Brother Baruch's eyes swept past him to Hana, and his face reddened to the color of a brick. "You...need me?"

"I lied to you and your friends," Hana said quietly. "I do love you. But I am not worthy—"

Brother Baruch shot forward and wrapped his long arms around her, muffling any words that might have followed. "My Hana!" he said, and there was no doubt in Ari's heart that he would do anything, anything for her.

Ari looked at his watch. Perhaps it would be wise to find something else to do for the next few hours. It was now noon. Rivka would return in time for the evening meal. They would share a joyful supper together with Brother Baruch and Sister Hana.

In the meantime, Ari knew a market not far from here with several bookstores. Not books, actually—scrolls. Books with pages weren't invented yet.

It didn't matter, though. Ari wanted to go investigate. He slipped away from the happy couple and smiled.

Ari Kazan, you performed a commandment today—a mitzvah. Blessed be HaShem!

Rivka

In early afternoon, a young man arrived at the house of Gamaliel. Rivka recognized him at a distance, and shivered. He was the Temple guard who had nearly arrested her. Was that only two days ago?

She turned and hurried away up the street, stopping only when the young man entered Gamaliel's house. Was he one of the forty conspirators intent on assassinating Paul? Or just a friend? What should she do? Try to talk to him? Avoid him?

This waiting was driving her crazy. She hated standing around. It was much easier to obey God when He said, "Fight!" or "Argue!" or "Sacrifice yourself!" But when He said, "Wait!"— that made things hard. Ari was good at that sort of thing. He was patient. Strong. Stubborn as a two-headed mule.

Half an hour later, the young Temple guard left Gamaliel's house, going back the way he had come. Rivka might have caught him by running, but she had no idea what she would say to him. She felt she belonged here, waiting for Gamaliel. Waiting. A fate worse than death.

Time passed slowly. Rivka's stomach ached. She had eaten little that morning, and nothing at noon. She stood in what little shade she could find, and tried to look as if she were going somewhere whenever anyone approached on the street. This particular neighborhood was not very busy, unfortunately. She could have blended into a crowd, but there was nothing to blend into here, except dust and stones.

Late in the afternoon, a girl of about ten arrived. Gamaliel's grandmother Marta spoke to her briefly at the door, then sent her off running. Minutes later, Marta came out again, locking the door behind her, then scurrying after the girl.

Rivka stayed. And worried. What was Dr. West up to? Where was he? What was his physical condition? What was his plan?

He would try something. He had to, or this whole sorry venture of his would fail. And Dr. West was not the sort of man to give up easily.

Rivka clenched her fists. She didn't give up easily either.

Another half hour passed. The sun hung just above the horizon. A woman hurried up the street, stopped at Gamaliel's house, unlocked the door, and entered.

A woman? Not Gamaliel's relative. According to Marta, he didn't have any.

Then who? A friend? It was not likely that a female friend would visit alone. A secret lover? No. This woman looked to be in her forties. She was probably old enough to be his mother. And a lover wouldn't be much entertainment for a man as sick as Gamaliel.

Rivka batted the possibilities around for half an hour. Should she knock at the door and try her luck with this strange woman? But what if Marta returned? There might be a nasty scene. Some gut instinct told Rivka to wait.

By now, she felt very hungry. Soon it would get dark, and this street would become unsafe. Her feet ached from standing and walking all day. Was she crazy? Maybe Ari was right. She had gotten fixated on stopping Dr. West, and now she couldn't let go, even after she had won.

Just as the sun went down, the door opened. The woman came out, looked left and right, then locked the door and hurried down the street.

Rivka waited impatiently. A certainty had formed in her mind. Dr. West did not know where Gamaliel lived, or else he would have come here. Therefore, Gamaliel would play his role. She need only wait, and he would come out. Then she could follow him and see what game Dr. West would play.

There was only one problem with that. How could Dr. West play games if he didn't know the other player? What did Dr. West know that she didn't? What if Dr. West—

The door of Gamaliel's house opened. In its frame stood a stocky young man wearing a light cloak. His eyes were closed and he swayed slightly.

Finally, he drew a deep breath, opened his eyes, and lurched out onto the street.

Rivka sucked in her breath. The waiting was over. The game was afoot. The pieces were moving. And her teammate looked sick as a dog.

Damien

Damien drew his right hand out of the cold water. The cold had helped with the swelling. He took another pain pill, checked his watch, and stood up. It was time.

He rechecked his gun, his spare ammo, his victory cigar. *Houston, all systems are go.*

Damien wanted to laugh. Rivka had gotten lucky twice. No, she had made her own luck twice. This time, she would not, because she didn't know where the battle would be fought.

What if they held a war and only one side showed up?

Damien went to the door and stepped out into the darkness. According to his calculations, a week and a half had passed since the new moon. The moon should be halfway up in the sky and giving good light.

Yes. There it shone. Perfect. Cloudless. Enough light for a marksman to kill at a hundred yards.

Damien closed the door and locked it. He had expected problems all along. And he had gotten them—double what he feared.

In the end, persistence paid off. That, and always having a backup.

Damien fondled the gun in his left hand. *Okay, Rivka Meyers, let's see you top this one.*

THIRTY-FOUR

Ari

Dark was falling when Ari arrived back at Brother Baruch's house. He tried the door and found it locked. He knocked several times. Silence.

Presumably Baruch and Hana had gone to visit someone. But where was Rivka? She had agreed to eat supper with him and Brother Baruch this evening. A lot had happened since then. Could Rivka have gone somewhere with Baruch and Hana?

No, impossible. She would insist on waiting for him.

Ari glanced at his watch. 7:12 P.M. He was a bit late for an evening meal, but not overly so in a city without clocks.

Fear slipped a blade into his heart. Possibly, Baruch and Hana had gone somewhere together, forgetting him in their joy. But Rivka should be here. She would have waited for him, unless something had gone wrong.

What had she told him this morning? He began pacing. Rivka had said something about a certain nephew of Paul. Ari hadn't really paid attention at the time, and much had happened to drive her words from his mind.

He remembered the number *9*. That was a time. What was supposed to happen at that hour?

Ari looked up and down the street. The light of the nearly full moon washed the streets in a glittering, metallic light.

Think, Ari! What did she tell you? Think!

His memory was strange here. Sometimes he could not remember something for days, and then it blazed into view in his mind's eye. But he didn't have days. He only had a couple of hours.

God of our fathers, help me.

Rivka

Rivka padded silently after Gamaliel, no more than fifty yards behind him. He staggered along, sometimes pausing, leaning against a wall to rest. He seemed oblivious to his surroundings. Not once did he look back.

They turned left on a broad avenue, retracing the steps Yohanan ben Zakkai had taken with Rivka that morning. This street was wider but more forbidding than the residential district where Gamaliel lived. Here, shops and warehouses jammed together on each side, silent now after the end of the business day.

The moon provided plenty of light, but Rivka took no comfort. In these deserted streets, she felt exposed. Ari had told her of his encounter with a bandit. If someone attacked her, she had no defense except a good scream. Would anyone hear?

Gamaliel would, of course, but he couldn't fight a mouse in his condition. If somebody attacked her, she would be on her own. By now, she felt thoroughly spooked. Every sound behind her caused her skin to crawl. Her muscles tensed up.

If anyone bothered her—anyone—she would scream blue murder and fight like a tiger.

Rivka looked behind her. Again, she saw nothing. She shivered, and looked forward to check on Gamaliel.

Something moved behind Gamaliel in the shadows on the right side, between two large granaries.

Rivka blinked. Her heart leapt into double-time. *Dr. West?*

A cloaked shadow darted out into the street and rushed at Gamaliel from behind.

Rivka sprinted toward the two men.

The attacker slammed into Gamaliel. They fell into the street.

Forty yards. Thirty. Too far!

At twenty yards, Rivka screamed, "Damien!"

The man's head jerked up, and he twisted around to look at her.

Rivka leapt in the air. She would kick him in the face if she could.

Then she saw the man's thin, pinched face, his filthy black beard. In the split second that she realized this was not Dr. West, her foot missed its mark, driving into his shoulder, twisting him further around.

He screamed.

Rivka crashed to the ground.

The stranger rolled in the dust, moaning. Gamaliel lay in the street beside him.

"Gamaliel! Are you well?" Rivka said.

Gamaliel slowly pushed himself up into a sitting position. "Who are you? Who is this man? And where is the *daimon* you were shouting about?"

"I am a friend of Yohanan ben Zakkai," Rivka said. "Also a friend of your uncle Saul. HaShem has sent me to make sure you complete your errand." She pointed at the man who had attacked him, now crawling away. "As for this man, I think he is only a bandit, and perhaps not a *daimon* as I first thought."

Gamaliel nodded wearily.

"Are you well?" Rivka asked.

He shook his head. "I am sick, and my knee hurts. But I must speak to my uncle tonight."

Rivka stood and extended a hand to help him up.

He simply stared at her.

"Can you stand?" she asked.

He pushed against the ground and grimaced. "Yes." His face turned pale as he slowly rose to his feet. Most of his weight seemed to rest on his left leg.

"Can you walk?"

He took a step forward, and his right leg buckled.

Rivka caught him before he fell.

He pulled away from her. "Please. It is not fitting for a woman to touch a man."

"It is not fitting for a man to talk to a woman, and yet you have done so," Rivka said. "Can you walk?"

"It is only a bruise." He stepped forward again, and stopped. Sweat formed on his broad forehead.

Rivka moved to Gamaliel's side and threw his right arm over her shoulder.

He tried to pull his arm back. "It is not fitting—"

"Hush!" she said fiercely. "It is not fitting for your uncle to die at the hands of unrighteous men, but that is what will happen if you do not act now. So walk!"

Gamaliel walked. Rivka groaned inwardly with each step. He stood only a few inches taller than she did, but he was a large man, powerfully built, heavily muscled.

Fortunately, they were already fairly close to the Antonia Fortress. Rivka guessed it lay about an eighth of a mile away.

They walked in silence. With each step, Gamaliel seemed to be strengthening, leaning on her less. Rivka guessed that he had been correct. It was only a deep bruise.

As they hobbled into the open space near the steps of the fortress, Rivka let go of his right hand and moved away from him. "Go in peace and do your task," she said. "All generations will remember what you do tonight."

Gamaliel stopped for a moment and eyed her pensively. "*Shalom*, little sister. As the mountains are around Jerusalem, so may the Lord be around you, to bless you and to watch over you."

He turned and limped toward the fortress. Rivka waited until he had climbed a dozen steps, pounded at the gate, and been admitted into the complex. There was nothing more she could do. Now she could leave Paul in the hands of HaShem.

She shivered. The memory of Gamaliel's blessing warmed her a little. Two fragments of it began running a footrace through her mind. *The mountains around Jerusalem. Watch over you.*

Why did that ring a bell?

Rivka heard a faint noise behind her. Before she could move, two strong arms wrapped around her.

CHAPTER
THIRTY-FIVE

Ari

Ari hugged Rivka to his chest. "I've found you at last!" Blessed be HaShem that he had found her and she was safe.

She squirmed and chuckled. "Ari, what's gotten into you?"

Wondering the same thing himself, he loosened his grip a little. "I was worried about you, Rivka. Do you know what time it is? It's dangerous out here after dark."

"Big girls aren't afraid of the dark," she said lightly. "And besides, it doesn't matter what happens to me now. I've done my duty."

He held her at arm's length. *Had she been playing Wonder Woman again?* "What have you been up to? Who was that young man with you?"

"That," Rivka said in a mock dramatic voice, "was the nephew of Renegade Saul. I told you about him, remember? He came here tonight to save his uncle's life."

Ari narrowed his eyes. "And you wanted to make sure he did his job?"

"He was sick as a dog, and then some creep attacked him." She gazed toward the Antonia. "If I hadn't helped him out, he would never have made it."

"Well, congratulations." Ari felt sick to his stomach. *Great, Rivka. You've just ensured twenty centuries of persecution for our people by the followers of That Man.*

Rivka seemed not to notice. Her eyes focused on something far away.

"Rivka, I've got to tell you about Baruch and Hana. You'll never believe it."

"What happened. Did they elope?"

Ari jabbed her playfully. "As a matter of fact, I think they did."

"What?" Her head spun around to stare at him. "You're joking."

"No joke. It was truly bizarre. This morning, some friends of Brother Baruch and Sister Miryam found out that Hana is a *zonah*." Ari told her the whole story.

By the time he finished, Rivka's eyes glittered with happiness. "Ari, you did a wonderful thing! Weren't you worried about interfering with history and all that?"

He shrugged. "I've told you my theory already. We can't interfere with history. The fact that we're here means we *are* history."

She studied him for a long moment. "We really can't go back, can we?"

He shook his head, took a deep breath. *Finish it, Ari. Do it now, or do it never. If Baruch had the courage to ask, and Hana had the courage to answer, you can, too.*

"We're stuck here, Rivka. You stayed here to finish a task. I stayed here for you." His eyes locked on hers. "I want you to be my wife. Will you...marry me?"

Rivka stared at him for a moment. Then she burst into tears.

Rivka

Rivka had never felt so confused in her life. Here she was, trapped in a doomed city, cut off from her old life, living among her own people, and yet a foreigner. Only one man in all the world would ever come close to understanding her. He was kind, gentle, and humorous. He put up with her moods and her sass. And yet he had made it perfectly clear that he didn't understand the one thing most important to her. He couldn't tolerate her religion. And he had sworn never to follow That Man.

What would life be like with such a man as Ari?

And suddenly, she couldn't see anything, because tears came squirting out of her eyes, and he must think she was a terrible fool to be crying at a time like this, but who cared what he thought anyway?

And the answer was that she cared. She cared what he thought of her. She liked him—had always liked him—but she had thought there was no danger of falling in love with him because he was off-limits.

And now?

Now he was the only man left in-limits. And she did care about him, though she had been trying so hard not to.

She felt Ari's arms around her, and she hugged him.

"I'm sorry," he said. "I didn't mean to ambush you like that. It was—"

"Wait!" Rivka pushed him away and stared up at him. "Say that again, Ari."

His eyes showed puzzlement. "I'm sorry, Rivka. I should have waited a little before I—"

"No, the other thing!" Rivka wiped her eyes with her sleeve. "Ambush. You didn't mean to ambush me."

"Yes, it was too sudden, and I'm sorry—"

"It's okay, Ari! But I just thought of something." She suddenly felt light-headed with fear. "Dr. West! I've been wondering all day where he is. He didn't show up where he was supposed to be."

Ari's eyes probed hers. "That depends entirely on who does the supposing. Don't you think it's time—"

"I guessed wrong. And look how high the moon is, and how bright. It's perfect for an ambush."

Ari looked exasperated. "Rivka, with what is he going to ambush anyone? Sticks and stones?"

"I don't know," Rivka said. Again, that irrational certainty gripped her soul. "Sticks, no. But stones—maybe. I don't know. He's crazy, Ari. He'll keep trying as long as he's alive. I know it."

"Rivka, with respect, a rational person would conclude that *you* are the crazy one."

"Fine. I'm crazy, Ari. Maybe you're crazy, too, for wanting to marry me. We're all a little crazy, right? So humor me. Just for one more hour, and then I'll forget about it. Okay? Can you do that, Ari?" She was babbling, and she knew it, but she didn't care.

She started walking along the avenue that led toward Gamaliel's home.

Ari's footsteps scuttered along behind her. "Rivka, where are you going? It's dangerous out in these streets at night."

"I just remembered something Gamaliel told me. He was quoting the psalms, about the mountains being around Jerusalem, about watching."

Ari caught up with her. "This is a surprise to you, that mountains surround Jerusalem?"

"Historically, those mountains have been the site of numerous ambushes, am I correct? In the year 66, Josephus tells of an ambush at the pass of Bet Horon."

"Every schoolchild knows of that ambush," Ari said. "There have been many in those hills, right up to the War for Independence in 1948."

"That's where he is, then." Rivka continued marching down the avenue. She passed the street where Gamaliel lived and continued straight, her eyes set on the gate far ahead, at the northwest corner of the city. The way to Caesarea. Paul would be going through that gate in less than an hour with four hundred infantry and seventy horsemen.

Dr. West would have to be crazy to attack that many men.

But he would have to be crazy to try to come back through time, too. If he was wacko enough to try that, then he would try anything. What did he have to lose?

"Rivka?" Ari caught her sleeve, slowing her.

She rounded on him and pulled away. "Listen up, Ari! I am serious about this. We're in the endgame of this little chess match. Dr. West is alive, and he's out there somewhere and he has a plan. You're not going to lead, and I don't expect you to. You have two choices: Follow me, or get out of the way."

Ari blinked and stepped back. "I'm just trying to protect you."

She started walking again. "I'm safe as long as I'm doing what HaShem tells me to do."

They marched on in silence toward the gate. Before they reached the halfway point, Rivka felt her bravado crumbling. *What made her think she had a clue what HaShem wanted her to do? When had she asked Him lately?*

Damien

Damien sat at the top of the bluff overlooking the road, which was lit up by the full moon for a quarter of a mile. The road passed by him at right angles, less than thirty yards away. At that distance, Paul would be a duck in a shooting gallery.

He pulled out his victory cigar and lit it, then leaned back contentedly and took a puff. This was better than that movie *Independence Day* which he had liked so much. This was a victory for all time.

We're going to win this one, Stu. Do you hear? We're going to win it.

Eyes locked on the road, he let his imagination drift. He remembered that Sunday night, years and years ago, when he had gone to liberate Stu.

The window had been cranked full open, just as Stu had promised. Damien peered in. He had chosen this night because it was a new moon, which would make him less visible. It also made everything else less visible. He could just make out the white uniform pants in Stu's Michigan State football posters. Stu lay in shadow, but Damien could hear his slow, even breathing. Lucky guy was asleep. He would never wake up again, that was for sure.

Damien looked around one more time, his heart thumping. If anyone caught him, he'd be in deep trouble before you could say "Boo!"

The coast was clear. He hauled himself up and set his knee on the windowsill. He listened intently. Nothing abnormal. He eased himself into the room and then listened again.

His heart was hammering like the drums in *2001*.

Do it now, or don't do it. He reached into his shirt pocket and pulled out a pencil-thin flashlight. "Stu, you awake?" he whispered.

The lights flicked on. Damien blinked, his eyes momentarily stunned. "What the..."

Two very large hands grabbed his arms. "Young man, would you care to explain what you're doing here?" A deep voice. Not Stu's.

"Stu!" he said, closing his eyes against the brightness. *Stay cool and make something up.* "What's going on? I got the beer you wanted me to bring." Lame, but better than nothing.

He opened his eyes again. Two orderlies stood beside him, each gripping an arm. In Stu's bed sat...oh, no! "Dad! What are you doing here?"

"I might ask you the same question." Dad looked like he was going to cry.

"Where's Stu?" Damien said. "I brought him some beer."

"Is that right?" his dad said, raising an eyebrow and staring at Damien's hands. "Where is it?"

"Where's Stu?"

"Somewhere else," Dad said. "We checked him out yesterday and put him somewhere safe. We know what you brought."

Which meant the game was up. Damien wondered how they had found out. Probably Stu had let something slip.

The door opened and a big cop walked in. He wasn't smiling.

A cold chill ran through Damien. They were going to lock him up and throw away the key. It wasn't fair! He was a hero—doing the right thing for Stu. Weren't you supposed to do unto others? Stu would have done it for him.

It didn't take long for them to get an admission out of him. They already knew most of the truth, and the drugs in Damien's pockets confirmed their suspicion.

As it turned out, no charges were ever pressed. Stu got locked up in some other dirt hole in some other city. Damien spent a couple of years trying to find out where, and then gave up.

Over the years since then, he had found a thousand reasons to hate Western society. Technology was ruining the world. The moralists kept shoving their Christian virtues down everybody else's throats. Between them, the technocrats and the religiocrats had mucked up Stu's life beyond repair. And until now, there had been nothing Damien could do about any of it.

Tonight, Damien would take care of that. At the root of the problem. Not only had Western religion set the stage for modern science, it had also set the moralistic tone which gave people the idea that they could decide that someone must live when that someone wanted to die.

Damien puffed on his cigar. *This one's for you, Stu. Wherever you are.*

Rivka

When they reached the city gate, they found it locked. Of course. The city officials locked the gates at sundown. The Romans would have a key when they got here with Paul, but Rivka couldn't wait that long.

She remembered that this section of the wall had lain unfinished since the time of Agrippa. A few years from now, when the war started, the Jews would make a belated attempt to finish the wall.

She followed the line of it south.

"Where are you going?" Ari asked. "I thought you wanted—"

"This." Rivka pointed at the wall. It had been twenty feet high, but beyond the first bend, it suddenly decreased to about six feet. "Help me climb this, Ari."

He grumbled something, but boosted her up. She climbed onto the wall and walked to the other side. "Are you coming along?"

No answer. *Let him sulk.*

Rivka sat down on top of the wall and then dropped to the ground.

Her right foot landed on a fist-sized stone. Her ankle twisted, and pain shot up through her leg. "Auggh!" She fell to the dirt, clutching her ankle.

A moment later, Ari's face appeared on the wall above her. "Rivka! Are you all right?"

"No." She gritted her teeth. "I think I've sprained my ankle."

"Don't move. I'll be right down." Ari turned around and lowered himself to the ground.

Rivka sat up and took off the veil she had been wearing.

"What are you doing?" Ari asked.

"I'm wrapping my ankle," Rivka said.

"Let me carry you."

Rivka tried to object. He scooped her up and held her in his arms as if she were a baby.

"Now, how do we get back into the city?" he asked.

"We're not going back in," she said. "Not yet, anyway. I want to look for Dr. West. Let's go back to the road."

He heaved a sigh that told her he thought she was an idiot. Which she already knew, but it was too late to worry about that. She had made up her mind, and she was going to carry through.

Half a minute later, they reached the road. "Take a left here," Rivka said. She snuggled closer to Ari. It felt nice to have a strong man holding her. She wished they could walk like this all night.

"How far are we going?" Ari asked.

"Until we find Dr. West, or until the Romans pass us."

"And how long will that be?"

Rivka looked up at the moon. Paul would be leaving at the third hour of the night—three hours after sundown. Approximately. "I would guess we've got half an hour yet before they leave. That should give us plenty of time. I don't think Dr. West's going to go far up this road."

"Agreed," Ari grunted. "We can go a long way in half an hour."

☾ ☾ ☾

The short man climbed onto his horse. All around him, Roman soldiers stood quietly at attention, awaiting the order to move out. It came soon enough.

The northern gate of the Antonia swung open. Two hundred foot soldiers marched out, javelins poking up out of their backpacks, rising high above them like an evil forest. Behind them came seventy horsemen. The short man rode in the exact middle of these. Following in the rear guard marched another two hundred infantry.

The soldiers had made good time in assembling. The commander of the fortress had ordered them to be ready to leave by the third hour. They had beaten that command by a good half hour.

As the last of the men filed out, the fortress gate began swinging shut. The moon shone clear and bright in a cloudless sky.

It would be a fine night for traveling.

THIRTY-SIX

Ari

Ari felt his senses prickling. A cliff loomed on the right side, casting the road into shadow. It was ridiculous to believe that Damien was really up there. But if he were, he could easily bombard them with stones from above. It wouldn't take a very heavy rock to kill one of them from that height.

Fifty meters shy of the cliff, Rivka whispered, "Stop. I think he's close. Put me down."

Ari lowered her to the road.

She kissed him on the cheek. "That's for being a good sport. My ankle's feeling a little better. I think I can walk now." She hobbled toward the side of the road and examined the hillside carefully.

"What are you planning to try?" Ari asked.

She gave him a determined look that told him she was not merely *trying*. She was *doing*. "I'm going to climb this, of course. It's not so steep here, and I think I can get up this way and get onto the top of that cliff from the back side."

Which was crazy. *Meshuga.* "No," Ari said. "Let me do it, please. If there is anything to see up there, I'll find it."

"And then what will you do?"

"I will protect you from harm," Ari said, and he meant it. He studied the hillside for a moment, and then chose his path. He had done a fair bit of climbing while in the Israel Defense Force, but that had been almost a decade ago.

Half a minute later, he looked down and smiled at Rivka. Already, he was six or seven meters high, and the view made him just a little dizzy. He had always had trouble with heights.

Don't look down, Ari Kazan. Focus on the goal. The goal is to reach the top. The goal is to secure the ground. The goal is to satisfy the lady's curiosity. The goal is—

He stopped short. The goal was not to save the life of that man Paul. That would be to sign the death warrant of countless millions of fellow Jews. The words of Dov echoed in his ears. *The prime minister of the State of Israel commands that you must do your duty as a member of the reserves of the Israel Defense Force.*

What was that duty? To block Damien West?

That would be to aid and abet Paul, to enable the crimes of the church against world Jewry.

But it could not come to that anyway. Damien could not succeed. The trajectory of the universe through phase space was single-valued. Nature would not permit Damien to change the past.

Unless they now lived in an alternate universe, in which case Damien could do anything he wanted. In that universe, if Damien killed Paul, history would take a different path. Would it be better or worse? In either universe, Jews would still suffer and die. They were good at that sort of thing.

It would be an interesting experiment, though, to see if Damien succeeded or failed. If he succeeded, then clearly they had tunneled to a different universe. If he failed, then that would prove nothing, since surely there must be many universes in which Paul survived this night.

But, of course, Damien would not be atop this cliff. He had to be asleep, somewhere in Jerusalem with a very sore right arm. He was simply not capable of mounting any kind of an attack tonight on Paul or anyone else. How, for example, would he climb this hill with only one good hand? Ari found it difficult enough with two.

Finally he reached the top. As Rivka had guessed, it was easy to walk around to the back side of the cliff. There he saw...nothing. No Damien. No human. Not even a rabbit.

Ari leaned over the edge of the cliff and peered down to the road, waving at Rivka.

But she was gone. He could see the whole stretch of road all the way back to Jerusalem. Nothing.

Ari's head began spinning, partly from the height, partly from the fact that Rivka was not where he had left her. He turned his head slowly from left to right, scanning the road as it bent around the cliff before continuing on west toward the Mediterranean coast.

It was empty. Rivka had disappeared.

God of our fathers, bring her back to me safely.

Rivka

By the time Ari had climbed a third of the way up the hill, Rivka decided he wasn't going to find anything. If Dr. West were up there, he would have seen them, heard them. And he would have done something.

Therefore, he must be somewhere else.

She couldn't wait for Ari. His heart wasn't in this anyway. She would have to take on Dr. West alone.

She limped slowly around the bend and down the road, keeping in the shadows on the right side. Her ankle felt lousy, but at least she could walk. After a couple of minutes, her eyes caught a red glow up ahead, a tiny pinprick of light that shouldn't have been there. She pressed deeper into the shadows, hobbling along a few feet off the road. It cost her time, but she had a little extra of that. She needed surprise.

Her eyes stayed glued on that red dot in the night. What could it be? It floated well above the road, and a couple of dozen yards off on the right side. *Careful, Rivka. Quiet.*

Then she smelled it—the disgusting odor of a cigar. The same smell that had made the lab smell like goat breath last Sunday morning when she had gone looking for Ari and found Dr. West alone. *Was that only six days ago?*

By now, she stood within fifty yards of him, and the shadows had run out. She could stay here and wait for Paul and the Romans. But what good would that do? Would they listen to the warnings of a woman? Dr. West must have a plan or he wouldn't be here. She needed to find out that plan. If she waited for Ari, he might arrive too late. Or he might argue with her. Delay would play into Dr. West's hands.

She had no other option. She would have to step out into the light now. But then what?

Obviously, she had to confront Dr. West. He was wounded. She was wounded. Neither had a weapon. Neither knew what the other intended. It would be a battle of wits alone. Assuming her mind was at least as sharp as his, she had a fifty-fifty chance of winning, right? Whereas she had no chance if she did nothing.

Dr. West sat atop a bluff. It looked nowhere near as steep as the one Ari had climbed, and it offered a much easier route up. In fact, it looked like a rock slide waiting to happen.

Was that the plan? Did Dr. West hope to level Paul with a rock slide? It didn't seem quite plausible. The timing would have to be perfect. But if that was his plan, Rivka's very arrival would ruin things. If she climbed up to Dr. West, he would have two options.

He could do nothing, and then she could set off the rock slide early, before Paul arrived. Or he could trigger it himself, killing her, but wasting his only weapon.

Rivka stepped out into the light and limped as quickly as she could toward the base of the bluff.

At once, the cigar tip went out. She heard the sharp intake of breath from up above.

No doubt of it now. That wasn't a shepherd up there with his flocks. No time to waste being afraid. She had to go now.

She reached the base of the slope and studied the climb. It looked steeper up close. She had thought it was forty-five degrees. Now it looked like sixty. *God, give me strength.*

Damien

Damien gasped when Rivka suddenly appeared on the road below in an exotic red outfit. Where had she come from? He stubbed out his cigar and peered down at her. Had she seen him?

Luckily, she was alone. There wouldn't be any Lone Rangers riding to her rescue this time.

She wore something on her right ankle. It looked like a bright red Ace bandage. No, it had to be part of that costume she wore.

Rivka's eyes glinted in the moonlight as she scanned the bluff around him. Then she began climbing.

Insanity! What could she be thinking of? Damien looked at his watch. Paul could come along anytime in the next hour or so. Impossible to predict.

One thing was sure. Damien couldn't afford to have Rivka standing around when Paul and the cavalry came riding around the corner.

Damien cocked the hammer on his gun. Some would sneer at this plain vanilla Colt .45 revolver, six bullets, hand loaded. He rather liked it. Simple. Clean. Reliable. He studied the barrel for a moment. Unfortunately, he had not been able to find a silencer on the black market to fit his backup gun.

This would make a lot of noise, so the quicker he got it over with, the better. If Paul and the Romans came around that bend right now, a gunshot might give them a good scare. They wouldn't recognize the sound, but still, it would be better that they not hear it at all.

By now, Rivka had climbed a dozen feet and showed no signs of stopping. Close enough. *Time for your reward, my dear.*

Damien calmly raised his gun.

Suddenly, Rivka stumbled.

An instant later, Damien fired.

THIRTY-SEVEN

Ari

A gunshot!

Ari's head jerked around to the right, his heart leaping with fear. The shot sounded close, but not too close. Perhaps a couple hundred meters away.

His mind began spinning wildly. Damien must have brought a second gun. He must have shot at Rivka. Why did he not shoot again? He must have hit her. Why did Rivka not scream? She must be...

Panic blinded him for a moment. He clenched his fists. Possibly, she was unconscious. She could not be dead. She could not be dead.

She could not be dead.

Ari raised himself to a low crouch and began slinking through the brushy country above the road. He saw no sense going back down there. Damien would have the high ground, would be watching the road from this level.

But he would not be watching behind him. He would never hear Ari creeping up, would only feel strong hands close around his throat. Whatever feelings of reconciliation Ari had felt for Damien a few days ago, they were gone now.

371

Damien had hurt Rivka. Probably seriously injured her. For that, he would pay.

A sharp, burning pain knifed through Ari's chest. Rivka had been right. Damien was here. *Oh, HaShem, why did I let her out of my sight? HaShem, please let her scream so that I can know she is alive. Please, HaShem. Let her be alive.*

Rivka

A dozen feet up the slope, Rivka's ankle had begun sending warning signals. But she had no time for pain. She ordered her body to keep moving.

God, help me. God, give me the victory. God, work Your will in this somehow, someway. When I am weak, then You are strong. You must be awfully strong, Lord, because right now I'm feeling awfully weak. Do Your stuff, Lord.

She stepped up again, reached a narrow ledge of rock. She looked down. She had climbed high enough that falling would really hurt, though it wouldn't kill her. A waist-high rock now confronted her. The climb looked easier to her right. She took a small step in that direction. *Ouch!*

Pain shot through her ankle.

She collapsed in agony.

As she fell, something brushed against the hair over her left ear. An instant later, she heard a gunshot, then the ricochet of a bullet off rock down below.

He's got a gun!

Rivka lay on the narrow rock ledge in a panic, afraid to make a noise. Where had Dr. West got another gun? He must have brought it with him. He was just the sort to have a backup to a backup to a backup. Why hadn't she thought of that?

For a moment, she lay very still. The rock she had been trying to climb shielded her from Dr. West's view. And shielded him from hers. What was he up to?

She pricked up her ears, listening for the faintest sound.

Then she heard it. The sound of rock against rock. The sound of a man climbing down a steep slope. Very, very carefully.

Rivka looked around. She lay on a ledge of rock about three feet wide and a couple of body lengths long. On one side, a wall of rock rose straight up. On the other, she faced a drop of a dozen feet down to a rocky floor. If she rolled over the edge, she would completely disable herself. Plus, she would be even more exposed than she was now.

Rivka closed her eyes. There was no back and no forward, no left, no right, no up, no down. Ari was too far away to be any help.

There was only God and Dr. West. And the one with the gun seemed a lot more real.

Rivka's head pounded with fury. She had blown it, and she had nobody to blame but herself. God had given her this game to win or lose, and she had lost it. Damien was going to win, all because she was an idiot. She hadn't thought that he might have a second gun, and now she was going to pay.

Well, not if she could help it. She had gotten herself into this mess, and she would get herself out. She wouldn't go gently into that dark night.

Rivka crawled along the ledge until she found what she needed. A few small shards of rock. Not much, but enough for God's First Tiger!

Okay, God, I'll show You what I'm made of. You sent me here to do the impossible, and I'll get it done. I won't give up.

Unlike David.

Oops! That was a mistake, to think of her stepfather at a time like this. Rivka felt her eyes misting. What kind of a First Tiger was she, anyway, crying when the game was on the line?

Damien

Damien stared in fury and disbelief. He had had to rush his shot when she stumbled. How had she known to fall down just in time? If God existed—and He didn't, but *if* He did—that was just the sort of stunt you would expect Him to pull.

Damien listened for a moment. Anybody nearby ought to be raising a ruckus right now.

Silence.

So Rivka had come alone. Good.

Obviously, Rivka hadn't fallen far, or she would be screaming her head off. So she must be hunkered down behind that big rock where she would have an excellent view of the road. She could still mess up his plan unless he did something quickly. When Paul got here with his bodyguard, all she would have to do would be to start screaming. That would alert the Romans, and they would come investigate. And Rivka spoke Latin.

She would screw things up, and Paul would get away again, and then he would have to go to his last backup: the kill zone in Caesarea. He didn't want to do that. He wanted Paul dead tonight.

Damien saw an easy way to solve this problem, but he had to do it quickly.

He popped open the cylinder, tapped out the cartridge he had fired, and replaced it with another bullet. Very good—a full deck again. He jammed the gun in his shoulder harness and began climbing down the hill. He had to go carefully. These rocks were loose, and he didn't want to break his neck in some sort of an avalanche. His right arm throbbed painfully.

Ignore the pain. Take your time and do the job right. That way you won't have to wait for another chance.

❨ ❨ ❨

The commander had sent a runner ahead with a key to unlock the gates. When the men of Rome arrived at the northwest gate of the city, it stood open. They marched out without stopping.

The short man at the center of the column swayed on his horse. A close observer would have seen that his eyes were shut, his lips moving.

Paul was praying.

Rivka

At the end, when the cancer had spread through his whole body, Rivka's stepfather David had given up. He had told the family to stop praying, to quit begging God for a miracle, because there wasn't going to be one. He wanted to go home.

That had irritated Rivka but good. What had happened to David's fight? His will to live? His courage?

His answer only infuriated her. "It takes more courage to do nothing for God than to fight like a tiger. Someday, Rivka, God is going to call you to do nothing."

Gutless. That's what she had called him.

He had just smiled through the pain and asked her, "Who's in charge, Rivka? You or the Big Guy?"

Rivka heard the crunch of shoes on loose rock. Dr. West was coming for her. For her, God's avatar, the one He had picked to save the world. So far, she had done just fine. She had stopped Dr. West twice. This was the third time that should have been the charm. And all she had was a handful of stone shards.

Why had God done this to her?

Or had He? She had stopped Dr. West twice this week. Both times, she had heard God's voice pushing her on, telling her to stop Damien, providing the opportunities. But had she been listening this morning?

Not really. She had just figured out what needed doing and gone off and done it.

Had God been in it? She couldn't remember. She had kind of assumed that He would help out when she needed it, as He had all week. He would be there to get it done after she had done her best.

He would be *her* avatar.

Who's in charge, Rivka?

Rivka buried her face in her sleeve. The truth was that she was in charge tonight. She was the player, moving the joystick, telling God when to jump, and how far, and how high. She wanted to fight. Wanted to call the shots. Wanted to win.

God wouldn't let Dr. West screw up the whole history of the church just because she had an ego. Would He?

She didn't know. But she wasn't going to move another finger without asking God first.

She flung her little handful of stones over the side. They clattered noisily on the rocks below.

Okay, Big Guy, You win. You're in charge; I'm not. I won't even remind You that I've got a very nasty bad guy coming at me with a gun. You tell me what to do, or not to do, and I'll do it. Or I'll do nothing.

Rivka calmed her heart and waited for that quiet voice within her soul that sometimes spoke when she allowed it.

She expected a reply she wouldn't like.

But she didn't expect it to be absurd.

THIRTY-EIGHT

Ari

Ari squinted in the moonlight. Where was Damien?

His nose caught the scent of a cigar. He crouched lower and hurried forward. His fingers itched to wring Damien's neck.

On a rock near the edge of the bluff, he found a half-smoked cigar, snuffed out but still pungent.

Ari dropped to his knees and crawled to the brink. A dozen yards down the steep slope, Damien hunched behind a large stone. Tonight he wore Western clothing, and he looked oddly out of place, like a cowboy in a kung-fu movie. A gun harness looped over his left shoulder.

Damien's right arm hung limply at his side. His left hand gripped the stone in front of him while he slowly raised his head to peer over it.

Where was Rivka? She had to be down there somewhere. Ari had heard nothing since the gunshot a few minutes earlier. *Oh, God of our fathers, let her be only unconscious and not dead.*

What to do about Damien? He had a gun and Ari had none.

It would be easy to start a rock slide here—the place seemed made for it. But Ari feared to take any action at all. A rock slide would have two disadvantages. Rivka was down there somewhere, so a rock slide might bury her, too. But worse, Damien would probably be killed, and Ari did not want him to die quickly. Death was too good for that lunatic.

Keeping his eyes on Damien, Ari felt for a stone. His hand finally found one—smooth and hard and roughly the size of a baseball. The rock felt quite a bit heavier than a baseball, though. The physics would be favorable—for maximum energy transfer, you wanted a projectile of about the same mass as your own arm.

Some premonition warned Ari to look toward the city. He saw at once what Damien could not. From this angle, the gate of Jerusalem was clearly visible. That explained why Damien had chosen this spot.

On the road, midway between the gate of the city and the bend in the road, a long ribbon of Roman soldiers stretched out. In a few minutes, they would be on the road directly below him.

In his mind's eye, Ari saw a long train of his Jewish brothers and sisters, two thousand years of innocent souls, persecuted, tortured, and slaughtered by Christians.

Christians enflamed in their anti-Judaic attitudes by that man Paul. Tears of rage formed in Ari's eyes, and suddenly he found that he could not breathe, could not see well enough to throw his stone. He brushed madly at his eyes.

Could Damien kill Paul? Could he prevent the madness?

And where was Rivka? If Ari waited, would she be caught in the middle of a battle between Damien and the Romans?

At that moment, Ari noticed that Damien seemed to see something. He saw Damien freeze for a moment.

Ari held his breath. Was Rivka dead or alive? *Oh, God of our fathers, protect her!*

Rivka

Rivka had just made her decision when she heard a scraping sound. Her heart hammered in her chest. Fear tore her hands away from her face and forced her eyes open.

A couple of yards away, just beyond the large rock, Dr. West slowly stood up. A grin covered his face.

Rivka swallowed hard. She had no retreat, no weapon, no defense. Either she would obey that still, small voice now, or she would never have a chance. It didn't make sense. It was a foolish gesture, and yet she felt compelled.

She drew in her breath and shouted the stupidest words she had ever uttered.

"Dr. West! I love you! God loves you!"

Damien's face froze. A moment of indecision clouded his eyes. Then a slow smile crossed his face.

Rivka immediately saw that she had lost. No, God had lost. The words hadn't worked.

Dr. West awkwardly reached with his left hand and pulled out a gun strapped to his left shoulder. "Sorry." He cocked the gun one-handed. "Lovey-dovey stuff doesn't work on me."

Terror shot through Rivka. She had failed. She was an idiot to believe she had heard from God. She looked up the barrel of the gun. With every ounce of willpower at her disposal, she did nothing.

Ari

Ari heard Rivka's beautiful voice, so pure and light and full of faith. *So alive!*

Damien drew his gun.

Ari threw his stone.

It smacked Damien in the left temple. His arm jerked. The gun discharged. Then he toppled over the edge and vanished.

Rivka screamed. Not a scream of pain, but of fear.

Damien landed heavily somewhere down below, swearing.

"Rivka!" Ari shouted. "Are you hurt?"

"Ari, is that you? I'm fine, but do something! Dr. West is just a few meters below me!"

"Hang on!" Ari shouted. "The Romans will be here in a couple of minutes. Can you see the road? They're rounding the bend right now!"

"There's a lip of rock here. I can see over it if I raise my head."

"Then for goodness sake, keep down." He dropped to the ground himself. Injured or not, Damien might still take a pot-shot at him from below.

The Roman force crested a small rise in the road, finally coming into full view.

"Here they come!" said Ari. *Blessed be HaShem.*

A harsh laugh at ground level stabbed the night silence.

Ari peered over the edge.

Damien West darted across the road to take cover behind a huge boulder.

THIRTY-NINE

Damien

Damien crouched behind the boulder and loaded another bullet into his gun. His years of training in martial arts had paid off. He had fallen twice his height onto a rough surface and landed well. Tomorrow, his knees would let him know they didn't appreciate him, but never mind that. He had a job to finish. Ari had been fool enough to warn him of the Romans coming.

Damien studied the road. He gauged the distance to the soldiers at two hundred yards. Perfect. He had a plan that could still give him victory.

A strange sense of calm settled over Damien. Be here now. Forget Ari and Rivka. They had no weapons, and they huddled in fear too far away to present him with any opposition. To get closer, they would have to cross the road. He could shoot them dead before they got near him. Ari couldn't throw anything from his vantage point without standing up, but then he would be clearly visible in the moonlight.

So that left Damien against a few hundred ignorant soldiers. He had made a plan for this very eventuality. Not even a fair fight.

The Romans only *seemed* to have overwhelming numerical superiority. But did they? No. They had four hundred men, but they could march only five abreast on this narrow road. His initial battle would not be with four hundred, but with five.

Those five were key. Destroy them with extravagant force, and confusion would mount. The Romans would stop, try to regroup.

Then he would attack again, and the confusion would turn to terror. The soldiers would not understand the horrors they saw—the heads of fellow warriors exploding.

They would think some supernatural force had invaded the planet. And wasn't that essentially the case? Some sci-fi writer once said that any sufficiently advanced civilization was indistinguishable from the gods. Damien had a couple of thousand years of advances to draw on. His gun would be the magic wand that flung terror into their hearts.

They would flee, with the fastest escaping first, the slowest last.

Who would be the slowest? Obviously, the oldest. Which meant Paul. He had to be in his fifties or sixties by now. He could not keep up with the fit, young Romans, and he could not outrun Damien.

The whole thing would take five minutes. It all depended on being able to reload quickly. If he still had his semiautomatic, that would have been much easier. No matter. Damien had been reloading guns all his life, and he could do it quickly enough for the job at hand.

The only way the Romans could defeat him would be to use archers. And the Roman infantry didn't use archers. Damien had checked. When they needed bowmen, they used auxiliaries raised from conquered peoples.

It took just about two seconds for all this to pass through his head. He had been planning it for so long that the fallback procedures were automatic. If this attack failed, he had yet another backup plan. But he wouldn't fail.

Damien raised his head for a moment and pointed his gun in the general direction of Ari. It was a warning, intended to freeze Ari in his place. *I know where you are and I can shoot you if you move, so don't try.*

A wave of the gun in Rivka's direction accomplished the same objective with her.

Now, back to the Romans. He would wait until they got to about a hundred and twenty yards. It was a long way, but they presented a huge target. If he missed the first row, he would hit someone in the second, or the third. At that distance, a .45 bullet still had a lot of raw stopping power, body armor or not. A hollow-point bullet exploding through somebody's face would get that person's attention.

He waited.

Waited.

Now.

Damien raised his gun and fired.

Quintus

Quintus had not yet resigned himself to this long night march. Why the sudden orders? Who was this man they were assigned to protect? Why had so many men been rousted from their games of dice or their cups of cheap wine?

They would march upward of thirty Roman miles tonight, and as many again tomorrow night before reaching Caesarea. Then, if the goddess *Fortuna* did not smile on them, they might be ordered back to this dark city of white stones and bloody hearts.

Quintus had not always hated Jews. Back in Rome, he had known them as a strange people who kept to themselves in their own districts and followed their primitive customs. But the Jews of Rome were as nothing compared to these savage folk in Judea.

The Jews of Rome kept to themselves, but at least they treated other peoples as humans. The Jews of Judea did not. They threw the evil eye at Romans, provoked them with insults, and attacked them with stones at every opportunity.

The Jews were an evil race, and Quintus hated them.

And now this strange march for no reason at night, taking one Jew in custody to Caesarea to protect him from other Jews.

Apparently, Jews were as vile to their own as to strangers.

The road bent to the right as it passed by a sheer cliff. Quintus marched on the right corner of the lead row. The country here looked wild, strange, eerie in the moonlight—as savage as the people who lived here. A hot, humid wind had been blowing all day, keeping tempers ugly. It would only get worse as they marched down into the lowlands near the coast. Tomorrow would be intolerable. There would be little sleep—

In the distance ahead, something scurried across the road. A wild animal? A man? Quintus estimated the distance at a hundred Roman paces. He squinted into the darkness.

Nothing. Perhaps some wild dog, but nothing more. The men of Rome continued forward at the same pace.

Beside Quintus, his gambling buddy Sextus spoke up cheerfully. "Quintus, when we reach Caesarea, we'll go to the games, get drunk, and find a woman."

Quintus spat in the road and half-turned to look at his friend. "I would not choose that order. And I suggest we find two women."

A bright flash shattered the darkness, then a boom split the night quiet. Half a heartbeat later, Sextus jolted backward, then collapsed in the road.

Quintus stared down at his friend. Half of his face was gone, the other half badly bloodied. Quintus had never witnessed anything like it. Sextus lay without moving in the dust.

The man behind Sextus stumbled over him. Quintus choked back bile. What new savagery was afoot?

Sudden shouts rippled backward through the force. "Keep moving, fools!"

Another noise boomed across the desert landscape. Marcus, the middle man in the row, screamed and tumbled to the ground, clutching his belly. His abdominal armor hung in shards.

Now the first few rows had stopped, staring at the two men on the ground.

Quintus spit bile onto the road. Something evil had been loosed in this evil land. It was like the old tales of gods who threw lightning and roared thunder at mortals. Cold fear slid a dagger down his spine.

The centurion appeared at a run. "What's going on?" he shouted. "Why has the march stopped?" His eyes fell on the two soldiers. "What—"

Another boom echoed. The centurion pitched backward as though a mule had kicked him in the chest. A gaping hole appeared in his body armor below the heart.

He collapsed on the ground and lay there screaming.

Ari

Ari's mouth hung open. His eyes were riveted on the scene playing out before him. *Damien has a chance to win this battle. A good chance. And I can't do a thing about it.*

Ari knew he could make a mad dash down this slope at Damien, but he would probably kill himself in the process. If he made it to the bottom, then he would have twenty meters of open ground to cover. But Damien was obviously a skilled gunman. Ari wouldn't have a chance.

Alternatively, Ari could find some more stones and throw them at Damien. But he would have to stand up to do so. With the moon behind him, he would be a perfect target for Damien.

Ari knew he could escape, no matter what happened. If he crawled back a few meters, he could stand up and slink away from this battlefield.

But Rivka couldn't do that. She was stuck down there somewhere. She could not leave without making herself a target. Ari could not go to her without becoming a target himself. If Damien completed his mission, what would he do next? Leave in triumph? Or take revenge on Rivka?

A bead of sweat rolled down into Ari's eye. If the Romans won, then all would be well. If they lost, then Rivka would die. Ari knew he would not abandon her. If Damien came after her, he would have to fight Ari first.

Until then, there was no point in doing anything.

Damien poked his head out from his hiding place and fired up toward Ari. The fact that Ari heard the shot told him that Damien had missed.

It was a warning shot, then. A reminder that Damien had superior force, and that Ari had better keep out of this.

Ari was already lying in the dirt, exposing just enough of his head so he could see the battle. He eased himself back a few centimeters to lower his profile even further.

At that moment, the Romans made their move.

Quintus

Fear tore through the ranks. Quintus could feel it like a cold wind. The three men in the dirt bore horrible wounds. The two still alive would not survive long. Who could do such things, except the gods?

A second centurion strode forward. "Men of Rome, our road lies ahead, not behind. We will attack. Unloose your javelins."

Quintus fumbled with the two javelins he carried in his pack, their twin points like fingers jabbing at the heavens. His nerveless hands would not work.

Another blast echoed in the hills. Another soldier's face exploded.

Master your fear, Quintus.

Suddenly, hot anger surged through his veins. This enemy was destroying the great army of Rome, one by one, affronting the gods of his land. And the gods of Rome ruled the earth. No enemy could stand against them. Quintus yanked his javelins up and out of his pack.

"Raise the standards!" he shouted. The standards would protect them. The standards were the gods of the legion. Normally, standard-bearers carried them on long poles wherever the legion went, shooting fear into the enemies of Rome. Here, in the vicinity of this city of the Jews, the standards had been lowered and covered, so as not to excite the anger of the Jews.

But now the standards must protect the army of Rome.

"Raise the standards!" the centurion ordered. Other soldiers took up the cry.

Quickly, the standard-bearer brought out the standards and uncovered them. He raised the pole and waved it aloft.

"I need fifty men," said the centurion. "The first ten rows. You will advance toward the enemy. Thirty paces from that boulder, you will launch javelins. At twenty paces, you will launch a second round. You will then draw swords and attack. Quintus, you will give the signal to launch."

Another burst of flame punctured the night. The man next to the standard-bearer screamed and fell to the ground, his arm shattered at the shoulder.

Quintus looked briefly at the wound. This wound might be mortal, or it might not. But if this enemy was a god, then he was not all-powerful. He could not kill every time.

"Go now!" said the centurion. "And may *Fortuna* smile on you."

Quintus found himself running, a javelin hefted in each hand, his eyes on the point from which the flashes of light had come.

The enemies of Rome had chosen the wrong night to attack her legions.

Damien

Damien reloaded quickly, stealing rapid glances at the turmoil on the road. Now they were unwrapping a long pole. He had no idea what it was—a totem pole? Crazy. Whatever it was, obviously they were counting on it as a talisman.

Damien fired at the man holding the pole. He missed, but the next man over fell in the dirt, screaming. Winged, by the look of him. That ought to send a fresh round of panic through the troops. A message from the god Damien. *Your magic is no use against my magic.*

That ought to get them panicked.

Instead, it appeared to have the opposite effect. Suddenly, a large group of soldiers made a dash toward Damien.

He smiled coolly and fired. *Bang!* Down went one of the leaders. *Bang!* Down went another. Still, they kept coming. The man with the pole ran in front, shrieking like a banshee.

Damien fired twice. Sweat gushed out of his armpits. He downed two more soldiers, but still they came on. Sixty yards away.

Damien aimed carefully and fired his last round.

The soldier with the totem pole staggered and fell. The pole fell with him. The attack stuttered to a halt.

Damien reloaded frantically.

Fools! Ten seconds more, and you could have overwhelmed me.

Instead, the men huddled around their fallen comrade, gibbering as if the great god Zeus had come crashing down to earth.

Damien shot another warning look up at Ari, and then at Rivka. He couldn't see either of them from here, but they could see him. That was what mattered.

Now for the finishing touch. He had stopped the advance. Time to put them on the run.

Damien raised his gun and began firing again.

Quintus

Quintus felt frantic with fear. The god of the legion was downed! What evil lurked behind that rock?

Another flash. Another boom. Death slammed another soldier in the face.

"Down!" shouted a voice in Latin. A woman's voice. "Get down!"

The goddess Fortuna?

A second flash. Another soldier fell.

On impulse, Quintus dropped to the earth.

Several of the soldiers did likewise.

The woman's voice shouted again. "After six flashes, the evil one must rest!"

The bright light flashed again. Another soldier fell in a shower of blood.

"Fall to the earth, fools!" Quintus hissed.

More of them did so.

The light flashed again, but this time not at the soldiers. Now it stabbed across the road in the direction of the woman's voice. A great boom echoed off the nearby hills.

Quintus thought feverishly. *The goddess had spoken true.* The flashes came in groups of six, and then there followed a pause. Like the Jewish god, who slept each seventh day, so it was said.

Another flash.

Another soldier fell, screaming.

"Prepare to attack!" Quintus said. "The evil god must rest after the next one."

The god spat forth his lightning again.

"Now!" screamed the goddess. "Now attack the evil one!"

Quintus leaped to his feet, hefting his javelins. "Follow me!" he bellowed.

Behind him, he heard the roars of his enraged comrades. "Attack the evil one!"

Quintus sprinted forward, raising his right arm. "Launch javelins, men of Rome!"

An instant after he released his own weapon, a dozen more sailed over his head in a shower that converged on the lair of the evil god.

Damien

Damien couldn't follow what Rivka shouted because he didn't know Latin. A quick warning shot shut her up. He didn't need to hit her, if he could keep her silenced. He fired twice more at the Romans, bringing down two more men. They had stopped. But why didn't they retreat?

He began reloading rapidly. Midway through, he looked up. He swore.

A small cluster of Romans had crossed half the distance. The gun slipped from Damien's hands and fell in the dirt. The lead soldier shouted something, and then a volley of spears came hurtling toward him on a high trajectory designed to clear his boulder.

Damien backpedaled furiously to get out of range, then spun and ran. He heard the weapons raining down behind him. One had been badly overthrown, and hurtled into the earth alongside him, an arm's length away.

They had missed!

Now all he had to do was outrun them. He had the better shoes, and they all wore heavy armor and would probably be winded after sprinting a hundred-plus yards.

Damien heard a shout behind him. He risked a look over his shoulder. No!

Ari

Ari peered over the edge of the cliff. Incredible! They had put Damien on the run! He watched as the soldiers launched their second volley of javelins.

At that moment, Damien looked back over his shoulder. Instantly, he dived to his left.

The weapons swarmed down around him. One javelin pierced his torso just as he hit the ground.

A terrible scream ripped the night air. Damien writhed on the ground, the javelin flopping about frantically.

The lead soldier drew his sword as he ran toward Damien. Ari held his breath and instinctively closed his eyes. The horrible screams cut through his soul. He had thought he hated Damien, had wanted to give him a long, slow death. Now he realized he could not have done so.

Suddenly, Damien's cries stopped.

Ari's eyes flew open. The soldier yanked his sword out of Damien's chest, then wiped it on the dead man's clothes.

Ari turned his head and retched.

When he looked again, several dozen men had gathered around Damien's body. Two of them pointed at something on this side of the road.

Rivka!

They had heard her shouts while Damien had been fighting them. Now they would come looking for her.

But the men waited quietly, talking in excited voices in a language Ari did not know. He wondered why they didn't come to investigate Rivka. Then he saw that no officers stood among the men. Probably, they thought themselves in no danger and awaited orders.

Soon enough, the main body of troops arrived.

Their discipline impressed Ari. Hundreds of men stood in neatly ordered ranks. A centurion strode forward to confer with the men.

In the middle of the force, a small man in Jewish garb sat on a horse, his shrouded head bowed. Was he praying?

The centurion pointed in Rivka's direction. Two of the soldiers drew swords and crossed the road toward her.

The small man on the horse shouted something. Latin? Greek? Ari couldn't tell.

The soldiers stopped. The small man dismounted and walked slowly toward the centurion. After a brief discussion, the officer beckoned his soldiers back.

Ari suddenly realized that he had not been breathing. *Blessed be HaShem.* Paul had saved Rivka from…something.

Paul stepped toward Damien's body. The soldiers moved out of his way.

Paul knelt beside Damien's dead body and closed his eyes. Then he stood and began to pray. It was impossible to make out the words at this distance, but Ari didn't care. In a few minutes, Paul would finish, the soldiers would all pass on, and he and Rivka would be free to get on with their lives.

Just then, one of the soldiers pointed toward Rivka and began jabbering excitedly to his commander.

Ari's heart slipped into a full gallop.

Rivka appeared. Coming out of hiding! Voluntarily!

Rivka, you crazy woman, don't go down there! Ari wanted to shriek. Instead, he watched in horrified silence.

Rivka

Rivka simply couldn't help herself. Something terrible might happen if she went. But what if she didn't? She would never be this close to Paul again. She had to join him, to pray with him.

As she climbed down, she heard the soldiers chattering in Latin. Ordinarily, she would have been terrified of walking among this many men alone at night. But Paul would protect her, she felt sure.

When she reached the bottom of the slope, she marched toward Paul, ignoring the soldiers. They separated before her, eyes downcast as if she were a queen or a goddess.

She reached Paul's side. Suddenly, she found herself crying. Dr. West had tried to kill her, but she could not hate him. He was a man, a living soul, a son of Adam.

Paul continued praying, oblivious to her. Not the *Kaddish*, but something else. Either his own extemporaneous prayer, or one which had not survived to modern times. Rivka remembered that the *Kaddish* would not be used by mourners for another thousand years or so, though some early form of it probably existed in this century. Paul had never heard that great and beautiful prayer, at least not in the form Rivka knew it.

When Paul finished his prayer, Rivka immediately began praying the *Kaddish*. She closed her eyes and recited the words, and as she did, their meaning expanded to fill her whole hungry soul.

Let His great name be magnified, be sanctified, in all the universe that was created by His word.

Soon and swiftly, let Him reign—in our days and in our lives—in all the house of Yisrael; and all will say, "Amen!"

Let His great name be blessed—forever and forever and forever.

Let Him be blessed, let Him be praised, let Him be honored, let Him be worshipped, let Him be glorified, let Him be exalted—the Holy One, the Blessed One—He who rises far above any blessing or anthem or honor or worship of mortal men; and all will say, "Amen!"

Let His peace and let His life pour out from the heavens on all Yisrael; and all will say, "Amen!"

He who makes peace in the heavens, let Him make peace in us—in all Yisrael; and all will say "Amen!"

After a moment of silence, Rivka heard a voice say, "Amen!"

She opened her eyes.

Paul stood there, his eyes still shut, tears running down his cheeks into his beard.

"Beautiful, my daughter," he said. "That touches my soul deeply." He pulled the prayer shawl away from his head.

Rivka stared at him. His skin looked parched and weathered from long travel under wind and rain and sun. A deep indentation on the left side of his forehead reminded her that he had received a stoning more than once.

Paul opened his eyes.

Rivka gasped. The left eye socket gaped empty. Was this Paul's "thorn in the flesh?" *What suffering he's been through!*

His right eye looked at her knowingly. "My daughter, you see my weakness, and you feel pity. Do not. The Lord has shown me this—that His strength is revealed in my weakness. When I am weak, then He is strong."

A strange peace settled over Rivka's heart. Yes, evil flourished in her world. Yes, trauma filled her life. Yes, confusion reigned in her heart. But it was nothing compared to what this man had suffered. Through it all, let God's great name be magnified.

Rivka smiled. She looked for a long minute into Paul's good eye. He was ugly—far more than she had expected. And she loved his beautiful ugliness.

"Go in peace, daughter of Zion," he said. He touched her forehead. "Blessed are You, Lord our God, King of the universe, who brings forth beauty from ugliness, strength from weakness, wisdom from foolishness."

Then he turned and limped away toward his horse.

Two soldiers came and grabbed Dr. West's legs. The burial detail, Rivka guessed. They made quick work of him, dragging his body onto a thick cloth, wrapping him up.

Rivka went to sit on a rock by the side of the road, her legs wobbly, her mind spinning.

Within minutes, the soldiers trundled Dr. West off toward the city. Dozens more went with them, carrying the bodies of the night's dead.

The rest of the troops formed up. A centurion gave the order. The procession started forward. Soon it disappeared into the night. Rivka sat alone with her thoughts.

My strength is made perfect in weakness.

A shadow appeared above her.

Rivka stood up and fell into Ari's arms. She gripped him, letting the sharp release of tears consume her.

Ari said nothing, just held her tight.

She cried until she was finished. Really finished. Then she let go her grip on Ari.

He released her at the same moment. "Rivka," he said, "we must talk."

She nodded. "Fine. But not here. Let's walk."

"Can you walk on that ankle?"

"Not very well, but I can walk. I don't want to stay here."

"Wait." Ari strode over to the boulder that had given Dr. West cover during his attack on the Romans. He came back a moment later, holding a gun. He flipped open the cylinder and ejected the cartridges into his hand.

"Any bullets left?"

Ari held them out for her to see. "Three."

"Keep them," Rivka said. "They may come in handy."

Ari

Ari and Rivka ended up walking most of the night, resting now and again. Ari felt mentally exhausted but physically charged. Rivka's ankle made it impossible to walk very fast, but she felt too restless to sit still for long. She refused to try climbing the wall back into the city, and they could not get in through the locked gates.

So they walked.

Near morning, they found themselves atop the Mount of Olives, sitting on a large stone, facing the Temple Mount. Here and there the torches of Temple guards lit up the Temple's stony blackness.

"So," Ari said. They had talked about Damien, about Brother Baruch and Sister Hana, about HaShem. Now it was time to talk about themselves. "I'm still waiting for an answer to my question." He shivered in the predawn chill. If she wasn't going to even think about marrying him, then he wanted to know quickly.

"We've still got a problem," Rivka said. "Remember? I'm a Christian, and you tell me I'm therefore not Jewish. And you're...What are you? I need to know, Ari."

Ari sighed. "I don't even know what to think anymore, my friend. But I fail to see why you take the name of Christian so lightly. Think how many of our people died at the hands of... those people. At the hands of men like Constantine. The Crusaders. The inquisitors. Hitler."

"None of that has happened yet, Ari. In this time, Christians are still the dregs of society. They haven't become conquerors or Crusaders or inquisitors yet. And Hitler was a pagan, not a Christian."

"What about Brother Baruch?" Ari turned to look at her. "Is he a Christian? Would he sign any of those creeds that Christians will someday fight wars over?"

Rivka sat silent for a moment. "The Athanasian Creed he probably wouldn't understand. The Nicene Creed might be a stretch in a couple of places, although I would need to talk to him to find out. The Apostle's Creed—misnamed, by the way—I think he would be fine with that one, but again, I would need to talk to him. But all those are decades or centuries down the road. Those Greek creeds just aren't relevant to these Jewish people."

"So Christianity doesn't exist yet?" Ari felt a grin tug at the corners of his mouth. "And if that's the case, how can you be a Christian? You don't exist?"

"I'm a throwback, I guess." Rivka returned his smile. "No, a throwforward. But let me clue you in on something, Mr. Defender of Judaism. Have a look at that Temple. Is that Judaism? Judaism as you know it? They kill animals in there, Ari. They say prayers you've never heard, and they don't know the ones you and I learned in *shul*. They don't recite the *Kaddish* at funerals. Synagogues are something fairly new, and the liturgy is just getting off the ground. You're right that Christianity as we know it doesn't exist yet. Neither does Judaism. Not as we know it."

"So I'm a throwforward, too?" Ari scratched at his beard. "Well, just tell me this, then. Do you really believe HaShem is both one and three?"

"First you answer a few physics questions for me," Rivka said. "Do you really believe in multiple universes? Electrons that are both waves and particles? Wormholes that let you be both today and yesterday at the same time?"

"Manifolds need not be simply connected—"

"Manifolds, shmanifolds, Ari! Maybe HaShem isn't simply connected, either, whatever that means. The universe is a funny place, isn't it? I don't understand it, and neither do you. So how do you expect to understand HaShem?"

Ari sighed. "I just wish..." *Never mind. Better not to say it.*

"You just wish what?"

Ari didn't say anything.

"Listen, Ari, any guy who wants to marry me had better learn to answer my questions, because I don't take no answer as an answer."

"I just wish...I understood why HaShem showed such poor judgment in choosing His friends," Ari said.

"You mean the Christians, Ari?"

"I mean all of them. The Christians. The Muslims. The *Haredim.*"

"Some of them are nice people, Ari."

"And some of them are evil."

"Really? I'm shocked—shocked to hear there are bad people in the world."

"Bad religious people, Rivka. People who claim to be friends of HaShem. Why does He put up with them?"

"And His choice is what, exactly, Ari? Zap them with lightning? Turn them into pillars of salt? Drown them? Been there, done that already in Genesis. None of that works very well."

"So why did He do it the first time? You're not making much sense, Rivka."

"Neither are you. I think we're both tired." She leaned heavily against him. "Where do we go from here, Ari?"

"We can't leave," he said. "We're stuck."

"I know that. I mean, what do we do now?"

"I'm going to learn a trade," he said. "Brother Baruch is teaching me to be a scribe."

"Want some advice?"

"If you have it."

"Get a sword and learn to use it."

"I'm a pacifist, remember?"

"You're a member of the Israel Defense Force, aren't you?"

"The reserves. Everybody is."

"Didn't you have orders from your prime minister?"

"Yes. My orders are to take whatever steps are required to preserve the State of Israel. I haven't done very well, have I?"

"But Ari, there won't be a State of Israel unless the Jewish people survive for the next two thousand years."

"They'll survive. No thanks to a certain religion which shall remain nameless."

"Jews will survive only if Judaism survives, Ari."

"You told me Judaism doesn't even exist yet."

"It's forming now. One man will make it happen."

"Rabban Yohanan ben Zakkai," Ari said. "Every schoolchild knows about his Torah school at Yavneh."

"There's a story about him, how he barely escaped alive from Jerusalem during the Jewish revolt—"

A sudden burning filled Ari's heart. He grabbed Rivka's shoulder. "We don't know if we're in our own universe or a parallel one, do we? Rivka, what if Yohanan doesn't get out?"

"He's a sweet little man," Rivka said. "I met him yesterday and—"

"What if he doesn't get out?"

"According to the history books, he will—"

"In our universe. But what if he doesn't in this one?"

"Nothing much changes. The city still falls. The Temple burns. The sacrifices end. No more dead animals. No more priests. But there'll be no Torah school. No *Haredim.*"

"No Jews," Ari said in a flat tone. He hated the *Haredim,* but they had kept his people alive for two thousand years with their inflexible ways. "No Zionism. No State of Israel."

At that moment, the golden roof of the Temple lit up with the first rays of the rising sun. Ari stared at it. The roof blazed red.

It's all going to burn. My city. My Temple. My people. Perhaps nothing I do can change that. Perhaps the currents of history are too strong to change what will be. And yet to do nothing is to do something.

Ari closed his eyes—too late. The hot tears spilled out, burned down his cheeks, burrowed into his beard. He would live to see Jerusalem aflame, and that was unbearable. How much worse if Torah died out in Israel? Then Israel would die, too. He covered his face with his hands.

He felt Rivka's arm around his shoulders.

"Yeshua wept here also," she said.

Ari had never heard that before. "Oh?"

"Could I tell you about it sometime, Ari?"

"Sometime, yes, maybe. But not—"

Something brushed the back of Ari's neck. He flicked at it. An instant later, he felt the sudden, sharp lance of a hornet sting.

PART V:
TESSERAE

tessara (noun), plural tesserae

1. Each of the small pieces used in mosaic work.

2. A small square of bone, wood, or the like, used
   in ancient times as a token, tally, ticket, due,
   etc.

—*Webster's Encyclopedic Unabridged Dictionary*
of the English Language

EPILOGUE

Dov

"So they're dead, aren't they?" Jessica said.

Dov stopped the car and shrugged. "After talking to Ari's colleagues, I do not know how to assign a meaning to that word. They talk about reference frames and coordinate patches and things which I do not understand. In our reference frame, they have been dead for many centuries."

"But in their own?" Jessica asked. She opened the door on her side but just sat there, her eyes seeming to look far beyond the dusty parking lot of the dig.

"They are still alive in their own frame," Dov said. "They have gone to their final rest already, but not yet, my friend. That is all I can say."

Jessica wiped her eyes. "Can't somebody make another time machine and go rescue them?"

"The physicists believe it is really impossible. Again, I do not understand the details, but they have no plans—"

"Dov! Jessica!"

Dov turned to look. Luke Morgan, a big, ruddy-faced American with a blond ponytail and piercing blue eyes, strode toward them. He wore a curious expression on his face.

"Welcome back to the dig, you two! Have you finished your fifteen minutes of fame yet?"

405

"Fifteen minutes?" Dov squinted at the big man. "I do not understand."

"Never mind." Luke opened the door and thumped Dov on the shoulder. "I want to show you guys something." He went around to the passenger side, helped Jessica out, and gave her a big hug.

"What is it?" Jessica asked.

Luke simply turned and began walking. Something in his step seemed strangely light.

Dov and Jessica hurried after him.

They reached the grid of squares that formed the dig. Luke strode out onto one of the meter-wide earthen walls that separated the squares. Dov waited for Jessica and motioned for her to go first.

Luke zigzagged along the grid until they reached the square where Dov had been digging with Rivka only three weeks earlier.

Dov's heart felt hollow and cold.

Suddenly, Luke spun and faced Jessica and Dov, gesturing with a flourish toward the mosaic. A number of volunteers stood around the edges of the square, admiring it. Dov saw that the earthen wall on the far side had been cut through to uncover the top part of the mosaic.

"Ladies and gentlemen!" Luke said. "I present to you the famous Rivka Meyers Memorial Mosaic, now complete, with the exception of some minor damage at the southwest corner."

Dov's eyes dropped to the mosaic. It was beautiful, the colors incredibly vivid, the details perfect, each tessera exactingly cut—

"Oh my gosh!" Jessica said.

Dov sucked in his breath.

"Look at the faces, Dov!" she said.

Dov could look at nothing else.

The mosaic was a portrait of Rivka and Ari—under a wedding canopy.

Randall Ingermanson earned his Ph.D. in theoretical physics at the University of California at Berkeley in 1986. He lives in San Diego with his wife and three wacky daughters and works full time as a physicist. He thinks he can read Hebrew, and he speaks Fortran, C, C++, and Java fluently. *Transgression* is his first novel and his second book on the intersection of science and religion; several more are in the works. If you'd like to know more about him and his books, then you are incurably nosy and your sentence is to go visit his Web site at www.rsingermanson.com.